P9-CNG-841

THE FREEDOM RACE

BOOKS BY LUCINDA ROY

FICTION

Lady Moses

The Hotel Alleluia

The Freedom Race

POETRY

Wailing the Dead to Sleep

The Humming Birds

Fabric

NONFICTION

No Right to Remain Silent: What We've Learned from the Tragedy at Virginia Tech

THE FREEDOM RACE

LUCINDA ROY

A TOM DOHERTY ASSOCIATES BOOK
NEW YORK

This is a work of fiction. All of the characters, organizations, and events portrayed in this novel are either products of the author's imagination or are used fictitiously.

THE FREEDOM RACE

Maps on pgs. ix and x created by Lucinda Roy
Map on pg. xi by Jon Lansberg

A Tor Book
Published by Tom Doherty Associates
120 Broadway
New York, NY 10271

www.tor-forge.com

Library of Congress Cataloging-in-Publication Data

Names: Roy, Lucinda, author.
Title: The freedom race / Lucinda Roy.
Description: First edition. | New York : TOR, a Tom Doherty Associates Book, 2021. | Identifiers: LCCN 2021009144 (print) | LCCN 2021009145 (ebook) | ISBN 9781250258908 (hardcover) | ISBN 9781250258892 (ebook)
Classification: LCC PR6068.O96 F74 2021 (print) | LCC PR6068.O96 (ebook) | DDC 813/.54—dc23
LC record available at https://lccn.loc.gov/2021009144
LC ebook record available at https://lccn.loc.gov/2021009145

First Edition: July 2021

Printed in the United States of America

0 9 8 7 6 5 4 3 2 1

In loving memory of my father, Namba Roy,
Jamaican Maroon carver and factory worker, whose stories,
sculptures, and paintings dreamed of the Cradle

For the young, whose future deserves a more inspired
imagining

And for Larry, who dreams with me always

AUTHOR'S NOTE

The Freedom Race is a story about both the endurance of the human spirit
and the horrors of slavery.

It is about where we could end up in the near future,
and about the stories that have sustained us in the past.

Because the most deep-rooted hope is honed by suffering,
and because oppressive systems premised on prejudice demand an honest depiction,
this book contains difficult subject matter,
including but not limited to violence, abuse, rape, and lynching.

Please read this survival narrative when you feel ready to enter the
challenging world it depicts.

CONTENTS

PLANTING 437
IN THE
HOMESTEAD
TERRITORIES
3 WISE MEN
THE MARGINS
FOREST
FRY-FENCE
PASTURELAND
LOTTER'S FATHERHOUSE
LOTTER'S SEED QUARTERS
MAIN HORSE BARN
HOMESTEAD 3
HOMESTEAD 1
BLUEGLASS LAKE
WILLIAMS' SEED QUARTERS
HOMESTEAD 2
DINING HALL
HOMESTEAD 4
SEED QUARTERS
STEADER DWELLINGS
CROPMASTER HALL
SYLVIE
BART'S MOUNT
LOOKOUT TOWER
FACTORY ROW
PLANTING ROW
LEGACY SCHOOL
HOMESTEAD 5
HOMESTEAD 8
PEN-PEN
THE COMMONS
RESTRICTED
DOOM DELL
HOMESTEAD 7
MURDER-MOUTH/ (AKA ARSENAL)
PIG FARM
SHOT TOWER
PLANTING FLYING COOP
HOMESTEAD 10
HOMESTEAD 9
PETRUS' SEED QUARTERS
HOMESTEAD 12
HOMESTEAD 6
BART'S POND
FLOOD LAND
HOMESTEAD 11
SNARLCATS
BRINE'S SEED QUARTERS
STRIPERS
G-J

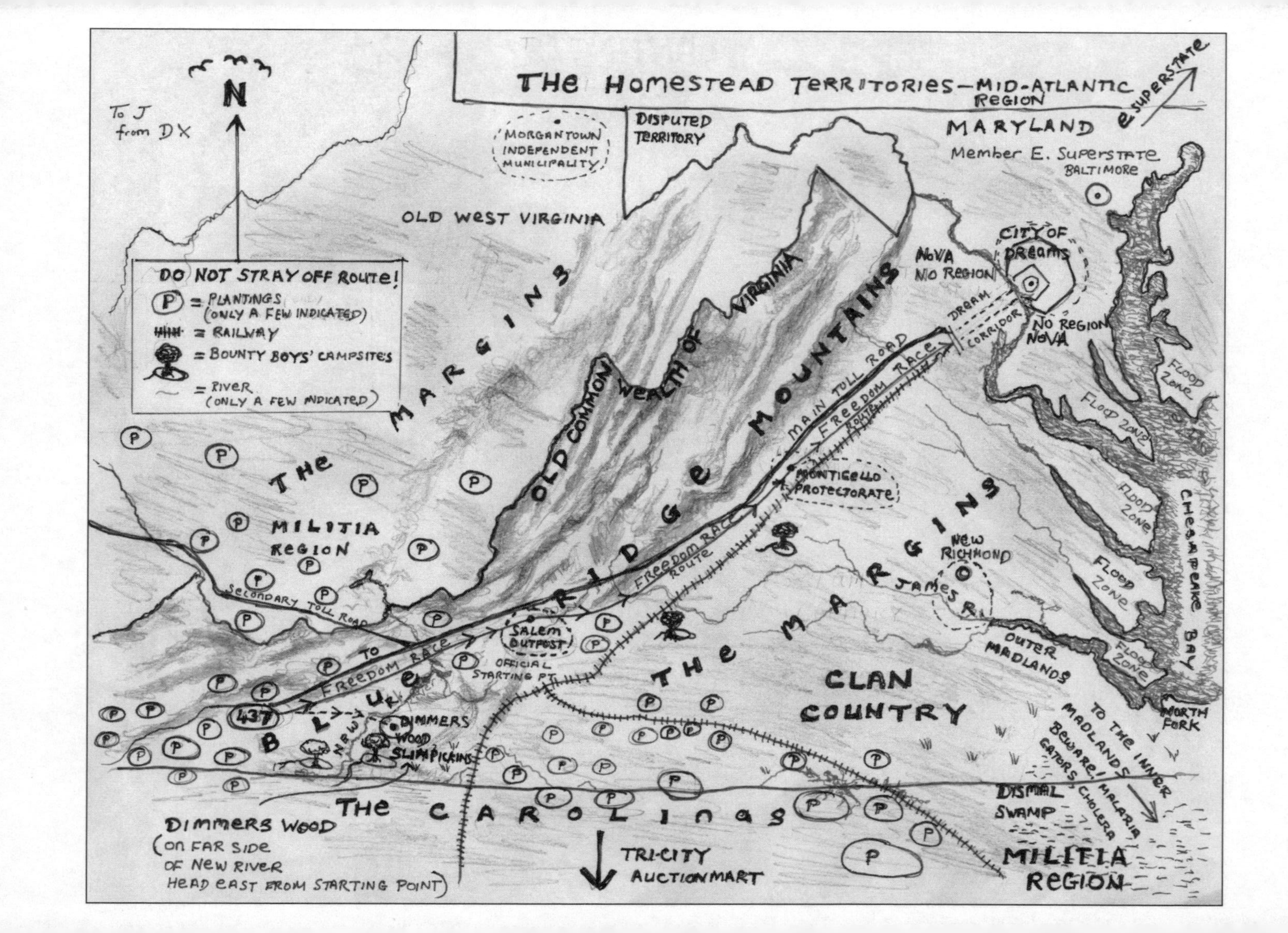
THE HOMESTEAD TERRITORIES—MID-ATLANTIC REGION
N
To J from DX
MORGANTOWN INDEPENDENT MUNICIPALITY
DISPUTED TERRITORY
MARYLAND
Member E. Superstate
E. SUPERSTATE
BALTIMORE
OLD WEST VIRGINIA
DO NOT STRAY OFF ROUTE!
P = PLANTINGS (ONLY A FEW INDICATED)
= RAILWAY
= BOUNTY BOYS' CAMPSITES
= RIVER (ONLY A FEW INDICATED)
THE MARGINS
OLD COMMONWEALTH OF VIRGINIA
BLUE RIDGE MOUNTAINS
CITY OF DREAMS
NOVA NO REGION
DREAM CORRIDOR
NO REGION NOVA
MAIN TOLL ROAD
FREEDOM RACE ROUTE
FLOOD ZONE
MONTICELLO PROTECTORATE
THE MILITIA REGION
SECONDARY TOLL ROAD
FREEDOM RACE ROUTE
NEW RICHMOND
JAMES R.
THE MARGINS
CHESAPEAKE BAY
SALEM OUTPOST
TO FREEDOM RACE
OFFICIAL STARTING PT.
OUTER MADLANDS
CLAN COUNTRY
437
NEW R.
DIMMERS WOOD
SLIMPICKINS
NORTH FORK
TO THE INNER MADLANDS
BEWARE! MALARIA
GATORS, CHOLERA
DISMAL SWAMP
THE CAROLINAS
DIMMERS WOOD (ON FAR SIDE OF NEW RIVER HEAD EAST FROM STARTING POINT)
TRI-CITY AUCTION MART
MILITIA REGION

THE DISUNITED STATES FOLLOWING TRIFURCATION
WESTERN SUPERSTATE
UNALIGNED TERRITORIES
HOMESTEAD TERRITORIES
THE MARGINS
THE MADLANDS
EASTERN SUPERSTATE
Seattle
Tacoma
Spokane
Portland
Salem
Eugene
Sacramento
Oakland
San Francisco
Fresno
Bakersfield
Santa Barbara
Los Angeles
Long Beach
San Diego
Reno
Boise
Helena
Butte
Billings
Sheridan
Idaho Falls
Ogden
Salt Lake
Provo
Cheyenne
Boulder
Denver
Colorado Springs
Pueblo
Las Vegas
Phoenix
Tucson
Santa Fe
Albuquerque
Roswell
El Paso
Fargo
Bismarck
Pierre
Rapid City
Sioux Falls
Duluth
Minneapolis
St. Paul
Madison
Waterloo
Milwaukee
Davenport
Omaha
Des Moines
Chicago
Lincoln
Peoria
Kansas City
Topeka
Springfield
Wichita
Tulsa
Oklahoma City
Amarillo
Wichita Falls
Dallas
Ft. Worth
San Angelo
Austin
San Antonio
Houston
Laredo
Brownsville
Springfield
Fort Smith
Little Rock
Greenville
Shreveport
Jackson
Baton Rouge
New Orleans
Lansing
Detroit
Gary
Ft. Wayne
Indianapolis
Cincinnati
Louisville
Frankfort
Cleveland
Columbus
Washington
Charleston
Roanoke
Richmond
Norfolk
Nashville
Asheville
Knoxville
Durham
Charlotte
Raleigh
Memphis
Greenville
Atlanta
Columbia
Birmingham
Augusta
Wilmington
Charleston
Montgomery
Savannah
Albany
Mobile
Tallahassee
Jacksonville
Orlando
St. Petersburg
Tampa
West Palm Beach
Miami
Key West
Buffalo
Montpelier
Augusta
Portland
Concord
Albany
Boston
Hartford
Providence
New York City
Philadelphia
Harrisburg
Pittsburgh
Trenton
Atlantic City
Dover
Fairbanks
Anchorage
Juneau
(UNALIGNED TERRITORIES)
(WESTERN SUPERSTATE)
Honolulu
Armistice
Urban Independents

PART ONE
PLANTING 437

Dreams are promises your imagination makes to itself.

—Toteppi proverb

Out of the cradle endlessly rocking,
Out of the mocking-bird's throat, the musical shuttle,
Out of the Ninth-month midnight . . .

—Walt Whitman

PROLOGUE

The best stories contain the best secrets, but Ji-ji and her friend Tiro knew that secrets could kill you if you shared them with the wrong people. So when Tiro's great-uncle Dreg said he would retrieve a treasure-cloth tonight and recite a story from the Cradle, Ji-ji and Tiro slapped their hands over their hearts and swore not to repeat any of it to anyone for as long as they resided in the Homestead Territories, even if that meant keeping the story secret to the end of their days.

Satisfied by the earnestness of their pledge, Uncle Dreg nodded. The two of them didn't need to be told what to do next. They dashed over to their lookout posts. Ji-ji stood guard at Uncle Dreg's poky, genuine-glass window, while Tiro eased the cabin door open a little and peered out into the night. Uncle Dreg's cabin sat in an out-of-the-way location he favored. But that didn't mean they were safe. Seeds were never safe on a planting.

Ever since her little sister Luvlydoll had taken her last rattle-breath beside her in the middle of the night, Ji-ji had been terrified of the dark. She could still hear it—the din of the silence after sweet Luvlydoll stopped breathing. And now, as Ji-ji stood by the window, she imagined the darkness moving toward her, eager to snatch away one of her last remaining sources of joy. If Darkness was out to get you, her mam said, you couldn't outrun it. Yet in spite of her terror, Ji-ji wouldn't go down without a fight. Uncle Dreg would expect no less from her. She clenched her hands into fists, then into claws, curling her fingers furiously until they ached. If any parrot-spies were lurking about outside, she'd lunge for their eyes the way Tiro had taught her to do. She was half Toteppi, after all, and Toteppi were the bravest tribe in the world.

"All clear, Uncle," Tiro announced.

As usual, Uncle Dreg wasn't convinced. "Are you sure there are no parrots around? It is easy for a boy of ten and a half to miss things of significance."

Ji-ji turned from her post at the window: "He's ten and three-quarters," she said.

"Eleven almost," Tiro boasted, cracking the door open a little farther so he could get a better view of Uncle Dreg's flower garden and vegetable patch in case a spy lurked there.

"You are like most seedlings your age," Uncle Dreg said. "Unable to perceive the danger waiting to ambush you. Are you sure there are no parrot-spies lurking out there in the dark?"

"Yeah, Uncle. I'm a thousand percent sure."

Uncle Dreg shook his head and muttered something in Totepp. One of only a handful of imports from the famous Toteppi tribe, he still remembered the old language. To Ji-ji's ears, certain words sounded like gobbledygook, horses' hooves, or clucking. But she loved the sound of it anyway, because it told her another world existed, where things were different.

Tiro objected to his great-uncle's skepticism. "Don't see even one parrot, Uncle. Not a one. I can perceive danger good as anyone."

"Sadly, that is a lie," Uncle Dreg stated, his Toteppi accent stitching his vowels and consonants together in spite of his many decades in the Territories. "If it were true, Coach Billy would not have told me he caught you and Amadee in the flying coop yesterday, acting like fools."

"We wasn't actin'," Tiro insisted.

Ji-ji giggled. "*Weren't* acting, with a *g*," she said.

"Wasn't, weren't—who cares? Amadee did this crazyass move an' the other fly-boys applauded. S'why Coach B caught us. Man, we was *good.* Even Coach B forced to admit it."

Uncle Dreg remained unimpressed: "Who but a pair of birdbrained twins would encourage each other to take a risk as foolish as that? You know what the penalty is for Precocious Elevation?"

Ji-ji jumped in. "You're not allowed to fly," she stated, resentment rising inside her as she thought about all the things she was forbidden to do. Females weren't permitted to fly in the coop at all. Risky enough, her mam said, allowing males to soar above their station. If females were allowed to do it, all hell would break loose.

"You're not eleven yet," Ji-ji said. She was almost yelling.

"Keep it down," Uncle Dreg said. "You want to wake every seed in the quarters?"

Ji-ji wasn't ready to let go of the argument. "Males gotta be eleven to fly—right, Uncle Dreg?"

"I *am* eleven . . . almost. So's Amadee . . . almost. Wait till you see Amadee soar in the fly-coop. That Mule ain't scared o' nothing."

"*Is*n't scared of *any*thing," Ji-ji corrected him.

"He ain't scared of those fancyass words neither," Tiro said, keeping his eyes glued to the darkness like someone who expected a pandemonium of parrots to leap out at him at any moment.

Ji-ji didn't have an answer for that and turned her attention to Uncle Dreg. Why was he taking so long? She craved another story the way a drug-sop craves another high. She snuck a peek at the old Tribalseed as he pushed his single bed out of the way and pulled back the tattered navy rug he'd salvaged from the garbage. It was unclear what had once adorned the rug, but Ji-ji liked to believe the faint white circles on it were moons. Tiro, who delighted in getting a rise out of her, claimed they were the white eyes of Dimmer ghosts peering at them through the dark. "Nothing worser'n a demon Dimmer," he'd tell her. "Make regular ghosts look like angels. Cling to you like a constrictor snake. Suck the soul right out o' your body." Ji-ji eyed the rug nervously. She'd never seen a Dimmer, of course. Everyone knew you only had to take one look at their moon-white eyes to be struck blind. No, Tiro was wrong. Those weren't Dimmer eyes. Those circles were kind. They were moons, one of the few pale bodies on the planting that weren't out to hurt her.

As he labored to unearth the stories, Tiro's great-uncle looked very ordinary, not at all like a Cradle wizard—though everyone, including Ji-ji's mam, who wasn't easily persuaded about anything, swore he was. With his shock of wiry white hair, his bony knees and missing teeth, the Toteppi wasn't someone you'd normally take note of. But looks could be deceiving. That was what Charra said, anyhow, and experience had taught Ji-ji that her elder sibling was usually right.

Earlier, in preparation for the storytelling, Uncle Dreg had taken his Seeing Eyes from under his pillow and hung the clunky wooden necklace around his neck. The wild eyeballs painted onto the beads enabled him to see through the Window-of-What's-to-Come. He could step backward into the past too, if he wanted, moving through time as if it were a place without fences, or any other obstacles for that matter. Ji-ji hoped he would teach her his time-travel trick one day.

Uncle Dreg removed four floorboards and reached down into what lay beneath: a treasure trench he'd dug underneath his one-room cabin years ago. His hand disappeared into the hole, then his forearm, then his entire arm. He groped around for a moment before pulling up a large leather case. Like everything else in Uncle Dreg's cabin, including Uncle Dreg himself, the case was very old. He blew off some of the dirt and wiped the rest off tenderly, the way you would wipe tears from someone's cheek. He opened the case and removed a single, rolled-up piece of cloth.

"Only one story?" Ji-ji asked.

"Only one," he replied. She must have looked disappointed because he added, "This is our Origin Story—the one that makes the others possible."

"Oh," she said, unsure of what he meant but trusting him to deliver even so.

"Come and sit," he told them, beckoning to them with his large-knuckled hand.

Ji-ji and Tiro hurried over to where Uncle Dreg sat cross-legged on the floor. They plopped down on either side of him and stayed still, knowing he wouldn't tell them anything if they fidgeted.

With great solemnity, Uncle Dreg proceeded to unfurl the cloth scroll until it was almost as long as Tiro was tall. A pale moth fell out, followed by a black beetle, both dead. As always, he placed a rock on each corner to prevent the story-cloth from rolling itself up again. Stories had minds of their own, he said, which made them hard to pin down.

A whiff of cedar and mothballs greeted Ji-ji. It was a smell she'd grown to love—a smell that whispered *story* and *magic, homeland* and *hope.* Though she was only half Toteppi and Tiro had even less Toteppi blood than that, Uncle Dreg routinely assured them that Ji-ji's half and Tiro's quarter were more than enough to grant them entry into the story-cloths. Didn't their eyes and mouths and hair testify to the fact that they were descendants of genuine Cradlers? They had to agree it was true. Well then, he would say, these stories belong to you too.

Uncle Dreg set the oil lamp closer to the cloth so they could make out the images on it. A long time ago, the reds would have been bolder, the greens more insistent, the blues deep enough to swim inside, the yellows infused with sunshine, and the browns as pretty as Ji-ji's mam's face. But now the colors were muted, like colors in moonlight or colors underwater, which only made them more mysterious. Ji-ji reached out and touched the rough cloth and ancient dyes, then sniffed her fingers so she could smell the *long-ago closeness* Uncle Dreg was always talking about.

As the lamp's fluid light danced on his face, the old man began to weave the story, running his fingers across the cloth like a blind man reading braille.

"Long ago, before we kept time with Time, there was One Being in the world."

Uncle Dreg placed his boomerang thumb near a large circle with a dot in the center. The dot looked like a tiny black star. Ji-ji figured that must be One Being's one eye. After the story was over, she'd have to remember to ask why It only had one.

"The One Being was lonely beyond lonely. It therefore made of Itself Two."

Uncle Dreg's gnarled fingers tapped two circles that lay side by side, each with a single eye. The eyes were bigger this time—more like the yolks inside a fried egg. Ji-ji asked why Two's eyes were bigger than One's. Uncle Dreg said this allowed It to see each other and know They weren't alone in the universe. To Ji-ji, this seemed reasonable, though the way he'd explained it was confusing. She wished she'd come up with this interpretation herself so she could impress Tiro. Although he was nearly two years older than she was, he was lousy at fathoming a story.

"The breaking of the One was terrible. A rupture so powerful we find echoes of it now when the earth erupts or shakes, and when the sky rumbles across our heads like a herd of buffalo."

Uncle Dreg pointed to other images—bolts of lightning, rain . . . and were those buffaloes?

"But because It was Two instead of One It was less lonely than before, though there were still times when Two yearned for more. So They made a Third—like Them, only smaller."

Ji-ji spotted a third circle, much smaller than the others. A seedling.

Tiro joked, "Guess it was smaller cos it was only a third."

Ji-ji laughed. She couldn't help herself. Uncle Dreg snorted disapprovingly and they settled down again.

"After many ages, there were countless others, each smaller than before, until tribes resided all over the world. As they multiplied, something peculiar happened. The Earth tribe grew arms and legs and walked on land; the Fish tribe grew gills to breathe in the water; and the Bird tribe grew wings and took to the air."

This middle section of the story-cloth was filled with figures. Ji-ji spotted footfolk, fishfolk, and birdfolk.

"The One-Who-Became-Two took great delight in the tribe of birds, blessing them with land and bounty. But the tribes tethered to the earth were sick with envy. For why should some rise while others were unable to do so?"

He let the question hang there for a while, the way he did when he wanted them to ponder something. Ji-ji attempted to look like she was thinking hard, though all she wanted him to do was keep telling the story. She was inside the story-cloth by now, far away from the planting.

At last, the old wizard continued: "Their chief was a skinny man with fat ambitions." Uncle Dreg pointed to a stick figure in a funny-looking hat. He was indeed very skinny. "The chief ordered his warriors to make war on the Bird tribe. The slaughter was immense. Such wailing! Such purple tears!" The artists had painted a blizzard of purple tears. They fell around the stick figures like leaves. "Those they did not kill were clipped so they could no longer take to the air, or chained to the ground so they would no longer recall the exaltation of flight."

Uncle Dreg paused. For a moment, Ji-ji was afraid the story was over, that it ended inside a circle of sorrow. If it did, she couldn't bear it. To her relief, the story wasn't over.

"The chief's wives knew that without the birds there would be a great wound in the world. For how can there be cooling breezes, the wives reasoned, without the flapping of wings to move the air? And how can there be songs unless there are birds who teach us how to sing? And how can there be joy if those who must rise are shackled to the earth? So, with the help of the wives—who bickered all day among themselves but who eventually decided they were stronger together—a few of the Bird tribe escaped up into the mountains, where the clipped ones took root and the chained ones dreamed of a New Breaking. Being close to the sky, they naturally sought the protection of the One-Who-Became-Two."

Ji-ji saw the wives huddled together like sisters, plotting their revolt. She saw the mountains beckoning in the distance.

"Because they were not seen, the other tribes forgot about the Bird tribe, though they still appeared in stories borrowed and retold—not exactly as they used to be, of course, but mutated into the likeness of those who told them. And so it was that the Bird tribe became a disobedient boy who flew too near the sun, or rebellious angels who disobeyed their father. And some became Middle Passengers who rose into the air as a spontaneous, wingless flock of ripened need. For always at the heart of every story worth telling is the elemental desire to rise.

"In all the world, there was only one people, the Rememberers, who did not forget the Bird tribe. They still knew where they made their nests. They brought them offerings so they would fill the world with song. It is said that some of the Rememberers journeyed up, up, up to the mountaintop to make a home with the birds, and that some of the birdfolk forsook their wings and swooped down to be with Rememberers they had seen from above and fallen in love with. Because falls engendered by love are not necessarily tragic.

"In Totepp, *to* means 'bird,' and *teppi* means 'to remember.' And though there has not been a full-fledged Wingchild in so long that even our elders' elders' elders do not recall exactly what they look like, the story has not lost its power. Stories are the wings of dreamers, and that is why some of the Passengers found their way back home to the tribe of lost birds whose songs filled their dreams."

Uncle Dreg stopped speaking. The First Story had been told. A silence fell over the listeners. This story was theirs; no one could snatch it from them.

For a few moments, riding the wake of the wizard's dream, Ji-ji Lottermule thought she heard birdsong. For a few moments, she wasn't afraid of the dark, or rats, or steaders, or her father-man, or the future. For a few blissful moments, she wasn't afraid of anything at all.

1 THE CRADLE

A convulsive wail catapulted Ji-ji awake. Oletto had woken to nurse. The wailing reached a crescendo. Each night her little brother woke at ten and two, guzzled from her mam's teat like a drunkard, then fell back to sleep so rapidly it looked like he was faking it. Only he wasn't—not according to Ji-ji's mam, who welcomed the wailing, said it assured her that her lastborn was still with them. "Don't ever leave a seedling to purple-wail like that, Ji-ji," Silapu would warn. "Unanswered yearning can split you wide open, force you to spend the rest of your life searching for foolish ways to plug up the wound."

Ji-ji rolled over to face the tattered curtain hanging over the doorway that separated her bedroom from the main room. For a few seconds, she tried to convince herself her name wasn't Jellybean Lottermule. She was Ji-ji Jubilation, the *j*'s in her first name pronounced like the *g* in *gee whiz*. She'd chosen it because it sounded cute and sassy, neither of which she was. "Brown as dung" the steaders called her, nothing like her dark and pretty mam, or Charra, her light-skinned, pretty sister. Not that she gave a damn what dumbass steaders thought. The only name worse than Jellybean was Lottermule. Thinking about it made her want to gag.

Oletto's wails turned to hiccuping whimpers. Sleep had deserted her, so Ji-ji took refuge in her pretend life. She was living *Free! Free! Free!* in Dream City . . . or up in the Eastern SuperState maybe, where rumor had it they'd rebuilt some of the iconic skyscrapers, locating them farther back from the coast this time cos SuperStaters didn't blame floods on the wrath of God like steaders did. She pictured herself living in a penthouse—a term Father-Man Lotter used to describe the main offices of the Territorial Headquarters in the Father-City of Armistice, a.k.a. the City of Cages. (*Don't think about their disgusting capital. It'll drive you crazy. Go back to where you can live Free. . . .*) She found a place of refuge again.

She was a half-Toteppi princess living high on the hog with her mam and little brother in a penthouse hundreds of miles from the Territories. No man could ever touch her or beat her. Ji-ji Jubilation was her very own self on her very own terms. . . .

Her brother's whimpers turned to shrieks. The truth gnawed like rats, severing the hope-rope she clung to. They weren't living in a liberty Super-State or an Independent oasis; they were trapped at the butt end of the Old Commonwealth of Virginia on one of the hundreds of plantings homesteaders established following the Civil War Sequel. She was Jellybean Lottermule, chief kitchen-seed. . . . It would never be enough. . . .

Ji-ji grabbed her wristwatch from the small bookshelf Tiro had made for her fourteenth birthday. She'd won the watch in one of the planting races. She stared at the hands on the watch's face. It was a child's wind-up watch, which explained why the steaders had given it as a prize to the fastest female runner. A tiny, coal-black cartoon mouse pointed his white-gloved, chubby fingers at the numbers on the watch face. The mouse was grinning so hard it looked painful. He reminded Ji-ji of the black-faced minstrels who played at the barn dance during the Harvesting Festival. Two A.M. Only three more hours to go before her morning run. By six thirty, she'd be preparing Lotter's breakfast at the father-house. He liked to eat early: poached eggs cooked just right—never hard-set but not undercooked either; coffee smooth not bitter—no milk, no sugar. Father-Man Lotter didn't go in for diluting anything.

Oletto's whimpers turned to screams. If she didn't get an hour or more of sleep she'd be dragging all day. She tried to think of herself as lucky. At fourteen, she was one of the few postpubescent females still living in her mam's cabin. She recited the words Zaini, Tiro's mam, had taught her to raise her spirits: "*Our mother, which art the Cradle, may we know our hallowed names.*" She took a deep breath and blew it out slowly to calm herself, then stepped lightly out of bed. Yawning, she shuffled through the bedroom, careful to avoid the twelve dents in the floor made by the legs of her three lost siblings' beds. The dents they'd left behind were pretty much all she had to remember them by. Stepping on them would have seemed like blasphemy.

Ji-ji entered the only other room in the cabin. Silapu must have been up for a while because a crackling fireplace warded off the winter chill. Apart from Oletto's cradle and Lotter's fancy rocking chair, all their other furniture was junk: a rickety table on a tired rug whose edges curled up like fried bacon; three wobbly wooden chairs, one with part of its back missing; and a sink with a working pump—admittedly a luxury few seed cabins possessed.

Ji-ji glanced over at the one object in the room—apart from her brother's magnificent cradle, of course—that didn't make her want to scream. Tiro's mam Zaini had made the quilt as a grieving gift for Silapu after Luvlydoll died. It depicted blackbirds—three perched in a tree while a few dozen took off from the branches in a burst of something akin to fireworks on the Fourth of July. The quilt almost convinced you the seedmate cabin was home, almost made you forget that behind it was Lotter's seeding bed. Not that her mam used it much. When Lotter wasn't paying her a seeding call, Silapu didn't sleep in the mating bed, opting instead for a makeshift bed on the floor. However hard she scrubbed, she claimed, it was impossible to wash Lotter's mating stench from the sheets.

Having dragged a chair over from the table, Ji-ji sat down beside the cradle. Woven from twigs fashioned into impossible patterns, it had solid black walnut rockers decorated with intricate carvings of beasts and birds. Six months before, a few hours after her mam had given birth, Uncle Dreg had shown up out of the blue to present Silapu with the magnificent cradle. When Ji-ji had asked him how he'd known her mam had seedbirthed, he'd pointed to his Seeing Eye necklace and smiled the way you do when you want to keep someone guessing. "This cradle will keep your offspring safe," the wizard had promised.

"Your brother is teething," Silapu declared with unmistakable pride. "His front tooth is sprouting, see? It is a sharp one. He will start biting down hard when he nurses. You were a biter. . . ."

Ji-ji poked her index finger into Oletto's mouth—not easy because he was snuffling around for the large dark nipple he craved—and found his wayward tooth. It had put down roots in the middle of his top gum.

"That center tooth is a sign," Silapu stated. Her Toteppi accent made her sound wise. "My own father's front tooth was in the center like this one. It is my father come to me again. 'Same mouth, same words'—that is what we Toteppi say. When this one is a warrior grown, he will sound like my father. His voice will boom out across the bush."

"We're not in the bush," Ji-j reminded her. "We're in the Homestead Territories."

"Only when our eyes are open," Silapu insisted.

Ji-ji smiled. It was good to hear her mam speak of her homeland, good to see her happy again. Tribalseed "imports" from the Cradle, shipped over to the Territories to address the severe labor shortage, sometimes wasted away or killed themselves soon after they arrived on transport planes or cargo ships. Silapu had been Ji-ji's age when she'd been snatched from the Cradle by pickers. Her mam knew the old words and the old stories, though unlike Uncle Dreg, she never spoke them aloud. "You know what memories are, Jellybean?" she'd said once to Ji-ji, after Clay had been auctionmarted. "Memories are knives—*slice, slice*!" She'd slashed her arms through the air and banged her head against the wall until Ji-ji and Charra coaxed her quiet. But tonight, as Silapu looked at her lastborn, there was a deep contentment and a Toteppi pride in her eyes.

"Do you hear that, Bonbon?" Ji-ji asked, suddenly happy. "Mam says all you need to do is keep your eyes shut an' you won't even know you're on a planting."

Ji-ji loved to use the nickname she'd given her little brother. She'd had a bonbon once—a dark chocolate one. It had slipped down her throat as easy as spit. She wished her lost brother and sisters could have seen him; they would have loved him too. But after metaflu took Luvlydoll, and they shipped Clay off to the auctionmart, and Charra—god knows what happened to Charra—Ji-ji was the only one left. Charra, the last of the three to be lost, had disappeared some months ago. Silapu, who'd been barely holding things together before then, was inconsolable. She blamed herself for what happened, though she wouldn't tell Ji-ji why. Crazy with grief, she'd drowned her sorrows in cheap whiskey from the planting store and pills she got from Lotter. She hadn't known she was pregnant until roughly the fifth month. When Doc Riff diagnosed her condition, she swore she'd never touch a drop of booze or swallow another of Lotter's pills—as long as her offspring was healthy and she was allowed to keep him. She sensed early that her lastborn was a boy, the seedling who would make her life bearable, she said. Silapu and Ji-ji had delivered Bonbon without a midwife or doctor in attendance. Ji-ji suspected her mam had somehow guessed her lastborn's secret.

When Bonbon slipped out of the seed canal into her hands, Ji-ji had stared at the seedling in disbelief. Unlike Silapu's other liveborns and deadborns, the infant was Midnight dark. Ji-ji had been "disappointingly dusky" herself, according to Lotter, her complexion aligning more closely with a typical Commonseed's than a Mule's. But Lotter reconciled himself to Jellybean's "dun-colored cheeks and nappy head." Bonbon's case was much more extreme, which was why both Ji-ji and her mam were terror-struck when they saw him.

Among Tribalseeds and products of Commonseed matings, very dark complexions were not unusual. Biracial Muleseeds, on the other hand, especially those begat by father-men, were supposed to testify to the strength of the patriarchal seed. Bonbon's complexion was on the Midnight arc of the official Color Wheel—a number 35 or 36. According to steader doctrine, Muleseeds on the duskiest arc (a.k.a. the *cuckold arc*) testified to the promiscuity of a seedmate.

Silapu and Ji-ji were thrown into a panic. They debated making a run for it. But how would they scale the electric fence without being fried? Even if they managed it somehow, the planting search hounds would hunt them down, or mutant beasts roaming The Margins would tear them to pieces. Silapu was terrified of the mutant big-cat and wolf species unleashed by the Territories to discourage trespass—an experiment gone hideously wrong. How would she protect her lastborn if they ran into a pride of snarlcats or a pack of stripers?

Ji-ji knew mutants and search hounds weren't the only horrors they would encounter. Because Uncle Dreg served as an errander for Cropmaster Herring (one of only four seeds on the planting who had a Right to Roam) he'd seen the world outside the 437th and had told her and Tiro how brutal it was, revealing things about his travels that made her blood run cold. She'd also read *An Abbreviated History of These Disunited States,* a book Miss Zyla Clobershay had given her days before she was fired for teaching things not on the seed curriculum. Though the Sequel had ended decades before, and some parts of the nation were at last beginning to emerge from the chaos created by the Long Warming, the former United States could be hell on earth for seeds.

Fueled by armed militias and taking advantage of the turmoil caused by shifts in climate, all of the Deep South and great swaths of the country's Midwest had seceded from the union to form the self-governing Homestead Territories. After the Sequel, the Eastern and Western SuperStates and the Homestead Territories had signed an uneasy truce, to the consternation of many urbanites in the Territories who were ready to die rather than submit to Territorial rule. Cities like Atlanta, Chicago, TriCity, Birmingham—and smaller places like Oxford, Mississippi, and Fayetteville, Arkansas—rebelled. In a coordinated effort that took the Territories by surprise, city mayors signed DUIs—Declarations of Urban Independence—broke ties with the Territories, and formed militias of their own. At first, flush with their own success, the Independents had welcomed refugees. But that soon changed when they understood the precariousness of their situation.

What Ji-ji learned from the history book she kept strapped to the underside of her bed refuted everything on the seed curriculum. The United States wasn't "reformed and revitalized," as the steaders liked to put it. It was a fractured, jittery nation teetering on the edge of total anarchy.

Ji-ji might have been afraid to tell Silapu the unvarnished truth, but Uncle Dreg had no such reservations. When he'd visited them to deliver the cradle a few hours after Silapu had given birth, he'd also delivered dire warnings about the dangers that awaited them should they try to run (though how he knew they'd been thinking about doing so, neither of them could figure out). He painted an alarming picture: the SuperStates and Independents were turning away hordes of asylum seekers; outbreaks of metaflu, cholera, and malaria had turned the squalid shantytowns that had sprung up around the Independents into death traps. If they made it to Dream City without entry papers, they would join the thousands of other refugees in the No Region. They would live in sight of a Dream they could never enter and a wall they could never climb.

The old wizard had taken Silapu's hand tenderly in his own. "Place your trust in the Freedom Race," he'd told her. "And in your courageous offspring. I have never seen another racer fly as fast as your thirdborn. When Ji-ji wins, she will petition for you and the infant."

In a tone brimming with certainty, Uncle Dreg had told Silapu her lastborn had come to him as a grown Freeman during one of his journeys through future-time. "He stood tall in the Cradle, like your father. His voice echoed across the land. I have also seen Ji-ji in the Window-of-What's-to-Come, wearing the Freedom Race logo and running like the wind. So you see, Sila. All will be well."

After Dreg had left, Silapu—no slouch herself when it came to manipulation—said it was ironic that the old wizard had used Ji-ji's gift as a runner to persuade them not to run. Then she'd said something else that still haunted Ji-ji: "Let us hope we do not regret placing so much faith in your abilities, Jellybean." Ever since, Ji-ji had thrown herself even more aggressively into her training, often going on late-night runs in addition to predawn ones, running till her feet bled and her heart was a piston in her chest. She was their only hope now; she had to succeed.

Deciding not to make a run for it had meant facing Lotter. In hopes of avoiding him, Silapu hadn't ventured out during the day, not even to the outhouse, for fear one of Lotter's parrots would spot her and relay the fact that she'd seedbirthed. On the seventh night, however, without warning, Lotter had barged in like a man possessed. Before they could stop him, he'd snatched up Bonbon and examined him from head to toe, rubbing his thumb over his seedling's back and shoulders like someone who could erase the blackness completely if he worked at it hard enough. After Lotter had finished rubbing, he'd done something they'd hardly ever seen him do before. He'd *laughed*—a full-throated guffaw. By this time Ji-ji was certain Lotter was drunk, high, or both. He'd wrapped his seedling carefully in the mushroom-colored seeding quilt Zaini had made and eased himself into his rocking chair. Still chuckling, he'd taken out his pipe and puffed contentedly while he rocked his dusky seed in his fairskin arms, as if Oletto were his Son-Proper instead of his Mule.

"Little bugger's black as pitch, Mammy Tep," he'd said, addressing his dumbstruck seedmate. "Black as an import. . . . But pretty as the devil in spite of that. See those big black eyes round as moons? *Damn!* You ever seen a seedling prettier'n this one?" Lotter assured his favorite seedmate she could keep her lastborn. Said he'd "figure out the rest later." It was the first time Ji-ji could remember her mam looking at her father-man with something approaching affection. It had always been the other way around—Lotter needing her so much he'd try to beat the love out of himself by beating her. That's what her mam said anyhow. Ji-ji wasn't convinced a selfish bastard like Lotter was capable of loving anyone.

In the six months since Bonbon's birth, every day had been a celebration. Whenever Bonbon grasped Ji-ji's Chestnut finger in his Midnight ones, everything felt right.

Ji-ji and Silapu were laughing at Bonbon's ecstatic gurgling when they heard footsteps outside the rough-hewn wooden door. They knew at once who it was: Lotter making one of his late-night seeding calls. He'd likely be high or drunk. Mean too.

Reluctantly, Silapu placed her sleeping offspring back in his cradle. In his dreams, Bonbon was sucking on an invisible nipple as though his life depended on it.

Ji-ji rose hurriedly. She stood next to the cradle in her flimsy cotton nightshift. Scared the light from the fire behind her would make it see-through, she covered herself with her hands.

Arundale Lotter thrust open the door and stood stock-still in the doorway. His thick blond hair was pulled back, his steader's beard neatly combed.

Ji-ji was hurrying toward her bedroom when something made her stop dead.

Lotter took one step forward. Usually, when he entered one of his seedmate cabins, he swallowed everything whole; this time something was different. He was hesitant, if she could apply a word like that to a father-man like him. Behind him, the night was pitch-black: no moon, no stars. Lotter stood inside a headstone of gloom. A feeling of dread enveloped her. *It's only the night,* she thought, tamping down her sense of foreboding. But the shadows writhing on the uneven walls looked sinister. More sinister still were the shadows licking the rocker Lotter had gone to enormous lengths to have custom-made because he wanted to sit in comfort when he made a seeding call. Neither Mam nor Ji-ji used Lotter's rocker, unwilling to plant their asses where his had been. Silapu had eaten a late supper; her plate and fork were still on the table. He wouldn't like that. He liked things clean and put away in their rightful places.

Lotter's scent wafted toward Ji-ji on night breeze—a lavender-citrus, musky fragrance that preceded him like a warning shot. He had the man-scent shipped all the way from Armistice. It arrived in a brown velvet box whose color would fall squarely in the middle of the Burnt Sienna arc of the Color Wheel, exactly where her mam's complexion did. In gold calligraphy on the inside of the box was the perfume's fancy name: *Dark Essenceial.* Because she hadn't known any better as a seedling, Ji-ji used to repeat that name to herself, swishing it around in her mouth like spring water on a hot day. Father-Man Lotter was the only one of the thirteen father-men on the 437th who wore scent. Not even Cropmaster Herring—who, like every cropmaster on every planting in the Territories, had the right to lord it over his disciples—indulged in that kind of vanity.

Without warning, two tall men stepped out of the shadows and took up positions on either side of Lotter. Ji-ji recognized them at once. The brute on Lotter's right went by the name of Vanguard Casper. He was Lotter's chief overseer—a man of immense height and girth who always, for some inexplicable reason, made Ji-ji think of shovels. Van Casper's beard reached almost to his waist. The one on Lotter's left was Matton Longsby, the blond guard only a few years older than Ji-ji, whose beard was more of a promise than a fact. Everyone commented on how much the guard looked like Lotter's Son-Proper, if he'd had one, which he didn't. (When drunk or high, Lotter complained to Silapu that his Wife-Proper in Armistice was as frigid as a glacier and as barren as a desert. *No point in dragging the bitch down here to the boondocks,* he'd say, *if she can't be put to good use.*)

Seconds passed. Ji-ji felt panic rise inside her. Everything seemed to be scurrying for the exits—screams, even piss. . . . She held them in, knowing how disgusted Lotter would be if she didn't.

It was when Lotter turned to give instructions to 'Seer Casper that Ji-ji and her mam saw it. Lotter's long blond hair was pulled back into a ponytail with a fat black seizure ribbon!

"*NO!*" Silapu cried. "*I kill you if you do this thing!*"

To Ji-ji it seemed as though someone had fired a starting pistol. Everything took off running as Silapu leapt toward Lotter, screaming like something on fire. Lotter pushed her roughly to the side. Silapu recovered and flung herself toward the cradle. Casper grabbed her before she could snatch up her seedling.

Ji-ji rushed to help her mam but found herself hoisted off the floor by the blond guard as she kicked and screamed. It was useless. Matton Longsby's grip was as strong as hope-rope.

Mad with terror, Silapu punched the overseer in the eye. 'Seer Casper reeled back in fury. He came at her again, cinching her so tight round the waist she gasped for breath. Silapu let out a mother's agonized roar.

Casper yelled at her: "Shut the fuck up, bitch!"

Immediately, the overseer realized his mistake. Still trying to shield himself from Silapu's crazed attack, he looked over at his boss and began to apologize.

Lotter interrupted him: "Overseer Casper, have eighty rebel dollars in an envelope on my desk by dawn." No one doled out an eighty-dollar fine for cussing, but Casper knew how foolhardy it would be to argue with a man like Arundale Lotter. "And another thing. You hurt one hair on my seedmate's head and I will kill you. Is that clear?"

Van Casper, his face a thunderstorm, nodded. The overseer gritted his teeth and held Silapu tight, wincing as her frenzied kicks made contact with his shins. Bonbon was screaming bloody murder. Every seed in Lotter's quarters and beyond could hear his wails.

When Lotter yanked open the flap of his leather satchel and drew from it a white wooden wheel the size of a dinner plate, Silapu's agonized cries echoed around the small cabin. Glued at regular intervals along the wheel's rim were thirty-six color swatches made from small squares of cloth—paler swatches first, followed by light tans, deeper tans, browns, black-browns, and finally the darkest shades of all, on the Coal and Midnight arcs. Bending over the wizard's beautiful cradle, Father-Man Lotter held the Wheel to the seedling's face, beginning with the lightest swatches and rotating it until he reached the shade that matched his seedling's skin color.

He read the official ruling in a tight, emotionless voice: "I, Arundale

Lotter, First Father-Man on Planting 437, hereby decree the fifth seedling of botanical Silapu Lotterseedmate to be a number 35 on the Midnight arc of the Color Wheel. He fails to testify to the strength of the patriarchal seed, attesting instead to the hussification of his mam and the blatant disrespect she has shown to myself, her fathermate and benefactor. Accordingly, the seedling will be removed from Planting 437 and shipped to a server camp where he will be raised nameless to serve the Territories as a Cloth-35. May his mam understand the error of her ways. May all who witness her shame be mindful of the authority of the Color Wheel and the divine hierarchy of the Great Ladder."

Lotter reached back and tore off his seizure ribbon. Set Free, his blond locks cascaded to his shoulders. He picked up Bonbon and draped the black worm of a ribbon round his seedling's chubby neck. Lotter hadn't looked at Silapu when he'd read the pronouncement, but he did so now. His handsome face was battered by the firelight; it looked like he was crying. Ji-ji didn't give a shit if he was. Her mam would never survive this. Might as well put a gun to her head.

Ji-ji tried to utter Bonbon's name, but she was choking back tears and struggling against the viselike grip of the bastard guard who held her.

Just then, Uncle Dreg arrived with his niece Zaini. Ji-ji knew why Lotter had ordered them to be there. Left to her own devices, Silapu would kill herself.

"Get her out of my sight, Dreg!" Lotter ordered. "Don't make me whip her quiet."

Lotter's voice cracked when he said this. She looked over at Uncle Dreg. He and Zaini were trying and failing to calm Silapu. Using her eyes, Ji-ji pleaded with Uncle Dreg to intervene. Uncle Dreg was an Oziadhee, a Toteppi wizard from the Cradle, the person who'd told her magical stories and fooled her into believing anything was possible. "Please," she whispered. "*Please!*" But he only shook his head and said something to her mam in Totepp—some worthless drivel about hope.

Zaini and Uncle Dreg dragged Silapu from the cabin as she called out to Bonbon and flung curses at Lotter, who ordered Casper to escort them safely back to Zaini's cabin. "Not a hair on her head, Casper—understand?" Lotter warned again.

"Yessir," Casper said, and followed them out. It took a long time for Silapu's screams to fade into the night.

"Stay here, Longsby. I've sent over to Petrus' quarters for . . ." Lotter paused. "What's that Mule's name? Lua? Sent for her mam too. They'll be here soon." He addressed Ji-ji. "Don't do anything stupid, Jellybean. You're your mam's Last&Only now."

Ji-ji spat at him. The arc of spittle fell short and landed at his feet. If Guard Longsby hadn't spoken up at that moment, Ji-ji suspected her father-man would have beaten her bloody.

"Let me carry the Serverseed, sir," Longsby suggested.

Although Lotter had given Bonbon that designation, he looked daggers at the young guard when he uttered the word *Serverseed*. Lotter, who never cussed in front of his men, said he'd carry his own damn seedling himself.

Ji-ji snatched at straws. He'd used the possessive to refer to Bonbon. Did that mean he wouldn't issue a Public Condemnation against her mam for whoring? What did it matter either way when he'd already snatched the one person her mam needed to keep on breathing?

Lotter tucked an apoplectic Bonbon under one arm like a bag of cornmeal.

As he stepped into the headstone doorway, Ji-ji made one last plea: "*Please*, Father-Man! Let me kiss Bonbon goodbye!"

Lotter didn't seem to know at first who Bonbon was. He glanced down at the screaming seedling as if he couldn't imagine how he got there.

"Oletto you mean? Her lastborn? You want to kiss him?"

Lotter seemed to think about it; then he shook his head. Without another word, he tore out into the gloom.

Her father-man had ripped her arm off. He'd torn open her chest and excised the last sliver of hope. Wrenching herself from the guard's grip, she fell to her knees, gasping. She would never see her little brother again. Bonbon, the last of her four siblings, was gone.

2 TONGUES OF FLAME

"Your brother'll be okay," a voice said.

Guard Longsby squatted down beside her. He was patronizing her—employing the term *brother* even though he knew seeds weren't classified as Siblings-Proper.

"*The hell he will!*" she cried, half hoping Lotter would hear her and return to teach her a lesson. If he did, she would rip his throat out. She gulped back tears and added, "You know what they do to Serverseeds in those camps? Treat 'em worse than dogs!"

"He'll be okay," the young guard repeated. Stupid, empty words. Platitudes.

They'd wound up next to the table. And there it was—Mam's fork, exactly where she'd left it. Ji-ji reached up and grabbed it. She brought it down hard, aiming for Longsby's hand. He jerked it away before she could stab him.

Quick as a flash, he grabbed her wrist, thrust his left knee into her abdomen, pushed her down, and flung his body on top of hers. He pounded her right hand into the floor until she dropped the fork. He was as heavy as lead.

"You itchin' to wind up roped to the whippin' post!"

Longsby's face was close to hers. So close. His eyes—she could see them clearly now—were as icy blue as Lotter's. She could smell his beard, almost expected it to be lavender-citrusy like Lotter's. It wasn't. It smelled waxy from the planting soap.

Ji-ji blurted out the first thing that came to her: "Your stupid beard looks like *shit*!"

"What the *hell* . . . ? You're beggin' for a whippin'!"

The young guard retrieved the fork and bounded up off the cabin floor in a single, agile move. "Who d'you think you are, Mule? I could have you strung up for that stunt."

Before she could think of a way to dig herself in deeper, Lua and Aunt Marcie arrived. Lua ran to Ji-ji and flung her arms around her neck.

Longsby looked at Ji-ji like someone who couldn't decide whether to smack her, report her, or forgive her. She didn't want his forgiveness. She wanted to stab his hand with her mam's fork until that weird smirk he often wore was torn from his face. The guard seemed to know what she was thinking. "Mind your mouth, y'hear?" he said, though she hadn't said anything out loud. He placed the fork back on the table and hurried out.

Her attack had been stupid. No one attacked a guard and got away with it. If he reported her, she would be hauled up in front of Inquisitor Tryton and sentenced to solitary in PenPen. The fork would be deemed a deadly weapon. Unless Lotter intervened, she would be classified as a Wild Seed and stripped of her plum position as chief kitchen-seed—could even get shipped to the mines in the neighboring parishes of Appalachia. Ji-ji's fury was mixed with an almost uncontrollable grief. Why had she and her mam assumed they could trust Lotter when everything told them seeds don't get to hold on to something as beautiful and precious as Bonbon?

Thirty minutes passed . . . an hour. Lua and Aunt Marcie tried to comfort her, but Ji-ji was desperate to be alone and begged them to leave—said she had to get an hour or two of sleep before her early shift at the planting dining hall. They both protested.

"We don't feel right 'bout leaving you, Ji-ji," Lua argued. "You sure you ain't about to do nothing reckless? Don't forget you got something to cling to. Next year's Big Race ain't far off. Fourteen months." Lua frowned. Math wasn't her strong suit. "Fifteen months tops. You an' Tiro'll both be eligible next year. You the best runner we ever seen on the 437th, an' Tiro's the best flyer. Better'n any we got this year. Tiro flies like a bird in that coop—right, Mam?" Aunt Marcie nodded in agreement. "An' you give a snarlcat a run for its money, Uncle Dreg says. After you win, you can petition for your mam. Petition for Bonbon too."

Ji-ji wanted to scream—an earth-shattering scream, powerful enough to split open the crust of the world. Instead, she took out her fury on Lua.

"How can I petition for Bonbon, dumbass, when I don't know where they're taking him?"

Lua looked as though she'd been hit. Ji-ji came to her senses. Her best friend was even worse off than she was. Her eight siblings were dead or auctioned off to other plantings, and Lua had been mated to Petrus last year. Petrus was in his fifties; Lua wasn't yet fourteen. Petrus expected his seedmates to be on call every night. If he found her cabin empty there would be hell to pay.

"Sorry, Lu," Ji-ji added. "I didn't mean—"

"S'okay." Lua always forgave everyone. Even Petrus.

"We know you're hurting," Aunt Marcie added, which made Ji-ji feel even worse.

"Promise you won't do nothing dumb?" Lua urged again. "*Anything* dumb's what I mean."

"I promise," Ji-ji replied. She forced herself to sound calm. "Go back to your quarters, Lua. Petrus'll hit the roof if he finds you missing. Last&Onlys like us—we got a special duty to keep on breathing. You told me that once, remember?" Lua nodded. "I'll be okay, Lu. I promise."

When at last Ji-ji had the cabin to herself, she checked to see the door was firmly closed, walked over to the fireplace, and picked up the sturdiest log she could find from the pile near the hearth. She raised it above her head and let it fall over and over again until all that was left of Uncle Dreg's beautiful cradle was a mound of splinters.

She wanted to hate him for filling her head with dream stories when she was little, yet she already knew she wouldn't find much comfort in that. She sat on the floor by the fire and rocked back and forth, recalling the vicious rhyme steaders liked to throw in seeds' faces:

The only way for a seed to be Free
Is to swing on high from a penal tree.

She remembered something Uncle Dreg used to say about not letting words like that ricochet around in your head because they could smash you to pieces. And now, she'd smashed Uncle Dreg's beautiful cradle, the one precious thing she had to remember Bonbon by!

"Oh Bonbon!" Ji-ji moaned. "How will you ever know how much you were loved?"

She placed a hand over her heart and gazed deep into the flames. Imitating the steader vows she'd grown up with, she made up one of her own.

"I, Jellybean 'Ji-ji' Lottermule, reared in captivity on Planting 437 in the Homestead Territories, hereby swear to find my little brother Oletto 'Bonbon' Lottermule, a designated Serverseed, an' set him Free!"

A series of loud sparks leapt from the fire.

"I'm coming for you, Bonbon," she whispered. "You'll never grow up to be a Serverseed, I swear. Don't cry. Your big sister's coming to save you."

The fire whispered, hissed, and crackled as wild yellow tongues spoke to her. In a trance, she fed twig after twig into the raging fire. She watched, eyes aflame, until it devoured every last one.

3 LAST&ONLY

Bettieann Plowman, the most senior of Planting 437's senior midwives, uttered the same sentence she'd uttered a dozen times: "Lua's pelvis is as narrow as a male's, Marcie."

Ji-ji would have liked nothing better than to tell the midwife to shut the hell up. It wasn't poor Lua's fault her pelvis was narrow. But it was dangerous to spar with the crabby midwife. As a certified African-American Indigenous, Bettieann Plowman enjoyed rights botanicals could only dream about. Her status entitled her to a multitude of luxuries: a salary—in trade dollars if she wanted; a generous food allowance; the right to wear clothing in any color; the right to come and go as she pleased, as long as she had a halfway decent reason for roaming; the right to keep her offspring (not that she had any); and the most relevant right of all in the current situation—the right to lodge complaints against botanicals and have them adjudicated by Inquisitor Tryton. Ji-ji had already infuriated Bettieann by sneaking into Father-Man Petrus' seed quarters so she could be by Lua's side. She didn't dare make matters worse. As Bettieann often boasted, she was in possession of documents that traced her lineage back to the first Civil War—far more than the three generations required for African-Americans and Native peoples in the Territories to petition for Indigenous status. She might be darker than most of the botanicals on the planting but she was a "certified human," a "genuine, old-school American."

Bettieann had a marked preference for abject humility in botanicals. Seeds—especially arrogant ones like Uncle Dreg, Silapu, and Ji-ji—pushed every button she had. She had two people she could feasibly call friends: Doc Riff (whose tolerance was legendary) and Aunt Marcie (who would befriend the devil himself if he asked her to). Ji-ji wondered if Bettieann's long-standing friendship with Marcie helped explain why the midwife was jumpy. Twice she'd dropped her instruments. Once her face had glazed over completely. She'd begun muttering to herself like a loon—scared them half to death. Ji-ji suspected she was drunk—an even better reason to stay on her good side.

When she'd burst through the door of Lua's seedmate cabin yesterday afternoon, Ji-ji had braved a torrent of abuse from the midwife, been greeted by a grateful smile from her best friend, and received a warm embrace from Aunt Marcie. Against Bettieann's express wishes, Ji-ji had been permitted to remain, though she'd had to swear on a copy of the seeds' version of *The One True Text* that she would hide if Father-Man Petrus came to check on how labor was progressing.

"Last thing Petrus wants to see," Bettieann had declared hotly, "is his archrival's uppity Mule near his seedbed. Like to accuse you an' me both of witchery if things go south."

"Are things going south?" Ji-ji had asked, triggering Bettieann's wrath.

"Jellybean Lottermule, you surely are the most annoying Mule on the 437th! No wonder your mam's slid down the whiskey chute again."

After that, Ji-ji didn't say much. She had to content herself with holding Lua's left hand while Aunt Marcie clutched her right. She tried to quiet the little voices in her head whispering that this seedbirth would be doomed too, like the one she and Lua had witnessed a few months back when their friend Mbeke had expired in a pool of blood and pus after thirty hours of agony.

Searching for reassurance, Ji-ji looked from Bettieann to Aunt Marcie—not her real aunt by blood but an aunt in the best sense of the word nevertheless. A devout Commonseed who accepted her lot with the stoicism of Job (the copy of *The One True Text* was hers), Marcie rocked back and forth in agitation, muttering invocations to the god steaders required seeds to worship—a god who was in agreement with steaders about everything.

Unlike Bettieann, who was built to last, Lua's mam could be toppled by a puff of wind. Marcie's eyes, which must have been striking once, were heavy with exhaustion. In honor of the seedbirthing, Marcie's tight braids shone with coconut oil. She'd braided Lua's hair too. The whorled-galaxy style mirrored her own. Lua had been thrashing about for ages; several of her braids had come undone. Ji-ji was reminded of Afarra, her mam's little Serverseed, whose hair was always a mess.

She looked at Bettieann, who was perched on her midwifery stool in her bulky, blood-spattered apron. Maybe she would inspire confidence? The apron's roomy kangaroo pocket held her seedbirthing instruments. Every so often she coughed a wad of phlegm into a handkerchief, but at least her handkerchief was reasonably clean. Not for the first time, Ji-ji wished Miss Clobershay hadn't taught them so much about hygiene.

By now there was no denying it. Lua's bigheaded Piglet was stuck. *Piglet* was the secret name Ji-ji had given Petrus' seedling—a nod to the father-man's porcine nostrils and prized pig farm. It pleased Ji-ji to think about how incensed he would be if he knew. She allowed herself to gloat over the name for a moment, before fear pulled her back to memories of Mbeke's nightmare seedbirth.

Ji-ji's friend Mbeke had been bound to a fairskin Liberty Laborer—an itinerant, work-for-hire steader. On that dreadful night when she'd pushed and strained to expel the laborer's fat-headed seedling, Ji-ji had been petrified. Mbeke's humble status as seedmate to a low-class itinerant laborer, albeit a fairskin, meant she wasn't entitled to the ministration of a senior midwife. Instead, Midwife Carolann—the least skilled and most frequently drunk of all the midwife-Anns on the planting—had tended her. Ji-ji reminded herself that Lua's case was nothing like Mbeke's. Lua had Bettieann, renowned for snatching seedmates and their offspring from the jaws of death. Nothing tragic was going to happen while she was in attendance. Yet Ji-ji would have felt much better if Doc Riff had gotten back from the 500s to help Lua through this. The Native Indigenous doctor was so skillful that Cropmaster Herring himself had been known to call upon his services.

When Lua let out another ear-piercing scream, Ji-ji's breath caught in her throat. Silently, Ji-ji cursed Danfrith Petrus. The Sixth Father-Man of Planting 437 was rabid for a male seedling, preferably on the lighter side. He'd plowed Lua regularly, sometimes calling her away from her fieldwork so he could implant his seed in her womb. Though all nine of his female Muleseeds by his four other seedmates were thriving, his male seedlings had never made it past the toddler stage. "You deliver me a male," Petrus had told Lua, "an' could be I'll get those ugly teeth o' yours fixed by that Tribalseed dentist at the Salem Outpost. Cost me a pretty penny, but if the whelp lives past three, could be I'll give you new teeth as a Fruition gift." Ji-ji would have been tempted to grab a knife and gut him for uttering something as crass as that. But Lua, who didn't have a mean bone in her body, had been grateful.

Lua and Ji-ji had played together as seedlings before they could even walk. Over the years, as they'd each lost one sibling after another, their relationship had deepened. Lua was the one who believed Ji-ji could succeed when Tiro and Uncle Dreg urged her to compete in the Freedom Race.

Ji-ji had always known she could run like the wind, but her mam had been dismayed when she'd learned she wanted to compete. "The Freedom Race is rigged," Silapu had warned, working herself into a lather. "Female runners cannot succeed. The male racers are different. Fans are desperate to see fly-boys like Tiro strut and preen in the flying coops." Then Silapu had repeated the story she'd told a hundred times, her eyes narrowing as she recalled how much had been taken from her. "Clay was almost chosen to represent the 437th. That bastard Herring robbed him of his chance to fly. Packed him off to the auctionmart. Males should not be called racers anymore. It is a joke, is it not? How far do they run? A few miles of sprinting in between battles in the flying coop so the pretty fly-boys do not get injured. And how far must females run? Two legs and each one a marathon! It is the same all over. Females carry wood and water while males drink palm wine and whiskey. Only stupid, gullible female seeds enter that stupid race, is it not so? . . . And whores. And sluts too. You would not reach Dream City, Jellybean. You would fail."

But with Uncle Dreg, Tiro, and Lua urging her on, Ji-ji had defied her mam and begun training, pushing herself to run a little faster each day. When she rose in the dark and slipped on her worn running shoes, it was Lua's voice she heard in her head urging her on. Lua believed tomorrow would be an improvement over yesterday, although nothing in her own ragged life gave her a reason to think it would be. Within six months of the start of her training, Ji-ji had broken the planting record. Lotter didn't take kindly to her running at first. Eventually, however, he reconciled himself to it—as if there were some new flaw in her he'd learned to accept.

Whenever she ran, Ji-ji felt as though a light had been switched on inside her. At last there was something—apart from cooking meals for steaders—she was *really* good at. Running helped her cope with Charra's disappearance, consoled her when Bonbon was Serverseeded, helped her stay sane after Silapu washed down half a bottle of pills with a bottle of whiskey. After Bonbon's snatching, she'd drifted apart from Uncle Dreg. She was civil to him, but she couldn't trust him anymore. When it had mattered most, he'd let her down. Throughout those lonely, bitter months, Lua's faith in her kept her going.

Lua groaned. Ji-ji felt guilty again. She'd been miles away. Lua's groans intensified. Fear grabbed Ji-ji by the throat; she wouldn't succumb to it. She tried to think of something to raise her spirits. . . . She found it. A few months ago, Bettieann had delivered Orchard's conjoined deadborns when it should have been impossible. Lauryann and Pennyann, Planting 437's other senior midwives, had given up—concluded Orchard was a goner and called Pastor Gillyman to administer last rites. But Bettieann had stormed in like the cavalry, pushed the pastor aside, birthed the joined deadborns, and saved Orchard's life. Saved her womb too, for subsequent plowing. Last Sunday, Ji-ji had run into Orchard on her way back from her shift at the planting furniture factory. Orchard, melon-bellied and grim-faced, said she was due any day. "I'd as soon be dead as seeded," Orchard told her. "Birthing's like dying, only more drawn out. Wish old Bettieann had never come to the rescue, interfering old cow. When you get plowed an' seeded, Ji-ji, do yourself a favor an' insist on Carolann. She guzzles more whiskey than your mam. Mbeke got Carolann an' look how lucky she was. Be over quick as a flash if you ask for her."

"Is it almost over?" Ji-ji ventured to ask.

"Stop your inquisiting, Lottermule," Bettieann replied from between Lua's legs. "Think I got nothing better to do than respond to the likes o' you, with them fancy airs an' flaunty blouses?"

Chastened, Ji-ji looked down at her yellow blouse. She'd worn it under her jacket so Lua could see it. Had planned to surprise her best friend with it. No chance of that now.

When Lua had first seen Ji-ji in her buttercup-yellow blouse, she'd clapped her hands together and declared she looked like a glass of sunshine. Perhaps to compensate for snatching Bonbon, Father-Man Lotter had gifted the blouse to Ji-ji for her fifteenth birthday. Said the blouse could be their secret. Reminded her (as if she needed reminding) that the only permitted colors for those on her Chestnut arc of the Wheel were blacks, browns, rusty reds the color of dried blood, storm grays, and dirty tans, so she could only wear the blouse indoors. Ji-ji had no intention of wearing it at all. But the color—a yellow so vivid it made your eyes water—seduced her. She'd worn it to visit Lua once, and her friend hadn't stopped talking about it. Said it was the most beautiful blouse in the world. Ji-ji had pictured her wearing the blouse indoors when she nursed her new seedling—a ridiculous idea because Lua would be flayed alive if Petrus caught her flauntifying herself. But maybe just taking it out and gazing upon it once in a while would make Lua happy?

As soon as Ji-ji arrived and saw the state of things, she forgot all about the blouse. If she'd had her wits about her, she would have changed into the dun-colored shirt she'd brought with her. As it was, she was still wearing Lotter's flaunty blouse. After hours of labor, it was hopelessly soiled. Stank of sweat too. She would need to find another seeding gift. Maybe she would draw a picture of Lua with the sketch pad and pencils Miss Clobershay had gifted her? She wasn't a very good artist yet but Lua would love it even so. Or maybe she would draw the seedling? Yes. Lua would treasure that, whether or not she got the mouth right. So far, every mouth she'd drawn looked like it contained a set of dentures a couple of sizes too large.

Ji-ji's gaze fell on her friend's bloody seedbirth shift. Lua's half-black, half-white Muleseed symbol took root in the center of her chest. Lua was very fair-skinned, which was why Petrus had selected her as his fourth seedmate. There was a decent chance Lua's seedling could fall on the lightest arcs of the Wheel and thereby testify to the potency of Petrus' seed. Creating sons in one's own image was viewed as a godly trait in a father-man, a sign that he was blessed. It could accelerate his ascent into positions of power. Father-Man Petrus was sixth in line for the cropmaster title. He would need all the help he could get if he wanted to leap over his rivals and move up the ladder. At Petrus' discretion, the offspring—assuming it was male and fair-skinned, of course—could be granted True Hybrid status, in which case he would be given a stipend for his work. A portion of his earnings would go to his father-man in perpetuity. Rather than being publicly auctioned, a True Hybrid was discreetly traded to wealthy patrons. Unfortunately, Lua had made the mistake of confessing to Ji-ji that she was praying for a True Hybrid. Ji-ji had lost it. Accused Lua of "buying into steader propaganda" and "swallowing wholesale the steaders' corrosive caste system." After she'd calmed down, Ji-ji realized she'd sounded like an asshole. What was wrong with a seed as long-suffering as Lua dreaming of a better life for her offspring? Instead of being forced to work fourteen-hour shifts in the fields or the factories, he would have a Right to Roam throughout the Territories. . . . He'd still be a botanical, but he'd sit on the highest rung above all the other seeds; his life would be bearable. Ji-ji had made her cherished friend feel guilty. Now, as she looked at the bloody sheets, she was awash in guilt herself. "I'll make it up to you, Lu. I promise," she whispered. Lua didn't seem to hear her.

Clang! Clang! Clang! The planting toll bell rang out across the twelve homesteads. The sickening sound flayed the skin off the back of every seed on the planting. Aunt Marcie nodded at Ji-ji, reminding her it was time for her to leave. Ji-ji shook her head.

Bettieann could hardly believe it. "You telling me you plan to skip the traitor's Culmination? You crazy? All seeds gotta attend—you more'n most. Father-Man Lotter'll whip you bloody if you're not in his viewing coop. You listening to me, Mule?"

Ji-ji swallowed hard. She knew how bad the punishment could be if she didn't get to the Circle in time. But she would never forgive herself if she abandoned Lua. She squeezed her friend's hand tighter while Bettieann continued to berate her. What troubled Ji-ji far more than Bettieann's insults and the beating she would almost certainly get from Lotter was breaking the promise she'd made to Tiro to stand by his side during the Culmination. At the Circle, all the seeds from each of the twelve homesteads were herded into giant viewing coops to view the proceedings. The dividing mesh between Tiro's coop (Homestead 2) and hers (Homestead 1) would prevent them from holding hands, but at least the tips of their fingers could touch. They could comfort each other that way.

Lua grabbed Ji-ji's arm and pulled her in close. "*No race!*" Lua cried hoarsely, her eyes so wide that a rind of white encircled her hazel irises. Lua's voice didn't sound like Lua. It sounded like she was impersonating someone else.

Ji-ji wanted to pull away but Lua's grip was unnaturally strong.

"*No race!*" Lua repeated, desperately. "*No race till we dream with the dead!*"

"Don't you go scaring your poor mam with that cadaver talk," snapped Bettieann. "Don't want no Dimmer-dead wafting around in this cabin. Marcie, you tell your seed to shush."

But Lua wasn't listening. "The *boy*!" she exclaimed, in that deep, unnerving voice, pointing to something she saw hovering above Ji-ji's head. "The boy with the head of wheat! *See?*"

Ji-ji looked up over her shoulder, half expecting to see some Dimmer behind her.

"Poor mite's delirious," the midwife said. "Do something useful an' check her brow, Lottermule. Let's hope it's not an infection."

Bettieann wiped her forehead on her sleeve, shifted her stool closer to Lua's pelvis, and got back to work between Lua's scrawny legs.

Ji-ji placed her hand on Lua's brow. "She's real hot," Ji-ji said.

"Keep cooling her with that wet cloth," the midwife ordered.

"Don't let her do it!" Lua murmured, listlessly. "*Don't!* No race . . . till we fly from here!"

"S'okay, Lu," Ji-ji assured her, realizing she was referring to the Freedom Race. "I promise I'll choose you an' Aunt Marcie for my kith-n-kins. When I reach Dream City, I get to petition for six, remember? Tiro an' me'll have twelve between us. You can bring your seedling too."

Bettieann snorted derisively. "What world you living in, Jellybean Lottermule? Overdreaming's a fool's game. *Jesus,* Marcie! I got no room to maneuver! This'll be a forceps, for sure."

Lua raised herself up on her elbows. In a voice unrecognizable, the timid Muleseed who had never yelled at anyone shrieked at the midwife: "*Don't you DARE hurt my angel-boy, you fuckin' BITCH! Me an' Silas'll Dimmer you if you do! DIMMER YOU DAY AN' NIGHT!*"

Aunt Marcie was horrified: "Hush, Lua!" she pleaded. "Pay her no mind, Bettie. She don't mean it. My Lua never swore in her life! Must be crazy with pain."

Bettieann looked rattled, but she assured Marcie it was okay. "Heard a lot worser in my time. Labor turns angels into devils. But it don't last, an' I learned long ago not to take it personal."

"In the *book*!" Lua cried, staring at the smoke-stained mat ceiling above Ji-ji's head before shifting her crazed eyes to focus on Ji-ji. "I *see* you an' him swinging! An' her—the *Listener*! In a cage of monsters! His seeing eyes seeing lies from afar!" She paused, then looked directly at Ji-ji and said, "Bye, bye, Blackbird. . . . Bye-bye."

Lua's strange goodbye sent shivers through Ji-ji. Zaini's quilt popped into her head—the one that hid her mam's seeding bed. The entire flock took off from the tree, leaving nothing but absence behind.

Bettieann's voice: "She's torn good an' proper this time. Marcie, c'mon down here an' help me staunch the bleeding."

Another chill ran through Ji-ji when she heard the midwife's anxiety. Aunt Marcie placed Lua's other hand in Ji-ji's and moved swiftly to join Bettieann at the foot of the seedbed.

"C'mon, you little bugger!" Bettieann urged, ramming a bloody hand up into Lua's seed canal. "That's it . . . that's it. . . . No more messing around. C'mon out!"

The toll bell rang out again—*clang-a-clang, clang-a-clang clang!* The final D-Day summons.

Suddenly, *gluck!* A shock of jet-black hair!

"You done the hard part, Lua!" Bettieann cried. "Head's out! Shoulders is coming too. Just relax now, honey pie. I got this one. Leave it to me. Scoot on up there an' check on her again, Marcie. Keep her calm. Tell her I got this. Go on now. *Scoot!*"

Marcie hurried back up to the head of the seedbed to relay the message.

Out of the corner of her eye, Ji-ji saw the old midwife's eyes grow wide, as if she'd seen a ghost or something. She shook her head and bit her lower lip. Looked like she was about to blubber. Was there something wrong with Lua's firstborn? *Please god, don't let there be anything wrong with it. . . . Petrus'll surely toss it in the garbage if it isn't perfect. . . .*

Bettieann reached into her kangaroo and pulled out a . . . a what? A tiny pair of forceps? A pair of miniature scissors? Ji-ji heard her snip something. Then she snipped again. Sometimes the cord was wound round a seedling's neck. Maybe she had to cut it Free? The midwife slipped the instrument back into the bloody kangaroo pouch. A few seconds later, Bettieann, her voice still shaky, told Marcie to shuffle back down to the seeding end and help her again.

"Shoulders is out now, Marcie. Hard part's done. Hold her legs steady. That's it."

The toll bell was still ringing: "*Shut your damn mouth!*" Bettieann yelled in the direction of the door. "Damn bell! Christ in heaven, we all know it's Death Day. Don't need reminding."

In an instant, Bettieann's tone switched from wrath to tenderness. She patted Lua's knee, crooned, "C'mon now, pumpkin. How 'bout we make it Birth Day instead?"

Lua ignored her and grabbed the front of Ji-ji's blouse. With a shocking surge of strength, she pulled her friend down to the seeding bed. Ji-ji felt as if she were being pulled underwater. She caught a whiff of something strange. Lua smelled like . . . like what? Like earth? No. Not just earth. Her best friend smelled like the grave.

Lua croaked out a warning: "No race till you dream with the dead! *They see you! In the book!* Death . . . rising! Bough broken! Weepings in the trees! Seeds don't die—they fly! Kings 'n' queens! Fly away from here! Oh, the *rising*! From the cradle to the grave! See it? *See?*"

Exhausted, Lua relinquished her grip around Ji-ji's neck and slumped back onto the pillow. "Bye-bye, Blackbirds," she murmured softly. "Bye, bye. . . ."

A few moments later, *gluck, gluck!* Lua's seedling was Free!

Ji-ji turned to stare at its black, limp form. She didn't have to ask whether or not it was a deadborn. She turned back to break the news to her friend.

Lua's pretty, unblinking eyes were fixed on the ceiling.

Over Ji-ji's shoulder, Aunt Marcie began to scream.

4 DEATH DAY

"It's no good, Bettie," Marcie said. "I can't close 'em. Can we leave 'em open a while longer so I can see their prettiness?"

Bettieann, who looked more upset than Ji-ji could ever remember seeing her, shook her head sadly. "Petrus'll be here after the Culmination, an' Lord knows he won't take the loss of his seedmate well. The least he'll want is her cleaned up an' resting peaceful with her eyes closed. Poor thing'll turn ghost an' spy on him if she's still bug-eyed." Marcie's face fell. "Oh, what the hell!" Bettieann added. "For now I guess it's okay to keep 'em open. But we gotta close 'em soon, Marcie hon. Don't have a choice."

Ji-ji couldn't bear to look at Lua's wide-open, accusatory eyes. To avoid them, she glanced over at the cardboard box Bettieann had placed on a battered old chest in the corner of the one-room cabin. A crude drawing of a pair of steader work boots had been glued to one end. The box reminded Ji-ji of the confessionals father-men kept in the basements of their father-houses—coffinlike cages for punishing recalcitrant seeds. Checking first to see the growns were occupied with readying Lua for inspection, Ji-ji crept over to the box. She almost slid on the floor, slippery with birthing fluid and blood. She took a deep breath and removed the lid. All that was visible was a bundle of swaddling clothes. With trembling fingers, she pulled them back as gently as she could.

Lua's deadborn was a male as dark as Bonbon. Given how light-skinned Lua was, Ji-ji should have been surprised. Yet somehow she'd known all along he would look exactly like her little brother, and that this too would be an accusation. The seedling was lying on his back, covered in blood. The box was bloody too. If she were to lift it, the deadborn would drop out through the sodden bottom. Funny thing was, the seedling didn't look dead. Looked like he was sleeping.

Ji-ji couldn't bear to see him all bloody like that. Because she couldn't think of anything else to do for Lua, she decided to clean him up so he could take his rightful place beside his mam. There would be a special harvesting service in honor of the sacrifice Lua had made for the Territories. Coffins were usually left open for viewing, so Lua's newborn had to look his best. Ji-ji realized her mind wasn't functioning properly. Petrus would rather cut off his arm than acknowledge this dark-skinned seedling as his own. Still, for Lua's sake, she felt compelled to clean him up. She was reaching into the shoebox to lift him out when Bettieann shunted her roughly to one side.

"Lord in heaven, Mule! You itching to be barren? Your mam never warn you to steer clear of a deadborn?"

The midwife scooped up the seedling, bloody swaddling cloth and all, and grabbed a clean cloth from the back of a chair. She bundled it around him, covering everything, including the face, then lowered the tiny form back into the box and slapped the lid on.

Ji-ji burst into tears. Lua's deadborn was alone in his bloody steader boot box.

"Let Ji-ji see him one last time, Bettie," Marcie urged. "My Lua would've wanted that."

Bettieann looked from Marcie to Ji-ji and back again. Grumbling, she lifted the lid, adamant that Ji-ji not touch the deadborn or remove his swaddling clothes. She drew back the swaddling just enough so Ji-ji could see his face.

"Better pull yourself together, Jellybean," Bettieann warned. "You seen death before, an' Lord knows you'll see it again 'fore this morning's done." The midwife leaned in and lowered her voice so Marcie couldn't hear her. "Server material, for sure," she said. "A 35 on the Wheel. Could be a 36. Petrus'd never acknowledge a swarthy newborn that don't testify to the strength of his seed. If you got any sympathy for that grief-laden mam over there, don't you go saying nothing to nobody 'bout what you seen here today. It'll rankle Petrus now the shoe's on the other foot. He's been mocking your father-man on account o' that black seedling your lunatic mam suckled for months—" Catching sight of Ji-ji's expression, Bettieann broke off and mumbled something about being too old for this type of work. She ordered Ji-ji to get her ass to the Circle. Ji-ji, unnerved by the deadborn swaddled in his shoebox and the terrifying corpse gazing up at the ceiling, obeyed.

IIIIIIIIIIIIII

She was out in the fresh air at last, some fourteen hours after she'd entered Lua's claustrophobic cabin. It was way past dawn on Death Day and her Lua was never coming back.

She was running, running. . . . A stiff breeze whipped up the grass and tussled with Ji-ji's regulation skirt. A bloody sun hung low in the sky. Grief gnawed at her insides. She and Lua had enjoyed a friendship devoid of secrets and filters. They'd told each other everything. Even their cycles had been aligned. They had grown up together, bled together, but they hadn't died together. Lua had left her behind. *Don't think. . . . Run. . . .*

She was a dumbass for sure. Lua's pelvis was roughly the size of her own waist. Why hadn't she known Lua would need a C-section? Why had she let the seedling lodge itself in Lua's narrow seed canal? It wasn't simply Death Day, it was also April, the month of the Propitious Gleaning, the time when a new crop of adolescent male seeds was sent to the auctionmart. The month seeds called the Weeping Month. *Oh Lua! . . . Did you know how much I loved you? Come back. Don't leave me here. . . .*

The irony of it all punched her in the gut. From out of her mouth came the same bitter laugh her mam had. She was running away from death and toward it at the same time. Behind her, Lua lay in her deathbed; ahead was just as bad. She'd blocked it out till now, refused to let herself think about why that blasted bell had summoned seeds and steaders to the Circle. She let the thought enter her like a knife.

Tiro's uncle Dreg, the only male who's ever treated me like a daughter, is about to be executed.

Young Death lay behind her, Old Death lay ahead. She got the weird sensation that she wasn't running *toward* Execution Circle but instead running around *inside* it, propelled back to the same bleak destination by the gravity of the planting. She was stuck on repeat—like those scratched-up gramophone records Uncle Dreg used to play on the few occasions when he had fuel for his small generator. She thought about black holes like the ones described in *Everyman's Guide to Intermediate Science,* another textbook her teacher had secretly given her. Black holes lay in wait all over the universe ready to swallow you up. "Shit, shit *shit!*" Ji-ji cried. How would she live without her best friend's pretty face and her endearing, ridiculous, inexplicable joy? After Ji-ji won the Freedom Race, they were meant to live in Dream City together—she and Tiro and Lua, along with Mam, Lua's seedling, and others they loved. Lua had vowed to help her find Bonbon too, however dangerous it might be. Couldn't be happy, she said, unless her Ji-ji was happy.

Pastor Cam Gillyman would reprimand her for her despair. Citing scripture, he would remind her it was a female seed's duty to be hopeful. But Ji-ji had stopped listening to the old fart years ago, and today the word *duty* made her want to vomit. Lua had "done her duty" and it had butchered her. Now she lay dead, and her pretty deadborn—who looked so much like Bonbon it tore at Ji-ji's innards—was bundled up like a stale sandwich and stuffed into a cardboard box.

A sob rose in Ji-ji's throat. She gulped it back down. If she indulged in grief now, she'd never make it to the Circle. She glanced at her minstrel watch. The mouse's hands pointed to 7:40. Time was taunting her. Could be the Culmination was over. Usually, most were by now to preserve the workday shift. It would take ages to navigate the circuitous route through the planting, with its manned boundary gates between homesteads. She was never going to make it.

From somewhere off in the distance came the frantic bleating of a goat. A kid, sounded like, tethered to a post in Petrus' seed quarters. "*Maaa, maa!*" it bleated. Lua's deadborn calling for his dead mam. As she ran past the Petrus pig farm, Ji-ji wished she'd never named Lua's wombling Piglet. She hadn't said the name out loud but she'd thought it. Guilt stung her. She wanted to punish herself, fling herself into a ditch and lie there gazing up at the sky. . . . An image of Lua's lifeless eyes accosted her again. She mustn't think about her eyes. They would slay her if she did. She needed to take refuge in something—find a lifeline, a crutch.

Uncle Dreg had taught her how to comfort herself by conjuring up what he called "a moment of translation." But finding something comforting in the carnage of Lua's cabin was like sifting through ash in the vain hope of discovering a rose in bloom. At last Ji-ji lit upon something she could cling to. While Bettieann and Aunt Marcie washed Lua's ravaged body, the midwife had started singing one of those ancient, spiritual songs old-timers sang at funerals when there were no steaders around. Marcie had joined in. It felt to Ji-ji as if her own sorrow had composed the music. The song braided everything together—the pain, the blood, Lua and her deadborn seedling. . . .

The goat bleated again, farther away now. Ji-ji took an eraser to the kid's pitiful bleating. You had to learn to shut things out on a planting else they killed you. Trouble was, she was so goddam *tired.* Her legs didn't want to propel her forward. It was like running through water. Forward was backward, circles were cages, and sweet Lua was dead. All that kindness obliterated from the world. . . .

For a moment, Ji-ji couldn't remember why she was desperate to get to the Circle. . . . Tiro, the fly-boy she'd loved since she was a seedling—he was the reason. She'd promised she'd stand beside him. But after all the other things she'd witnessed that morning, she wasn't sure she could.

Footsteps! Ji-ji turned to look behind her. The sharp bend in the path didn't allow her to see who it was. Someone was running at a clip, puffing as they came. Before Ji-ji could come up with an excuse for why she wasn't at the Circle, the figure rounded the bend and pulled up sharply.

"*Afarra!*" Ji-ji exclaimed—relieved at first, then angry. "What the hell are you doing here?"

Afarra was panting so heavily Ji-ji was afraid she would pass out. Half her braids had come undone and the rest were heading in that direction. The server looked up at Ji-ji and smiled nervously, revealing two missing teeth.

"I am . . . following you . . . Missy Ji," Afarra confessed, breathlessly.

Four weeks after he'd snatched Bonbon, Lotter had presented the server to Silapu. In a fit of bad taste, he had wound a ghastly scarlet ribbon round Afarra's head and tied it in a huge, droopy bow, even though servers were forbidden from wearing any colors except charcoal, dark brown, and black. Silapu had asked Lotter if he thought a "stinking little outcast" would make up for every shitty thing he'd done to them. Ji-ji had expected Lotter to strike her mam for her insolence but he hadn't. "You know how many seedmates get their own servers?" Lotter had told her. "Took me a month to persuade Herring to let you keep the Cloth. Try being grateful for a change." When Silapu had grunted in disgust, Lotter had raised his hand to strike her, then thought better of it. "Do whatever you want with it," he'd said. "It's yours now."

Ji-ji soon began calling the server Afarra because she came from afar. She hated the generic name Cloth given to all servers—a reference not only to the cloth swatches on the Color Wheel but also to *girlcloths* and *boycloths,* steader terms for underwear. Ji-ji hoped that naming the little server would put a dent in her mam's hatred. It hadn't. In the months since, Silapu never once referred to the server as Afarra, or showed her a grain of compassion. On the contrary, Ji-ji's mam took Lotter at his word and did whatever she wanted with the little female known as Cloth-33h/437, a combination of her numerical designation on the Wheel and the planting number. (The final letter *h* distinguished her from the other Serverseeds on the planting with the same shade designation.) Unless Ji-ji was there to intercede, Silapu beat the crap out of Cloth-33h in much the same way as Lotter beat the crap out of her.

"You been shadowing me all along, Afarra?" Ji-ji demanded.

"Uncle Dreg is the one telling me to watch over. He is saying you are needing it. He is saying do not be afraid. So I wait in the bushes in the darken. I hear the moon rise. It is very loud weeping. I hear Lua scream. I say, 'Do not be afraid, Afarra.' And then I am here with Missy Ji."

Afarra stared down at her bare feet, callused and dusty from the road. Half of her left big toenail was torn off. There was blood on her other foot too.

Maybe because of Afarra's pitiful feet, or maybe because she felt so lonely at that moment, Ji-ji reached out and grabbed Afarra's hand. The Serverseed broke into a smile so filled with gratitude Ji-ji had to look away. Ji-ji knew she was being impulsive taking Afarra's hand. You weren't supposed to touch outcasts. As a reminder of how unclean Serverseeds were, they were only given a scratchy shift to wear and two measly pairs of underwear. Not surprisingly, servers stank, which was why Ji-ji would rise at midnight when there was a halfway decent moon to see by, fetch Afarra from the shed in the back where she slept, and lead her down to the stream to bathe. She would wash her shift and underwear too. Afarra was always thankful. "I am not being a pungent in the water," she would say.

Ji-ji took a deep breath. In for a penny . . .

"Okay, Afarra, listen up. We run together. I'll help you but you *got* to keep up. I can't hang back for you, okay?" Afarra nodded so hard Ji-ji feared she'd pull a muscle.

As they raced down the permissible path, Afarra called out breathlessly, "I am being very sorry for your sorrowing! Lua was a goodness voice inside your heart. I am being sad for him too."

"Sad for who?"

"For Silas. Her angel-boy."

"How do you know her deadborn was male? An' who told you she planned to call him after her brother? You hear her scream at Bettieann?"

"It is easy," Afarra explained. "I am seeing the pretty wombling in my other eyes in the dark. He is peace time. He is smiley. He is looking like the other ones. I am seeing him in here too." Afarra beat her chest with her fist, striking the broken-seed symbol on her potato sack of a dress.

The scrap of jet-black fabric designated her as a Serverseed. Stamped below it was her designation: CLOTH-33H. The symbol looked like an ugly nailhead, which made Afarra's fist the hammer.

Ji-ji sank down on the grass beside the path and buried her face in her hands.

Afarra squatted down beside her. Like most imports from the Cradle, Afarra could squat with her feet flat on the ground for hours. The little server pulled Ji-ji toward her so she could rest her weary head on Afarra's shoulder.

After she'd recovered a little, Ji-ji shared what had happened. Afarra smiled when she heard how insistent Lua had been about a boy with a head of wheat, a book, blackbirds, and dreaming with the dead. Seemed to think it all made perfect sense.

"Culmination must be over by now," Ji-ji stated blankly. "We missed it."

"No cannon fire," Afarra pointed out.

"What?" Then Ji-ji remembered. The planting cannon fired thrice to signal the completion of the convicted's Death Spiral.

At last, something merciful.

"C'mon!" she cried, brushing her hand roughly across her cheeks and gripping the server's hand in hers again. "We can still get there before the end. C'mon, Afarra! *Run!*"

IIIIIIIIIIIIII

Ji-ji thought she saw something—there in the shadows! She ordered Afarra to take cover. They crouched down behind a lethal-looking thornbush. Ji-ji blinked hard. Didn't do much good. What the hell was it over there near that tree? How many times had her mam warned her never to venture into the Doom Dell? In spite of the sun-filled morning, the light had a muddy, purple cast to it. The Dell made her feel worse than she had before, if that was possible. It was as though all the long sorrow and deep grief of the planting had congregated here. As soon as they'd set foot inside this unnatural place, she'd had to resist a growing urge to dig a hole and bury herself alive.

Taking the forbidden path meant she'd done the other thing her mam was always scolding her about—acted on impulse, a luxury seeds couldn't afford. The forbidden path ran down through the Commons Lowland and into the restricted area of the planting. She'd decided to take it because it would shave a hunk of time off their journey. If they sprinted along the narrow path, they could reach the foot of the hill bordering the southwestern edge of the Circle in less than twenty minutes. When they got there, a permissible path intersected with the forbidden one—at least, that's how it looked from what Ji-ji could recall from glimpses she'd gotten of Lotter's security maps. Granted, they would have to creep past PenPen, the planting's penitence penitentiary. But they were unlikely to be spotted today because almost all the guards would be at the Circle.

Ji-ji thought about the other reason why the Doom Dell put the fear of god into seeds—because something terrible was located there. Dubbed *Murder Mouth* because it spewed acrid black smoke from its chimneys, the facility—used as an arsenal way back when—was even more notorious than PenPen. Some seeds claimed it was where steaders manufactured chemicals to use in ongoing skirmishes with the SuperStates and Independents; others whispered of more unnatural goings-on. Lotter told her the area was contaminated by radiation, but she suspected he'd said it just to scare her. If it were true, the steaders who worked there would all have been dead long ago.

The deeper the two seeds had descended into the Doom Dell, the colder and darker it had become. A slick green mold covered everything, including the footpath. It was like walking on slimy fur. Being barefoot, Afarra suffered the most. She'd tried running on tiptoe but couldn't keep it up for long. Every so often, she cried out, "*Slimy toes! Slimy toes!*" Her exclamations would have been funny in another place. But nothing was funny on Death Day in the Doom Dell. A pasty morning light seeped through the canopy of thick, dark leaves. A rotting stench lodged in Ji-ji's nostrils, like the planting slaughterhouse on a sweltering summer day. Not even flies buzzed here, and Ji-ji soon realized she hadn't heard any birdsong either.

Ji-ji peered through the gloom. She still couldn't make out what it was. A snarlcat? No. This wasn't a snarlcat or a striper. The monster stood upright on its hind legs. A bear? Big and black enough. But there was something odd about its fur. She tried not to give in to panic and instead to think it through rationally. As far as she knew, only two mutant species had been successfully bred by the steaders—snarlcats and stripers. This gigantic beast was neither. What was it then?

To Ji-ji's relief, she noticed the beast was limping. If they took off into the woods to avoid it, then caught up with the forbidden path later on, chances are it wouldn't be able to catch them. The beast's back was turned. It hadn't spotted them yet. Time to make a run for it!

Ji-ji signaled to Afarra it was time to leave. They crept out from their hiding place and headed away from the path and into the woods. They'd nearly reached the safety of the shadows when the monster heard them! It turned its bulbous head and let out a kind of shocked grunt.

Before she took off like a bat out of hell, Ji-ji caught a glimpse of its apelike face. She threw a frantic command over her shoulder: "*RUN!*" Afarra obeyed.

A second later, the awful truth dawned. Afarra had run in the wrong direction! She was heading straight for the monster with her arms outstretched like it was some long-lost pet!

"*NO!*" Ji-ji screamed, and took off after her. She caught up quickly and thrust her arm out to stop her. The two of them skidded to a halt not twenty feet from where the monster stood.

Ji-ji stared at it in disbelief. She still didn't know what it was. Seven feet tall or more, it was covered from head to toe in hair. Its foot was wet—blood, looked like. Its mournful face looked like the faces of gorillas in photos Ji-ji had seen, but it certainly wasn't a gorilla. It was badly injured. Not just its foot either. Its entire body was covered in wounds. Its stench was overpowering.

Ji-ji grabbed Afarra's hand and tried to drag her away. Afarra wouldn't budge!

"What the fuck are you doing?" Ji-ji hissed. "Are you nuts? We gotta get out of here!"

Afarra set her mouth in a stubborn line. Like someone fluent in Monster, Afarra spoke to it: "They are hurting—yes? We help—yes?" She moved toward it.

"*No!*" Ji-ji cried, and jerked her back.

The creature raised a huge hand . . . paw? . . . hand? Waved it in their direction. Ji-ji didn't know exactly what it meant but the gesture didn't strike her as aggressive, just bone-weary like she was. The beast turned suddenly and loped off in the direction of the fry-fence. They watched it disappear into shadow.

In the throes of her fear, Ji-ji raised her hand to smack some sense into her mam's Serverseed. Afarra didn't try to shield herself from the blow. Ji-ji caught sight of the gap in Afarra's mouth where two teeth used to be before Silapu knocked them out in a drunken rage. What was she doing? She came to her senses. Flushed with shame, she lowered her arm.

"Sorry. . . . I was scared shitless. That's why I . . . Sorry. That thing was huge. Could've ripped us to shreds. You gotta stay close. You *got* to promise me. . . . That thing could've killed us both."

"Drol is not being a thing. He is for living. He is for Free."

"What do you mean? Is Drol its name? How do you know that?"

Before Afarra could reply, a blast shook the air, followed by another, then a third. *BOOM . . . BOOM . . . BOOM!* Cannon fire.

"*Uncle Dreg!*" Ji-ji cried. She had broken her promise to Tiro. She had never broken a promise as sacred as that. Could Death Day get any worse? Yes. It could. Because up ahead, another monster more terrifying than the one they'd just seen straddled the path: a steader guard in riot gear.

The guard raised his rifle and pointed its bloodthirsty, circular eye at their heads. Another black hole from which nothing could escape. They were doomed.

Afarra rushed toward this monster too, begging him not to shoot. Ji-ji tore up beside her, terrified the guard would pull the trigger. She attempted to shield the little server. Afarra wasn't having any of it. She pushed herself in front of Ji-ji in an absurd attempt to protect her instead.

We look like a comedy routine, Ji-ji thought, remembering the crappy shows on Lotter's homescreen. Then it hit her. Comedy wasn't what the guard saw—far from it. *We look like prey,* Ji-ji thought. *Mam was right. There's no escape for seeds. We fall along the path and the buzzards devour us.*

Ji-ji forced Afarra behind her and focused on the just-in-case-of-rape knife she had strapped to her thigh. A knife sharp enough to slit a man's throat. Sheathed. Hidden. Ready to wage war. . . .

5 A PURPLE PATH

The guard's beard was bushy and full below his helmet—the only part of his face they could see. A reflective visor covered his eyes and nose, but they didn't need to see his expression to know how eager he was to pull the trigger. A sudden, painful stitch gripped Ji-ji. She clutched her side as the pain migrated to her back. It lodged there, throbbing.

Rage blossomed inside her. Rage for Lua, lying dead with her deadborn; rage for Cloths like Afarra; rage for Bonbon and her other lost siblings; rage for Uncle Dreg, murdered by steaders; and rage for Tiro, whose beloved uncle—and his brother before that—had been murdered by father-men. Most of all, she directed her rage against herself. In her reckless arrogance, she'd taken a forbidden path and led herself and Afarra to their doom. It was one of the dumbest things she'd ever done. The words of a poem Miss Clobershay used to recite leapt into her mind: "Rage, rage against the dying of the—" She couldn't remember what came next. It didn't matter. Rage was rage and dying was always. She was left with a single option: draw as much steader blood as she could on her way down.

Afarra sensed her plan and whispered to her not to do it. Ji-ji ignored her. Beneath the beard was the guard's throat—a sliver of vulnerable flesh. She would take him by surprise. One quick swipe and, whatever the outcome, it would all be over.

The guard roared at them: "Cut the crap or I'll shoot!"—his voice so menacing that Ji-ji and Afarra stopped jostling for position. His rifle's unblinking eye watched them. The guard was nervous; his short, quick breaths betrayed him. It took a special kind of viciousness to blow off a young seed's head at close range. A nervous guard was vulnerable but also unpredictable. He could overreact—shoot first and ask questions later. Ji-ji had to get closer.

Afarra launched into an explanation: "So this is why we are not being over there at the Circle. The juvis push Missy Ji into the ditch. See her blouse? Very filthy to look at. It is proof."

"Shut your trap, Cloth!" the guard warned.

Afarra kept on talking. "We get lost. It is easy. We are taking the wrong path. Missy Ji is poor eyesight and I am very stupid. We are not seeing the sign. Cloths do not go to legacy school. The alphabet is very squiggly. Like worms."

"Tell her to shut her trap!" the guard yelled from under his helmet.

All at once Ji-ji understood. Each time the guard warned Afarra to shut up, he lowered his rifle slightly. Afarra was trying to help her. She told herself, *It's now or never.*

They were little more than a corpse-length from the guard when Ji-ji faked a stumble. For an instant, he dropped his rifle to his side and instinctively reached out to break her fall. Ji-ji's knife was in her hand, though she had no memory of reaching for it. Something ripped. Her dress? Flesh?

Ji-ji leapt toward him, aiming for his throat. *Go in for the kill*—what Lotter used to say when he took Ji-ji on hunting expeditions as a seedling. *You hesitate and you're dead. Nothing more dangerous than a wounded mutant.* She homed in like a missile, letting out a cry as she slashed her knife from right to left, funneling every ounce of energy into one lethal movement.

Ji-ji knew she had failed miserably before she saw the result of her attack. The guard had been looking down at her; his neck hadn't been exposed. All she'd managed to do was slice some beard from his chin. The guard cupped a gloved hand over his jaw and swore at her. She saw herself reflected in his visor: a feeble seed thrashing on a slick, black sea. *Am I really that small?* she thought.

It felt as if it took an age for him to wrench the knife from her hand, yet she couldn't prevent it. Using one arm, the guard wheeled her around, encircled her waist, and heaved her bodily off the ground. He still had his rifle in his right hand ready to blow their heads off. His left arm held Ji-ji as tight as a noose.

They'd forgotten about Afarra. The Serverseed lowered her head like a bull and charged at the enemy. Before she could make contact, the guard batted her away with his rifle. It was like batting away a mosquito. Afarra landed hard several feet from them. The guard flung Ji-ji after her.

Ji-ji crouched down over Afarra, who struggled for breath, shielding the server's frail body with her own. "You gotta get through me first!" she cried, and waited to be shot in the back. *Let it be quick!* she thought.

Her courage would fail if she had to wait much longer. Another second passed . . . another. . . . Ji-ji looked up.

"Are you *nuts*?" the guard asked. "What the *hell* you think you're doing?"

The guard wrenched off his helmet. His long blond hair cascaded from beneath it. Blood had turned some of his blond beard red. She understood why they weren't dead. The man under the riot helmet was none other than Matton Longsby.

"But you . . . you left!" Ji-ji blurted out in amazement, adding stupidly, "Your beard . . . it grew!"

"That's what you got to say after you try to slice my fuckin' head off!" He ran a hand through his bloodied beard. She'd excised a bigger chunk of it than she'd thought, sliced his chin too. "Yeah, it grew. So what? Things grow if you let 'em be. S'not some miracle. You almost slit my goddam throat!"

"But why come back to this place?" she blurted out.

"Are you *insane*? Who gives a fuck why? Where'd you get that knife? From the kitchens, I'll bet. Know what the penalty is for seeds on a forbidden, never mind the other crap you pulled?"

Ji-ji nodded gravely, but inside her hope sprouted again. This was the same guard she'd attacked with a fork over a year ago. He hadn't parroted to Lotter then, maybe he wouldn't parrot this time either? They were *not* dead. A miracle.

Together, Ji-ji and Afarra staggered to their feet. Ji-ji noticed she'd ripped her skirt in her frenzy to get at the knife. She was lucky she hadn't sliced her thigh open.

As soon as they were upright, Afarra exclaimed, "Guard Matty! You are back!"

"Shut your stinking mouth, Cloth! How many times I gotta tell you don't call me that. You know what the penalty is for attacking a guard? A date with Sylvie, that's what. Want your neck stretched like Traitor Dreg? Soon as they catch him they'll—"

Ji-ji cut in: "Uncle Dreg's been executed. We heard the cannon fire three times."

Longsby spat on the ground to signal his disgust. "New recruits screwed up. Morons fired three times for a kill instead of two for a runaway. Dumb as logs. Dreg's still missin'."

Ji-ji tried to fit the news into her head but it was too large or her head was too small. Either way, it wouldn't fit. "He's . . . you mean . . . he's not dead? Uncle Dreg . . . escaped? That's impossible!"

Afarra didn't wait for Matty to respond. She danced around like a mad thing. Clearly, the dance was original—more like convulsions than dancing, the kind of dance you would do if you had hardly ever seen yourself in a mirror. Longsby ordered her to cut it out. Ji-ji placed her hand on Afarra's arm and she stopped dancing. Longsby dabbed at his chin. It was still bleeding.

"Wait till your father-man hears what the two of you—"

Afarra cried out in alarm: "Do not report, Guard Matty! He will be killing us!"

"Not my problem," he told her. A cluster of beard hairs came off in his hand. "*Shit!* You sawed off half my beard. *Jesus!*"

Ji-ji noticed again how startlingly blue Longsby's eyes were, as unnaturally blue as Lotter's. The fairskin had grown several inches in the months since she'd last laid eyes on him. Like most of the other young recruits enticed to the far-flung homesteads, he hadn't remained on the planting for long. A couple of months after Lotter presented Afarra to Silapu, Longsby had set out to find work somewhere less remote. Ji-ji's father-man was irate when he learned that the young guard wouldn't be renewing his contract, complained to Silapu that Longsby was a rarity among recruits because he only needed to be told once what to do. Much to Ji-ji's surprise, Afarra had wept when Matty left—something she almost never did, whatever abuse was heaped on her. Apparently, Matty had given Afarra an orange when he'd run into her after one of Silapu's beatings. Kindness from a male steader was so alien to Afarra that she'd never forgotten it. Ji-ji couldn't imagine what could have enticed him back to the remote Southeast Territories.

During his months away, Matty had hardened. It wasn't just his beard that was different or how much meatier he was in the chest and shoulders, it was his attitude—something flinty behind his eyes, something steaderlike. Ji-ji had assumed at first his compassion had prevented him from firing. But looking at him now as he weighed his options she could see that self-interest was uppermost in his mind. Probably angling for a reward from Lotter, trying to prove himself in hopes of a speedy promotion. Ji-ji wouldn't be surprised to learn that the inside of a prison cell was responsible for his transformation. Chances were good he'd gotten into trouble with the law and been sent back to serve out his time as a guard. Few young fairskins were willing to serve on a planting voluntarily, and the severe labor shortage brought about by conflict, disease, and other disasters meant steaders couldn't be too picky about hires.

Most young guards were delinquents, ex-cons, or zealots. She'd need to proceed with caution.

Hurriedly, Ji-ji explained how they'd strayed onto a forbidden, elaborating on the story about the juvis Afarra had invented earlier. Longsby stuffed a wad of chewing tobacco into his mouth, groaned and spat a bloody glob onto the ground at their feet. His mouth was bleeding. She'd done more harm than she thought. She started to elaborate further on their delay. He cut in.

"What part of shut-the-fuck-up don't you understand? Walk ahead, both of you. One false move an' I aim for the Cloth." He turned to Afarra and added, "Hear that, Afarra?"

Immediately he realized his error. No steader was allowed to call a server by a proper name. It was tantamount to calling her human. He cursed, looked away. The guard pushed them both in front of him, where he could keep a close eye on them, he said. When he shoved Ji-ji ahead of him, he made contact with her back. Ji-ji yelped in pain.

"You hurt?" Longsby asked. Another thing he shouldn't have said.

"I'm fine," Ji-ji lied, trying to conceal how much her back was now hurting. "Bruised is all." She prayed she wasn't injured so close to the race—not now there was still a chance she could be selected.

He grunted indifferently and ordered them to get moving. They began walking in the direction of the Circle, Longsby close on their heels, a rifle aimed at their backs.

Soon they emerged from the wooded section of the Dell and reached the wall surrounding PenPen. Above it, Ji-ji could see the upper stories of the brooding penitentiary where Uncle Dreg had spent the past fourteen days and nights while Tryton conducted his sham investigation. And then he'd escaped! Up and flew away like a Middle Passenger, just like he'd said he would, if the fancy took him. If only Lua were here to witness the miracle.

The Doom Dell was dungeon-dark, but, if anything, shadows got even deeper around PenPen. Almost no light could penetrate into that part of the Dell. The stench of leaking sewage came from a semi-submerged, rusted-out septic tank. The rottenness seeped into Ji-ji's pores. The pain in her back intensified as they hurried past it. She needed to relax the muscles in her shoulders . . . take some deep breaths . . . keep the pain a secret. If Uncle Dreg could be confined in PenPen for fourteen days, she could endure some minor discomfort for a few minutes.

They traipsed alongside the prison's outer wall, which was topped with barbed wire and embedded with glass shards. Afarra murmured, "It is too doomy in the Dell." She was right.

Built on an old landfill, PenPen had flooded more times than anyone could count. Each year it sank a little more. In the dank basement reserved for solitary confinement, penitents drowned whenever the nearby creek overtopped its banks. Ji-ji caught sight of a column of rats squirming through a hole in the outer wall—hunters searching for prey. Seeing PenPen up close made the wizard's feat even more impressive. Tiro must be leaping for joy. Lotter, on the other hand, would be homicidal. As chief of security, he would be blamed by the cropmaster for this fiasco. If habit was a fortune-teller, Lotter would make his favorite seedmate pay for his humiliation.

Ji-ji's thoughts were pulled back to Uncle Dreg's miracle. Just like he urged her and Tiro to do, Uncle Dreg had "dreaminated" the future. The word *dreaminate* always made Ji-ji think of *ruminate,* only *dreaminate* was weightier because it was pumped full of hope. It also made her think of *germinate.* Only, according to Uncle Dreg, you dreaminated with your imagination instead of placing your faith in time and botany. Ji-ji suspected *dreaminate* wasn't a legit word, that Uncle Dreg had invented it so she and Tiro could chew on it like comfort food and convince themselves they had the power to make good things happen. To verify her hypothesis, she'd attempted to look it up, but *do* to *du* was missing from the *American Heritage Dictionary* she'd filched from Lotter's garbage, so she couldn't prove it. Didn't make no never mind either way. Uncle Dreg had dreaminated the future he wanted by pulling off the most miraculous escape in planting history.

Afarra, whose right leg had been injured during the attack, walked with a slight limp. She also had an ugly knot like a partially buried egg on her temple. Ji-ji whispered to her, asked if she was okay. Afarra nodded. Ji-ji didn't trust her. The little server never complained about anything. Before they reached Execution Circle, Ji-ji *had* to find out what Longsby planned to do with them. If you knew what lay ahead you could combat it. Ignorance was never bliss for seeds.

"You plan to let Father-Man know where you found us?" Ji-ji asked, without turning around.

"Shut yer trap an' keep movin'."

His bullying tone made her fearful again. What could she say to convince him not to parrot to Lotter? They emerged on the other side of the Doom Dell. She only had a few minutes left to come up with a plan. They climbed up to a long embankment that ran parallel to the forbidden. At the top, they found the remnants of rail ties. Most of the ties had been pulled up by seeds and used for scrap or even firewood—a serious mistake, Lotter once told her, because the ties were toxic, full of black creosote. Back in the day, the old rail line used to run right through the planting to the arsenal. On the other side of the rail tracks was a ramshackle chicken-wire fence. Longsby propelled them to a rusted-out hole in the fence and ordered them to climb through it. They did as they were told. On the other side of a steep slope was a permissible path. A stone's throw from that lay the Circle. Ji-ji had been correct: the forbidden *was* a shortcut.

The bellicose notes from the planting's brass band hijacked the breeze. Cropmaster Herring was fond of playing military marches at Culminations. Ji-ji saw the segregated band in her mind's eye. To the right of the massive tree, Rightcause Fansom, the band's official leader and Herring's first cousin, would be waving his baton in the air while Jeremicah Williamsseed (the band's real leader and a far more talented musician) would be leading the band discreetly from behind. But it wasn't the band that made Execution Circle the most dreaded place on the planting for seeds. It was the enormous tree at its hub.

Sylvie sat in the lowest part of the Circle, but Ji-ji could see her hefty crown already. Ji-ji often wished the steaders had never baptized her. The name made Culminations more vengeful, as if Nature herself enjoyed conspiring with steaders to make seeds' lives hell. As wide as she was high, Sylvie served as the planting's most potent symbol. According to Uncle Dreg, who made the claim with a wink and a nod, the great tree was a hybrid—the offspring of a live oak from the Deep South and a kapok tree from the Cradle, an example of the "unadulterated magnificence produced by unauthorized miscegenation." Ji-ji was never sure whether Uncle Dreg was pulling their leg, but she liked the idea that the steaders worshipped an entity that mocked them. Coach Billy Brineseed—Uncle Dreg's best friend and the planting's chief arborist and volunteer fly-coach—had a simpler explanation. Coach B said Sylvie was a species unique unto herself. There was not another like her in the entire world. You couldn't pin a fine specimen like Sylvie down to type without doing her a grave injustice, he'd tell them. In the face of two conflicting assertions, Ji-ji had done what Miss Clobershay had taught her to do—accept nothing on one person's say-so and go on a quest for truth. Her research on the Grubby Pipe, the seeds' ruthlessly censored network, was inconclusive. Sylvie did indeed look like she was the giant offspring of a live oak and a kapok tree, but she couldn't find anything like Sylvie anywhere. The penal tree was a mystery that would certainly have been awe-inspiring if the steaders hadn't co-opted her. As it was, they'd turned her into a freak.

Ji-ji couldn't make out Sylvie's hateful adornments yet, but she pictured them dangling from Sylvie's branches. The names of executed seeds were etched onto brick-sized metal expiration tags that functioned as grisly wind chimes. Steaders referred to the tags as Sylvie's *purple earrings* because the metal reflected the penal tree's pinkish-purple blossoms in the spring. Among themselves, seeds never called them earrings; instead, they called them *purple tears*.

Nowhere on the planting was more sacrosanct to steaders than the Circle. When Founding Cropmaster Bartholemew had come upon the natural amphitheater and freakishly large tree, he decreed them to be signs from God and informed his coastal flock that their exodus up from Inner Tampa had ended. The sea would not rise in wrath in this place, he assured them. The Endless Strife and Long Drought would be over. By the grace of God, extended growing seasons would make the land bountiful. (The strife and droughts continued, as did flooding and fallout, but he'd gotten the last part right: the growing season in this part of the country was surprisingly long.) Bartholemew's god was as merciful to steaders as he was merciless to seeds. When Ji-ji had questioned Miss Clobershay about him, her teacher paraphrased a poem by a feminist poet—a fairskin from way back when. If you were to ask the spider what god is, the spider would tell you, "God is a spider." In other words, Miss Clobershay told her, the steaders' god was a steader through and through. It was a comfort to Ji-ji to know that God might not be a vicious bastard after all.

Closer and closer they came to the place where Uncle Dreg would not be lynched today. Among seeds—and some steaders too—Execution Circle was known as Dimmers Ditch because it was rumored to contain so many vengeful ghosts. Even when there were no executions going on, an oppressive sensation hit as you descended into the natural amphitheater, with its large wooden platform encircling Sylvie like a stage and its terraced viewing coops. The steaders sat on white bleachers flanking the penal platform. All those not on essential duty would be in the bleachers this morning, and all of them would be fuming over Uncle Dreg's escape. Ji-ji sized things up as fast as she could.

They had entered from the southwest, about fifty yards behind the coops reserved for the six lower-ranked homesteads. To reach Viewing Coop 1, Lotter's coop, they had to work their way round to the other side of the Circle, where the coops for Homesteads 1 through 6 were located. The Outcast Coop was way off to the east, at the crest of the hill. In other words, the odds were lousy they could sneak in unnoticed. They would need Matty's help. Yet she still didn't know if he planned to parrot to Lotter. Panic fluttered in her chest as martial music blared across the Circle. However loudly the band played, they couldn't outdo the shouting, laughing, and carrying-on in the viewing coops. Ji-ji had never seen anything like it. Granted, it wasn't mutiny, but it was close. For once, the seeds weren't cowed and the steaders weren't crowing. The world had been upended by a funny-looking, nappy-headed, necklace-wearing wizard from the Cradle.

Matty ordered Ji-ji and Afarra to halt. To Ji-ji's relief, no guards patrolled the upper tiers, which explained why they hadn't been spotted yet. Eager to get a good view of the penal platform, the seeds had surged forward to the front of their coops. The guards must have taken up positions farther down inside the well of the Circle to monitor them.

Ji-ji looked at Longsby. "You plan to report us? Father-Man'll beat us or worse if you—"

"Keep your damn mouth shut, Mule, an' let a man think."

Ji-ji was desperate. She played a hunch and spoke again: "We didn't know it was you."

Longsby looked at her strangely. She'd got his attention. "You tellin' me it would've made a difference if you had?" he asked.

"*Yes!*" Ji-ji and Afarra insisted in unison.

Ji-ji decided to risk it and tell the truth. "You're right, Guard Longsby. We weren't lost. It was me made the Cloth take the forbidden."

"Missy Ji is a liar of the worst kind. *I* am the one. It was my idea entirety. I am very ideaful. This is another bad case of it."

Matton Longsby looked away. For an instant, Ji-ji thought he was smiling. But when he looked back at them, his face was a wall. He addressed Ji-ji.

"Okay, here's the deal. . . . I'll let you into your viewing coop, an' I won't tell your father-man what you did." Before she could thank him, Matty grabbed her arm and pulled her in closer. "But if you don't stop acting the fool, Uncle Dreg won't be the only seed dangling from Sylvie this week."

Matty Longsby's ice-blue eyes drilled into hers. He squeezed her arm so tight it hurt.

She had to ask him one more favor. "Please, I beg you. Can you take Afarra to her coop?"

The young guard pulled Ji-ji even closer. She smelled weed on his breath. "Call her by that ridiculous name again an' they'll accuse you of befriending an outcast. You want Tryton to ship her off to the Rad Region?" Ji-ji shook her head, opting not to remind him that he had called her by a proper name himself. He added too softly for Afarra to hear, "You owe me for this, understand? I expect . . . gratitude." He glanced down at her chest. "Yeah. Things sure do grow if you let 'em be."

She was an idiot. For a few stupid minutes she had almost trusted him.

Not long afterward, Ji-ji was inside Viewing Coop 1, and Matty had marched off with Afarra toward the Outcast Coop. As a guard in Lotter's security contingent, he would have a plausible excuse for her tardiness. Afarra was safe. Ji-ji tried not to worry.

In Viewing Coop 1, seeds were packed in like sardines. Ji-ji pushed her way to the front and scanned the next-door coop for the top of Tiro's head. At six-two, Tiro was taller than most seeds on the planting. Seeds' reaction to the miracle varied greatly. Some were weeping openly, some were laughing, and others looked stupefied. A palpable tension hung in the air. Dozens of guards patrolled the well of the Circle with high-powered rifles, semiautomatic handguns, zapper sticks, and stun staffs. Most wore grenade pouches. *Bad kangaroos,* the seeds called them, as if the contents of these pouches would be less lethal if they had a harmless midwifery name.

After multiple pleas to let her pass, Ji-ji worked her way to the front of Coop 1. She spotted Tiro, standing near the mesh separating the two coops. As soon as he saw her, his face lit up.

The ordeal had taken its toll on him. He had heavy bags beneath his bloodshot eyes, but he'd taken pains to prepare himself that morning. His Sand-Tan skin and close-cut hair shone with oil. He wore his regulation fly-boy T-shirt—something he'd told Ji-ji he would do if he suspected Uncle Dreg could pull off a miracle. The T-shirt—with the planting crest in orange on the chest, and a pair of wings, the flyer's symbol, underneath it—was Tiro's way of saying his great-uncle would fly from this place. On the back of his T-shirt in all caps was the name he despised: T. WILLIAMSMULE. (Tiro had repeatedly threatened to rename himself Tiro Dregulahmo after his uncle. But Auntie Zaini, knowing that Father-Man Williams would hit the roof if he did, wouldn't hear of it.) Like Longsby, Tiro had grown in the past few months. The Gleaning diet that fattened up the juvis had transformed him from a gangly sixteen-year-old to a muscular seventeen-year-old. Someone—Marcus or one of his other fly-boy buddies probably—had shaved the flyers' wings symbol onto the left side of Tiro's head. The wings were barely visible because his hair was so short. Nevertheless, Ji-ji was uneasy when she saw it. As Planting 437's flying champion, Tiro could get away with a lot. But Inquisitor Tryton enjoyed accusing male seeds of dandification almost as much as he relished accusing female seeds of flauntification. Still, Ji-ji couldn't worry about that now, not when she saw Tiro rushing toward her, grinning from ear to ear.

"Where you been, Ji? Look like you been rolling with the hogs!"

Before she could answer, he confessed he went crazy when he couldn't locate her in the coop. Without taking a breath, he launched into an account of the past few hours.

"He *did* it, Ji! Flew off like he promised! Like those Passengers from the old days! Herring swears he won't let us out o' these coops till they find him. Been stuck here going on three hours. But hey, who cares? Uncle Dreg's magicked himself Free!"

At last Tiro noticed something was wrong. "Hey, you okay? We'd given up on you."

Haltingly, making sure she kept her voice low, Ji-ji told him about Lua and her deadborn, leaving out how dark he was and the strange things Lua had said.

"Oh Ji, I'm real sorry. Lua never had a bad word to say 'bout anybody. I know what she meant to you. An' here I am carrying on like—"

"No, don't be sorry. No one would be happier than Lua. She loved Uncle Dreg."

Auntie Zaini, Tiro's mam, came up to the dividing mesh with Bromadu and Eeyatho, Tiro's two young brothers, in tow. She looked drained, but as always she held her head up proudly. Tall like Tiro, with a soft brown complexion that placed her firmly in the Raw Umber arc of the Wheel, Auntie Z had taken Ji-ji under her wing after Bonbon's snatching, when Silapu dove headfirst into a depression more purple than any before. Though Silapu and Zaini weren't related, they'd been as close as sisters at one time.

Ma Merrimac joined the group on Ji-ji's side of the dividing mesh. One of the matriarchs of the planting, Ma Mac had lived on the 437th even longer than Uncle Dreg. As an elder on Lotter's homestead, she was responsible for calling roll in Coop 1. She checked Ji-ji off her list and asked where Silapu was.

"You mean Mam's not here?" Ji-ji asked.

Ma Merrimac shook her head. "An' you know how nasty Dale Lotter gets when his Mammy Tep goes missing."

Auntie Z told Ma Merrimac the tragic news about Lua and her seedling. The older woman groaned in sympathy, put her big arm around Ji-ji, and pulled her to her ample chest. Ma Mac worked the night shift in the planting's furniture factory and smelled strongly of sawdust and glue.

"Poor Marcie," Ma Merrimac said. "Lua was her Last&Only. Well . . . least we got one thing to celebrate on this mournful Death Day. No one escapes PenPen, but the Oz found a way. Never underestimate a wizard, that's my motto."

Tiro couldn't contain his excitement: "We always believed he'd find a way to defeat the bastards—right, Mother?"

"Hush, Mule!" Ma Mac scolded. She put her face up close to the dividing mesh and hissed a warning: "Call your mam by that steader name an' you'll be flogged! You know how picky they are 'bout their terminology. Parrots got ears, an' they love nothing better than squawking to steaders. Don't know what you were thinking shaving those dandified wings onto your head! Good-looking don't compensate for stupid."

Ji-ji was about to intervene on Tiro's behalf when she felt the mood suddenly shift in the coops. Seeds were pointing and yelling. Cries went up from those with a clear view of the platform.

The seeds in Coop 2 fell back to allow Tiro and his kin to move forward. In Coop 1, Ma Merrimac used her impressive bulk to bulldoze a path for Ji-ji so she could squeeze closer to the front and stand beside Tiro on the other side of the mesh.

There, being led up onto the platform by two guards, was the Toteppi wizard who was supposed to have flown away. Only he hadn't flown anywhere. The wizard had been caught!

Zaini hugged her little ones closer and placed her hand on Tiro's arm like someone who'd always known they would lose Uncle Dreg to Sylvie in the end. Bromadu and Eeyatho began to wail.

Tiro appealed to Ji-ji: "That's some imposter, right? Don't even look like him! He escaped—right, Ji?"

Ji-ji's expression told the awful truth. Tiro ripped off his T-shirt and ground it into the dirt.

Ji-ji knew now her mam was right after all. There was no escape. Round and round seeds went, lashed to the Wheel of Misfortune. The steaders' sick rhyme ambushed her again.

The only way for a seed to be Free
Is to swing on high from a penal tree.

Not even a wizard from the Cradle could break a spell as powerful as that.

6 THE WIZARD

When she saw what they had done to him, Ji-ji wanted to weep.

The two guards pushed Uncle Dreg forward. He stumbled to his knees to an outcry from the coops. As an errander, Uncle Dreg had dozens of opportunities to seek asylum in the Independents or the Eastern SuperState, yet he'd chosen to return again and again to Planting 437. He'd spoken Toteppi death rites over seeds' graves and made them believe their dreams weren't futile. The old warrior, who didn't know exactly how old he was, had done the impossible—convinced steaders to trust him while he cultivated hope in his fellow seeds.

Up on the penal platform, however, Uncle Dreg looked defeated. They'd stripped him almost bare and wrapped a filthy loincloth around his privates. He was one of the few male seeds permitted to wear his hair long and uppity. To humiliate him, someone had smeared muck in his wild gray hair and shaved sections off to reveal his scalp. Yet for some reason, his knobbly knees devastated Ji-ji the most. They looked like two ashy, wrinkled faces.

The wizard wasn't wearing his mystical necklace of colorful wooden beads with a single eye painted on each. The steaders had settled for mockery instead. They'd placed two big round balls around his neck, strung together with thick rope. On them they'd painted two crude, insane-looking eyes. They dangled from his scrawny neck like an obscenity.

Cropmaster Herring marched up to the podium. Under the shadow of Sylvie's huge limbs, he paused for effect. Outfitted in the heavy black robe and cloak he wore on Death Days, Michael Prinshum Herring looked every inch the cropmaster. His massive chain with its gold and silver links glinted on his chest. The chain was heavy, but he stood upright, shoulders pulled back. Like Father-Man Williams and the four other bald or balding father-men, the cropmaster wore a gray ceremonial wig tied back with a black seizure ribbon. As far as Ji-ji knew, no one had ever seen Herring smile; he didn't ambush them with it now.

On Herring's right stood Lotter, disconcertingly handsome in his olive-colored robe, his blond hair corralled by the infamous black ribbon. On Herring's left stood Father-Man Williams. The tallest and meanest of Herring's twelve father-men, Williams was even more vicious than Petrus. At his father-house while she was preparing his meal the other day, Ji-ji had overheard Lotter say he was opposed to lynching the Toteppi, warning it could incite a riot like the diviner warned. A pragmatist, Lotter had lobbied instead for expulsion to the Rad Region, saying the Tribal would die slowly—a fitting punishment less likely to cause unrest. But Herring wanted blood.

The other father-men took their designated stations in a half circle around the wide trunk of the penal tree. The group faced Viewing Coops 1 through 6, which gave Coops 7 through 12 a rear view of the ceremony. To enable the lower-ranked coops to get a frontal view of the proceedings, a camera caught the action and displayed it on a giant screen attached to scaffolding. Though steaders were wary of employing technology, Herring, who relished seeing himself enlarged on a big screen, decreed that it could be used "to instill an appropriate reverence for rites and rituals."

No one observed Territorial rites and rituals more obsessively than Inquisitor Tryton, a bumblebee of a man in a crimson robe, who functioned as chief justice for the planting and reported directly to Armistice. Tryton was buzzing around the wooden platform, fussily checking and rechecking that everything was in order. Pastor Cam Gillyman, Tryton's toady, who could have passed for a fairskin, stood at the foot of the penal platform. In a nasal whine, the True Hybrid implored the Lord to inflict eternal damnation on those who betrayed the Territories.

Herring hated being duped. Like many other steaders, Herring called the wizard "Uncle Dreg" and listened to his counsel. He'd held him up as an example of loyal service, afforded him extra privileges—allowing him to wear his Seeing Eyes in public on occasion, for example. Bad enough that the Tribalseed betrayed him, but the revelation that the affable wizard was a Friend of Freedom had shaken Herring to the core. Already eccentric, Herring's behavior at the hearing had been downright strange.

Ji-ji wasn't surprised by Herring's outrage, though only paranoid fools would think that Uncle Dreg was a Friend of Freedom. The Friends raided plantings throughout the Territories on their quest to liberate seeds and reunify the states. Many Friends were ex-seeds themselves, willing to fight to the death. Some went on suicide missions, blowing themselves up at steader checkpoints or infiltrating homesteads as spies. Four burnt-out trucks not far from the fry-fence testified to an unsuccessful raid Friends had launched on the planting six years before. Though the attack had been thwarted before any seeds could be liberated, a dozen steaders had been killed, including Herring's eldest Son-Proper. Many more had been wounded. The raid prompted an official reprimand from the Lord-Father of Lord-Fathers in Armistice, a blot on Herring's record as cropmaster, and one reason why his application to serve on the Supreme Council in the Father-City had been denied. No—Uncle Dreg wasn't a warrior in that sense. He was an avowed pacifist, spiritual and long-suffering. Ji-ji suspected he was framed. Father-Man Williams was the most likely person to do it too. His animosity toward Tiro ran deep, and he'd wanted to topple Uncle Dreg from his pedestal for years. The other day, Ji-ji had overheard one of Lotter's guards say that Herring had wept with fury when he'd learned of Uncle Dreg's betrayal. She couldn't imagine the cropmaster weeping any more than she could imagine him laughing. But as she looked at him standing like a rod of iron in his somber black robe and cloak, she could tell how desperate he was to see the old Toteppi lynched. For Herring, this execution was personal.

Cropmaster Herring reached down into his black robe and drew out the Sacred Tablet, a screen reader roughly the size of a man's palm. In a tone of indignation, he read the sentence.

"I, Lord-Father Michael Prinshum Herring, Eleventh Cropmaster of Planting 437 in the Fourth Judiciary of the Homestead Territories, hereby proclaim Dregulahmo Williamsseed, a Tribalseed botanical, commonly known as Uncle Dreg the Oziadhee, to be a traitor in the first degree."

A few seeds dared to shout their disapproval. The Serverseeds in their cramped Outcast Coop way off up at the top of the Circle protested as loudly as any of them. Uncle Dreg had always treated them with respect and encouraged others to do the same. Ji-ji was heartsick to hear the servers' protests. No doubt they would pay dearly for them.

"*QUIET!*" a voice boomed out. The sound system screeched in protest. Father-Man Williams leaned over the mic. Because Uncle Dreg was a seed on his homestead, Williams was charged with maintaining order. The coops fell silent, but Ji-ji could feel them simmering around her. Williams stepped back to his station to the left of Herring, his deep-set eyes two sadistic pixels in his head.

Cropmaster Herring strode forward again. His black cloak made it look as though he were dragging behind him the shadows of seeds he'd executed in the past. The wind picked up, became gusty. His cloak swirled and bucked around him.

"By the power vested in me by the glorious Father-City of Armistice, the esteemed Lord-Father of Lord-Fathers, and the twelve noble father-men of Planting 437, I, Michael Prinshum Herring, convict you, Dregulahmo Williamsseed, of acts of treason against the Homestead Territories. I hereby sentence you to swing from the penal tree until all breath has been taken from you, and the traitorous poison in your veins is expunged."

Herring stepped to one side. Williams, in his role as Aggrieved Patriarch, replaced him at the podium. He drew his own tablet from a robe of purplish blue, the color of a bruise. The gusty wind shifted his gray horsehair wig. It sat lopsided on his head, making him look tipsy, a state that was completely out of character. Williams retrieved his reading glasses from another pocket and slipped them on. He hesitated, which didn't make sense to Ji-ji because there was no steader less hesitant than Drexler Williams. You could hear a pin drop in the coops and the bleachers.

"What's that sonuvabitch doing?" Ma Merrimac wondered softly. "Giving us poor seeds some damn lecture we don't need, I bet."

"I, Drexler Williams, Second Father-Man on Planting 437 in the Fourth Judiciary of the Homestead Territories . . ." Williams paused to glance over at Herring, who nodded for him to continue. Still, Williams was reluctant. He looked over at the bleachers where his fellow steaders sat—the laborers and carpenters, lumberjacks and factory supervisors, accountants, engineers, dairymen, and others who worked on the planting. No. It wasn't a lecture. It was something else.

"I hereby proclaim," Williams continued, "that Cherub Holleran, also known as Chaff Man II, Executioner for Parishes 400 and 500 in the Homestead Territories, has disobeyed a Cardinal Command by refusing to hang a traitor. Holleran, you are hereby sentenced to swing from the penal tree until all breath has been taken from you, and the traitorous poison in your veins is expunged."

At first there was dead silence, then gasps, then a gathering roar from the coops as seeds surrendered to the dizzying excitement of vengeance. They whooped in delight and stomped their feet. Apart from Father-Man Williams, Chaff Man II was the most hated fairskin on the planting. Until now, no steader had ever been flogged in front of seeds, let alone hanged.

Ji-ji couldn't imagine why Chaff Man had refused to hang Uncle Dreg. It wasn't clear either why Williams had been selected to deliver the verdict when Lotter, chief of security, would have been the logical choice. Ji-ji hadn't noticed the executioner until now. But there he was standing next to Uncle Dreg, his stocky torso heaving with sobs. Seeing Chaff Man's freckled face and curly mop of rust-red hair without his customary execution mask was like seeing the devil naked.

Williams wasn't finished. He started reading from his screen again. His grim voice echoed around the Circle: "I, Drexler Williams, Second Father-Man on Planting 437 in the Fourth Judiciary of the Homestead Territories, hereby proclaim . . ." Williams glanced over at Cropmaster Herring again, who waved his hand in the air impatiently. Williams continued, speaking fast: "I hereby proclaim the canine known as Circus to be in league with the executioner, Chaff Man II. Accordingly, I sentence you, Circus the Pomeranian, to swing from the penal tree until all breath has been taken from you, and the traitorous poison in your veins is expunged."

A cry of anguish went up from Chaff Man, who prostrated himself and begged for mercy for his beloved dog like dozens of prisoners had begged for mercy from him in the past.

Laughter erupted in the coops, but Ma Mac was livid. "They've turned this into a farce!" she said. A chant rose up from the coops, "*Kill the killer! Kill the Chaff! Kill Circus! Lynch 'em NOW!*" Seeds doubled over with laughter as steaders shifted in their seats in the bleachers. Clearly, this turn of events was a surprise to them too.

Tiro shouted at the seeds around him: "What the hell you laughing at? They're executing Uncle Dreg! You too dumb to remember that?"

The executioner began shrieking about "heinous and unnatural acts," about a secret that would bring down the Territories and lead to Armageddon. "Don't lynch my Circus!" he begged. "He's innocent! I'll lynch the fuckin' wizard if you spare Circus! Show some mercy, for pity's sake!"

Chaff Man finally caught on that pleading for mercy from Cropmaster Herring was like pleading for mercy from an executioner. He changed tactics and yelled hysterically at the coops. "Y'know what these bastards're doing in that arsenal? They're—"

Herring gave a signal and Chaff Man was gagged mid-yell.

"What was that about?" Ji-ji asked.

Ma Merrimac offered her own theories: "Could be the Chaff's referring to the weapons they say they're making in there—arming themselves for the Doomsday. Could be the bastard was just stalling. Every minute's precious when you can count the ones left on one hand."

Father-Man Williams looped the noose over Uncle Dreg's head. The crowd quieted. Ji-ji tried again to get Tiro to look at her, but he'd traveled to the same desolate place he'd gone to after Drexler Williams dragged his brother Amadee behind the penal tractor two years earlier. Ji-ji knew how dangerous it was to go to a windswept place like that. Her mam lived there. Sometimes she did too. A place like that could kill you. . . .

The time for the Denunciation arrived. As usual, Inquisitor Tryton invited Mistress Shadowbrook, the planting diviner, to the podium to read it.

The woman everyone knew as Old Shadowy hesitated. One of only a handful of fairskin females on the planting, she had spoken up in defense of Uncle Dreg at his hearing. If she hadn't been so eccentric, so aged, and so useful to the steaders (the octogenarian had successfully predicted two droughts, five floods, a raid, and three tornadoes), Silapu claimed, Old Shadowy would have been fired on the spot for a traitorous move like that—pilloried too, probably. But the weather was too capricious for them to risk losing her. Besides, a rival planting would have snapped her up in a second. With a nod of his head, Tryton invited her up again. Ji-ji could tell from his gesture that the inquisitor's patience was hanging by a thread. Would Old Shadowy refuse? Would she swing from Sylvie too? No. She wasn't prepared to die today. Shakily, the diviner rose from her chair, walked to the mic, and began to read. The blustery wind caught her long white hair, which waved over her head like a flag of surrender. Her voice quavered but she fought through it and kept reading.

"I, Emmeline Shadowbrook, Diviner for Planting 437 . . . call upon the demon-dead to stalk you three traitorous souls to the ends of the earth. . . . From this day forward, when your names are uttered anywhere in the Homestead Territories, those who utter them must spit upon the ground to testify to your desecration. Thus will your names be forever reviled. . . ."

As Old Shadowy heaped curses on the convicted, Ji-ji searched for something to whisper to Tiro to distract him. In desperation, she lit upon the only thing she could come up with.

"We saw a mutant—me an' Afarra. An ape . . . a *thing.* Don't know what it was. Huge. This'll sound crazy but I think Afarra knows it . . . him, I mean. She knew his name."

Tiro looked at her through the mesh. It was the same look of agony he'd given her after Amadee had been tractor-lynched and Uncle Dreg had wrestled the butchering knife from Tiro's hand so he couldn't go through with his plan to kill his father-man.

Tiro had seen his mam gather up his twin brother and hold his ruined body in her arms. On his way to revenge-kill Father-Man Williams, Tiro had run into Uncle Dreg. He said later he couldn't believe how strong the old man was, how easily he'd wrenched the knife from his hand and hurled him to the ground as if he were a seedling. Ji-ji found Tiro some two hours later on Father-Man Brine's swampy homestead, sitting on the edge of the Jimmy Crow's Nest high above the ground ring in the dome of the planting flying coop. Tiro and Amadee had been fly-boy partners. They'd shared a dream of entering the Big Race together as flyers and petitioning for their mam, their great-uncle, and their siblings to join them after they'd flown their way to Freedom. Ji-ji had crept along the upper walkway toward Tiro as cautiously as she could. She'd have one chance, and one chance only, to save him. In spite of the fact that she was scared shitless of heights, she'd clambered up onto the rim of the nest and sat down next to him. She'd taken his hand in hers and told him the truth. "If you jump, Tiro, you'll take me down too cos I won't let go of your hand. You gotta have someone to dreaminate with, else you shrivel up and die. You're my dream partner, Tiro. My dream twin. Please don't kill us." And then she'd raised his trembling hand to her lips and kissed it because she hadn't known what else to do. When he'd agreed to come down from the edge of the nest, Ji-ji had never been more relieved about anything.

Since that time she'd known Tiro had a gaping hole inside him, the same kind of hole left in her mam after Lotter snatched Bonbon. The same hole she had inside herself. That was why she'd risked everything to get to the Circle—to save Tiro from being pulled into that black hole of emptiness for good.

In a desperate effort to get through to him, Ji-ji whispered through the mesh: "They're crazy if they think Uncle Dreg's a Friend of Freedom."

Tiro pressed his head so hard against the mesh that it left indentations on his forehead. He looked at her. He didn't need to say anything because she could see it in his face. Uncle Dreg *was* a Friend of Freedom!

When Ji-ji found her tongue again, all she could sputter was "But . . . but he's not like that. He's a pacifist! An' he's . . . he's way too old!" Once again, Tiro's expression convinced her she'd got it wrong. "How long's he been—?"

"Decades," Tiro replied. "Never shoulda been caught." He bit his bottom lip so hard it started to bleed. "It's worse. . . . It's me he's taking the fall for. Should be me up there."

"You mean you're a—?"

"*Ssh!*" Tiro said. "Parrots everywhere."

Ji-ji stared at him in disbelief. Tiro and Uncle Dreg. Both rebels! Both Friends of Freedom! They had kept this terrifying secret from her. Before she could begin to digest the shocking news, the Denunciation was over. Old Shadowy, head bowed, shuffled back to her seat.

Master-Guard Falrenn ascended the platform with the Grim Reaper, the colossal blade used to mark the end of the Death Spiral. He handed the Reaper to Herring. Meanwhile, the twelve chief overseers carried the Crow Man scarecrow in on a litter and set it down at the feet of the crop-master. A cry went up when Herring raised the giant blade in both hands and aimed for the top of Crow Man's head. In one dramatic stroke he sliced the straw dummy in two.

On cue, the band launched into a military march. As the music crescendoed, Inquisitor Tryton scurried up the spiral staircase leading to the pulpit and drew back the red lever to activate the pulley system. Circus let out a squeal of abject terror as he, Uncle Dreg, and Chaff Man were hoisted into the air.

Horrified moans went up from the crowd. Tiro cried out like someone who'd been shot. Auntie Z pulled her youngest sons close and recited a Toteppi prayer. Ma Merrimac, tears streaming down her face, put her arms around Ji-ji.

CRACK! For a split second, Ji-ji assumed it was a gunshot. It wasn't. It was Sylvie!

The sturdiest of her limbs—the one the ropes were looped over—had broken off from the rest of the tree! The three traitors fell like leaves!

Tiro leapt so high he slammed into the roof of the viewing coop. "I *knew* it!" he cried. "I *knew* they couldn't kill an Oziadhee!"

Pandemonium broke out in the coops: "*The Oz broke off Sylvie's limb! You see that? Uncle Dreg UNHANGED himself!*"

The only one who didn't react was Auntie Zaini, who stood there while her male offspring rejoiced around her. Ji-ji thought she heard Zaini say, "It's not over," and thought she knew what she meant by it. Uncle Dreg had prophesied during his trial that the earth would give up its dead to wreak havoc on a land "despoiled by injustice." It was the only time Ji-ji could recall him saying something about the need for violence. He was going to call up an army of Dimmers! He was going to Free them all! *This is really happening!* Ji-ji thought. *The Rising is coming to pass!* The wizard had defied death, the most powerful demon of all. There was nothing he couldn't do.

Uncle Dreg and Chaff Man staggered to their feet. Chaff Man gathered Circus up into his arms and bawled into his fur.

Ji-ji didn't see the semiautomatic until Herring raised his arm and took aim. The bleachers yelled at the cropmaster, "*Shoot! Shoot!*" The coops begged him not to.

Uncle Dreg stared at Herring; Herring stared at Uncle Dreg. Even then, when all seemed lost, Ji-ji was sure the Toteppi wizard would find a way to cheat death one more time.

Uncle Dreg's voice boomed out across the Circle. He addressed the bleachers first, bewitching them—or so it seemed—into silence. Time seemed to stop while the wizard spoke.

"Homesteaders, I tell you truthfully—kill us and you kill yourselves. You must destroy the cage you have nightmared into being. Murdered bones take root! Graves are full to blossoming! The slave-dead riot under the earth! You have written this poisonous story before. You know the Rising will come. Your *One True Text* has sown these seeds."

Uncle Dreg turned to the coops. "My beloved children, you are destined to fly! I have seen it in the Window-of-What's-to-Come. A blessed awakening! Black, brown, and white flocking together! Heads of midnight, heads of earthlight, heads of moonlight! Faith and Hope will nourish you, but only Love can dream you Free! My beautiful birds of paradise, you are destined to fly the coop and bring together the tribes of the world! I tell you truthfully, you will all—"

Cropmaster Herring had heard enough. He pulled the trigger. The blast sheared off the top of Uncle Dreg's head.

Even then, Uncle Dreg's story wasn't over.

The bullet struck Sylvie and boomeranged back to hit the cropmaster. The force of the bullet swiveled Herring round 180 degrees to face Coops 1 through 6 again. He looked at the terraced coops in surprise, as if he couldn't figure out how he'd been spun around.

Slowly, the way a tree would fall, Lord-Father Michael Prinshum Herring, Eleventh Cropmaster of Planting 437, keeled over.

"Holy Mother!" Ma Merrimac exclaimed. "Dreg smote the sonuvabitch!"

Father-Man Lotter and Father-Man Williams ran to the cropmaster and bent over him.

Ji-ji looked from her father-man to the man who had been father to them all. Uncle Dreg had landed with his back propped up against Sylvie. What remained of his brain was spilling from the side of his head and out of his empty eye socket. Ji-ji half expected the wizard to find his eye, gather up the shards of bone and pitiful globs of brain, and stuff them back into his own shattered skull. He didn't, of course. Uncle Dreg wasn't Uncle Dreg anymore. They'd killed him.

The coops exploded with grief.

On Sylvie's heavy branches, an agony of purple tears fluttered in the wind.

7 SEEDS OF REBELLION

The gift on her sleeping mat reminds Afarra that death is not everlasting. Her friend Uncle Dreg told her that and he was right.

If Sylvie hadn't sung to her this morning, Afarra would have wept to see her friend's head shattered, his one remaining eye staring-staring-staring. . . . But Sylvie with her pretty purple tongues told her not to cry. . . . *He will rise for certainty,* Sylvie said. *Look for your friend. He is already on his way.*

And here is proof waiting on the sleeping mat in the shed out back near the outhouse where Afarra sleeps most nights when Missy Ji can't sneak her into her bed—something she does whenever Missy Sila is passed out behind the quilt Missy Z made to tell them the way.

So many lessons from the wizard. She must remember every one, count them off like the forget-me-not treasures she keeps in a wooden box Tiro made for her and Ji-ji painted with forget-me-nots—treasures inside a treasure. Inside the box the red bow. . . . Not demon-red like Inquisitor's robe or dead-red like the wizard's (*don't look!*) blood. Pretty-red like tomatoes. Missy Sila ripped off the tomato bow but Missy Ji found it and presented it to her in the beautiful box. Inside the box in a real plastic bag, dried orange peel—Guard Matty's gift, Freely given. She keeps her forget-me-nots in order so she can remember when wonderful things happen and go back in time by touching each one. The other times she makes herself forget. She can forget anything if she labors at it cos she can turn herself on and off like a light switch when Fear approaches—become *Not Here, Not Now.*

When Fear calls her a filthy-stinking-Cloth or beats her like a rug, she is someplace else—sitting under Sylvie, or lying with Ji-ji in her warm bed, or bathing in the whisper-sparkle river. It's a clever trick she's mastered. It explains why Cloth-33h/437 isn't there whenever Fear barges in, taking up all the space in the shed as he shoves *Not Here, Not Now* to the edge of the sleeping mat. Sometimes Fear is a tall skinny seed with sandpaper hands and a dirty mouth; sometimes Fear's a heavyset steader who wants to sample something not yet bled. That's how come he's willing to demean himself, he says, and do it with a Cloth.

Missy Ji who isn't scared of any damn thing in the world caught that steader and chased him away with a stick. Here is a part of the stick, her next treasure, right there under the orange peel. The steader is giving Missy Ji a black eye for interference but Missy Ji is saying she doesn't give a rat's ass cos she's the chief kitchen-seed and she will be reporting him to her father-man for unauthorized mating without a mating slip if he tries that shit again. And the steader is telling her fairskins don't need no fuckin matin slip to sample a fuckin cunt Cloth. And Missy Ji is saying tell that to my father-man an' use those exact same words an' see what he does to you! An' don't come sniffing round here again! (Afarra wants to say the steader wasn't sniffing and neither was she, but words don't grow in her mouth like they grow in Missy Ji's. *Not Here, Not Now* holding her breath so she wouldn't smell his spurt on her belly this time. A hard thing to describe so she doesn't.)

Some important lessons Afarra has learned. On a planting always the plow. Fear may look different but he is always the deep-down same. "Hope is you," the wizard said. "Remember."

During the bad times, Afarra does not say to herself *I am being plowed.* She doesn't think about it. If she did, her seed canal would be furrows and grooves and ruts and potholes, and she likes things smooth and pretty. . . . Fly-boy Tiro is pretty. Nice ears . . . kind. Missy Ji doesn't know—no one knows—that Tiro stood guard outside the shed for two whole weeks after Missy Ji told him about the steader she chased away. He kept Afarra safe and the steader never bothered her again.

Afarra looks at her gift. She doesn't know who left it on her sleeping mat, but her suspicion is Sylvie. Or Uncle Dreg the Dimmer. Or Tiro. Or Missy Ji. Or one of the quilt birds. Either way is not a problem because she has never had a gift as wonderful as this in her entire life—a gift that changes everything! She takes a deep breath and reaches for the necklace, slips it over her head.

If Fear comes, he will see the scary wizard staring with his many eyes and run the fuck away like a chicken. She will laugh to see him run. She will grab a stick and beat his ass to pulp. She is Afarra from afar and she is holding in her hands the world's greatest treasure. A secret. *Her* secret.

She has never felt so powerful before.

IIIIIIIIIIIIII

"You do not run tomorrow, you hear me, Jellybean?" Silapu pulled the pick impatiently through Ji-ji's hair. She hadn't attempted to domesticate it in years and it wasn't going well. "You must be presentable for the harvesting," Silapu added. "You look like a scarecrow."

"But I gotta practice, Mam. Ratification is less than three weeks away. *Ow!*"

"You think I am stupid, yes?" Silapu's Toteppi accent became more pronounced as her irritation grew. "You will ignore the prohibitions and make a beeline for that beat-up fly-coop where that fool fly-boy loops through the air like some buzzbuzz."

"Buzzbuzz drones don't loop. I saw one on a hunting trip. They fly in a straight line. More to the point, Brine has hardly any guards. Too miserly to pay them. An' there's no way Stinky Brine will catch me. He's blind as a bat and deaf as a post. Pees every few minutes. Has to be near a bathroom or an outhouse."

"And if he catches you, he will haul you off to PenPen."

PenPen. A wave of guilt washed over Ji-ji. Telling her mam why she was late to the Culmination meant admitting she'd been with Afarra on a forbidden. Silapu would hit the roof, beat Afarra bloody if Ji-ji wasn't there to stop her. Adamantly opposed to the idea of her Last&Only competing in the race, Silapu would intensify her opposition if she discovered that a new class of mutants existed—if that's what Drol was. Matty hadn't parroted—not yet anyway. Ji-ji learned from her mam who learned it from Lotter that, in addition to continuing her service as chief kitchenseed for the planting, she would continue serving as Lotter's personal cook. Lotter had relocated to Cropmaster Hall, a dour edifice on the top of Bart's Mount. He scorned the stodgy dishes made by Dumpty Heringseed, the former cropmaster's eighty-year-old cook, and wanted Ji-ji to continue cooking his meals. It was a lucky break. With so little time till the Race Ratification Ceremony, Ji-ji could keep her ears and eyes open at Cropmaster Hall, make Lotter his favorite meals (assuming she could get hold of the right ingredients) and plead her case if she got the chance.

In anticipation of what lay ahead, and in mourning for what lay behind,

Ji-ji could barely sleep and had to force herself to eat. She'd bitten her fingernails to the quick. Had spasms in her back too. She hid the pain from her mam, who was desperate for any excuse to tell Lotter she wasn't raceworthy. If only she could see Tiro at Lua's harvesting this morning. The strict prohibitions Lotter had placed on inter-homestead movement meant she hadn't seen him since Death Day. Unlike the female runners, the male flyers had a special dispensation to practice, so she knew she'd find him in the flying coop practicing with Marcus. He would be there today, unable to attend Lua's harvesting. The thought of seeing sweet Lua in her coffin without Tiro there for support gutted her. But his recklessness scared her even more. He could be in a downward spiral of vengeance. All seeds knew that vengeance pain was the kind most likely to result in catastrophe. She and Tiro had always planned to race together. They knew they'd be separated most of the time—males in the fly-coops and the sprints, females in the marathons. It didn't matter. Living the dream inside Dream City meant nothing if they couldn't do it together. However much Silapu objected, Ji-ji would run the six miles to the flying coop on Brine's homestead before dawn tomorrow to check on Tiro. If she stuck to the quieter permissible paths she'd be okay.

Ji-ji wished Silapu had chosen a less inconvenient time to reprise the role of Mam. Silapu wasn't oblivious to a damn thing anymore. Sober for *three whole days*—the longest period of sobriety since Bonbon's snatching—she was eerily alert and watched Ji-ji like a hawk. Funny how much Ji-ji had yearned for a sober mam again, prayed for it each night when she wasn't pissed at God. Now it had happened at last, proving the old adage "Be careful what you wish for."

Ji-ji took another crack at persuading her mam: "Marcus says Stinky Brine's too miserly to hire many guards. Says there's no chance of getting caught if you trespass on—"

"Marcus Shadowbrookseed is a dandified drug-sop! Smokes more weed than a steader guard! Emmeline Shadowbrook spoils him. Juvis like him wind up swinging from Sylvie's branches."

Ji-ji moaned aloud. Silapu stopped attacking her hair. "What is wrong?" she asked.

"I see him, Mam. After that bullet tore into his skull. . . . In my dreams. Lua too. She wanted to call him Silas, after her brother. . . . So pretty. . . . Could've been Bonbon's twin almost."

Silapu listened intently. For Toteppi, dreams weren't mere fantasy; dreams were windows, guides, mysteries to unravel.

Ji-ji replays the nightmare she's had three nights in a row, ever since Death Day.

Dead-eyed Lua clutches her deadborn. Not Silas but a miniature version of Uncle Dreg. His skull is open like a lid, brains spilling out—pink oatmeal and cottage cheese. Lua tells her no one in Dimmers Ditch has been able to revive her seedling. At that moment, the deadborn's eyes spring open, scaring Ji-ji half to death. In his grandfatherly voice, Infant Dreg tells Ji-ji only the living can fix the dead and only the dead can fix the living, after which he asks if she will do him a favor. Can she gather up his blown-out brains and carry them home to the Rememberers before they forget for good? Next thing she knows, Infant Dreg turns into a full-size Uncle Dreg, who turns into Lotter, who commands her to stop fucking around. (Which proves she's dreaming cos Lotter only swears when he's drunk or high, and in the nightmare he's cold sober.) Three seconds later—or is it three days?—she's swinging back and forth from one of Sylvie's branches. She turns her head and sees Tiro swinging beside her. Tiro keeps his head, but his body turns into Circus the Pomeranian's. She looks to her other side and sees Afarra, who is smiling. And dead. She expects the branch to break like it did at the Culmination and save them all. Bettieann is below, waving a tiny pair of shears in the air and singing, "*When the bough breaks, the Wild Seeds will fall. Snip! Snip!*" Only the bough doesn't break and the rope cuts into her neck . . . choking her. Above her, filtering through the leaves, she hears Sylvie whispering. A singer's voice (her own? Uncle Dreg's? Lua's?) orders her to decipher Sylvie's language. "*She's the key to everything,*" the singer says.

At that point in the nightmare, Ji-ji wakes up. She hasn't included all these grisly details—can't bring herself to recount them. But she's conveyed the gist of the dream to her mam, who has taught her dreaming isn't a pastime, it's a path outside of time.

Back in the here and now, Silapu laid the pick on the table. She slipped her rough, chapped fingers under Ji-ji's chin and tilted her offspring's face up toward her own. Ji-ji caught a glimpse of the ridged scar on her mam's wrist from the time she slit them. Even after years of abuse, Silapu is still beautiful, with her rich brown skin, high cheekbones, almond-shaped eyes, and full lips. Lotter, who prizes female beauty, has been careful not to leave any marks on his favorite seedmate's face.

"Listen to me, Ji-ji. The corpse on that penal platform and the corpse in your dream, those were not Uncle Dreg. Those were evil spirits trying to make you believe death is a locked door."

"It was him, Mam. I saw what they did to him. It was awful."

"Exactly. What *they* did to him. That is not who he was. Your dreams are speaking the steaders' words—is it not so? Cage him in that butchery and you kill him all over again. Let him live. Free. In here." She touched Ji-ji's forehead. "And here." She tapped the center of Ji-ji's chest over her black-and-white Muleseed symbol.

Silapu took up the pick again while Ji-ji pondered her mam's words. Was that why Silapu had been able to resign herself to Uncle Dreg's death? Had she translated grief into something bearable?

"Jellybean, sit up straight. You know how your father-man feels about a slouching Mule. Vexes him as much as bad grammar and cussing."

And just like that Silapu switched from a sage Toteppi who had it all figured out to a cowering seed. Her mam was a hodgepodge of contradictions. No point in confronting her about it either. Wouldn't do any good. Ji-ji settled for a rehash of an old complaint.

"I hate the name Jellybean. You gave your other offspring pretty names."

"I love Jellybean," Silapu stated, the same nonanswer she always gave. "Stop wriggling. You show up at his harvesting with uppity hair and Petrus is sure to fine you."

"It's not *his* harvesting. It's Lua's an' her deadborn's."

"Everything on this planting belongs to the father-men." Silapu tugged at a clump of tangled hair. "We play their game and follow their rules. If we don't we die."

Ever since Death Day, the steaders had been steeling themselves for a revolt. A failed uprising at a planting in the 500s and two raids on plantings in the 300s by Friends of Freedom in the past couple of months had made them antsy. Herring's death made them more so, which was why it was a surprise last night when Silapu slapped two inter-homestead roaming passes on the rickety table and announced they were going to Lua's harvesting, the first harvesting Silapu had attended since Bonbon's snatching. The wagon would pick them up at 6:30 A.M., she said.

Silapu was reclusive, misanthropic even. Apart from her work at the planting's textile factory and her visits to Lotter's father-house, she rarely ventured beyond their vegetable garden. So why the sudden desire to see other people? Silapu hadn't explained why she'd been absent during Uncle Dreg's Culmination either, nor had she explained why Lotter appeared to have excused her for it. Didn't make any sense. Ji-ji hadn't asked whether Afarra could accompany them, knowing full well Serverseeds couldn't attend as guests. Besides, Afarra had to pull an extra shift in the fields, even though this was meant to be her one day off from hard labor this week.

Well before dawn this morning, Ji-ji had run out back to the shed to take breakfast to her friend before her long stint in the fields. Fortunately, Afarra's leg had healed, and the egg-sized lump on her forehead had shrunk considerably. Afarra spoke like someone who expected to run into Uncle Dreg at any moment. Talked in riddles and kept saying they were watching—though who "they" were exactly, Ji-ji couldn't figure out. Ji-ji had questioned Afarra about the mutant again and received the same impenetrable response: "Drol is not being a killing thing. He is for living. The Drol is for hope. Like Uncle Dreg." When Ji-ji had asked Afarra if she'd ever seen him before, she'd mumbled through a mouthful of bread and milk, "I am being fond of cow- and pig-talkings. But bird-word and tree-chat is my favorite. You are liking them too, isn't it? You are having their dreams." Ji-ji hadn't asked her to explain. Questions only led you deeper into the bizarre maze of Afarra's mind. The truth was, Afarra scared her at times. She seemed to be on another planet, as if their lives here on the planting were only a dream or a trick of the light.

Sometimes Ji-ji envied the outcast, who managed to live in harmony with her circumstances, pitiful though they were. Ji-ji didn't live in harmony with anything. Right now she was as consumed by vengeance as Tiro was. She could barely contain her fury at the steaders for lynch-killing Uncle Dreg and birth-killing Lua. Petrus had plowed Lua like she was dirt. . . .

Ji-ji gritted her teeth as her mam yanked on her hair. The increasingly aggressive combing told Ji-ji she was in for yet another of her mam's mood swings. She braced herself. Sure enough, this time, instead of speaking reverentially about Uncle Dreg, Silapu lit into him.

"Hold still!" Silapu scolded. "You want me to gouge you with this pick? And don't forget, if Petrus discovers you saw Lua's deadborn he will skin you alive! Your hair is a bird nest! Dreg should never have told you all those foolish things! Filling seeds' heads with crap. 'Seeds of midnight'! Nothing but foolishness!"

"*Heads* of midnight."

"Foolishness! Telling the Cloth she is special. What kind of nonsense is that?"

"Afarra *is* special. There are things she knows, things she sees that none of us—"

"I know what the Cloth is. If I catch her in our cabin again without permission I will—"

Ji-ji couldn't take it any longer. She needed to inflict pain. "Bonbon's a Serverseed too."

Silapu slammed the pick down on the table. "You think I do not know what they do to him? You think I do not hear how he purple-wails for us? You have seen Dreg's face for a few nights! I have seen my Oletto's face for four hundred and twenty-four!"

Ji-ji looked away, ashamed. Why had she brought up Bonbon? She didn't want to admit to herself that Silapu hadn't been able to drink and drug her way into oblivion, that she'd been counting the days all this time. Jesus!

Ji-ji focused on the only thing in the cabin's main room that didn't depress her: the blackbird quilt Auntie Zaini had made—three blackbirds nesting, a dozen more flying away. As long as she didn't think about what went on behind the curtain-quilt, she could live inside the white-turned-yellow squares with the blackbirds, perch with them on the tree—an Immaculate, her mam used to say, like the tree near her village in the Cradle that had never been violated by lynch ropes. But as she stared at it she realized that the quilt was no refuge. "Bye-bye, Blackbird," Lua had said, before blackness was all there was. Ji-ji decided to risk asking another question—anything to interrupt the silence.

"How come you're . . . different?"

Silapu pulled up the chair and plopped down in it. "Do not worry. It will not last. I made a promise to Dregulahmo to stay sober until after the Ratification. That is what I am doing—fulfilling a final promise to the dead."

At last something made sense. Her mam's sobriety was temporary, the result of a promise she would feel obliged as a Toteppi to keep. Ji-ji risked another question.

"Did you know Uncle Dreg was a Friend of Freedom?"

Silapu stood up and hurried to the door, tugged it open and peered out. Satisfied, she closed it again. In lieu of a lock—botanicals weren't entitled to privacy—Silapu stuffed a wooden wedge under the door. She came back to where Ji-ji was sitting, sat down, and spoke softly.

"Lotter's blasted parrots are everywhere. . . . Yes, I knew. I have lived with the danger his choice posed to him and those around him. It is a burden I carried. Do not let males choose your burdens, Jellybean. If you do, you will be forced to carry them for the rest of your life. He asked me to promise to . . . when I saw him the last time . . . after he was captured."

"Wait! What are you talking about?"

"I visited him. In PenPen."

"But . . . that's impossible! No penitents get visitors."

"Normally that is true. But a few nights before his Culmination—after you snuck that stinking Cloth into the cabin when you thought I was sleeping—I rose in the middle of the night. Zaini and I took to him his favorite stew. Zaini made it. Delicious. Gru'nut soup from the Cradle."

"The PenPen guards let you visit at midnight? That doesn't make sense."

"It was later than that when we got there. Diviner Shadowbrook had some of her own guards on duty. Emmeline and Uncle Dreg have always been . . . close. They let us see him."

Ji-ji prided herself on how observant she was. How had she missed all this?

"What happened?"

"I gave him the soup."

"Is that it?"

"I gave him a spoon. What do you expect? A miracle?"

"Was he still predicting he would escape?"

"Yes. That is why he did."

"Not for long. They caught him."

"No they did not. Dregulahmo escaped . . . then he chose to return."

"But . . . that's *crazy*! Why would anyone choose to come back to a hellhole like this?"

"Because he worried about what Williams would do to Zaini and her offspring if he left. And because he still had things to accomplish—is it not so? And clean up your mouth and watch your grammar too. You know how your father-man feels about—"

"But I don't understand . . . how did he escape from PenPen?"

"Better not to know how he did it. Dreg was a fool to enlist in the Friends in the first place. And a bigger fool to get caught."

"It wasn't his fault," Ji-ji replied.

"Whose fault was it if not—"

Silapu stopped midsentence and eyed her offspring suspiciously. She stood up, grabbed hold of Ji-ji's shoulders, and shook them hard.

"It was *not* Zaini he was covering for! That is what your eyes are saying! Who then? *Argh!* Your fool fly-boy! Tiro is a Friend of Freedom! Of course!

Why did I not see it? Dreg betrayed me after he swore to keep my offspring safe, swore Tiro would never join the rebels! He *promised*! He and Zaini duped me! I will never forgive her for this! You will *never* see that fly-boy again!"

"Mam, I can't live without—"

"Of course you can! You think that foolish, empty-headed fly-boy loves you? If he makes it to Dream City he will be snapped up by the Dream-fleet. You think he will have eyes for a plain-looking dusky like you after he sees those flaunty city whores? His nappy head will spin."

"Please, Mam," Ji-ji pleaded. "Please don't."

Charra used to say their mam said things like that cos she didn't want Ji-ji to get her heart broken. Yet Ji-ji had no illusions about how she looked: no cheekbones to speak of, no dimples, an ordinary mouth, average eyes often with dark circles under them, rebellious hair, and a muddy complexion decidedly dark for a Muleseed. Her sisters—beautiful Charra and pretty Luvlydoll—took after their mam and father-man respectively. She didn't.

Silapu spoke with venomous irritation, spitting out her words and pulling on her fingers like someone who wanted to dislodge them from their sockets. "Tiro's devil father-man makes Lotter look like a saint! You think a seed from Williams' loins will exercise self-control? Swinging around in that coop like some brainless bird! Those vulgar wings on his shirt! Using cheap tricks to fly! An illusion—is it not so? A game steaders play to pacify seeds—trick us into forgetting we can never fly from here. They've snatched our history like they snatched us! You think that lousy equipment in Brine's rusty coop—the Douglass Pipes and Marshall Mazes, the Rosa Parks Seats—"

"Perches. They're called Rosa Parks Perches."

"What? Seats, perches, who gives a damn! You think the King-spins and that ridiculous crow's nest are tributes to the likes of *us,* a recognition of *our* struggle? You think most steaders—and most seeds for that matter—remember the Passengers and the old stories of flight? You know how many Toteppi are left in the world? A few hundred at the most! Genocided by war and famine and disease and drought and betrayal and more war! You think it is only the fairskins who are evil? The old wizard glorified it, made it sound like paradise. It is not. It is still the Africa of old—the Dark Continent of strife and terror. How do you think so many of us wound up in the Territories? One tribe sells the other to the highest bidder. . . . Freedom Race! *Huh!* It is a *joke*! The males do not even race anymore. Two short sprints, that is all. The coop is for fairskins' entertainment—and those fly-boys are too dumb to know they are being exploited! Why do you think the only time juvis are called 'boys' is when the word is chained to flight? It is smoke and mirrors, mockery! The race is a way to cage Freedom, a trick to distract us. And dumb seeds like you and that fly-boy of yours fall for it every time."

Ji-ji leapt from her chair. "You're *wrong*! When Tiro soars in that coop he's magnificent!"

Silapu's disgusted laugh stung more than her words: "*Ha-ha!* You are a fool, Jellybean. Fly-boys like Tiro live for air and applause, not for some homely-looking seed. How does the rhyme go?

"Love a fly-boy, if you dare.
He'll fly from you. Beware! Beware!"

"That's a stupid rhyme. Doesn't mean a damn thing. Tiro loves me more than—"

"Lotter loves his Mammy Tep too. The sonuvabitch has poured that poison into my ears for twenty years." Without warning, Silapu shoved the chair behind her farther back from the table. It toppled with a clatter. She high-kicked her right leg up onto the table, which lurched like a rowboat.

"Didn't know you were still that flexible," Ji-ji said, instantly concluding it was one of the dumbest comments she'd ever made.

Silapu grabbed hold of the back of Ji-ji's neck and pushed her face down until her cheek brushed up against her mam's raised ankle. "See that?" she cried. "Look at it. *LOOK!*"

Silapu jammed Ji-ji's nose against the copper seedmate band, which had worn a cracked path around her ankle. Lotter's name and planting number were engraved on it in bold capitals: ARUNDALE LOTTER, 437. Her planting name, Mammy Tep Lotterseedmate, was written in small font under his. All seedmates were called "Mammy." Silapu was a Toteppi import, so Lotter called her "Tep" for short. Ji-ji had asked her once if it bothered her that Lotter never called her Silapu. She'd said she was glad. Didn't want the bastard swilling her Cradle name around in his mouth.

"You want one of these pretty little bands on your ankle for the rest of your life? Well? Neither did I. Got one anyway. I am a Tribalseed, an import. You are a Muleseed. You wear a black-and-white seed symbol and I wear a black one. That is all there is. Nothing but that and purple tears. . . . Lotter has enemies—that bastard Williams most of all. If your father-man keeps favoritizing you and me they will accuse him of Unnatural Affiliation. Tryton's already suspicious, itching to summon every inquisitor in the region to investigate Lotter's unnaturalness."

"Think I care 'bout what happens to Lotter? I *hate* him!"

Relinquishing her hold on Ji-ji's neck, Silapu laughed scornfully again. "Dale Lotter is the only thing standing between you and calamity. I will not wait for you to come back in some box."

"A box is better than a cage! It's not *me* Lotter favoritizes, it's *you*. If it weren't for you he wouldn't even know I existed."

Silapu groaned. "Oh, Ji-ji. Why must you *always* fight?"

The answer flew out of her mouth before Ji-ji could prevent it: "Why did you stop?"

Silapu reached over and took Ji-ji's hand. "For you. And for the others I seedbirthed."

It was true. All the sacrifices Silapu had made over the years had been aimed at keeping her five offspring alive and close by. Ji-ji wanted to forget the scalding anger that bubbled from her mam's mouth, forget the drinking and the drugs and the beatings. She wanted to forget finding her on the cabin floor, wrists slashed . . . finding her in the seeding bed beside an empty bottle . . . When you got right down to it, she, Ji-ji, wasn't enough to persuade her mam to stick around.

Ji-ji clutched at the only thing she had to cling to: "The race is coming up an'—"

Silapu rapped Ji-ji's forehead with her knuckles as though she were knocking on a door. "Anyone in there? You got to grow up, Jellybean. Most Mules your age have two seedlings by now."

Silapu's fury always came in waves. For now, it had subsided a little. She seemed to notice her toppled chair for the first time. She righted it, then grabbed the pick off the table as if it were a weapon. She started in again on Ji-ji's hair. Whenever Ji-ji squealed in pain, she scoffed at her for being tender-headed, reminded her she was half Toteppi and needed to toughen up. The Cradle was suddenly paradise again: she boasted about how boys in her own village became men by walking on hot coals, while girls endured cutting to become women.

"Cutting is barbaric," Ji-ji countered. "They cut out the clitoris, the only part that matters."

"Barbaric, you say? And what is this?" Silapu said, indicating the planting with a wide sweep of her arm. "Now hold still! Your hair is as stubborn as you are."

Periodically, Silapu jammed her fingers into a jar of coconut oil and smoothed a dollop onto Ji-ji's head. When she protested, Silapu launched full-tilt into another scolding. "Your head's as empty as a seed's pocket! You are lucky Lotter did not punish you for arriving late to the coop. Yes. Ma Mac told me how late you were. You know how many botanicals would kill to make it to chief kitchen-seed? Even with your dusky skin and plainness, Lotter could have seedmated you to a father-man for a decent seed-price. He spared you for my sake."

"*Spared* me? How? To labor in planting kitchens fourteen hours a day for a few lousy seedchips? I'd rather be dead than demean myself like . . ."

The word *you* hovered between them, a tongue of fire.

Silapu slumped down into the chair again. She looked worn out . . . old.

"I didn't mean—"

"I would rather be dead too. But some of us do not run like the wind. . . . The steaders are spooked by what happened. You better be minding your p and q for the next month or two."

"P's and q's. It's plural."

"Why?"

"I don't know—what's it matter? Lotter is cropmaster now. He can ratify whoever he likes."

"*Whom*ever. And have you been asleep while I schooled you? In a million years he will *never* let you go! Herring wanted the cash reward. For Lotter it is all about power and control. If you are lucky, he will allow you to remain as chief kitchen-seed."

Silapu stood again and continued her battle with Ji-ji's hair. "So . . . Dregulahmo took the fall for his reckless nephew. I was a fool not to guess this. He knew I would help if it was for Zaini. . . . You know what they do to the kith-n-kin of underage traitors who are found guilty of cultivating an insurgent? They pyre females and lynch males. That fly-boy is as selfish as Charra!"

"Charra was brave. How come you hate her so much?"

Silapu put the pick down, said, "I do not hate her. . . . I have never hated her."

"They're all gone," Ji-ji said, desolately. "Charra, Clay, Luvlydoll, Bonbon. We lost them all."

Something seemed to register for Silapu. She tilted her Last&Only's face up to hers again and looked into her eyes. "Dregulahmo asked me to tell you this. I suppose it is time." She took a deep breath. "They did not kill your sister. Charra escaped. Made it all the way to Dream City."

Ji-ji dared not even blink as she waited for her mam to speak again.

"Last we heard she was in a place called North Fork in the Madlands, leading a group of rebels, raiding plantings. Dregulahmo said she is on the Southeast Territories' Most Wanted list. So much for escaping to the City of Dreams! Your selfish sister chose to live inside a nightmare. Dregulahmo helped her escape. He took her from me . . . my beautiful, headstrong Charra. That is why I could not speak to him much after that. And then Lotter snatched Bonbon and the feeble old wizard did nothing! Some things are unforgivable."

Ji-ji stared at her mam in disbelief. The sister she used to follow around everywhere wasn't dead after all. She was living Free!

"All this time . . . why didn't you tell me? Why didn't Uncle Dreg tell me? Does Tiro know?"

"That fool fly-boy knows nothing. Dreg wanted me to tell you, but it is my job to keep my Last&Only safe. Even with help from the Friends, Charra almost died. Shot in the back by Bounty Boys. Would have been mauled to death by snarlcats if Dreg had not found her. He and the Friends ran a secret trailroad. . . ."

"The Friends' Trailroad is real? I thought it was just a story."

Silapu wasn't listening. "Charra could have stayed in Dream City, been safe, petitioned for us to join her as asylum seekers. They let seeds do that sometimes. The Friends would have made it happen. Lotter would never let me leave, but he would have let you go if I begged hard enough. . . . Let Oletto go too. . . . But your sister forgot us. Charra left us here to rot. . . ."

"An' now she's in the Madlands?"

"What? Oh . . . who knows? Maybe. We heard she was raiding plantings in the Tidewater and down south. The Madlands region is a gator-infested swampland. Malaria is worse there than the Cradle. Dengue fever too. . . . Charra is like Tiro. Always putting her own needs first. . . ."

"An' Uncle Dreg asked you to tell me she's still alive?"

"Said your fate and hers intertwined. But Dregulahmo said many things. Most were lies."

"Mam, don't you see? This changes *everything*! You gotta help me an' Tiro get out of here! I can find Charra an'—"

"If you follow in her footsteps you will *die*! My Last&Only. . . ."

Silapu broke down and wept. Ji-ji had not seen her cry since she returned from Auntie Zaini's the day after Lotter had snatched Bonbon. For forty-eight hours, Silapu had purple-wailed for her lastborn. Then Bettieann had stopped by with a bottle of cheap whiskey, and Lotter had brought her whatever he had around the father-house, only some of which was legal—uppers, downers, killers, drifters, flukes. . . . Silapu hadn't wept since. Ji-ji attempted to comfort her.

"I'll send for you, Mam. I promise. We get six petitions each, remember?"

"Only if you make it all the way to the city inside the time limit. He will never let me go."

"He will if the seedmate price is right."

"You are not listening! For Lotter, it is not about money. It is about power. And love."

"That's not love, Mam."

"You are wrong. Love is a bludgeon, and a razor too. It beats you up then slices you open. Tiro will do that to you. I have seen the way you look at him. It is not the way he looks at you. I am sorry, Ji-ji, it is not."

Why did her mam always want to pluck out hope and cast it aside like there was so much of it to spare? Anyway, she was wrong. Tiro cared. She mustn't let her bitter mam snatch that away.

"You may have more schooling than me, Jellybean, and you can run like the wind and cook like a magician, but beauty is what a female needs to hold on to males like him . . . and even then. . . . Tiro is a Wild Seed. And Wild Seeds never belong to anyone."

"I don't want him to *belong* to me. Why can't we be two Wild Seeds together?" Ji-ji resolved to tell Silapu the truth while she was sober enough to hear it. "I'll *die* if I have to stay on this planting, Mam. I swear I'll walk into Blueglass Lake like Mbeke's mam. Sometimes it feels like I'm already swinging from Sylvie or burning on a pyre. I can't live as a seed for the rest of my life. I'd rather be dead. You *got* to persuade Lotter to let Tiro an' me compete. *You got to let me go!*"

When Silapu spoke next she sounded far away.

"Dregulahmo was planning to help you if you were ratified for the race. He had arranged for Friends to guide you along the way. Herring blasted a hole in . . . Shot the only man who ever . . ."

"Ever what?"

"Nothing. Without the Friends' help you will be as vulnerable as the rest of the competitors. The race monitors protect the fly-boys, ferry them from one sprint to another so they are rested enough to battle each other in the coops. It is not the same for female runners. Females are disposable. Only fourteen racers made it last year—out of a hundred and seventy-five! And only four of those were runners. They say steaders are sabotaging the race. Homesteads claim the reward for their female runners who are then snatched by pickers along the way and shipped to the auctionmart. The whole thing is rigged. You enter that race and I will never see you again. No. You stay here. Safe. With me."

Silapu took a step back to study Ji-ji's hair. "Well, it is not perfect, but at least it is not a nest for a bird. Come on. We must not be late."

The thought of burying Lua made Ji-ji want to vomit. She grabbed hold of Silapu's hand and pleaded with her one last time: "Uncle Dreg said we were destined to fly the coop."

"Was that before or after Herring blew his brains out?"

Silapu recognized how cruel that was when she saw Ji-ji's expression. "Sorry," she muttered. "Too long inside a bottle. I have soured worse than I thought."

Silapu took hold of Ji-ji's shoulders and gave her an odd, penetrating look, as if she suddenly understood what her Last&Only had been trying to tell her. To Ji-ji it felt like her mam was looking deep into her soul and arguing with herself about what she saw there.

Suddenly Silapu relinquished her grip on Ji-ji's shoulders, stood up, and brushed at her skirt like someone cleaning off years of dust. She ran her hands nervously over her braids, worn in a kind of crown on her head the way Lotter liked them.

"All right then, Wayward Daughter Number Two . . ." (She'd used the word *daughter*—a word reserved for fairskins.) "My miserable path does not have to be yours. What good has it done me to play by men's rules all these years? I have nothing left to hold on to but you. Dregulahmo was right. I am holding on too tight. Like a lynch rope. That is what he said. You must get out or this place will kill you as it has killed me. You can fly from here like your sister did. You can live Free."

Ji-ji wanted to get on her knees and thank her but she couldn't move, couldn't speak.

Silapu added with great solemnity, placing her hand over her heart, "I promise to help you fly from here. You are braver than me, my Ji-ji. You have always been."

She gathered her daughter in her arms and held her close—something she had not done since Bonbon had been taken. Her embrace lasted for ten whole seconds. Ji-ji counted.

8 A HARVESTING

Ji-ji stood with Silapu, Marcie, and Zaini in the dusty Central Yard of Homestead 6. She looked at her mam, who smiled with her whole face and looked as beautiful as Ji-ji had ever seen her. Pride swelled in her chest. Her mother—yes, her *mother*—looked alive again.

Silapu's arrival had surprised and delighted the other two. Though they were not related, the three females had embraced like sisters. "It's good to have you back with us, Sila," Zaini said. "We missed you." The mothers (a word that seemed to Ji-ji to bear the weight of the world) stood shoulder-to-shoulder, grasping each other's hands.

Auntie Z confirmed that Tiro was practicing in the flying coop. Though Ji-ji had braced herself for this news it saddened her, until Auntie Z pulled her aside and slid a piece of paper into her hand. Her heart racing, Ji-ji slipped the folded paper into her pocket. It wasn't easy for seeds to get hold of paper for personal use. Maybe Tiro had found some in Uncle Dreg's cabin? Unlikely. Williams would have laid claim to everything of any value Uncle Dreg owned after Herring decreed him a traitor. Tiro had probably obtained a sheet from Marcus, who had easy access to it. It was common knowledge that Old Shadowy required "Nature's Muse" in order to perform her divinations. Marcus, though not an official errander, was occasionally sent to nearby homesteads to purchase the hybrid strain of cannabis the diviner liked to smoke during her divination sessions. Yes—the paper likely came from him.

A little while later, as guests arrived, Ji-ji ran to an outhouse to peek at the note. Her hunch about the origin of the paper proved accurate: it bore the skunky-piney aroma of weed. Too risky to read it now. She would have to wait until she got home. Correspondence among seeds had to be authorized, each note stamped with a security seal by one of the twelve planting censors. Zaini had taken a risk delivering it to her. Ji-ji looked at it longingly. Then, employing every ounce of willpower she had, she slipped Tiro's note back into her pocket.

When she returned from her trip to the outhouse to stand again with the others, Ji-ji glanced up and saw Matty Longsby not forty feet away, his back resting against Petrus' horse barn. His beard, though full, was shorter, presumably to make the section Ji-ji had sliced off three days before less noticeable. His uniform announced that the young guard had been promoted to the rank of first lieutenant. Lotter must have removed Crux Manderby, Herring's lieutenant, and installed Longsby in his place. Matty's presence at the harvesting made her uneasy. But if he'd spilled the beans wouldn't she know it by now? More likely he was holding out for his "reward." Not long to go until the race. She must be certain to keep out of his way.

By this time, almost all the mourners had arrived. Petrus' other three seedmates, Layla, Hapsy, and Jilletta, were there, accompanied by his primary source of resentment, his nine female Muleseeds. Three dozen or so seeds from other homesteads attended too. Given the effort it took to obtain a harvesting pass and get time off from the factories, the fields, and the father-houses, the number of mourners proved how much Lua was loved. A smattering of fairskin Liberty Laborers showed up, much to Petrus' surprise. The father-man assumed they had all come for his sake, but everyone else knew they were there for Lua. Respectfully, the laborers doffed their hats and caps to Marcie, revealing deep tan lines from outdoor labor. In various accents from around the Territories and beyond, the fairskin laborers spoke of how good Lua was and how much they would miss her.

Just before the ceremony began, Doc Riff and Bettieann Plowman pulled up in the doc's sputtering Ford truck. Personal vehicles were hard to come by in the Territories. But the doc, a skilled mechanic, had salvaged the truck so he wouldn't have to rely on a horse-drawn wagon to travel from one planting to the next. The physician brought a gift for Marcie: a framed photo he'd taken of Lua after one of her checkups at the clinic, a practice he'd begun at his own expense because the mortality rate for seedbirths was so high, and few seeds—or steaders, for that matter—could get hold of decent cameras in the Territories. Ji-ji glanced at the photo and thought Lua looked as pretty as ever, with a wistful smile on her face. Yet it infuriated her. Petrus' seedmate looked like a child with a balloon stuck up her seed shift. Marcie didn't seem to notice any of that. Overcome with gratitude, she kissed the photo, which she planned to place next to Lua's official Seedmating Ceremony photo, the only other one she had. Ji-ji thought she knew which one Marcie would cherish more in the long run, and it wouldn't be the one with Petrus looming over Lua as he fastened a copper seedmate band around her tiny ankle.

Whenever he attended functions like these, Doc Riff—a striking man in his forties with a Native Indigenous' glossy black hair—caused a stir among the female seeds. The doc had always been kind to Ji-ji. She wished she could ask him to take a look at her sore back, but she dared not risk having him rescind his earlier certification of her for the race.

Bettieann Plowman shuffled over to Marcie and hugged her so hard Ji-ji was scared the midwife would crush her. Though Bettieann frequently attended harvestings along with the other midwives, no one could remember seeing her weep at one before. Under her breath, Silapu told Ji-ji that Bettieann's extreme reaction proved guilt was more powerful than sorrow. "One glance at Lua's pelvis and any fool would know surgery was the only option—is it not so? Bettie should have sent for Doc Riff when Lua went into labor. Blood is on her hands and she knows it."

Ji-ji wanted to blame Bettieann, but it wasn't that simple. Why hadn't she herself insisted they send for Doc Riff? Maybe her best friend would be alive today if she'd spoken up?

Apart from Petrus, the only father-man in attendance was Brine, the oldest father-man on the 437th. Clearly, Brine planned to ingratiate himself with Petrus in hopes that he would eventually be awarded a higher-ranked homestead. Homestead 12, the one Brine held currently, was a dump. Brine's father-house stood in a flood ditch. His house-seeds complained about the mildew and rats. His arable lowlands flooded during heavy rains, and most of his seeds suffered from lung ailments. Doc Riff said the neglected cabins in Brine's boggy seed quarters weren't fit for pigs. Brine must have figured that having an ally in Petrus—a known adversary of Lotter—could prove useful now that Lotter had been elevated to cropmaster.

Ji-ji recalled that last year Herring, encouraged by Lotter, had threatened to have Brine removed from the planting altogether for "perennial unproductiveness." As it was, Inquisitor Tryton had given Brine three citations for impotence. If he got a fourth there would be an official hearing. All steaders had an obligation to procreate to ameliorate the acute labor shortage, and a father-man's title captured the symbolic significance of his role. Decimated populations around the world had led to incentivized procreation elsewhere, according to Uncle Dreg, but the Territories posed new challenges. As the wizard had frequently pointed out, steaders were engaged in a delicate, unethical dance. They had to reseed the Territories without ceding power to those they begat. Everyone had to perform in their assigned roles; otherwise the entire system collapsed. So far, however, Brine had failed miserably in his appointed task. None of his four young seedmates had gotten pregnant—though the wizened steader swore up and down that several had miscarried. As was customary, he'd been asked to tender his preemie womblings as evidence. He'd offered one lame excuse after another for not doing so. Lotter despised Brine as much as he loathed Petrus and Williams. As Silapu put it, Brine was hanging on to his homestead by a thread, aware that the person in possession of scissors—i.e., the new cropmaster—considered him to be scum. It shouldn't surprise anyone that Stinky Brine sought out allies whenever he could.

The lowest-ranking father-man on the 437th tottered up to Ji-ji's mam and began making small talk with her, commenting on how "refreshed" she looked. Brine entreated her to extend his greetings to Lord-Father Lotter, and muttered something else to her mam Ji-ji didn't catch.

"The old fart has been lobbying to get into Lotter's good graces for years," Silapu informed the other mams as Brine slunk off. "He will never succeed. Lotter despises him—calls him a drain on the planting. Says a father-man who cannot father is like a bird that cannot fly."

Ji-ji turned her attention away from Stinky Brine. Talking about him was making her mad again. Her eyes were drawn to Lua's coffin, but the cheap-looking wood Petrus had ordered his carpenters to slap together looked pathetic. Set on a table up on the platform in the middle of the Central Yard, the coffin was a mishmash of uneven planks of wood. No one had bothered to stain or sand it. Lua's planting name, Mammy Lua Petrusseedmate, had been scrawled on the side.

Officially, Lua was Petrus' fourth seedmate, selected after Charra had disappeared. But if you counted Charra (who had been erased from the official roll as a seedmate due to her ingratitude), Lua was his fifth. Ji-ji had taken it personally—first her sister, then her best friend mated to a swine. She had conferred with Ma Merrimac, who, in her role as seed recorder, knew almost as much about botanical and Indigenous folklore as Uncle Dreg did. Unlike the Toteppi wizard, Ma Merrimac wasn't averse to placing ancient wisdom in the service of revenge. Following Ma's detailed instructions, Ji-ji had made a voodoo doll. She'd stuck so many pins in it that Petrus Doll looked like a porcupine. Soon afterward, Petrus had been thrown from his quarter horse. Fittingly, he'd landed on a thorn-bush. It comforted Ji-ji to know that the severe butt injury he'd sustained still caused him pain.

Danfrith Petrus stood up on the harvesting platform receiving mourners and feigning grief. Lua hadn't managed to escape his clutches, but Charra had. And Charra was alive! Ji-ji wished she could share the miraculous news with her dead best friend. Lua would have done a happy dance.

Charra had been horrified when she'd learned she was to be seed-mated to Petrus. Her seed-price had been a bone of contention for several months. Lotter knew how desirable Charra was; he expected her price to set a record. Petrus had balked at first, claiming no Mule was worth that kind of lucre. Lotter had been mildly entertained as he "stuck it to Petrus." Then, in a move that devastated Charra, they agreed upon a seed-price significantly below the one Lotter had originally demanded. What was worse, Silapu hadn't uttered a word of protest. In bed, the night before the Seedmating Ceremony—the last night Ji-ji would share the small bedroom with a sibling—Charra had vowed she would find a way to defy Lotter's ruling.

Ji-ji hadn't doubted her sister for a second. Beautiful, talented Charra had always forged her own path. When Ji-ji had asked her how she would escape, all Charra would say was "I won't let the bastard touch me. You'll see. Don't let any man convince you you're worthless, Beany." (Charra had been the only person who had called Ji-ji a bean in a way that didn't seem to highlight her seediness.)

"The steaders do everything they can to convince us we're small," Charra continued. "So we gotta scale ourselves up an' take on the world." Her voice turned to a whisper. "I'll tell you a secret. There's something about us—something about Mam and Uncle Dreg and the other Toteppi and their offspring—that scares the crap out of the steaders. Don't know what it is yet but I aim to find out. Listen to Uncle Dreg, Beany. He sees things in those Seeing Eyes of his. But for god's sake steer clear of that Tiro. No fly-boy can be trusted, an' Tiro's a fly-boy through an' through."

Accustomed to her mam's relentless criticism of Tiro, Ji-ji hadn't expected Charra to follow suit. She put it down to her sister's muddled state of mind over her pending union with Petrus. Every male must look awful to her. Who could blame her for not being able to differentiate between the good and the bad?

The last time Ji-ji saw her sister was a Sunday. They hadn't seen each other for months. Seeds who weren't working were required to worship at the pray center, but Charra had always found any excuse not to listen to Pastor Gillyman's whining sermons. Ji-ji knew she would find her sister in Petrus' seed quarters.

When Ji-ji knocked on the warped, termite-ridden door of the seedmate cabin, Charra had opened the door just enough to mutter "What are *you* doing here?" through the narrow slit. Suspecting something was amiss, Ji-ji had pushed on the door and wriggled inside to find her sister's lip badly swollen, and a fist-sized bruise on her lovely cheek. "I'll *kill* that pig face!" Ji-ji declared. Charra had laughed—more of a snort really cos her mouth was swollen. Then she warned Ji-ji never to confront Petrus. "He's crazy evil. Got a grudge against botanicals, 'specially if they let on they know more than he does. Stay as far away from him as possible, Beany. Promise me."

Seven days later, Petrus barged into Silapu's cabin at the crack of dawn, demanding to know where Charra was hiding and threatening to whip Ji-ji and her mam if they were in cahoots with the bitch. Less than a minute later, Lotter appeared as if by magic. Enunciating each word carefully, he'd informed Petrus that he would slice off his hairy balls and hang them round his neck if he ever dared to lay hands on his property. Petrus had been reaching for his handgun when Van Casper appeared behind Lotter, accompanied by three of Lotter's security guards. Four rifles were aimed at Petrus' head, who raised his hands in surrender, then attempted to save face by claiming all he wanted was a refund on the seed-price—something he never got.

After that, Silapu poured her offspring-love into Bonbon to make up for losing Charra—Charra being the offspring she'd lost after Clay had been auctionmarted, and Clay being the offspring she'd lost after Luvlydoll succumbed to metaflu. And then Lotter held up the official Color Wheel to Bonbon's pretty face, and Silapu lost her lastborn too. Yet here she was, standing tall beside Ji-ji's adopted mother-aunts. *All is not lost,* Ji-ji reminded herself. *If Mam can return to life, anything is possible.*

It was time for Petrus to deliver the Seedmate Harvesting Sermon. He delivered it from the platform, standing next to Lua's shabby coffin. He was dressed in business attire: beige carpenter pants and a father-man camo jacket, with the planting crest (a sheaf of wheat and a chisel plow) sewn onto the pocket, and a smaller homestead seal embroidered underneath it. Petrus rounded out his outfit with a pair of hefty work boots. He hadn't bothered to have them cleaned. Recognition slapped Ji-ji in the face. A picture of those same work boots had been glued to the end of Silas' boot-box coffin. It was all she could do not to throw up.

Danfrith Petrus was no wordsmith. Anxious to get the sermon over with, he spoke brusquely, praising "Mammy Lua" for her efforts to "do her patriotic duty and seed the blessed Territories." He extinguished the wreath of harvesting candles to symbolize the fact that Lua's life cycle was complete; his seedmate's soul had been harvested by God. Lua would now assume her rightful place on the Great Ladder of Meaning. (He didn't mention that her place would be on one of the lowest rungs with the other botanicals, just above the outcasts, beasts, and mutants. He didn't mention her deadborn either. Not once.)

Seedbirth coffins were regularly left open so that dead seedmates, clothed in martyr-white and holding white lilies, could inspire other female seeds, but Lua's coffin had been nailed shut with six enormous nails. *Either Lua's seedling is in the coffin with her,* Ji-ji thought, *and Petrus doesn't want anyone to see him, or Lua's being buried alone.* She prayed it was the former—couldn't bear to think of her best friend being buried underground without little Silas.

The mourners were invited to file past the coffin and pay their respects. When it was Ji-ji's turn, she placed one of Uncle Dreg's greenhouse roses on the lid. She had selected a blood-red hybrid tea rose from a bush labeled CRIMSON MOTHERGLORY, the kind of bloom that looked beautiful and angry at the same time. *Beauty for Lu and her deadborn,* Ji-ji thought, *anger for me.* The bloom was a blaze of red fire—so red it almost sliced you open when you looked at it.

Some of Petrus' seedlings scattered white rose petals on the ground to symbolize purity. Then Lua's child-sized coffin was hoisted onto the back of the burial wagon. Silent Pete, a seed who'd lost half of his left foot, an ear, and three fingers when he'd served as a child soldier in one of the many clashes that followed the Sequel (the mounds of corpses he'd seen had robbed him of his voice too, they said, which was why he rarely spoke and never touched meat), slapped the reins on the horse's rump. The burial wagon trundled off in the direction of the seed cemetery. Two of Petrus' seedlings played nearby. Their hands joined, they spun round in a circle. When Pete was out of earshot, their high voices trilled a familiar rhyme, one Ji-ji was ashamed to admit she had sung as a seedling: "*Silent Pete don't eat meat / Silent Pete ain't got two feet.*" As the wagon disappeared over the crest of the hill, Marcie let out a doleful wail. Bettieann sobbed.

While the other females gathered round to comfort both her and Marcie, something caught Ji-ji's eye. Her Crimson Motherglory had rolled off the lid of the coffin and been trampled by the seedlings. Lua wouldn't even have a rose to comfort her in the dark.

With a flourish of phony concern, Petrus presented Aunt Marcie with a mam-of-the-seedmate harvesting basket. The black ribbon snaked around it made Ji-ji think of seizure ribbons.

Vincent Fratt, Petrus' clerical assistant, recited a list of the contents like it was a regular grocery list: fruit, a large fry pan, a bag of seedchips valued at ten rebel dollars, a pair of sunglasses, hand lotion, a can of roasted peanuts, a stick of deodorant, genuine fluoride toothpaste, and a screen viewer. In addition to the basket, Fratt informed Marcie she would get electricity in her cabin next year or the year after, and a reception box too, to reward her for her "sacrifice to the Territories." The grieving mam would be able to watch the propaganda programs piped in through the Grubby Pipe from the Father-City of Armistice. Ji-ji hoped Marcie would spit in Fratt's face. She didn't.

After Petrus and Fratt moved off, Silapu turned to Ji-ji and muttered, "And that crap is supposed to compensate for the loss of her Last&Only. Absolute evil."

Soon afterward, Silapu and Ji-ji climbed into the mourning wagon along with four other seeds from various parts of the planting. Ji-ji spied Matty Longsby in the distance. He was sitting astride his horse, staring at them. She pretended she hadn't seen him.

A short time later, Ji-ji was alone in the cabin at last. Her mam, still railing about the hideous mam-of-the-seedmate basket, had set off for her shift at the textile factory. Ji-ji had thirty minutes before she had to leave for Cropmaster Hall to prepare Lotter's lunch. She stuffed a wooden wedge under the door so no one could enter and retrieved the note from her pocket. Her heart beat fiercely in her chest. *Let him be okay. . . . Let him be okay. . . .*

Tiro's sprawling handwriting took up two full pages. She had never received a letter as long as this from him before.

Dear Ji-ji—excuse all the mistakes in this note. I was never great at writing. Not bad for a juvi but nothing like you. And I dont have ackcess to an American ~~Heritij~~ H. dictionary like you either. Scared you will see how often I mess up when it comes to spelling and grammer and hold it against me!

I know this day is hell for you. Lua was good and you were a good friend to her. Real good. I hope that comforts you some. Wish I could be there but Coach B wont let up. You know how he is. I'm trying out this new move from the crow's nest. I ~~come~~ came up with it myself. Hoping it will seal the deal if I make it to the final.

You dont have to worry. I mean it. I'm OK. Well OK could be streching it, but I'm not crazy or anything so don't get it in your head to be going any place <u>you shouldnt be going</u> if you see what I mean cos I'm OK. I really am.

Funniest thing happened Ji. I kind of saw him. Uncle Dreg. I was so mad after what happened. Thats why I couldnt look at you. Couldnt speak either. But then I was sitting on the porch that night and I looked up and there was all these stars. Like thousands! And it made me think of what Uncle Dreg used to tell us. Those old stories he brought over from the Cradle. And then its like I fell asleep and then woke up and he was there in the sky. Like the night was a storycloth and he was flying across it and just stopped for a second to say hi before he takes off again.

Bet your dam sure I'm crazy now but I swear to god Ji if you could see it you would be crazy too. Happy crazy. And the old man was smiling and nodding and I thought he was pointing to the stars only he wasnt. He was pointing to the dark parts. The midnight in between. You see, he says all joyfull, I told you. Heads of midnight. And then I understood how he ment it was us seeds reaching for the stars. Does that sound corny? Guess it does. But corny can be truer than anything sometimes. Right?

And even tho I cant honistly say I know exactly what he ment by that and even tho it could be I made the hole thing up cos I was pretty messed up that night it made me feel like I was right to keep on flying in the coop after Amadee got tractor pulled, and right to hold on to you too even tho there are times when I think your mams right and I'm too messed up for you Ji but I hope thats not the way it turns out. Bet there should be about a hundred comas in that last sentence but I've looked it over and it beats me where I should plug them in. Seems to me punctuation and spelling too is a way to keep us seeds from writing things down for posteritty and thinking out loud on paper. A way to keep us quite. But dont worry Ji. I aim to get real good at both so I can keep up with you in Dream City and not show you up. (Feel Free to mark up this note and show me the corrections later. I wont be off-ended.)

Anyhow I'm kinda scared to send this now in case it proves I'm a ignorant nut job like your mam says. But I guess I'll send it anyway so you dont worry the way you always worry about me and about everything in this world cos thats how your made.

We can do this Ji. I know it. Keep to the curfew and dont do nothing wreckless. Just imagine Ji. Were almost there. Heads of midnight flying through the dark. Free.—T

Tiro was okay! Ji-ji felt like leaping for joy.

She got down on her hands and knees and, with difficulty, retrieved *An Abbreviated History of These Disunited States* from under her bed. She folded up Tiro's note and slipped it into the book, inside a chapter called "Promises Kept"—one of her favorites cos it described the old U.S. before Trifurcation, when it split into three self-governing entities. That chapter always made Ji-ji wonder if people knew how good they had it back then. Tiro's note would be safe there with the other coverts she'd lashed to the underside of the bed frame. Her books would outrage the steaders, of course, who would rail against the "sedition-fomenting texts." If her mam discovered them, she'd freak out as well, especially if she found out Ji-ji had hidden something even more seditious under her bed.

A not-to-scale map she'd drawn lay hidden inside *The Tempest,* next to the page at the end where the wizard Prospero pleads with the audience to set him Free. She treasured the map because it brought the planting down to size—with its fry-fence, corny wagon-wheel layout, forbidden paths, and pridefulness. Each time she added something to the map it felt like she had power over the planting—like she'd humbled it simply by consigning it to paper. Risky drawing something like that, but sometimes you had to do the stuff they said you couldn't just to prove to yourself you could. The map said, "A seed named Ji-ji Jubilation squeezed your entire sorryass planting onto a scrap of paper. Planting 437 looks downright pathetic cos that's exactly what it is."

Ji-ji wasn't the only one engaging in risky business. Zaini had taken a real risk too. If she'd been searched and Tiro's note found, she would have gotten a public lashing; so would Tiro. Worse, probably, given the contents. Yet that was what Ji-ji loved about them both—the fact that they would risk exposure cos they knew how much it mattered. Uncle Dreg might have been the wizard in the family, but Zaini was the one who sensed what others needed and found a way to get it to them. With her steady hands, Zaini steered Tiro away from despair and toward joy again.

When Ji-ji first set eyes on Tiro, she'd just turned six and Tiro was seven and a half. They'd been at the Seed Symbol Ceremony. Tiro had introduced himself with the words "Hi. I'm Tiro. When I grow up I'm gonna fly." And Ji-ji had replied, "Hi, I'm Jellybean. I'm scared of heights but I'm a fast runner an' I can spell already—a-l-r-e-a-d-y." Tiro had burst out laughing, and Ji-ji had known she would want to hear that laugh for as long as she lived.

At the Seed Symbol Ceremony, seedlings sewed seed symbols onto their shirts and blouses. If they failed to attach their symbols within five minutes, they had to start all over again. Ji-ji had been the quickest seedling in the Gathering Place that day; Tiro had been the slowest. It wasn't that he couldn't do it. He had purposely screwed up—made his stitches a mile long and as crooked as a broken finger. The last time the overseers had made him redo it, he'd attached the symbol to his shirt sleeve. When the seers had ordered him to put his shirt on so everyone could see how badly he'd screwed up, Tiro had slipped it on and thrust his arm dramatically over his heart. "*See!*" he'd exclaimed. "It *is* in the right place!" All the seedlings had laughed and a star had been born. Tiro would have been whipped raw for impudence if Uncle Dreg hadn't interceded on his behalf.

Ji-ji had been coming up on thirteen when Silapu convinced Lotter to delay seedmating her. Lotter knew she was a good cook, and after nonstop pleas from Silapu, he had her inducted as a kitchen-seed. It took her only a few months to be named to the chief's position, following the seedbirthing death of her predecessor, Harriett Herringseedmate.

Ji-j knew she was lucky. Being chief kitchen-seed was tons better than being seedmated. But knowing she wouldn't have access to education at the planting legacy school for seeds anymore sent her on a downward spiral. She started doing crazy things, taking risks whenever she could. Silapu got scared because Ji-ji wasn't scared enough. Training for the Freedom Race saved her life. Ji-ji began to run—a mile or two at first, then greater and greater distances. She discovered how freaky fast she was and realized how hard she could push her body without fear of it letting her down. And now, for the first time since Lua's seedbirthing, Ji-ji felt at peace. Every sign seemed to be pointing in the right direction. Tiro believed Uncle Dreg was still watching over him. He would be okay. She decided to do the sensible thing and heed his warning. She would not attempt to visit the flying coop tomorrow. She would let Silapu know that Tiro had persuaded her not to do it—prove to her mam that Tiro could be sensible when he wanted. As soon as Lotter lifted the restrictions on inter-homestead movement, she would visit the flying coop. In the meantime, she would have his words to comfort her.

A sudden, searing pain between Ji-ji's shoulder blades flung her onto her bed. After several seconds of unbearable spasms, the pain lessened. A few minutes later it all but disappeared.

Ji-ji tried not to panic. She stood up gingerly. Her back was still tender. She resolved to consult with Coach Billy. He knew all about sports injuries. "Don't let this be happening," she prayed, to anyone who might be listening. "Give me as much pain as you like after I get to the city. Just hold off till then, okay?"

Careful not to irritate her back, she changed from her pray-day outfit into her kitchen-seed uniform—a bulky striped skirt, a dun-colored blouse, and a dark brown apron with her name and CHIEF KITCHEN-SEED embroidered on the pocket. She set off for work.

During the long jog to Cropmaster Hall she kept repeating to herself, "You are not in pain and your back is fine. You are not in pain and your back is fine. . . ."

All she had to do now was make herself believe it.

9 THE FLYING COOP

Ji-ji set out before dawn from Lotter's seed quarters on Homestead 1 to Brine's quarters, directly south on Homestead 12. She tore along the permissible paths and cut across fields she had permission to traverse. The past few years of desperately needed, steady seasonal rain had ended the latest drought. Though she suspected the mild weather wouldn't last, she'd take it as a good sign.

Ji-ji wasn't surprised that she and her mam still resided in their cabin on Homestead 1, in spite of the fact that Lotter was serving as cropmaster. His seeds would likely remain there for weeks while the father-men squabbled over the tricky issue of homestead reassignment. In theory, the so-called Homestead Shuffle that took place after a cropmaster died enabled every father-man to move up into the homestead above his own; in practice, it wasn't that simple. Lotter could do whatever he wanted—reassign the majority of his seeds, or relocate them onto seed quarters he could construct near his residence. He could keep his homestead, or he could cede it to another father-man for a fat bestowal fee. Herring had surrendered his homestead after he was formally appointed as cropmaster. But Lotter, who never relinquished control of anything easily, had so far opted to retain Homestead 1, which was why the route Ji-ji was taking to the flying coop this morning was the same one she always took.

She had a lot to be thankful for. Mam was still sober and acting like a mother, and the paralyzing grief Ji-ji had felt over the loss of Lua and Uncle Dreg had morphed into an unshakable determination to succeed for their sakes. Yesterday, newly appointed Security Chief Williams' curt announcement about "the restoration of inter-homestead movement" had played over the loudspeakers. With inter-homestead movement no longer restricted, the Ratification Ceremony scheduled for tomorrow night would go ahead. To Ji-ji's relief, her back had almost healed. Not a single twinge in a week. After nearly three weeks, the longest time they had been apart in years, she and Tiro would see each other again this morning. She would have a chance to speak with him before Ratification—remind him not to do anything reckless. She had other things to tell him too.

Silapu had lobbied hard for Ji-ji's ratification and had even put in a good word for Tiro, under a dark cloud as the blood relative of a traitor. Apparently, Herring had let the planting drift into debt. The tithes payable to Armistice to secure the Territories were six months in arrears. You didn't mess with the Territorial Council, whose members dished out crippling fines to tardy plantings. Lotter had to find extra money fast. Though the recompense for runner reps paled in comparison to what competitors' home plantings received for fly-boys, the compensation for Ji-ji, particularly if she made it all the way to the city, would offset some of the debt. In light of this auspicious new development, Silapu said she was almost certain Ji-ji would be ratified. The planting trial records Ji-ji had smashed appeared to have made an impression on Lotter after all. Apart from Sloppy—Ji-ji's fellow kitchen-seed who'd crossed the finish line a few minutes behind her in the trials—no other female seed could come close to Ji-ji's time or match her endurance. As for Tiro, Silapu figured his chances had improved to, maybe, fifty-fifty. Not good, but considerably better than what they were before. Lotter was a pragmatist, and multiple payments would accrue to the planting at every stage of Tiro's ascent. The stars were in alignment at last.

Ji-ji poured cold water on her own excitement. She would jinx herself if she wasn't careful. *Remember Mam's warning,* Ji-ji thought. *If you're gazing too far into the future you fall on your ass in the present.* The day after the Ratification Ceremony, she and Tiro—*it had to be both of them*—would be transported to the Salem Outpost, where the first leg of the race would commence. Before then, she and her dozen full-time kitchen-seeds, along with a slew of helper seeds, would prepare the greatest feast of the season. If she served an unappetizing dish to the head table, or failed to take into account the dietary preferences of a VIP guest of honor, or—worse still—offended the taste buds of Planting Taster Lemmaging, she'd be toast. . . .

Ji-ji shivered—more with nervousness than with the chill. She'd come down from her high. Overconfidence was a seed's worst enemy. She had to keep it in check.

She reached the small bridge spanning the rock-lined drainage trench Coach B and his fly-boys had dug to reroute rain- and floodwater. Water pooled so badly in Brine's low-lying homestead that Tiro joked it would be easier to travel to the flying coop by ferry. Brine refused to spend a seedchip on maintenance, complaining that flying incited sedition by encouraging seeds "to de-rung themselves from their natural position on God's Great Ladder." The rusty old coop had been losing its battle with the elements ever since Brine had been granted fathership rights to Homestead 12.

Although females were not permitted to fly in the coop, that didn't prevent Ji-ji from falling in love with flight the first time she'd set foot there as a seedling. The dilapidated coop didn't look like much from the outside. A grimy canvas tent that had been repeatedly patched and mended covered its metal skeleton; a smell of mold, sweat, and gas fumes from the ancient generators permeated the space. Yet seeds and steaders alike flocked to the battles held there four times a year, spectators shelling out the hefty sum of seven seedchips each for tickets. The funds enabled Coach Billy and his Serverseed assistant Pheebs to make repairs and purchase fuel from the general store to feed the gas-guzzling generators. But each year, the father-men debated whether it was worth the upkeep, especially given the fact that no fly-boy from the 437th had made it to the finals for years. According to Marcus Shadowbrookseed, whose gossip was invariably accurate due to Old Shadowy's tendency to confide in him when she was high as a kite, Williams, Brine, and others lobbied for the coop to be demolished; Lotter was indifferent—no surprise there; and the other nine father-men, along with Diviner Shadowbrook, usually voted in favor of keeping it. Every seed knew privileges could be snatched away without notice, which was why the fly-boys lived in constant fear that they would wake up one morning to discover their one source of elevation demolished.

Ji-ji pulled back the frayed canvas flap that served as a door to the coop and stepped inside. As usual, a reverence she never felt at the planting pray center—or anywhere else, for that matter—filled her. Coach B's hollers and the creak of rusty equipment filled the cavernous space. Though one of the repurposed generators chugged away outside as usual, only a handful of lights were on. Almost immediately after he took over as acting cropmaster, Lotter had issued an order mandating frugality, which explained why it wasn't much brighter inside the tent than it was outside. No one had seen her yet. She paused to take it all in. This place meant so much to her.

Steaders claimed that flying coops had been their invention, but Ji-ji knew they lied. The first coop had been conceived of by seed-laborers at a progressive planting in the 600s, less than a generation after the conclusion of the Civil War Sequel. Risky even then for seeds to speak openly about civil rights, so those early seeds had to be creative. The two coastal SuperStates, reeling from a Sequel that wiped out a third of the population, and battling major disasters on multiple fronts, decided to believe the steaders' claim that the Territories would usher in a New Era of Civility. According to Swinburne Augustus, Supreme Commander of the Territorial Militia and the first Lord-Father of Lord-Fathers, it was a steader's duty to "obliterate the unrestrained thinking that brought God's wrath upon the world." During his famous Reversal Address to the Territorial Representatives, Augustus pledged to "usher in a glorious system of patronage." This necessary reversal, he promised, would revive the way of life established by our Founding Fathers.

Ji-ji had seen a photo of Swinburne Augustus in the history text she had strapped to the underside of her bed. She'd read Maeve Exra's book so many times the pages were falling out. In Armistice's Rotunda, gray-haired Augustus stood under portraits of Washington, Jefferson, and other father-men, a copy of the Bible in one raised hand, a copy of *The One True Text* in the other. An antique rifle lay on the podium. (Exra pointed to the odd fusion of elements in the steaders' *One True Text,* saying it was as if Margaret Mitchell, Augustus' favorite author, had wed St. Paul and *The One True Text* was their offspring.) Ji-ji knew Exra's description by heart: "To thunderous applause, Swinburne Augustus, bearded and steely-eyed, swore fealty to the Found Cause, to the Fathers and Daughters of the Sacred South, and to America's Blessed Rural Edens."

The importation of labor from other parts of the world wasn't sinister at first—just a logical response to the global labor shortage. Early waves of imported laborers signed bona fide contracts and worked for a wage. When their time was up, the laborers had the right to go wherever they wanted. Many opted to remain in homesteads in the Territories. With each successive wave of workers, however, Territorial laws calcified. Soon there were Liberty Laborers—mostly fairskins—recognized under the Constitution, and Indentures—mostly so-called duskies—who weren't. Importing laborers from Central and South America had concluded, for the most part, after pickers met with a unified resistance on the southern border. Attempts to recruit laborers from Asia had failed abysmally. As a result, toward the end of Augustus' tenure, the focus switched entirely to the place steaders called the Dark Continent.

The idea of a flying coop should never have survived an atmosphere as poisonous as that. But not all the early steaders were segregationists; many were just secessionists sick of taxation and centralized government and terrified of a future that looked like it was only going to get worse. The unionists were in as much disarray as the secessionists. As Exra put it, "The SuperStates, struggling for survival themselves, didn't have the time or the means to excise the cancer in the belly of the country." Ji-ji had repeated Exra's phrase over and over the first time she'd read it because it rang true. A cancer in the belly—which meant she and everyone she loved lived inside a tumor.

As the disunited states struggled to emerge as three separate-but-equal power centers, Augustus' successors pounded the final nails into the coffin in the form of the Necessary Reversal Acts—legislation that reclassified imports from the Cradle as botanicals. The reclassification wasn't confined to race, a point the Territorial Council emphasized whenever the system was challenged. It also reclassified others. Sexual deviants, occultists (especially witches), historians, librarians, Free thinkers—any of these and more could be reclassified as botanicals and obliged to surrender their rights as individuals. Scientists and clergymen who refused to sign a fealty pledge to the steaders' *One True Text* could also be reclassified as botanicals in the Territories, even if they were the fairest of fairskins—though the overwhelming majority of seeds were on the duskier arcs of the Wheel. How could such a system be based on race, steaders asked, if race was only one criterion for classification?

As she paused in the dark just inside the door of the coop, Ji-ji was thrust back into the recent past. She remembered Juan, a certified "Deviant," who'd been caught with Amadee in one of Williams' barns. Amadee should be here now, flying with his twin brother. Amadee tractor-pulled, Juan pyred—a female punishment Father-Man Williams insisted upon. The cancer had spread until there were hundreds of plantings throughout the Territories, a dozen homesteads on each. . . .

She breathed in the musty air, ignoring the staleness of it. Coach Billy had told Tiro, who'd told Ji-ji, that the first flying coop had been built as a response to the Necessary Reversal—the seeds' way of memorializing their own history. They believed, Coach B said, that if they didn't write their own story in canvas, metal, and wood, it would be lost. The seeds constructed the coop (or *flying birdcage,* as it was called back then) out of scraps they'd salvaged, working at night and in secret—though how they managed to do this, Ji-ji couldn't imagine, unless the early steaders were blind and deaf. The seeds devised the rules and named the equipment after figures they admired.

Legend had it (and so did Coach B) that a tornado leveled the first flying birdcage two years after it was built, but not before a few enterprising steaders discovered it and recognized its potential as a revenue-generating source of entertainment. The flying birdcage withstood the test of time, morphing into bigger and grander things but always—in Coach B's opinion, at least—adhering to its role as a memorial to not-to-be-forgotten stories.

Uncle Dreg used to tell Ji-ji that the coop was equally symbolic to seeds and steaders. To seeds it was a reminder that flight was possible; to steaders it emphasized the inescapable supremacy of the cage. When a symbol has two faces, Uncle Dreg said, it is potent *and* dangerous—liable to shift on you if you don't keep your eye on it. What mattered to Ji-ji was that the planting flying coop was the one place where her dreams were more powerful than her yearning.

Under the tent, the giant, domed flying cage took up the entire middle section of the coop. Like a circus ring, the sawdust-lined ground ring in the center was where Planting Coopmaster Mack-Jack Ferguson stood, calling out play-by-play commentary as the flyer-battlers fought overhead. In spite of what Mack-Jack would have you believe, the magic didn't happen at ground level where he stood; it happened when you saw caged birds fly.

As your eye traveled upward it encountered spiral staircases, trapezes, staging rings and platforms, sycamore copters, a rickety hamster wheel, Jacob's Ladders, Harriet's Stairs, Douglass Pipes, the Marshall Maze, X Boxes, Parks Perches, Colvin Coils, Lincoln Logs, Plessy Pulleys, Kingspins, hope-ropes, zip lines, and trampolines—all of them culminating in the Jimmy Crow's Nest, a woven basket modeled after the legendary lookout baskets on sailing ships. Located inside the dome at the pinnacle of the coop, the nest was roomy enough to hold four flyers. According to Uncle Dreg, the nest was a tribute to the Middle Passengers imported centuries before.

Ji-ji looked up. Tiro was perched on the edge of the Jimmy Crow. She waved excitedly, grinning from ear to ear and raising herself on her tiptoes as if she could reach him if she tried hard enough.

Tiro saw her, but the nod he returned was hesitant and he didn't smile. Ji-ji tried not to let it deflate her. He had to concentrate. If he didn't, he could plunge to his death.

The flying cage sat in the center of the coop and took up most of its volume. Encircling the cage were rows of bleachers where, two months before, hundreds of spectators—steaders in the fairskin sections and seeds in the dusky sections—had watched Tiro and the other fly-boys vie for the championship.

Ji-ji looked around cautiously, then walked to the main door of the metal flying cage. Her hands were shaking—god, she was nervous! If they caught her here, the day before Ratification, she'd be screwed. But she had to see him. . . . Her trembling fingers fumbled with the latch. The sound of metal against metal echoed through the coop as Ji-ji stepped inside. She closed the gate and sat down on one of the benches near the ground ring's low wall.

To prevent herself from obsessing about all the news she was desperate to share with Tiro, and to calm her fear that Brine's guards could enter at any time, Ji-ji tried to dwell inside the moment and take it all in. It would probably be the last time she would ever see Planting 437's flying coop. The thought made her happy and sad at the same time. Her eyes fell on the safety net directly in front of her. Raised twelve feet off the ground, it spanned the diameter of the ground ring but offered no protection should a flyer fall from somewhere other than the safe zone in the center of the coop. Fly-boys were supposed to wear safety harnesses, but these slowed them down, which explained why Tiro was notoriously irresponsible about wearing his. It also explained why Billy and his assistant Pheebs spent their nights strengthening the harnesses to ensure the old mechanical pulley system was functioning correctly.

Coach Billy stood beside the net, yelling instructions at his fly-boys. Four seeds flew in the coop this morning: Tiro, Marcus, Orlie, and Georgie-Porge, Billy's strongest flyer-battlers.

Like Tiro and Marcus, Orlie and Georgie-Porge partnered up during battles, though their aversion to each other resulted in constant bickering. Georgie-Porge had been known to drop Orlie into the net "by accident" instead of catching him on the high trapeze; Orlie had been known to grease Georgie-Porge's favorite staging platform. As usual, Ji-ji couldn't help but notice how odd Orlie and Georgie-Porge looked together.

Whereas Tiro and Marcus could easily have been mistaken for brothers, Georgie-Porge and Orlie couldn't have looked more different. In spite of the fattening-up process juvis underwent in readiness for the Propitious Gleaning, Orlie Mallorymule remained as skinny as a rake and almost as pale as his begetter, Father-Man Harold Mallory of Homestead 9. In fact, Orlie was so light-skinned he could pass for a True Hybrid or even a fairskin. Georgie-Porge Snellingseed, on the other hand, a Commonseed, was one of the darkest juvis on the planting, and one of the biggest too. Tom Snelling, the fairskin Liberty Laborer who begat Georgie, had mated with a Tribalseed import. His seed's ebony skin hadn't alarmed him, or made him suspect infidelity on the part of Issa, his mate. In fact, Snelling took enormous pride in his offspring—the only offspring from a union that had endured for more than twenty-five years, and one so full of obvious affection on the part of both Tom and Issa it would have resulted in a charge of Unnatural Affiliation had Snelling been a father-man. Fortunately for the couple, Inquisitor Tryton had better things to do than trouble himself with the love life of a lowly laborer.

Boasting about Georgie-Porge's prodigious strength and appetite delighted Tom Snelling (fined on several occasions for holding Issa's hand in public). Tiro had overheard Snelling confess to Zaini he was saving up to make a Patronage Claim for Issa. Planned to take her to live up in the Eastern SuperState near Buffalo. Figured it would take him a while to do it, so his fingers were crossed that Georgie-Porge would be on Tiro's petition list and reach the city before they did. (Ji-ji figured it would take Snelling a while too, given how regularly he gambled away his salary.) Like everyone else, Tom knew that Georgie didn't have anywhere near Orlie's quickness, but what his offspring lacked in agility he made up for in strength. Built more like a sumo wrestler than a flyer, Tom Snelling's pride and joy could bench-press all three of the other fly-boys at once.

When disputes broke out among the four, Marcus invariably sided with Georgie-Porge, but Tiro had taken Orlie under his wing and often spoke up for him. Ji-ji puzzled over Tiro's friendship with Orlie, a notorious whiner and a sulker. Marcus—the only seed on the planting who had more access to books and learning than Ji-ji—claimed Tiro didn't have to be fake-happy around Orlie. That was the glue, Marcus said, which made their unlikely friendship stick. "T. can grieve nonstop in the company of that pathetic crybaby. Doesn't need to get his shit together so there's no pressure." Marcus was right about most things. Could be he was right about that too.

Veteran coach Billy Brineseed stood in the center of the ground ring where Mack-Jack stood during battles in his multicolored coopmaster's outfit and jaunty top hat. Unlike the flamboyant coopmaster, Coach B wore dung-colored overalls. Even in the dim light, his bald head gleamed. He tramped over to Ji-ji and eased himself down on the bench beside her.

He didn't greet her; small talk wasn't his forte. They sat in silence for a while.

In his mid-seventies, Billy was still as lean as a racehorse and as strong as an ox. Though he had a full head of gray hair, each year he shaved it off before the Big Race and oiled his head to keep it slick, claiming baldness made him slippery as an eel and harder for juvis to catch hold of. Though Billy no longer battled on the high platforms or upper ring of the coop, he routinely bested juvis in hand-to-hand combat.

Ji-ji almost gasped when Coach B dug his hand into his pocket and pulled out a packet of cigarettes, withdrew one, then rummaged in his pocket for a box of matches. He struck a match. Ji-ji got a whiff of sulfur as it flared. In the flying coop, smoking was banned. Time and again, Coach B had ordered his fly-boys not to light up, warning them that the tent and the wooden pillars erected to help support the coop's corroding framework would go up like kindling.

Much of what Ji-Ji had learned about the veteran coach she'd gotten first from her mam and, later, from Tiro. Billy Brineseed's mother had been an import from the Cradle. His father was a Freeman, an African-American Indigenous with Proof of Ancestry documentation, which should have allowed his descendants to live with Indigenous rights and privileges in perpetuity. However, after his parents died from cholera just before Billy became a juvi at thirteen, he became a Ward of the Planting. Not long afterward, the planting "lost" his father's A-I documents. Being on one of the duskiest arcs of the Color Wheel meant he was vulnerable to reclassification not simply as a botanical Commonseed but as a Server-seed, an outcast. Billy's exceptional talent in the coop, along with his uncanny ability as an arborist, saved him. Eventually, he was traded to the 437th and assigned to care for Sylvie and other trees on the planting, and serve as flying coach.

There was another story about Billy too—one fewer seeds knew. Decades ago, Billy had appealed to have his A-I status reinstated. After years of tireless petitioning, he was reinstated to Indigenous by Saul Nickelback, Planting 437's eighth cropmaster. Billy had left the planting to live Free in the City of Dreams. But there was a problem: he was in love with a female seed back on the planting. After numerous unsuccessful attempts to petition for his beloved's Freedom, Billy couldn't stand it anymore. He returned to the planting to be with her. Cropmaster Nickelback was so offended by Billy's ingratitude he refused to allow him to pass through the perimeter gate. Undaunted, Billy had tunneled under the fry-fence, prompting Uncle Dreg to claim he was the only seed in history who had tunneled *into* rather than *out of* a planting.

Nickelback, impressed by Billy's determination, had permitted him to remain as long as he surrendered his claim to A-I status. Billy did so. Tragically, only two years later, Billy's beloved died.

"So," Coach Billy said, inhaling deeply and blowing out enough smoke to fill a slop bucket, "what do you think?"

Ji-ji had no idea what he was referring to. She did what she always did when growns asked a question she didn't have a clue about—repeated it. "What do I think?"

The tactic irritated the veteran coach. "You some kind of parrot, Lottermule?" Fortunately, before Ji-ji was obliged to respond again, Coach B explained himself: "Your fly-boy's acting like a moron. Careening round the cage then perching himself up there in that Jiminy Nest like he's got all the time in the world. We been on a restricted schedule. Still got four or five moves to refine. The Jefferson Coop in Monticello and the fancy new Dream Coop in the city are high tech. They got equipment in those coops like you never seen. Makes this place look like the scrap heap it is. Even the Salem Coop puts this one to shame. He's forgotten he's got to compete in all three and run the sprints too. You better knock some sense into him cos I've had it up to here." Coach B indicated a place near the top of his forehead to demonstrate his level of frustration.

"Bet you didn't know I smoked, did you?" Ji-ji shook her head. "April's a crappy time of year. I'm sick of watching juvis get fattened up for the auction. Only lucky one is Marcus. Wouldn't be surprised if Emmeline adopted him one day if he don't expire first from weed overdosing."

The coach blew a smoke ring. It held its shape for a few seconds in the nippy morning air before it faded into the gloom of the coop. Ji-ji decided that now, while Billy was getting solace from his death stick, would be as good a time as any to ask for advice about her back.

Billy Brineseed listened in silence, nodding a few times as he pulled on his cigarette. Dawn was breaking; daylight had started to filter in through the dome flaps at the top of the cage. To open them, Pheebs had to shimmy up the main hope-rope hung from the center of the dome, clamber onto a Parks Perch, and with the help of a hooked staff and fearlessness, roll back the unwieldy canvas flaps. No one could shimmy up a hope-rope faster than Pheebs, whose diminutive size (she was only four foot six) and extraordinary agility had earned her a permanent spot as Billy's assistant. Even some of the steaders referred to her by her proper name rather than Cloth-34b. Billy spoke of Pheebs with a reverence he reserved for only four others: Dregulahmo, his best friend; Silapu, whom he called a Toteppi princess; Zaini, especially after Amadee's death; and Amadee.

After Williams murdered Amadee, the old coach had been inconsolable for a while. There were rumors that he'd begun drinking again and that Pheebs had ferreted out his store of booze and poured the contents of every bottle into the flood drain. Tiro said Billy blamed himself, said he should have warned Amadee never to act on his impulses. It was common knowledge that Amadee wasn't "regular," as Billy put it, adding, "But if he was a Deviant, I'm King Tut. He wanted to love Free, that's all." Ever since Amadee's death, Billy was always reminding Tiro to look out for Zaini and his little brothers. "Zaini kept on living," Billy told him. "That's courage. An' that's why you don't do nothing dumb with some stupid butchery knife. That's why you fly your heart out up there. Not just for Amadee but for Zaini too. Cos she's the one held your tore-up brother in her arms and kissed his mashed-up remains. An' she's the one who birthed an' buried him, an' she's the one left behind. An' that's the goddam painfullest place of all. Sure, I know what you're thinking cos I'm thinking it too—Marcus can never be Amadee. Don't be fooled. When he's not high as a kite Marcus is one hell of a flyer. Same build as you an' Amadee, same recklessness. So be grateful he's willing to step up an' serve as your practice partner. From now on, you fly like you mean it. For Zaini. For Amadee. For all of us. Fly like you're heading home."

Having sufficiently pondered what Ji-ji had shared with him about her injury, Billy said, "Sounds to me like you got a pulled muscle. You say it feels okay now?"

"Haven't had a problem in days. The pain has disappeared. Ran all the way here from Lotter's seed quarters in record time."

"Don't overdo it. You don't want to reinjure it or get tuckered out either."

"I never get tuckered out."

Coach B looked over at her. "I don't s'pose you do," he said. "Guess there are advantages to being young an' dumb. Speaking of which . . ." Coach B shot up from the bench and yelled up at Marcus, Orlie, and Georgie-Porge, who were attempting to use their long staffs to bat each other off the lower staging platform. Tiro was still perched on the edge of the nest, staring down at them. "Damn *FOOLS*!" the coach bellowed. "I could do better with my eyes closed!"

Marcus, Orlie, and Georgie-Porge glanced down at their irate coach and proceeded to put more energy into their attack.

"An' what the *HELL* you think you're doing perched on that damn nest, Williamsmule? You think you got *ALL THE TIME IN THE WORLD*? You think the race monitors'll give you points for loungin' up there on your bony butt? Think they'll take one look at your pretty face an' say, give Williamsmule the prize jus' cos he's jus' so damn *cute*? What the *hell* is he thinking? Well?"

Ji-ji realized the coach's last comment had been addressed to her. She offered the first thing that came into her head: "Could be . . . he's tired?"

"Tired my ass! Juvi's been flying around like some demented hornet this morning 'fore you got here. Battled the other three one after the other. Tossed each of 'em into the net like they was seedlings. Tiro's always been a crazy sonuvabitch—no offense meant to Zaini. But this morning that fly-boy's acting ridiculous. An' *now* look at him! Sitting there like some comatose Buddha! I mean it, Williamsmule! *GET YOUR SKINNY ASS OFF THAT NEST AN' FIGHT!*"

The anger in Billy's voice seemed to register at last. Tiro grabbed hold of a hope-rope. In a risky maneuver, he swung down from the Jimmy Crow to the midlevel staging ring.

"What's that juvi up to now?" Coach B wondered aloud. "Mule's just showing off." He yelled up at Tiro again, "You a battler or a clown? You deliberately kamikaze-in' your way to oblivion?"

Billy turned to address Ji-ji: "Your fly-boy needs to learn the coop's a battlefield not a circus. His antics'll score him a few points, but it's battles earn you a win."

Coach Billy Brineseed knew more about flying than everyone else on the planting combined. He was right about the scoring, but Ji-ji would much rather watch Tiro fly than battle. Tiro was swinging from trapezes to hope-ropes, to trampolines, to King-spins, to staging platforms, slashing at his flying buddies with his wooden practice sword. He had removed his shirt, but round his head he'd tied the purple bandana he wore in honor of Amadee. He liked to fly shirtless, said he loved the feel of the air on his bare skin. Ji-ji understood. It was the same feeling she got when she ran barefoot, when all she heard was the sound of her heart pumping and her feet pounding the earth. At those times, the earth was the skin of a drum and she was its rhythm.

It didn't take long for Tiro to defeat Orlie. The Muleseed cried out in fury when Tiro flung him off the Parks Perch and left him flailing in his safety harness. (Orlie had only defeated Tiro twice—once when Tiro had a stomach bug, and once when Tiro had been drunk.) As he always did in defeat, Orlie stomped over to a bench on the other side of the ground ring to begin his moping ritual. A few seconds later, Georgie-Porge bit the dust when Tiro smacked the back of the Tribal's knees with his sword. Georgie's big knees buckled. He toppled from the platform to land safely in the net. Georgie-Porge—all six-nine, 285 pounds of him—took it in stride, laughing as he fell.

Billy Brineseed scratched his oiled head. In spite of their rebelliousness, the juvis heeded Coach B because they knew he could provide them with their one shot at Freedom. Over the years, five of his trainees had made it to the finals, which made him one of the winningest fly-coaches in the Territories. But his wins had petered out eight years ago, to coincide with Brine's procurement of Homestead 12. As the coop sank into disrepair, Billy's lucky streak went with it. Worse still, because all his fly-boys had won before their coaches were automatically granted Freedom, Billy was still trapped on Planting 437. There were rumors that he'd made it all the way to the finals when he'd been entered in the Freedom Race as a juvi but was robbed when the Third Territorial Offensive was launched on the outskirts of Dream City on the exact same day the finalists arrived at the city border. Pickers had snatched or slaughtered all the finalists that year—male flyers and female runners both. The competitors who survived had been hauled back to the Territories. Billy hadn't returned to captivity empty-handed. He'd brought his new nickname with him: Bad Luck Billy. Even through his lucky streak, the name had stuck.

Tiro did another crazyass stunt. Coach B roared up to him to practice his goddam battle moves with goddam Marcus. Tiro acknowledged his coach's cuss-laden command with a cursory nod and proceeded to ignore it. The coach flung another bouquet of cuss words up at Tiro.

"Guess he's trying to fly the rage out," Billy said, planting himself back down on the bench.

"Rage?" Ji-ji asked, as Tiro leapt from the midlevel staging platform, grabbed the center hope-rope, and swung himself back into the nest.

"Guess you ain't heard," Coach continued. "Tiro an' Zaini learned last night what those bastards did with Dreg's body. The day after D-Day the steaders threw him over the fry-fence. Let the mutants an' whatever else is out there tear him to pieces. There's rumors that Chaff Man, on the other hand, got off scot-Free with that pooch o' his. It's hard on Zaini—hard on Tiro too. Toteppi value their burial rites. Harder to make the journey back to the Cradle 'less you been afforded the right protocols. Guess the steaders thought the wizard would rise up if they buried him, bring a goddam Dimmer army with him too. . . . You ever run into a Dimmer?"

Ji-ji was still trying to recover from the news about Uncle Dreg. Seeing him killed was bad enough. Imagining him being torn to shreds by stripers and snarlcats appalled her.

"No," she murmured. "I never seen one."

"Your mam has, I bet. Pure Toteppi like Dregulahmo. Got better antenna than the rest of us. Dimmers're tricksters. Can fool you into thinking they're a tree or a river. My Salome came back as a boulder. But then Sal always was stout around the middle. . . ."

Uncle Dreg was to Billy what Lua was to Ji-ji, but it surprised her to hear the ornery coach speak so fondly and sentimentally of Dimmers. Passed from one father-man to another on the planting because fly-coaches came with their coops, Billy had learned to keep his thoughts to himself. When he wasn't training juvis to fly, he served as a garden-seed like Uncle Dreg. Whereas Uncle Dreg tended the father-men's gardens and grew magnificent roses, orchids, medicinal herbs, and other exotic flora in his greenhouse, Billy Brineseed served as Planting 437's chief arborist, overseeing the care of all the trees on the planting. Sylvie was his special charge. Seeds claimed that he spoke her ancient language and that it was like taking an axe to him every time Herring ordered him to hang another purple tear from her branches. For the first time, Ji-ji imagined him hanging Uncle Dreg's purple tear from one of Sylvie's branches. Unbearable.

Silapu used to say that Billy could hear Sylvie weeping in his dreams. Uncle Dreg told her that suffering as deep as the kind Bad Luck Billy and her mam had endured was a knife that whittled you away. Afterward, the wizard would remind them that the most blessed among the botanicals found a way to grow themselves back. Growing back what's been lost was the secret. Ji-ji would be inspired when he said that. But then she'd return to her cabin to find Lotter making a lustful seeding call behind the blackbird quilt while her mam tried not to plunge a knife in his back, and she couldn't believe in regrowth anymore. She'd rush out into the dark and run like something on fire. She would force herself to breathe—*in, out, in, out*—because the air was thin as tissue paper, and all she had was a pair of tired-out lungs, while despair gnawed at her insides like rats on a hope-rope.

Ji-ji asked the question she'd been reluctant to ask before now: "You think Uncle Dreg will come back? You think he's dead for sure?"

"Dead as a dodo," Coach B replied, grimly. "But could be he'll still come back."

"What's a dodo?"

"A hefty bird with stumpy wings. Been extinct for a long time. Looked like a goddam cartoon. You seen a cartoon, Lottermule?" She nodded, having snuck a peek at Lotter's homescreen many a time and seen things she wasn't authorized to view. "Well, that's what the goddam dodo looked like. A cartoon with a strong resemblance to Inquisitor Tryton—heavy round the middle with a limited IQ and a preference for sedentariness." Coach B looked up at Tiro. "Seeds gotta fly to live. Guess dodos did too. Stay too long in the wrong place and it's sayonara. Dregulahmo's dead but it don't necessarily mean he won't come back is what I'm saying. Think our kind could've gotten this far if a whole army of Middle Passenger Dimmers hadn't come to our aid?"

Ji-ji studied the coach's profile. Was he pulling her leg? It was hard to tell with Coach B, but she was pretty certain the Middle Passengers were as dead as dodos.

Coach B pulled harder on his cigarette, like someone in the desert sucking water through a straw. "You look after that fly-boy o' yours, y'hear?" Ji-ji promised she would.

As if to emphasize how necessary this was, Tiro leapt off the high platform and rode the zip line. Above the small trampoline he let go and dropped twenty feet to land plumb in its center. In a single bounce he landed on the hamster wheel, the twenty-four-foot fly-wheel Coach B and Pheebs had constructed from an old-timey Ferris wheel. Billy shook his head. "Mule's a suicider," he muttered.

A chill shot down Ji-ji's spine. She thought about the scars on her mam's wrists, and Mbeke's mam wading into Blueglass Lake. Meanwhile, Bad Luck Billy had moved on. He was going over the rules of the race, worried that Ji-ji could slip up on the oral qualification test.

". . . So if it's an inquisitor from the Territories, give him an answer suggests the whole goddam Civil War Sequel an' what came after was inevitable. Frame it so it sounds like the secessionists had a point. If it's a monitor from the city, be honest an' say the Sequel blew apart the greatest union in history and turned the nation into a bunch of small-minded principalities. If you're tested by both an inquisitor and a monitor, slice it down the middle an' be diplomatic. An' keep it clean. Don't go saying 'goddam' or any other cuss word cos inquisitors are pious bastards. An' for god's sake don't use too many o' them fancyass words you an' Marcus is prone to using. An' make a few grammar screwups to be on the safe side. Inquisitors can't stomach an overschooled Mule. Till you get inside the city walls you're classified as botanical. Forget that an' you're screwed."

Coach B looked up at Tiro, who had climbed back into the crow's nest at the apex of the coop. "An' don't forget. What's the prohibition you can't break as a female?"

"Prohibition 168. It prohibits female seeds from flying in the coop. But I don't fly in the—"

"Cut the crap, Lottermule. I seen you up there in the nest. *Twice.* Calm down. Haven't told anyone 'cept Sylvie. But if those race inquisitors catch you flying in one o' them race coops you'll be dragged back here so fast your little head'll spin."

"They got female flyer-battlers in Dream City," Ji-ji contended.

"Yeah, they got a few. An' are you in Dream City, Lottermule?" Ji-ji shook her head. "Correct. You're on Planting 437 in the Homestead Territories. You're a Muleseed like your fly-boy up there, an' his easygoing pal Marcus is an orphaned Mule who got lucky. Then there's Georgie-Porge, a Commonseed who's laughed his way through suffering, an' Orlie, a Muleseed who's moped his way through, cos reminding himself how hard done by he is keeps him from killing something—himself, most likely. When you reach the city don't assume what you see is what you get, or that folks there say what they mean an' mean what they say. The City of Dreams is screwed up too, in its own way. Calls itself 'the Nexus of Freedom,' the place where Abraham sits on his stone throne and oversees justice, the place where a King preached a people out of bondage. The city sees itself as the guardian of democracy. Could be it is. But it's also the last of the Independents to shake itself from Territorial rule, an' that makes it a goddam wishy-washy teeterer in my book."

"You saying we won't be safe in Dream City, Coach?"

Perhaps Billy saw how worried she looked because he put his muscled arm round her and gave her a fatherly squeeze—something he'd never done before in all the years she'd known him, not being predisposed to showing affection to anything other than trees.

"It's a lot safer than the 437th," Billy said, drawing back from her to watch his flyers. "But the City of Dreams is still deciding whose dreams it wants to invest in, an' that makes it prone to treachery. Keep your eyes peeled an' stay under the radar. Likely be a whole flock of parrots there ready to squawk on you to steader sympathizers. Be careful what you say an' who you say it to."

"But why would anyone be watching me? I don't understand—"

Just then, Tiro performed a risky move. Coach B swore up at him before turning to Ji-ji. "An' stop that jackass from killing himself . . . or killing those around him either."

Ji-ji shot Coach B a look. Did he know that Uncle Dreg had sacrificed himself for his great-nephew? Billy was Uncle Dreg's best friend. Could Bad Luck Billy be a Friend of Freedom too?

Because Uncle Dreg and Lua were gone and there was no one else she trusted enough to confide in (apart from Tiro, who had problems enough of his own), Ji-ji told Billy about the mutant they had encountered on the forbidden. She expected him to accuse her of lying, or at least scold her for being reckless. To her surprise he did neither. Instead, he squinted his eyes into slits and looked at her—looked *into* her almost, like someone trying to figure something out.

"The little server may've communicated with it, you say? *Damn!* Guess it's true then. Sounds like Afarra may be one o' them ant whisperers. One o' them seeds that speaks Mutant. They say some ant whisperers can talk to regular animals too. Dregulahmo suspected as much. Pheebs too."

"You saying you believe me? You think it happened for real?"

"Sure. Why not? You lying?"

"No!" After a few moments she added, "You ever seen a bear-ape mutant thing like that, Coach B? One that looked . . . like a person."

"Listen up, Ji-ji. If you want that little server to keep breathing, don't mention what you seen to anyone else. Not till you're safe in the city. Not even then, 'less you can trust the listener."

"Is Afarra in danger?"

"She's an outcast. Poor kid flirts with danger every second. Know how many times seeds an' steaders both took advantage of Pheebs over there? Ask Afarra what she's been through when you can stomach hearing 'bout the evil men do. Establishing a group lower'n us on their Great Ladder was masterful. Everyone gets a punching bag. Everyone 'cept those on the lowest rung."

Something else had been gnawing at Ji-ji. "Coach, you remember what Chaff Man said about the arsenal at the Culmination? That a secret could bring down the Territories? Seems like Herring couldn't shut him up quick enough when—"

Billy's voice eviscerated her. "Hush your mouth, Lottermule! Think I want to hang another purple tear from Sylvie?" He saw how startled she was and softened his tone a little. "Some things it's better not to query.

Not till you're miles from here. Even then—may not be safe." Billy looked around warily, then lowered his voice.

"Silapu stayed for you, y'know that? Had an opportunity to run with her lastborn. But she couldn't get to you in time to take you with her. Couldn't leave you behind neither. My theory is Lotter found out—some parrot squawked. You ever wondered why your father-man snatched her lastborn long after the probationary period was up? Figure it was his sick way of warning her never to try an' escape again."

Ji-ji stuttered out a protest: "But Mam never said anything about—"

"You think most people say important things out loud? That's not the way the world works, on or off a planting. That pretty father-man of yours can't decide if he wants to love Sila to death or kill her outright an' rid himself of his misery. Becoming cropmaster is a potent antidote to compassion. Cropmastery could prompt the bastard to end his pain for good. You petition for your mam soon as you reach the city, Lottermule, y'hear? Your mam may not make it otherwise."

"I will. I promise. . . . I'll petition for Afarra too. . . . Think Afarra will be okay till then without me or Tiro here to protect her?"

Coach B considered this for a moment, then said, "You sure you're the ones doing the protecting? Okay, tell you what. How 'bout Pheebs an' me take Afarra under our wing till your petition's granted—keep an eye on her for you?"

The offer was so unexpected that Ji-ji flung her arms around him. "*Thank you, Coach B!*"

The veteran coach laughed—a deep vibration in his broad chest. "Don't go thanking me till your kith-n-kin's granted an' she meets up with you the city." He pulled away from her embrace, but he was still smiling, so she felt reasonably certain she hadn't offended him.

Billy reached into his pocket and pulled out a folded sheet of paper. "Here. A map."

"The monitors give us an official race map at the start of the—"

"I know. This one's from Dregulahmo. Covers more than the race route. If you stray from the official route, you need to find your way to Dimmers Wood. See? It's directly southeast, on the far side of the New River." Billy pointed to a place called Slim Pickins.

"But I'm not straying from the route. It's dangerous to—"

"Yeah, that's what your fly-boy told me when I gave him his copy. But sometimes things happen we don't plan for. If they do, you meet up with him at Dimmers, understand?"

The name of the place sounded ominous, but Coach B didn't take kindly to arguing, so she nodded her head and slipped the map into her pocket.

"An' another thing," Coach Billy continued. "Afarra wasn't the only special one. Dreg called you the Triumvirate—you, her, an' that goddam blockhead up there. But Tiro's a blood relative so the old wizard could've been mistaken 'bout him. Sure looks like it this morning. . . . *GET BACK IN THAT GODDAM HARNESS 'FORE I COME UP AND STUFF YOU INTO IT MYSELF!*"

To Ji-ji's relief, Tiro obeyed. Coach B continued as though he'd never been interrupted.

"The Necessaries was another name Dregulahmo used for you, Afarra, an' that moron up there. Said there were wonders in store for you."

"Did you believe Uncle Dreg when he said all that stuff?"

"I'm a skeptic. But could be you an' Tiro got a special part to play. An' if it's true the server's an ant whisperer, who knows? Always been something different 'bout that one. Not just the funny way she talks either. Something otherworldly about her, something not quite in the here-an'-now."

Coach B threw down his cigarette and stomped it out with his foot as though he had a grudge against it. "Tell Birdbrain I'll see him at tonight's practice, soon as his shift in the fields is over and Zaini's fed him—assuming he hasn't broken every goddam bone in his body before then."

With that, Bad Luck Billy strode over to Georgie-Porge and Orlie, grasped Orlie by his drooping shoulders, and ordered him to suck it up. Pheebs ran up and joined the group. The four left together, Orlie trailing gloomily behind the other three. Ji-ji remembered too late that she'd wanted to ask Coach B about the strange things Lua had told her before she died. Maybe Tiro could figure out what Lua had been talking about?

Marcus plopped into the net soon afterward, unhitched himself from his harness, and strutted over to Ji-ji. It wasn't clear if Tiro had defeated him or if he'd simply called it quits.

As muscular as Tiro, Marcus was a year older than he was. Old Shadowy spoiled him. Apart from the slight swagger in his walk, however, he didn't rub it in your face. You'd never suspect he could get mating permission slips whenever he wanted, go on errander trips to nearby plantings, and watch any show he fancied on Old Shadowy's homescreen. He was tutored by Old Shadowy herself, which was why he was the most educated juvi on the planting. Marcus had always been kind to Ji-ji. Sometimes he reminded her of Clay, her older brother. Marcus knew how unlikely it was he would be selected for the Freedom Race ahead of Tiro. Like Georgie-Porge and Orlie, he was betting Tiro would keep his word and file a kith-n-kin for him.

"The Pterodactyl's in a foul mood this morning," Marcus complained, rubbing his shoulder and using the nickname he'd given Tiro the first time he saw him fly. "Can't be ratified soon enough far as I'm concerned. If he messes up this gorgeous face, my future as a stud is shot."

Marcus turned to head out, took a few strides, then turned back. He swept Ji-ji up in his arms and gave her a brotherly bear hug. "You're too good for that crazy fly-boy—y'know that?" he said.

"How come you're saying goodbye now?" she asked. "I'll see you tomorrow."

"You'll be rushed off your feet. Won't have time for a humble little fly-boy like me. You take care of yourself in The Margins, okay?"

"Could be Lotter won't ratify me."

"Sure he will. Emmeline says it's a done deal. She's warned Lotter if he doesn't ratify you both, calamity will fall on the planting. They listen to Old Shadowy—most of the time anyway. Some of the steaders think if they'd listened to her warnings about Dregulahmo they wouldn't have lost Herring. 'Sides, no one's faster'n you. Remember—don't stray from the race route. It's guarded from Salem to Monticello—most of the final leg too. But pickers have the right to harvest any stray seeds they find. Pickers're sly bastards. Hunt in packs. Worse than Bounty Boys. If it's anything like last year, they'll try to lure runners off the race route. Don't be fooled. Oh—almost forgot. Tell your fly-boy up there not to forget the little people—though if Orlie's kith-n-kin is mislaid, it wouldn't be the end of the world."

Ji-ji laughed. Marcus gave her a wistful smile and sauntered off.

Ji-ji sat for a moment in an effort to gather her thoughts after Billy's revelation about Silapu. Like Coach B, her mam had chosen captivity over Freedom—chosen it for her sake. Whatever it cost, she would find Bonbon and reunite the two. She owed her that.

She was about to shout up to Tiro and ask him to come down from the nest when she got an unsettling sense of déjà vu. He sat perched on the edge of the Jimmy Crow way up at the very top of the cage, just like he did after Amadee was killed. He was in pain, she knew that, but there was something crazed in the way he tore around the cage. For once in her life she hadn't been worried enough—chatting with Coach B like they had all the time in the world! She had to climb up the Jacob's Ladders and go to him—*now*! She rushed to a ladder and began to climb.

Ji-ji scanned the coop to make sure no one had entered. The planting's Elevation Prohibitions against female botanicals were rigorously enforced: no climbing above twelve feet unless it was to clean something; no venturing up mountains (not that there were any to speak of on the planting, all of them being beyond the fry-fence); no ascending into the toll-bell turret; no looking out of windows on the upper floors of father-houses; no heels even. . . . She devised a plan. If anyone caught her she would claim Tiro's harness was caught and she'd climbed up to give him a hand. Was he still wearing a harness? She glanced over at him as she climbed, but he was sitting in shadow and she couldn't tell for sure.

Afraid of startling him, she called out his name as she crossed the narrow walkway leading to the nest. Without turning around he said, "Climbing up here is way too risky." It was fairly bright by now, with light streaming through the sky flaps above them. Tiro's eyes looked bloodshot when he swiveled round to face her. He swiped his forearm across his face and Ji-ji realized he'd been crying. At least he was wearing a safety harness. She relaxed a little.

Quickly, she clambered into the nest and stood inside it. Without a harness of her own she didn't dare join him on the rim. She told him what she had been burning to tell him for weeks.

"That's great," he said, after she'd finished. "Can't believe Charra's alive."

The way he said it emphasized how far away he was. Maybe he was anxious about ratification? Ji-ji explained that her mam had decided to help them.

"You hear me? Mam is sure Lotter's gonna ratify—"

"Ji, I got something real bad to tell you." He joined her inside the basket. "Last night, Mother an' me . . ." He stood there searching for words.

"It's okay. Coach B told me what they did to Uncle Dreg. They should never have—"

"No, not that," he said, looking away. "Something worse. Been sitting up here trying to figure out how to tell you."

"You're scaring me. What is it?"

"There's a parrot among us . . . someone we know. This parrot betrayed Uncle Dreg to the steaders. S'why Uncle Dreg got lynched. . . ."

Parrots received no mercy on a planting. They were usually found

Pain welled up her spine; its roots fanned out to her shoulders. The burning sensation was buried deep beneath the skin, like an old injury come back to haunt her. She knew exactly what it was. At the worst possible time, she'd reinjured herself in exactly the same place as before.

Tiro asked if he could take a look. By this time, Ji-ji couldn't hold back her tears.

Gently, he eased her to a sitting position. She wasn't wearing a bra under her shirt because, apart from the bra she shared with her mam, she only had one other, and she'd washed it last night in readiness for tomorrow's Last Supper. As Tiro raised her shirt, his breath caught in his throat.

"Looks bad, Ji. Like your back an' shoulders got hammered. Should've caught you."

"It's done now," Ji-ji said. "It's over."

Ji-ji tugged at her shirt to lower it again. They sat together on the sawdust, shell-shocked. She glanced at Tiro. Looked like he was on the verge of tears too. She felt a surge of pity for him.

"It's easing up some," she offered, in an effort to lessen his anxiety.

Tiro looked absurdly relieved, then suspicious. "You lying to me, Ji?"

"No. It does feel better." A partial truth. The burning had been replaced by a dull throbbing.

"Okay if I take another look?"

She shrugged, her unimpressive boobs being the least of her worries right now. Tiro raised her shirt again and studied her back for several seconds.

"What's it look like?"

"Don't make sense. It's almost like . . . like it's healing itself. Don't get me wrong, you're all banged up, but it's a lot better than a few moments ago."

"Could be it's like hives or something," Ji-ji offered, feeling a small measure of relief. "You know how bad they can look. Then they disappear."

"Don't look like hives to me," Tiro replied, but he sounded less worried than before.

Ji-ji pulled her shirt down, grateful to be able to do it on her own this time. Moving cautiously, she turned round to face him.

"How's it feel when you move?" he asked.

"Sore," she answered honestly. "But not as bad as I thought it would feel."

He asked her if she could walk or if she wanted him to carry her over to the bench. She insisted she could make it under her own steam as long as he helped her up.

A few seconds later, they were seated side by side on the coach's bench.

Tiro wound his arm lightly around her waist to keep her steady. "Swelling's nasty," he said. "You gotta get ice on it fast. Doc Riff should take a look. If you don't take care of an injury like that it'll get tons worse tomorrow."

Ji-ji wiped her nose on the sleeve of her shirt. "Tell me about Mam."

As quickly as he could, Tiro described how kitchen-seeds Dip and Sloppy came to his mother's cabin last night to tell them what they knew. They would have come earlier, they said, only the prohibitions made unauthorized travel between homesteads too dangerous. The two said they'd overheard Silapu parroting to Lotter at his father-house a few weeks ago. Said Sila told Lotter she'd gone to lay flowers at the little shrine seeds had made by Blueglass Lake to honor Mbeke's mam. While there, she'd spied Uncle Dreg at around midnight, sneaking about with someone else. Sila swore she didn't know who the other male was because it was dark and she couldn't get a good look. All she could say for certain was that he had a beard, and the two men addressed each other as "Friend." Lotter had railed at Silapu when she couldn't identify the other traitor. Dip said Lotter shoved Sila across the room, but Sloppy said it sounded like he'd just dropped something. Ji-ji shuddered—didn't dare tell Tiro that she'd seen her mam's badly bruised arm around the time Uncle Dreg was hauled off to PenPen. When she'd asked her how she got it, her mam had made up some lame excuse about tripping at the textile factory.

Dip and Sloppy claimed to have eavesdropped through the vent in Lotter's kitchen at his father-house. At that time, Lotter was still First Father-Man, living on Homestead 1. Their story was plausible. Ji-ji had eavesdropped at that same vent in the past. Lotter hadn't known Dip and Sloppy were nearby. They'd only returned to his father-house after completing their cleaning shift because they'd forgotten to empty the trash. Fearful of a whipping, the two kitchen-seeds had hurried back to do so.

"Still doesn't make sense. Mam *hates* Lotter. Besides, what would Uncle Dreg be doing at Blueglass Lake?"

Tiro got a strange look on his face. "That's just it. Remember I told you he took the fall for me? I was the one s'posed to meet up with the Friend at Blueglass. . . . Uncle Dreg went in my place."

Ji-ji's heart fell as Tiro described how he had received a note from someone who'd identified himself as 9-0-2, who said he had to meet with Tiro urgently.

"Seemed legit to me cos number nine's the Friends' password number for this season, an' zero-two would've been his individual code. So I sent a confirmation to 9-0-2 over the comm."

"What comm?"

Tiro quickly described the secret communication system the Friends of Freedom used and made her promise not to repeat what he was telling her. "That was my major screwup. We'd been warned the comm may not be safe. Uncle Dreg found out. Raked me over the coals. Told me I'd put Mother an' the boys in danger. Then he read 9-0-2's note an' understood why I had to respond."

"What could've been so important that you'd risk—"

"The note was about you, Ji."

"*Me?* What are you talking about? I've never even heard of 9-0-2!"

"Well, he'd heard of you. Said you posed 'an existential threat to the Territories.'"

"That's nuts! Did you know what 'existential' meant?"

"Shit, Ji! I'm not a complete jackass . . . though I guess I may've asked Marcus what the hell it meant—without giving anything away, of course." He attempted a smile, but she was too upset to acknowledge it. "9-0-2 said the steaders're scared you'll destroy 'em."

"That's crazy!" Then Ji-ji remembered something and added, "Charra said the same thing. Not about me, about Toteppi. Said steaders were scared of us. But why? And who is 9-0-2?"

"Wish I knew. Thing was, I'd already used the comm, so it was too late to back out. Uncle Dreg said we had to go through with a meeting. Insisted on going instead. It's how come he met up with 9-0-2. He was gonna tell me what he'd learned, only they hauled him off to PenPen 'fore he could cos Silapu parroted. It's weird. Your mam has always hated my guts, but I never thought she'd turn parrot. Why betray us like that?"

Ji-ji wanted to insist that her mam would never parrot to Lotter but the words stuck in her throat. She struggled to think things through logically. Sloppy could be a pain in the ass when she set her mind to it. She was a snob too—treated Afarra like dirt. But her friend Dip Spareseed was as honest as the day was long. And Dip loved Silapu because she'd spoken up for her when Dip had been demoted to Tainted status following a bout with syphilis. Dip was eternally grateful to Silapu for persuading Lotter to obtain a position for her as a kitchen-seed in spite of her spoilage. *No,* Ji-ji thought. *Dip would never lie about this. She loves Mam too much.*

Ji-ji couldn't deny it any longer. "The other seeds'll kill Mam if they find out."

"That's why we petition for Silapu soon as we make it to the city."

"You mean . . . you'd still want her to join us, even though—"

"She's your mother, Ji. 'Sides, who knows what Lotter threatened her with? Bet he said he'd snatch you from her too, truck you off to the Rad Region or something. When someone you care about is threatened, you do all kinds of crazy shit."

"Yeah, I guess. But it feels like we're missing something. Like we don't have all the pieces. Why would anyone think I'm a threat?"

Tiro got a strange look on his face. "Hear me out, Ji," he said. "Some of this'll sound crazy, an' we don't have much time 'fore we gotta get to work, so just listen, okay?" Ji-ji nodded warily.

Tiro looked around the flying coop to check they were still alone. "Here goes. In the steaders' *One True Text,* there's this whole series of passages dealing with a Dark Scourge. They say it'll come from the Cradle. They use that word too. Not Africa, the Cradle. Our word. Some say the Scourge is the steaders' own creation, the planting system itself. That was what Uncle Dreg was saying 'fore Herring shot him, remember?"

"Yeah, I remember."

"But some steaders think there's more to it than that. Most of *The One True Text* is lifted straight from the Bible so those passages are ancient. But some parts ain't nearly as old as that. Swinburne Augustus—an' his Wife-Proper, the Friends claim—wrote great hunks of the *Text* during the secessionist campaigns, before Augustus became the first Lord-Father of Lord-Fathers. It's been added to over the years by others, which is how come there are all these different versions, an' steaders keep squabbling 'bout which one is genuine. Seeds get the abridged version, so the Dark Scourge ain't in our copy. They don't want to put an idea like that in our heads. According to their version, this Scourge would be led by 'an ancient, dwindling tribe,' the book says, a tribe 'who remembers where they came from.'" Tiro saw recognition spread across Ji-ji's face. "Yeah—sounded a lot like the Rememberers to Uncle Dreg too."

"It's like the Origin Story he told us about," Ji-ji said. "The Rememberers were the ones who could tell the old stories."

"Yeah. Anyhow, the steaders're spooked. Listen, Ji. What I'm about to tell you—for god's sake don't repeat it, okay? Friends ain't meant to share stuff like this. But I figure you have a right to know. So this is what's going down, far as we can tell. Some members of the Territorial Council are lobbying to take drastic measures. Only thing stopping 'em is the labor shortage." Tiro hesitated.

"Drastic measures? What do you mean?"

"Some of the steaders believe the seed population is contaminated. Needs to be purged."

"Purged? I don't understand what . . . Oh my god!"

"Yeah. They want to exterminate the bad seeds. Get rid of all the Toteppi. Seems like a planting in the 200s got impatient couple months ago an' took matters into their own hands. They executed four Toteppi for being Toteppi. Then they massacred their offspring and other seeds close to them. Two dozen or more. Seedlings too."

"But why would they target us now?"

"There's a new diviner advising the council. She's identified Toteppi an' their offspring as the source of contamination, persuaded many on the council that Doomsday is round the corner if they don't act fast."

"So we're all in danger then? You . . . me . . . your mam an' brothers?"

"Don't worry. For now we're okay. We got lucky. Planting 437's got a savior."

"Who?"

"Arundale Lotter."

"You're joking, right?"

"Nope. Marcus says Lotter convinced Herring Toteppi weren't a threat. Marcus gets his info straight from Shadowy, so I figure that's what really happened. Lotter can't stand the thought of—"

"—losing Mam," Ji-ji said.

"Bingo. Problem is, Death Day destroyed Lotter's argument. It shocked the hell outta steaders when the most revered penal tree in the Territories lopped off a limb and unhanged Uncle Dreg. That would've been bad enough. But when Herring's bullet deflected off Sylvie's baptism plate and blasted through the cropmaster's own heart, that looked to the steaders like black magic. Could be it was, of course, but that's not the point. Chatter 'bout Lotter being too attached to your mam is on the upswing. Williams'll almost certainly challenge Lotter for the cropmaster title 'less your father-man finds a way to persuade him not to. An' believe me, my father-man, bastard that he is, would be only too happy to exterminate a few Toteppi."

Tiro saw how anxious she looked and added, "Don't worry, Ji. If anyone can rise to the occasion it's Lotter. Never been a more manipulative asshole in the whole history of the Territories. Ol' Blue Eyes'll have 'em eating out of his hand in no time."

"But why would anyone think I'm a threat? I'm not a wizard or anything. Only thing I can do is run an' cook. Are they scared I'll chase after them with a spatula?" Ji-ji hadn't planned to make a joke, but when Tiro broke into his trademark smile she couldn't help smiling too.

Tiro's expression turned serious again. "There's this other passage, Ji. In their sacred text. Says, 'The Scourge will rise as One, an' she will seek to rend apart the blessed Territories.'"

"The Scourge is female?"

"Yep."

"Figures, I guess. How do you know all this?"

"Marcus. He's read the entire text. Not the doctored one seeds get either. The real version—one of 'em anyway. Old Shadowy's very lax when it comes to censoring. Course Marcus was too high on Shadowy's weed to remember most of it. Uncle Dreg filled in the rest."

Ji-ji thought for a moment. "Are there other Friends on the planting?"

"One or two I know of. Can't reveal who they are. But none of 'em goes by 9-0-2. Wish I knew who he was an' if he's really on our side."

"Did Uncle Dreg think the three of us—you, me, an' Afarra—had a special role cos of those passages in *The One True Text*?"

"Don't think so. He had his own theories—only he was real cagey 'bout the future. Said if you got too cocky 'bout what lay ahead you didn't need to dreaminate it into happening the way it should. Kept reminding me the future wasn't fixed an' that what he saw with his Seeing Eyes was a picture of what *could* be, not what *must* be. . . . They took 'em, Ji."

"Took what?"

"His Seeing Eyes. Some bastard must've stole 'em. Zaini got a package with his things—the stuff Williams didn't lay claim to. 'Fore you ask, Uncle removed the story-cloths 'bout a year ago—filled in the treasure hole under his bed. Said it wasn't safe to house the stories here anymore. Said they needed to go home. Anyhow, when they brought us his stuff, his Seeing Eyes weren't there."

Ji-ji could see that Tiro was thinking about how they'd discarded the wizard's body like it was a piece of trash. She was about to comfort him when he asked her a question out of the blue.

"You ever recall your mam saying where she went those times she went missing?"

"Missing? Mam? What are you talking about?"

"Silapu disappeared a whole bunch of times over the years."

"No she didn't."

"Oh yes she did."

"For how long?"

"Sometimes only a couple days. Once or twice more than a week, Mother says. You don't remember?"

Ji-ji thought about it. Yes . . . she did vaguely recall something. "Wait a minute. Did we come an' stay with you—me, Clay, an' Charra one time?"

"Yeah. That was one of the times she went missing."

"Where was she?"

"That's the million-dollar question. Was hoping you'd tell me. Wasn't with Lotter—we know that for a fact. Uncle had this theory—" Tiro stopped speaking and leapt up. "*You hear that?*"

"What?" Ji-ji stood up shakily, gritting her teeth against the pain in her back.

"*Ssh!* Someone's here! *Don't move!*"

While Ji-ji stood glued to the spot, Tiro rushed to the bleachers behind them. If they'd been overheard by some steader that was it. It was over!

After two agonizing seconds that seemed to last for an age, Tiro emerged from behind the bleachers with Coach B's enormous tabby cat in his arms. Something dangled from the cat's mouth.

"Looks like Marmaduke here found himself a juicy rat to chew on." Tiro put the cat down so he could feast. More relieved than she could say, Ji-ji sank back down onto the bench.

Worry soon came flooding back. "If Dip an' Sloppy tell anyone else—"

"They swore they wouldn't tell a soul. S'why they came to us in the first place. I don't think they plan to out her, Ji, I really don't. Think of it this way. It could be worse. Least your mam doesn't know it was me who was s'posed to meet up with—"

Ji-ji recoiled from him in horror and slapped an open palm over her mouth.

"What's wrong?"

"Mam knows Uncle Dreg covered for you! She knows you're a Friend! I told her!"

Ji-ji relayed how she had revealed the truth by accident only three days after Uncle Dreg's Death Day. She tried to reassure him that Silapu would never betray him, but her argument sounded weak even to her ears. If her mam had been willing to betray Uncle Dreg, who, in spite of their differences, held a special place in her heart, what would prevent her from betraying the fly-boy she despised?

"It's been three weeks since Mam found out about you. If she'd parroted, wouldn't the father-men already know you're a—"

"They *do* know. She's parroted. Whole thing's a setup."

"What are you talking about?"

Tiro buried his head in his hands. When he raised it again, he sounded as tired as she felt.

"I been seeing things I wanted to see, Ji. Williams been acting strange. Like he's happy for me or something. The other day he said I'd worked hard and deserved to get my just desserts. They plan to expose me at the Last Supper during the Ratification Ceremony. They got no intention of ratifying me. Bastards plan to lynch me instead."

She wanted to deny it, but all at once she realized he was right. Things had been falling into place too neatly. Luck didn't work like that for seeds on a planting. It wasn't just Williams acting strange either. Why would Lotter, who always played his cards close to his chest, reveal so much to Silapu about planting debt? And why would her mam say she and Tiro would be ratified when he'd been so opposed to it earlier?

"Okay," Ji-ji said, as she gathered her wits about her, "I guess we gotta assume the worst. So here's what we do. We run. Tonight . . . together. Hope that the fry-fence is on the blink. Lotter told Mam it's been shorting out again. Could be we'll be lucky."

The hammering pain in her back had resurfaced stronger than ever. She braced herself against it and stood up, said, "C'mon, Tiro. We got loads to do an' we gotta do it fast!"

Tiro stood and grasped both her hands in his. "Hold up, Ji," he said. "That's not plan B."

"We . . . we got a plan B? Didn't know we had a plan A."

"Course we do. Friends of Freedom always got a plan or two up our sleeves. Plan A was ratification for both of us. Plan B was ratification for you only. So plan B's the one we roll with. Look at it from this angle. I'm lucky. I get to escape from this crappy place 'fore you do."

"But you don't stand a chance! The fry-fence is powerful enough to kill a snarlcat—"

"S'okay. We got it covered. Listen, there's not much time to explain.

There's this Wild Seed Rule. I know you think I'm making this shit up but I swear I'm not. The rule's not well known cos the steaders've used every trick in the book to keep it quiet."

"But—"

"Just listen, okay. We don't got much time. The Wild Seed Rule allows flyers and runners to enter themselves in the Freedom Race. Don't need to be ratified. The Friends of Freedom lobbied hard for it for years. Gives runaways a shot at Freedom. For the duration of the race, the route's a sanctuary for competitors, right? Well, it's the same for Wild Seeds. They got the same rights and protections as regular entrants. Billy give you the map?" Ji-ji nodded. Things were slamming into her so thick and fast she felt like she was suffering from concussion. "Good. We meet up at the first checkpoint at the Salem Outpost on day one of the race. That's a Wednesday—four days from now. If we miss each other or plans change, we meet up in Dimmers Wood. Billy told you 'bout Dimmers, right? Wild Seeds are allowed to enter the race at Monticello too. But getting there on foot would be crazy tough. Monticello's a hundred and fifty miles from here. Salem's my best bet. Way closer an' forested mostly. I can steer clear of the Main Toll Road, take the trails, an' follow the old rail lines. Uncle Dreg prepped me for this. It'll be okay. We figured they could be on to us."

"S'pose I'm not ratified either?"

"Glad you asked, Lottermule. That's when we go to plan C. Billy's your escort if that happens. He'll find a way to get you out."

"Coach B? Why didn't he tell me he—?"

"The fewer people know the details the better. Now that Uncle Dreg's gone, there's no one I'd trust more'n Billy to pull it off. But my bet is Lotter *will* ratify you. Marcus says it's in the bag. Silapu sure as hell ain't lobbying for me to race, but I figure she's stayed loyal to you. An' don't worry. Lotter won't let 'em massacre Toteppi. Not as long as Silapu's around anyhow."

She opened her mouth to ask him something but he placed his finger on her lips.

"Sorry, Ji. No time for questions. Could be Williams already has his henchmen waiting to nab me. I gotta get to Coach B. He'll be tending Sylvie. Coach already knows I'm to blame for Uncle Dreg, but Silapu parroting—well, that's a different story. An' before you start worrying, Billy's the last person in the world would ever hurt your mam, whatever she's done. Think your back's okay?"

"Yeah," she lied. "Don't worry about me. Tiro, you *got* to make it. If you don't, nothing'll mean anything. . . . I'm sorry. It's my fault Mam knows about—"

"Ssh. Finding out the truth 'bout your mam likely saved my ass. Think Williams would allow me to reach Dream City? The bastard's wanted me dead for years. Figure that's why he murdered Amadee. He knew it was just about the worst thing he could do to me. . . . Don't cry, Ji. . . . Hey, listen up. I got an idea. How 'bout you stop blaming yourself for telling your mam I'm a Friend, an' I'll stop blamin' myself for what happened to Uncle Dreg?"

"Okay," Ji-ji said, knowing neither of them had a chance in hell of keeping a bargain like that. Tiro brushed her wet cheek with his fingers. Shyly, they kissed. It wasn't something they did often cos it was so risky. Ji-ji tasted salt and realized she was still crying.

Tiro cupped her tearstained face in his large hands. "Don't cry, Ji. We can do this. Uncle Dreg said we could, remember? Said we were destined to fly. Said he'd seen it in the Window-of-What's-to-Come. We get to bring together the tribes of the world. How many seeds get to do something like that? We got a mission. Now . . . you go first. I'll follow."

"No, you go first," she insisted, scared he wouldn't leave if he realized how much pain she was in. "I'm faster. You got to see Coach B, which means you got to take the long way round to the Commons, hug the woods. No working cameras there." She sounded much calmer and more logical than she felt.

"Guess that makes sense. Okay, I go first. Just got to get my stuff."

Tiro's fly-boy backpack was lying under the net. He hurried over to it and slipped it on. He'd glued a pair of purple wings to it, a private tribute to his brother's favorite color. At the door flap he turned to take in the old coop one last time. He'd spent more hours here than any other place on the planting. Ji-ji watched him linger as if he were waiting for permission to leave. They both knew how dangerous it would be for him in The Margins, and she still had no idea how he'd get over the fry-fence. There was a good chance they'd never see each other again.

She nodded at him once to let him know she was okay. He seemed to buy it. He placed his hand over his heart, smiled at her one last time, turned, and headed off. For a reason she couldn't explain, Lua's pain-crazed words popped into her head at that moment. "Bye, bye, Blackbird," Ji-ji whispered. Once again, the person she loved most had been snatched from her. It took every bit of willpower she had not to run after him.

She hurried to the exit as fast as her back allowed. When she reached it, she could still see him racing away from her. She glimpsed a pair of purple wings on a midnight sky before the pain in her back brought her to her knees. Tiro Williamsmule, the fly-boy she'd loved for nearly a decade, disappeared over the crest of the hill. For once, she was grateful he didn't look back.

11 KITCHEN-SEEDS

Stripped to the waist, Ji-ji sat on a stool in Storeroom 2 in the planting dining hall while Dip applied a numbing ointment to her back. Afarra, squatting on the floor by Ji-ji, took her hand and tried to stroke it better. Ji-ji didn't have the heart to tell the server her hand was one of the few places that didn't hurt. A short while ago, Ji-ji had revealed the awful truth about Silapu to the server, though it wasn't clear whether Afarra really understood what that meant. Sloppy, who'd accompanied them to the storeroom, had demanded to know why they were letting the Cloth in on the secret. It was just plain dumb, she'd said, to trust some outcast who couldn't even read.

Sloppy was lounging on a crate that held luxury foods—rare delicacies like olive oil, canned apricots, spices, pistachios, stuffed olives, and imported coffee beans, the type of fare only father-men and a few affluent steaders could afford to consume at feasts. The seal of the Father-City of Armistice (an image of a burly, bearded father-man straddling a planting, a rifle in one hand and an ear of corn in the other) had been burned into the crate.

Earlier that morning, Ji-ji had been late to the dining hall. If Silent Pete hadn't passed by in his wagon she probably wouldn't have made it there at all. She'd hitched a ride with the battle-ravaged veteran and his mongrel dog, Gesture.

Ji-ji asked the question she'd been burning to ask: "You gonna tell?"

"Course not!" Dip assured her. "Figure that cruel sonuvabitch Lotter says to Sila, 'If you don't turn parrot, your Last&Only'll be next.' It's how them bastards operate."

Though Dip was in her mid-twenties, she looked older. On the Raw Umber arc of the Color Wheel, she could only trace her lineage through a single generation and had therefore been unable to petition for Indigenous status. She had broad, strong features and a wide, honest mouth. Dipthong Spareseed never whined about anything. Her main talent was mothering, which was why it struck Ji-ji as so tragic that all four of Dip's own seedlings had been deadborns.

"Your back's all swolled up," Dip informed her. "Don't know how you'll race in this state."

"You need to see Doc Riff," Sloppy warned, polishing an apple on her apron. "Otherwise you'll toxissify and expire."

"Don't be a downer, Slop," Dip cautioned. "It ain't becoming."

"It's *not* becom*ing*," Slop countered, taking a large bite from the apple and wincing when it hit her bad tooth.

Dip didn't miss a beat: "No need to keep reminding every Tom, Dip, an' Harry you got second place in the Legacy Spelling Bee an' Vocabulary Contest. This Muleseed sitting right here beat you by a mile. Boasting ain't attractive in a kitchen-seed."

"Neither is bad grammar," Sloppy retorted.

"Ignore her, Ji-ji," Dip advised. "Slop's out to raise Cain this morning. That bastard Casper mashed her toe last night cos his biscuits an' gravy was cold. An' that rotten molar of hers is giving her fits again too. Why anyone eats a apple with a tooth as orn'ry as that is beyond me."

Sloppy gave Dip the evil eye and bit defiantly into her apple.

"Think Crabby noticed I was hurting?" Ji-ji asked.

Dip shook her head. "Crabby don't notice nothing 'cept his own appetite. An' his belly's gotten so big he has trouble seeing that these days."

Ji-ji hoped Dip was right. If Crabby reported her as Unfit for Labor, she was in deep trouble. 'Seer Crabstreet, kitchen overseer, liked to imagine he ruled with a rod of iron. He was fond of brandishing his braided leather bullwhip and striking it on the flagstone floor to instill the fear of god into the twelve kitchen-seeds who worked under Ji-ji. It didn't take long, however, for them to realize that Crabby talked a good game and that was about it. Crabstreet was first cousin to Homestead 3's father-man, Mickyjon Pratterly. Nepotism had kept him employed at the planting. The position of kitchen overseer had been created for him after he'd proven sublimely incompetent in his other roles as dairyman, factory manager, turbine operator, plumber, welder, fish farmer, and septic tank repairman. His seeding abilities were equally unimpressive. Like Brine, Crabby had been unable to successfully impregnate any of his young seedmates, for which they were all thankful. Since Ji-ji's appointment to chief kitchen-seed, he'd been coasting to fame and heart disease on her roast lamb, apple pies, chicken-n-dumplings, fresh-baked bread, and casseroles. Crabstreet complained he'd put on ten extra pounds—though all the kitchen-seeds agreed that Crabby's waistline had waved goodbye to ten excess pounds several dozen pounds ago. Crabby sweated more than a sautéed mushroom and rarely stayed in the kitchen for long when cooking was underway.

When Ji-ji had entered the kitchen through its wide double doors, the overseer had railed against her for being late. He'd caught himself cussing and stopped midsentence. Everyone knew how Lotter felt about swearing, everyone knew Jellybean was Lotter's favorite Mule, and everyone who worked in the planting dining hall knew that at least one of the surveillance cameras dotted around the main kitchen was in working order. (Herring, paranoid about poisoning, had insisted on monitoring food preparation.) Fearful his cussing had been recorded, Crabby had delivered his customary exit line—"If you can't stand the heat, get out of the kitchen"—with as repentant a tone as he could muster for the camera. He'd shambled off to commence his self-inflicted penance: weed smoking and food sampling. Crabby would be occupied out by the dumpsters for the better part of the morning.

Ji-ji knew she didn't have much time to recover. Seeds would be arriving that afternoon, assigned to help them prepare the biggest feast of the season. Tomorrow, the expanded cohort of kitchen-seeds would be joined by garden-seeds, a few partially deaf factory-seeds, field-seeds (some as young as six), and construction-seeds, all assigned to ensure that the feast went off without a hitch. Ji-ji had to be careful. There was almost certainly a parrot or two among the extras. Right now, however, she had to conquer the debilitating pain in her back.

Dip addressed Sloppy: "We got any o' those high-kick killers Doc Riff give us?" Sloppy shrugged. "Get off your lazy ass an' look, Slop. Can't you see the pain she's in?"

"We're all in pain," Sloppy grumbled. "We live on a fucking planting. Guess I know what your last servant died of, Dip, and it wasn't indolence. That's laziness, in case you're wondering."

Sloppy heaved herself up off the crate and shuffled toward a shelf labeled PHARMACY. She wore a ratty pair of brown slippers with a hole cut out for her swollen toe, but Ji-ji knew that Sloppy would find a way to cope with the pain. When Vanguard Casper, Lotter's chief overseer and her steadermate, had broken her jaw, Sloppy had only missed a day or two of work. When he'd torn a patch of hair from her skull, roots and all (not easy because Sloppy's hair was as short as mown grass), Sloppy had simply taken to wearing a headscarf. And when Casper had kicked her seedling out of her womb by accident—in his inebriated state, the overseer had forgotten his seedmate was carrying—Sloppy had shown up for work the next day. "Never wanted Casper's demon seed in my belly in the first place," she'd asserted. "Easier this way. Bastard saved me the trouble."

Four years ago, before Sloppy had even bled yet, Van Casper had selected her as his second seedmate. Sloppy's keen intellect soon exasperated Casper, who'd had little formal schooling to speak of and resented the fact that seeds on the 437th attended the legacy school for seeds two or three hours a day—till females reached mating age and males had to get in shape for the Propitious Gleaning. Casper had no idea how smart Sloppy was when he'd fastened his copper seedmate band round her ankle. He punished her for it daily.

Ji-ji couldn't think of a worse steader to mate with than Van Casper—the bastard she'd caught sniffing around Afarra. He'd been drunk as a skunk, and she'd had to beat him away with a stick. He'd already been pissed off at Silapu after the eighty-dollar fine levied against him at Bonbon's snatching. Being beaten and threatened by her uppity offspring solidified his animosity. Ji-ji knew it was only fear of Lotter, coupled with extreme drunkenness, that kept Vanguard Casper from slitting her throat that night. Poor Sloppy took the heat for every female seed Casper wanted to murder—namely, all of them. Ji-ji often pitied her. But if Sloppy ever detected pity, look out. By the time she'd finished her verbal sandblasting, your pity had turned to dust.

Sloppy pulled down a dog-eared cardboard box, retrieved a pill container from it, twisted off the cap, and peered inside. It was dark in the basement storeroom. The only light came from a transom above the door and a battery-powered lamp.

"So? How many's in there?" Dip asked.

"Six," Sloppy replied, squinting into the container. "Wait." She counted again. "Seven."

Afarra cheered and rushed over to where Sloppy stood. Sloppy held out her arm to prevent her from approaching further.

"Keep your filthy shadow off the pharmaceuticals! Think we want 'em contaminated?"

Accustomed as Afarra was to Sloppy's hostility, her excitement didn't diminish, though she did take several steps back. "These pills will be helping Missy Ji," she stated.

Sloppy grimaced in disgust and appealed to Dip. "Doc Riff left these for major injuries—cuts, burns, chopped-off digits. S'pose one of us needs a pain killed an' she's snatched 'em all?"

Dip told Sloppy to quit whining and give the pill to Ji-ji. Cussing, Sloppy complied.

"Promise me you won't say a word about my back to anyone," Ji-ji said to Dip and Sloppy, after she'd finally managed to swallow the oversize pain pill.

Sloppy bristled. "Since when did Dip and me turn parrot?"

Ji-ji couldn't blame Sloppy for being mad at her. They were taking a huge risk covering for her mam. Though Ji-ji had already thanked them numerous times, she did so again.

"No thanks warranted," Dip assured her. "We know you'd do the same for us if we had mams—right, Slop? . . . You got enough o' that ointment on your back an' shoulders to numb 'em for a while. I've rubbed it in good and it don't smell pungent. Take a pill with you for tonight else you won't sleep. Come down here to the pharmacy an' grab another tomorrow. An' after the supper's done, pocket the last four for the race."

"We got a big feast tomorrow," Sloppy pointed out. "Bound to be a few gets burned, chopped, or beaten."

"Sloppy's right," Ji-ji conceded. "I don't need all the—"

"It's us will manage," Dip insisted. "You want Freedom, Slop, or you decided against it? She asks the doc for painkillers and he'll suspect she's ailing. All three of us kitchen-seeds aim to bask in liberty in the near future, courtesy of Ji-ji's kith-n-kins. An' don't even start on why she shouldn't petition for the Cloth. You seen how they are together. Like sisters almost." Afarra beamed. "*Moreover,*" Dip continued, pronouncing her words with exaggerated care, "it's Ji-ji's right to choose *whomever* she wants."

Sloppy was thrown by Dip's grammatical curveball, which could be why she didn't heed the warning in it. "No guarantee she'll petition for us," Sloppy countered. "Her mam can't be trusted. Could be lying's genetic. Charra promised the same thing an' never came through when she reached Dream—" Sloppy broke off.

Ji-ji almost fell off the chair. "You knew Charra was alive!"

Before Sloppy could answer, Dip cried out, "Charra's alive? I don't believe it! Where is she?"

"*Hush!*" Ji-ji urged. "Lotter's got spies everywhere. Sloppy, who told you?"

In a defiant tone, Sloppy made her confession: "Sila spilled the beans a few months back. Was braiding my hair. Sila gets talky when she's braiding, 'specially if she's imbibing too. Made me swear to keep quiet. Swore she'd deny it an' tell the other seeds I was a parrot. Ironic, huh? So I kept my mouth shut."

Sloppy's expression gradually changed as it dawned on her how dire the consequences could be if she kept offending the one person she relied on for her Freedom. "Hey, Ji-ji—you're not planning to wipe me off your kith-n-kins? Your mam can be scary as hell. You know that. Gotta get out! Casper beats me nonstop! Bastard'll kill me if I stay here!"

Dip started to panic then too, said Sloppy hadn't even told *her* about Charra. "I bet my life she's telling the truth, Ji-ji. Casper's sure to kill her one o' these days. Twisted her pinky till it broke last month. She sucked it up like always. What she says 'bout Sila being scary—that's true. You know it is. Sloppy can be a bitch an' a half but she ain't no liar."

Sloppy, less than flattered by Dip's testimonial, looked at Ji-ji expectantly. Her jaw had never set right; her lazy eye where Casper had punched her gave her migraines. He'd knocked out a few of her teeth too. If anything, Sloppy was even worse off than Afarra.

"Wish you'd told me Charra was alive," Ji-ji said. "I would've appreciated that. But it's done now. Like I promised, I'll petition for you an' Dip, along with Afarra, Mam, an'—" Ji-ji broke off.

Guessing what she'd been about to say, Dip assured her that Lua and Mbeke would be happy for all of them if they made it out. "Don't you waste no more purple tears on grieving, Ji-ji. Folks who look back too often trip over the future—ain't that what your mam always says?"

Ji-ji was still struggling to get her emotions under control. Dip plugged up the silence.

"Can't hardly wait to sit on my porch in Dream City. Folks say planes zoom by up top once in a while. Got neon lights, an' restaurants where you can eat no matter where you fall on the Color Wheel. An' genuine theater screens. Not some blood-spattered bedsheet strung up in a field."

Dip placed a hand over her heart, imitating the gesture father-men employed in their rituals. The black contamination cross beneath her brown Commonseed symbol, identifying her as soiled goods due to her bout with syphilis, peeked out from beneath her fingers. Dip made a solemn vow.

"After I'm Freed, I, Dipthong Spareseed (who won't be a Spareseed after Freedom comes and likely won't be known as Dipthong either—hate that blasted name), swear never to cook another meal for no one 'cept these three individuals—Me, Myself, an' I. An' for adopted kith-n-kin like the three kitchen-seeds in this storeroom, including the little Cloth. Not cleanin' for no one 'cept friends neither. Not *ever.*" Dip paused to savor the idea. Even Sloppy seemed moved.

Reluctantly, Ji-ji roused them from their daydreams: "Come on. We been gone a while and there's loads of prep to do 'fore tomorrow night. . . . No spitting in the cake batter this time, Sloppy."

"I never went near the cake batter! Cakes are Dip's prerogative."

"I saw you," Ji-ji told her. "You're lucky Crabby was looking the other way."

"Huh! Lucky? Me? Since when?"

||||||||||||||

Twelve hours later, Ji-ji stepped down from the seed transport wagon and stumbled, exhausted, into her mam's cabin. She would have been in a worse state had Dip not insisted she take a nap. Ji-ji had slept for four hours straight on a cot in the storeroom. Dip had told 'Seer Crabstreet that the chief kitchen-seed was checking on produce for the feast and he'd fallen for it. Ji-ji had expected to see her mam when she entered their cabin—had been dreading it all day. It wasn't easy to pull the wool over Silapu's eyes when she was sober, and now there were so many questions she was burning to ask her. The first thing that greeted her, however, was a note on the wobbly table.

> *Jellybean—Your father-man sent for me. Gone to Cropmaster Hall. May not be back 2nite. Nothing to eat here. Hope you ate already.—Mam*

Ji-ji breathed a sigh of relief. Bone weary and sore, she climbed into bed. Nearly an hour later, she concluded that the long nap she'd taken had scuttled sleep. She thought about swallowing another pain pill but the pain was bearable. Wiser to save it.

Her mind kept looping back to Tiro. Had he escaped? Where was he now? Was he as scared as she was? Would the fugitive siren blast out over the planting tonight and alert everyone to the runaway? She still didn't have a clue how he would make it to Salem. Tunneling under the fry-fence hadn't been possible for years. They had cameras and sensors there; guards patrolled the perimeter fence night and day. She pictured Tiro touching the fence and shrieking in pain as thousands of volts fried his beautiful body. She needed to distract herself—focus on something else.

She returned to the questions plaguing her ever since D-Day, and to Tiro's shocking new disclosures. What did Lua mean when she talked about the book and the boy with a head of wheat? Was the book the steaders' *One True Text*? It sure sounded like it—but then how would Lua know what was in it? What was the secret Chaff Man wanted to spill about Murder Mouth? Could it be connected to the creature she and Afarra ran into on the forbidden? Rumors always swirled about how the steaders had cross-bred the mutants. Maybe they'd found a way to cross-breed apes? Yet why did Drol look almost . . . human? . . . And how could she possibly be an existential threat to anyone? Weren't there dozens of Toteppi females scattered on plantings throughout the Territories? Why her? And why did Silapu go missing all those times? Was she parroting? To Lotter? To others? Was that what Tiro and Zaini thought? Were Toteppi and those they'd seeded doomed? Had Lotter, the man she'd hated for years, really risked his own skin to save them—or save her mam, at least?

Ji-ji closed her eyes. Soon, if all went well, she could put this nightmare behind her and see the world beyond the fry-fence. Her thoughts wandered to one of the few times she'd left the planting. Three years ago, she'd been transported down south to the 300s as a loaner seed, along with eleven other seeds from her planting. She had assumed at first that the 368th was less cruel because their perimeter fence wasn't high-voltage. Her first impressions had been wrong. Seeds on the 368th weren't even allowed to talk much. When they did speak, they had to draw from a list of approved words. If they were caught using words not on the seed vocabulary list, they had to forfeit a week's worth of seedchips. Repeat offenders had a fingernail or tooth yanked out. For chronic offenders, especially females, it was their tongues. All the female seeds on the 368th had to wear black hoods to mask their entire faces except their eyes. Females as young as three were forced to wear these "modesty hoods" so they wouldn't "Eve-tempt" the steaders. When you saw the female seeds together, it looked as though Chaff Man had spawned a crop of clones. For weeks afterward, Ji-ji had a recurring nightmare about a hooded tribe of executioners who dragged her off to the Circle.

She kept swinging from hopefulness to fearfulness. She needed to get a grip. Uncle Dreg had warned Tiro and Ji-ji there would be times when hope would shrivel up like a dried apple, and he'd instructed them to look to the "Coreseed within," saying it was the essence of who they were—the tiny unfathomable element that enabled seeds to overcome horror and suffering. "The Coreseed can save you," he used to say. "Just like it saved the Passengers. But you got to know how to cultivate it so it can put down roots in your soul and enable your spirit to rise. You got to turn the name the steaders gave you into salvation."

Inspired, Ji-ji had tried drawing her Coreseed. But it resembled a bird dropping—or, worse still, the seed symbol she was forced to wear. She tried to picture the Coreseed inside her body, but soon she was thinking about the invasive seeds that took root in Lua and Mbeke—sperm-seeds that ambushed their eggs, occupied their wombs, and exterminated them.

The ghostly light of an almost-full moon seeped through the one small window in her bedroom. She remembered she still had Uncle Dreg's map in her pocket. She would have to be careful tomorrow. There could be extra security for the feast; they could frisk some of the kitchen-seeds. She climbed out of bed and hurried over to where she'd hung her kitchen-seed uniform on a nail on the wall. She pulled out the map and opened it up. There was the Salem Outpost, the first station of the race, and, to the northeast, up along the old interstate then east a ways, Monticello, the second station. Farther to the northeast was their ultimate destination, the place steaders called Dark City, seeds called Dream City, and residents called D.C. The place where dreams blossomed for seeds like her. Uncle Dreg had employed the name Dream City, the term seeds used.

Ji-ji brought the map to her lips and kissed the initials. Tomorrow she would be ratified. The day after that she would embark on her quest for Freedom—for herself and for those she loved. So many were depending on her. With the help of Doc Riff's killers, she wouldn't fail them.

She stared at the map again. Uncle Dreg had drawn Dream Corridor too, which ran for twenty-plus miles through the No Region. On either side of Dream Corridor was a wretched place teeming with refugees unable to gain entry into the city. On the map, the No Region was also called by its historical name: NoVA. *Like the stars,* Ji-ji thought, grasping at anything she could interpret as encouraging. With her index finger, Ji-ji traced the route separating her from Freedom. The distance was less intimidating when she did that, a matter of inches, not miles. She would stick to the official race route, even though Uncle Dreg's map had a broken line leading to Dimmers Wood, located deep in The Margins. Near Dimmers Wood sat Slim Pickins. As if to confirm how treacherous the area was, Uncle Dreg had drawn the Bounty Boys' symbol there—a penal tree with a thick noose around its trunk. Bounty Boys weren't known for their subtlety. She needed to hide Uncle Dreg's map under her bed. She would retrieve it before setting out for the race and burn her planting map and her covert books at the same time, painful though that would be. She could redraw her map from memory after she reached the city, buy books too. Imagine that. She planned to hold on to Tiro's note—hide it inside the secret flap she'd made in her regulation skirt. It was risky, but she couldn't bring herself to burn it. The race monitors would never find it there.

Ji-ji had piled all kinds of crap under her bed—empty boxes, hand-me-down clothing—so her mam wouldn't discover her coverts. Her candids—books like the seeds' version of the Bible and *The Planting Cookbook*—she could possess without risk of censure. They sat on the small bookshelf Tiro had made for her birthday. Her coverts, on the other hand, would be classified as sedition texts cos they contained ideas that ran counter to steader doctrine. *Things Fall Apart,* a gift from Uncle Dreg, the four others gifts from Miss Clobershay: *Wuthering Heights, A Midsummer Night's Dream, The Tempest,* and Maeve Exra's *Abbreviated History.* She'd hidden Tiro's note in that one. She would take it out and read it again right now. Her last covert, *Everyman's Guide to Intermediate Science,* she'd filched from Father-Man Lotter's garbage, which explained why she got a faint whiff of rotten eggs whenever she turned the pages.

With some difficulty due to the soreness of her back, Ji-ji lowered herself onto her belly. She pushed the junk aside and thrust her arm under the bed. . . . *Nothing!* She must be imagining things. Must be that horse pill of the doc's. She thrust her arm under the bed again. Her coverts, her map . . . everything! *Gone!*

Ji-ji ignored her aching back and flung the junk to one side. She braced herself against the pain and slid her entire body under the bed. She rubbed her hands over every inch of the underside of the bed frame. Her map, her cherished books, and Tiro's note snatched! Straining with the effort, she crawled out from under the bed and staggered to her feet. Surely her mam wouldn't take them to Lotter? Bet she'd hidden them to teach her a lesson. Ji-ji tore around the cabin searching for them. She did it all over again. She came up empty. *Nothing!*

Back in her bedroom, Ji-ji found herself sliding down the wall to a sitting position, the pain in her back so intense she wouldn't have been surprised if she'd left a trail of blood on the wall behind her. Imaging a planting was a cardinal offense, and her sedition texts violated a whole bunch of Elevation Prohibitions and Censorship Doctrines. Tiro's note snatched too! Why hadn't she burned it when she had the chance? Even if Tiro managed to escape and triumph in the Freedom Race, his kith-n-kin petition for her would never be granted. Any seed with a serious conviction was ineligible. She wouldn't live Free. Not now. Not ever.

The front door creaked open. Ji-ji knew who it was. "Hi, Missy Ji," the voice said.

Servers had to stay later than other seeds to finish the cleanup. Afarra must have surmised that Silapu wasn't there. She closed the door behind her and crept into the cabin.

She drew back the curtain to Ji-ji's room and said, "I am hoping to sleep in your bed tonight, okay?"

The terrible news spilled out of Ji-ji all at once. "Mam found it! That map I told you about, an' my books! An' Tiro's letter! Lotter's got them by now. *Oh god!* Tiro's run off to be a Wild Seed! After Mam tells Lotter about the map an' he sees my coverts I won't be ratified! An' the map—unforgivable! I can't save anyone. Not anymore. Not you . . . not Mam . . . not Bonbon! I'm toast!"

"We are being toast together," Afarra said, as if it were something to be desired.

In her distress, Ji-ji had crumpled up Uncle Dreg's map. Afarra took it from her and smoothed it out carefully. She slipped it back into a secret pocket in Ji-ji's skirt and plopped down on the floor next to her friend. After a few moments, Afarra scrambled up to peer out of the bedroom window.

"The moon is pretty moonlight," she said. "See? She is from afar. Like me."

Ji-ji hauled herself up from the floor and sank down onto the bed. She could see the moon from there. It made her think about something her teacher had pointed to in their history book. Great hunks of the text had been blacked out, but Zyla Clobershay had explained that once upon a time—long before Trifurcation, and before the Necessary Reversal and Faith Revival made unfettered scientific inquiry an offense punishable by death in the Territories—twelve fairskin men had walked on the moon. For all Ji-ji knew, Miss Clobershay had made that up. She liked to tell them inspiring tales, and the number twelve, considered sacred by steaders, seemed too coincidental. Yet it was one of the few stories about fairskins that made Ji-ji happy—made her believe, like Uncle Dreg did, that they could all rise together. Ji-ji wanted to pass the story on to the little server. Couldn't bear to think of her having no miracles to hold on to. So she told Afarra about Apollo, who had flown on a spaceship to the moon with eleven fairskin men and walked on its surface.

Afarra stared at her in disbelief. "A *fairskin*!" she exclaimed, as if that were the most stunning part of the tale. Then she seemed to realize what Ji-ji had said. "To the *moon*! In a *spaceship*!"

Afarra peered out of the window and held up her fingers to measure the size of the moon. "The moon she is small in between the dark. Small as my eye. I am thinking the ship was tiny, yes?"

"The spaceship was big when it left the ground, an' it could fly."

"Not a fish ship? A *bird* ship! With *wings*!" Afarra sucked in her breath in wonder.

"I've let you down, Afarra. Do you understand? I can't petition for you now. I'm sorry."

"No sorrowfuling. See the moon-eye. She is smiling. We fly there too . . . one day."

Ji-ji tried to see the smile on the moon's pale face, but all she saw was a blind eye suspended from an invisible lynch rope, reminding her of the journeys people like her would never make.

Exhausted, they climbed into bed. Afarra wrapped her thin brown arms around Ji-ji. As night raced toward dawn, Afarra prattled on, rocking her sad sister to sleep.

12 THE LAST SUPPER

When Ji-ji woke at five o'clock, Afarra had already left to begin her predawn shift in the dining hall. Beside her bed, Ji-ji found a cup of water and some bread and honey. Afarra must have left it for her before she took off. The cabin was quiet. Silapu hadn't come back. The absence of extreme pain in her back lifted Ji-ji's spirits a little. And there was something else to be thankful for: the fugitive siren hadn't sounded, which meant Tiro's absence hadn't been noticed yet.

In less than twenty minutes, Ji-ji had hitched a ride on one of the transport wagons. Soon she was hard at work in the main kitchen, where dozens of seeds were already peeling, baking, grating, and mixing. 'Seer Crabby strolled up to her, put his arm around her shoulders and squeezed.

"A juicy seed like you, Jellybean, is a testament to Cropmaster Lotter. He must be real proud." Crabstreet's eyes were glued to her boobs. "If you make it to Sodom, make sure you tell those turncoat Independents 'bout your privileges on the 437th. Not many plantings as generous as this one when it comes to seed pamperin'." Ji-ji vowed to spread the word about the planting, neglecting to be specific about which words she would spread.

As soon as they had a moment together, Dip asked Ji-ji how her back was doing. When she heard it wasn't hurting much anymore, Dip whistled softly in surprise. "Guess Luck's perched itself on your shoulder, Ji-ji. Let's hope, for all our sakes, it don't fly off anytime soon."

Ji-ji went to check on Sloppy, who was toiling over a honey-spice sauce to pour over the buttered carrots.

"You seen Tiro?" Sloppy asked.

For a split second, Ji-ji was rattled, but she didn't let it show. "Not for a while," she replied.

"Rumor has it Williams is mad as the devil with him. Good chance he won't be ratified."

Ji-ji almost gave herself away by not looking as surprised as the news warranted. She recovered quickly.

"No one flies like Tiro," she said. "He'll be fine."

"Just repeating what I heard, that's all. Thought you'd want to know."

Sloppy looked over at Crabby, who was out of earshot, running his chunky finger round a bowl of cake batter. "Wouldn't be surprised if Williams had something up his sleeve. I know you dreamed about competing with Tiro. I know how tight you two lovebirds are." Sloppy used to have a crush on Tiro, and there was a serrated edge to her voice whenever she spoke about him.

"Williams'll get a great payout if Tiro competes," Ji-ji replied, "so will the planting—"

"It's not about some lousy payout. It's *personal.* Male pride an' vengeance—that's what it's always about. You would've noticed if you'd been paying attention."

Dip slid up behind them. "Zip it, Sloppy," she said. "Your sauce is getting lumpy."

Dip guided Ji-ji down to Storeroom 2, handed her another pill, and said Sloppy was in a worse mood this morning than she'd been in yesterday.

"If you can only petition for one of us, pick Sloppy. Casper'll kill her if she don't get away soon. Me, I'd survive a holocaust. Like one o' them roaches—indestructible. Most steaders—seeds too—are wary o' messing with me when they see this black cross. Assume my love channel's a sewer, which it ain't, by the way. Doc Riff says my pipes are as clean as a whistle. So choose Slop over me, if you got to. I got this spoilage cross to protect me."

"You're a good friend to her, Dip. She doesn't deserve you."

"Don't underestimate Sloppy. Not sure I could go home every night to a monster like Casper. Poor seed don't even get a seedmate cabin of her own. Has to live in one o' Casper's falling-down side shacks. Not fit for an outcast, or a dog even."

"If I'm ratified an' if I make it to the city, I promise I won't forget you or Sloppy."

Dip and Ji-ji embraced. Ji-ji tried to pour all her love for the generous kitchen-seed into one hug so Dip would know how much she admired her.

"You seen the little server?" Dip asked.

"Not yet. Could be she's out by the trash. Crabby ordered all the servers to sort through it, remember? Make sure nothing goes to waste."

They were starting back for the kitchen when Dip put a hand on Ji-ji's arm.

"Hey, almost forgot. Your mam catch up with you?"

"Mam was looking for me?"

"Stopped by 'fore you got here. Seemed real eager to speak to you. Said you shouldn't worry 'bout nothing. Guess she figured you was real nervous an' wanted to buck you up."

Ji-ji nearly jumped up and down with relief. Her mam hadn't betrayed her to Lotter and didn't intend to. "I'll find her," Ji-ji said.

"Won't do no good. She'll be at Cropmaster Hall by now. Said Lotter's graspy again. Said she'd be back for the feast. Don't worry. I never mentioned we know about her being a you-know-what. Wouldn't be surprised if it was guilt motivating her to seek you out. Could be she wants forgiveness. Guess that's something we all of us want."

As they climbed the steep back stairs leading to the kitchen, Ji-ji decided Dip was right. Luck really had perched itself on her shoulder—for now, at least. *Let the same be true for Tiro,* she thought.

IIIIIIIIIIIIII

The rest of the day was a whirlwind of preparation. As dusk descended, Crabby inspected the food laid out on the enormous kitchen tables. He smiled approvingly, curled his hairy arm around Ji-ji's shoulders, and leaned into her. He reeked of booze; food was lodged between his nicotine-stained teeth.

"God knows you ain't the prettiest-looking plum on the tree, Jellybean," he told her, "but you done me proud tonight. Have to admit, thought you was too green for a chief kitchen-seed. Wouldn't be surprised if Cropmaster Lotter give me a bonus after he tastes these gastronomical delights. How'd you get those mushroom tarts so damn flaky?" Ji-ji pretended she had to rescue a saucepan of gravy before it spilled over and slid out from under the overseer's clammy armpit.

Throughout the day, Ji-ji had searched for Afarra whenever she had a spare moment, to no avail. Servers could be drafted for duty by steaders at any time. Maybe she'd been sent to the fields or to one of the factories? Ji-ji wouldn't be able to look for her until after the feast was over. Wherever she was, Ji-ji prayed she was safe.

At 6:00 P.M., the fifteen-foot-high, carved-oak doors to the dining hall were flung open. The planting crier, outfitted in his hunter-green garb, shouted the proclamation: "Honored Father-Men, esteemed guests, worthy steaders, Indigenous, and invited seeds! By order of Lord-Father Arundale Lotter, Twelfth Cropmaster of Planting 437, the Last Supper of the Spring will commence!"

Ji-ji stood in a corner, eager to catch sight of her mam. While the steaders ambled in, she surveyed the massive dining hall to check everything was in order. At one end, behind the raised platform where the cropmaster and his twelve father-men sat, was the Planting Mural—a series of idyllic pastoral scenes depicting the four seasons of planting life. Happy seeds toiled in the fields and factories while smiling steaders watched over them. In the center of the mural was a life-size version of the Armistice seal. Above the mural, the Territories' motto was carved in gigantic letters covered in gold leaf: ***Growing the Territories One Seed at a Time!***

The seating arrangements inside the hall reflected the planting's strict adherence to hierarchy. The cropmaster and the twelve planting patriarchs sat at a long table on the raised platform in front. Inquisitor Tryton, Diviner Shadowbrook, and the cropmaster's VIP guests sat with the father-men. Bearded steaders in their white shirts and fraternal neckties, along with other fairskin professionals who worked on the planting, sat at the tables closest to the platform. Fairskin work-for-hire Liberty Laborers, dressed in their pray-day best, sat behind them.

Two dozen African and Native Indigenous guests, all of them wearing their status ID pins—curlicued, silver-plated lapel pins with the letters *A-I* or *N-I* encircled by a harvest wreath—sat farther back from the platform. Ji-ji caught sight of Bettieann Plowman and Doc Riff. The doc looked dapper in his pray-day duds. He waved to her and mouthed, "Good luck." Dusky Liberty Laborers, along with Pastor Cam Gillyman and the other two True Hybrids on the planting, sat in this section.

Muleseeds, Tribalseeds, and Commonseeds sat at the back of the hall: twelve representatives from each homestead, together with the twelve Cropmaster Picks and seeds who had participated in the Glory Trials and were therefore eligible to compete for ratification. Some of the competitors' kith-n-kin had been invited too. No Serverseeds would be seated, of course. Servers were never permitted to eat in the dining hall, nor were they, in spite of their name, allowed to serve food, though dozens would be called upon to clean up after the feast.

The Cropmaster Picks entered last of all so they could be observed as they filed in. The group of twelve female unplowed seeds aged eleven to thirteen had received a special invitation to the Last Supper. A white card with fancy black lettering and gold edging, hand-delivered by the crop-master's assistant, signaled the Lord-Father's intention to mate with them at some point. The invitation served as a warning to other steaders not to mess with them. The Picks, their invitations hanging from gold ribbons around their necks, filed in. Their white, diaphanous gowns fluttered behind them like delicate wings. Mutterings echoed around the hall. Three of the Picks could be classified as belonging to the outcast arcs of the Color Wheel, where beauty wasn't supposed to reside. Those who didn't know Arundale Lotter would put it down to recklessness, but Ji-ji suspected Lotter wanted to assert his power by announcing to the planting that he could have any female he wanted.

As they slipped into their reserved pew at the front of the seed section, a few Picks looked excited; most looked petrified. Ji-ji, who knew Lotter as well as anyone, pitied them. Her father-man's cruelty could be subtle; some of them wouldn't catch on at first. They would mistake him for a man who could be easily read; they would imagine they could do things to please him. They wouldn't see his fist coming before it smashed into their jaws. They wouldn't be equipped to dodge his verbal grenades or know how to cope with his drug-induced tantrums. They would think his reticence stemmed from shyness rather than indifference. Chances were good they wouldn't discover the depth of his sick obsession with Silapu till it hit them, literally, in the face. Ji-ji stared at the procession of young females clothed in white and shivered when she recalled what Uncle Dreg used to say about white symbolizing death in the Cradle.

After most of the guests had been seated, Ji-ji scanned the hall again in search of her mam. She'd expected to see Silapu sitting next to Auntie Zaini or Aunt Marcie, but she wasn't there. At that moment, Ji-ji caught sight of Crabby making a beeline toward her. She glanced at her wristwatch to suggest she was in a hurry and hightailed it back to the kitchen.

It was Ji-ji's duty as chief kitchen-seed to serve the First Plate to the official taster. Ji-ji entered from a hidden door located in the mural and presented Taster Lemmaging with a platter piled high with appetizers: bacon-wrapped bay scallops, mushroom tarts in flaky pastry, and mini crab-and-goat-cheese soufflés for the head table. Friedrich "Fray" Lemmaging—a man Sloppy had dubbed "the Lemming"—had been the official tastemaster for the past fifteen years. Though he hadn't yet been poisoned, he seemed convinced it was only a matter of time. Big-jowled and easily affronted, he referred to himself as a *gourmand* and boasted about his discerning palate.

As the Lemming popped a mushroom tart into his mouth, Ji-ji stole a glance at Lotter as he gazed around the hall surveying his property. Ji-ji didn't recognize the guest on Lotter's right, though his crimson robe and the heavy gold chain he wore, set with a stunning ruby, told her he was high up on the Great Ladder. The inquisitor's hollow cheeks and deep-set eyes gave him an impenetrable look, as if he'd ferreted out the world's most important secrets and planned to keep them all to himself. Under his crimson skullcap, his closely cropped hair looked as if it had been painted onto his head. Surrounded by so many bearded faces, the inquisitor's face looked naked. He caught Ji-ji staring at him. Instead of being offended, the VIP nodded in her direction and smiled at her, revealing teeth that didn't have a right to be as white as they were. His smile unnerved her. She'd never seen anyone smile quite like that before. She nearly dropped the appetizer platter into the Lemming's lap. When next she looked in the VIP's direction, he was deep in conversation with Inquisitor Tryton.

As soon as Taster Lemmaging nodded his approval, Ji-ji told the kitchen-seeds to begin serving the guests on the platform. While she supervised them, she had another opportunity to observe her father-man and gauge his mood. If anything, Lotter looked even more handsome than usual. His hair lay on his broad shoulders in glossy locks. Some of the kitchen-seeds who worked regularly in Cropmaster Hall had mentioned that Lotter had taken to quoting from *The One True Text*. This had alarmed her; Lotter had never been guilty of piety. Could be he'd decided to put on an act for his VIP guest. She hoped so, for all their sakes. In her experience, zealots could be the cruelest steaders of all. She had to admit that from the moment he had assumed the mantle of cropmaster, Lotter had changed.

After the ricocheted bullet had taken out Herring, Lotter had been proclaimed acting cropmaster. To make it official, Diviner Shadowbrook draped Herring's blood-soaked cloak across his shoulders. Lotter was a germophobe. Normally, he would have been repulsed by a dead man's bloody cloak. That morning, however, no one would have suspected he had any qualms about wearing it. He had addressed the assembled steaders and seeds with confidence and worn the great black cloak and cropmaster chain like someone born to be Lord-Father. Lotter hadn't expected to assume a leadership role for years—decades, even—yet he'd taken to cropmastery with the ease of someone who seemed destined to rule. As luck would have it, he became the twelfth Lord-Father of the Planting. Already, superstitious steaders talked about the special role he would play in planting history as "the Twelfth." A cult seemed to be growing around him.

Ji-ji pulled her gaze away from her father-man and focused on the feast, which featured an ambitious menu and multiple courses. For the father-men and their VIP guests, nine courses; for steaders, including fairskin Liberty Laborers, seven; five for Indigenous, True Hybrids, and dusky Liberty Laborers; four for Cropmaster Picks; and three for the other invited seeds—soup, a meat dish, and a hunk of pie as large as Ji-ji could get away with serving them. The seeds, accustomed to rationing, devoured their courses in minutes. The lambs were roasted to perfection on the outdoor spits; the suckling pigs tasted sweet and juicy, their cracklings wafer-crisp; the casseroles, seasoned to perfection, disappeared as fast as she could serve them; and the pies had crusts so light that, as Dip put it, "They would surely fly away if they was left outside." The wine in the "only-for-VIPs" section of Herring's private store lived up to its billing. Lotter had taught Ji-ji how to select the best vintages, though Crabby didn't hesitate to take credit for the choices she'd made. She'd chosen well, as evidenced by frequent calls for refills.

Three hours later, after multiple rounds of toasts and announcements, Ji-ji and her kitchen-seeds served the last of the desserts to the seeds. So far, at least, things had proceeded as planned. She heard seeds whispering among themselves, wondering where Tiro could be. Ji-ji wished the VIP inquisitor hadn't accepted the invitation. Lotter would want to impress him. When he learned that Tiro had run away, Lotter would lash out. There was another thing gnawing at her too. Tiro had said there was a desire to purge plantings of Toteppi. The inquisitor was from Armistice, she was certain; no one else would wear a chain like that. Was he here to persuade Lotter to give up Toteppi for slaughter? If so, would Lotter play savior again?

Confident that Crabstreet had imbibed copious amounts of alcohol, Ji-ji decided to risk inquiring about the VIP's identity when she ran into the kitchen overseer near Storeroom 1. Crabby, who loved being thought of as "in the know," eagerly divulged what he knew.

"Honorable Inquisitor Fightgood Worthy is the most powerful cleric in the Territories. He's Lord-Secretary of the Supreme Council, which makes him the right-hand man of the Lord-Father of Lord-Fathers. Herring invited him to the planting a dozen times but all he got was regrets.

Then along comes Dale Lotter who asks once an' he accepts the very first time. That's why your father-man was so hell-bent on making sure we served only the best of everything tonight. Fightgood's got more power in his pinky than all those other councilors combined. They say he can conjure too. Cures are his specialty. A bona fide healer, they say, with half a dozen certified miracles. The Lord-Secretary does real conjurin'—not that dumb shit Tryton does at the pray center."

Crabby stopped blabbing. He'd said far too much.

Ji-ji pretended the din coming from the kitchen had prevented her from catching most of what he'd said and asked him to repeat it. Crabby got all huffy and told her he didn't have time to jaw with a Mule. He strolled off in the direction of the dumpsters. Ji-ji watched him go, then hurried down the corridor to Storeroom 2. The pain in her back was returning. She needed to get some more painkillers—take them with her to the race.

He was behind her in the dark storeroom before she knew it—shoving her against the wall, his arm pressing into her back! She tried to see who it was but when she turned her head he slammed it into the wall so hard she almost blacked out.

He ran his hands over her back and shoulders. She tried again to turn around. He shoved her harder into the wall. A planting guard—must be. She didn't have her knife. Matty did. Was he claiming his reward? He'd threatened her. Why had she come down here alone? *Stupid . . . stupid!*

He rubbed his hands over her back and shoulders again before pulling up her skirt and slapping his clammy hand up between her thighs. He dug around her girlcloth, tried to finger her. Rubbed his swollen dick against her buttocks. She felt his wet stiffness against her and decided to scream. Would Dip hear her? Would Sloppy? Would they come running if they did? She screamed.

Her attacker jerked his hand away from between her thighs and used it to smother her quiet. She smelled herself on his fingers. He pressed down harder on her nose and mouth. She couldn't breathe! She bit his fleshy hand and he squealed like a pig.

Charra's voice echoed in her head: "Fight, Beany! *Fight!*" Charra had taught her how to reach down and grab their crotch if they came at you from behind. She fought to get the bastard to release her hand. *Done it!* Before he could confine it again, she reached back behind her. She couldn't find his balls so she found something else instead. His baton? *No, fool!*

She grabbed it with her fist and twisted with all her might, digging in with her nails. As he shrieked in pain, she managed to get hold of a ball too. "*You stinking little bitch!*" he cried.

Not Matty! Definitely not. Who then? In his rush to protect himself, her attacker relinquished his hold on her. She was able to turn at last. She swiveled round to face him.

Inquisitor Tryton stood before her, his crimson robe puddled round his feet.

Stunned, Ji-ji relinquished her hold on his privates.

At that moment, through the slit in the storeroom doorway, Ji-ji caught sight of another man observing them. Tryton had slammed the door shut but the man must've inched it open.

Tryton followed Ji-ji's gaze to the deep-set eyes of the witness. He slapped a hand over himself and sputtered, "It's not how it looks. . . . I mean, I wasn't . . . The slut grabbed my—"

"Yes. I saw that she took matters into her own hands," Lord-Secretary Fightgood Worthy said. "Tell me, Inquisitor Tryton. Did I ask you to rape her?"

Tryton's eyes bulged out their sockets. "*Rape?*" He looked at Ji-ji in utter disbelief. "How could I rape *that*? It's not possible! I was just checking, like you commanded. She's a Mule! How can it be *rape?*"

Fightgood Worthy nodded. "Of course, Inquisitor Tryton, you are correct. She is indeed a Mule. . . . And you are a servant of God."

"The Mule grabbed *me*! She's a lustful *bitch*! I swear on *The One,* Your Honor, *she* accosted *me*!"

Tryton stopped speaking. A look from the Lord-Secretary had silenced him.

"Pick up your robe," Fightgood Worthy said. "Leave the feast and come see me tomorrow at six A.M. on the dot to discuss your future—assuming, of course, you have one."

Tryton made a pitiful attempt at an apology. His superior raised a hand to stop him.

"Say another word and I will defrock you here and now, and announce both the defrocking and the reason why to the assembled gathering. I am sure the new cropmaster will be fascinated to learn you decided to plow his seed without his permission. Or mine."

Tryton picked up his robe and rushed out.

"Did he hurt you, Toteppi?" Worthy asked. Ji-ji shook her head. "Good. Make yourself presentable. Say nothing about this to anyone. For your own sake." As he headed down the corridor, he called back over his shoulder, "And for the sake of your pretty mam."

IIIIIIIIIIIIII

At the end of the meal, as the seeds nursed their cider, the steaders their beer and wine, and the father-men their coffee and brandy, Ji-ji took up her position toward the back. She'd stopped shaking as soon as she realized Fightgood Worthy didn't plan to participate in what he'd called a rape. She'd started shaking again when he'd made the threat against her mam and called her Toteppi. It was the way he'd said it that put the fear of god into her.

The Lord-Secretary sat at the head table. He hadn't once looked in her direction since she'd returned to the dining hall. When he wasn't conversing with Lotter, the Lord-Secretary made small talk with steaders who came up to the platform to pay their respects. Tryton's seat was empty. No one seemed to miss him.

Nothing added up. Everyone knew the term *rape* couldn't be applied to the plowing of botanicals, but he'd used it anyway. Why? Had he sent Tryton down there so he could watch the assault? No—that wasn't it. Ji-ji had a feeling Fightgood Worthy wouldn't be interested in entertainment as crude as that. Was he spying on Toteppi? Was he trying to find out if she was a threat? One thing she did know: if Worthy hadn't shown up, she wouldn't have been able to fight off Tryton for long. Planting 437's inquisitor would have entered her from behind like a dog.

Ji-ji wasn't a seedling. She'd been hard-groped before, and undergone invasive searches by planting guards. A drunk Bounty Boy, a guest of Herring's, had tried to rape her. Pushed her into a pantry and ripped her shirt off. Grabbed her breast and stuck his tongue down her throat. Dip had saved her by purposely catching fire to a dish towel and screaming "*Fire!*" This was different. Although Inquisitor Tryton was supposed to act as the planting's "moral compass," everyone knew he was a disgusting rodent. What did he mean when he said he'd been asked to check on her? Why would Lord-Secretary Worthy ask him to do that?

Dip and a few of the other kitchen-seeds joined Ji-ji and wished her good luck. 'Seer Crabstreet, meanwhile, wobbled back and forth in the center aisle marking the end of the steader and beginning of the seed sections, ready to take credit for the kitchen-seeds' culinary excellence. Ji-ji scanned the hall. Still no sign of Silapu. Dip asked her if she was okay. She noticed the bump above her left eye. "You fell or something?" she asked. "Or something," Ji-ji replied. Dip squeezed her hand like a mother.

Diviner Shadowbrook rose. As always after major feasts, she spoke first. Giant screens had been placed on either side of the platform. They sprang to life as she approached the mic. The dining hall broke into applause when the two screens lit up. Steaders, always sensitive about Territorial inferiority when it came to modernization, applauded with vigor. It was disconcerting, however, to see Old Shadowy's face enlarged to the size of a small tree. "You could ride a tractor up her left nostril," Dip joked. "Always assuming you could make it through that thicket o' nose hair."

Diviner Shadowbrook thanked 'Seer Crabstreet and his kitchen-seeds for the wonderful food. Crabby, relishing the applause, bowed so low in acknowledgment he would have toppled over had it not been for a quick-thinking steader whose arm shot out to steady him.

Williams, the newly appointed chief of security, rose next. The camera followed him to the podium. His grim figure appeared on the screens. The hall fell silent when he bent to the mic. Because the occasion wasn't as formal as a Culmination, none of the bald father-men wore their gray ceremonial wigs. Williams' pale head and oversize ears looked enormous on the screens; the large mole by his right ear had the diameter of a saucer. Animosity toward the sadistic father-man churned in the seed section.

Williams singled out a few steaders and Indigenous for their accomplishments. Among them was Doc Riff, cited for his work at the seed clinic. He stood to appreciative applause from seeds and steaders alike. Williams droned on, congratulating his fellow father-men on the number of liveborns so far this year, and listing each one by name, weight, and number on the Color Wheel.

Dip prodded Ji-ji in the back. "Sila's here," she whispered.

Sure enough, Silapu must have entered by a side door. She stood all the way on the other side of the seed section, trying to get Ji-ji's attention. She looked tired and worried. Ji-ji couldn't make out what she was trying to tell her. Had she spilled the beans about her coverts after all? Was that what she was trying to warn her about? Silapu began to make her way across the hall but was waylaid by Zaini, intent on speaking with her.

Williams began his lengthy introduction of Lotter, whom he called "Brother Lotter," as though they hadn't been undermining each other for years. Williams announced the date of Lotter's Inauguration: May 15th. Lotter's ascension would be uncontested; the other father-men must have pledged allegiance to him. Thank god! With any luck, Toteppi wouldn't be purged anytime soon.

At the conclusion of Williams' introduction, Lotter rose to sustained applause. On the huge screens, Lotter's tumble of blond hair and his striking blue eyes made him look younger than he was—kinder too. But Ji-ji noted the clenched cruelty of his mouth and the total absence of smile lines round his eyes. He wore an exquisitely tailored suit in the traditional style; the gold cropmaster chain, a necklace of intricate gold and silver wreaths, hung from his neck. The hall fell silent.

"Welcome to the Last Supper of the Spring. We are honored this evening by the presence of a very special guest who comes to us all the way from the Father-City of Armistice. Devout secessionist Inquisitor Fightgood Worthy has been a tireless advocate for law and order, evidenced by his steadfast opposition to the lax laws of the Eastern and Western Super-States, and the waywardness of some of the Independents. His visit signals a new era of collaboration between this planting and the great Father-City on the great lake." Ji-ji didn't like the sound of that.

"My fellow Freedom Fighters, we must never forget that the danger posed by the so-called Friends of Freedom is real. They are conspiring with reunionists to rob us of our hard-won Freedom. They would strip the Homestead Territories of its autonomy and force us to abandon our values. Fightgood Worthy is leading our Holy Crusade of Resistance. Esteemed Lord-Secretary, may Planting 437 prove as worthy of this honor as you have proven worthy of your name." Lotter held up his glass. "Guests, please join me in welcoming the distinguished secretary of state to the Lord-Father of Lord-Fathers, Lord-Secretary Fightgood Worthy."

The steaders shot up from their seats as one, raised their glasses and mugs, and cheered. The seeds, who understood that exultation was expected of them but not elevation, remained seated. The hall rang with steader applause, stomping, and cheering. Lotter raised his hand to indicate the steaders should take their seats again.

"We are blessed," Lotter continued. "A planting is the only safe haven for seeds. Our botanicals are protected from the horrors of The Margins. Should vicious mutants seek to attack us, the perimeter security fence has enough volts to deliver a fatal charge in an instant. . . . A new species of mutant was recently spotted roaming not far from here. A biped of enormous strength and size. The rabid creature managed to lure a hapless guard beyond the fry-fence and rip the hero to shreds."

Ji-ji shot Billy a look; his eyes were glued to the platform.

Lotter went on: "Have no fear. Inquisitor Worthy has informed me that this new rabid species is being systematically wiped out by the militias. The Lord-Father of Lord-Fathers, in his wisdom, has dispatched buzzbuzz drones to locate and annihilate them. You are safe on the 437th."

Did Lotter know what Ji-ji and Afarra had seen? Had Matty ratted on them? Dip, aware of her agitation, whispered to her not to worry. "You're a shoo-in," she said.

"And now," Lotter continued, "it is time for Ratification."

Ji-ji's heart clenched in her chest. Dip squeezed her hand again as Lotter continued.

"This year, two young Mules performed exceptionally well in the flyer-runner trials. Tiro Williamsmule, seeded by First Father-Man Williams, won the championship title for flyer-battlers." A cheer went up from the seed section. Lotter raised his hand for quiet. Ji-ji remembered sitting on Lotter's lap as a seedling and combing the tiny tufts of blond hair below his knuckles. The same fine, blond hair that sprouted on his arms.

"The second contestant, Jellybean Lottermule—my own Muleseed—won the Planting Long Race in record time and took the runner title."

More cheers. Dip patted Ji-ji on the arm, careful to avoid her back.

"First Father-Man Drexler Williams has requested that Tiro Williamsmule, his legitimate Muleseed . . . *not* be ratified for the Big Race."

The hall fell silent, but Ji-ji already knew what was coming.

"I have granted Father-Man Williams' request."

Ji-ji remembered to look devastated. Auntie Zaini broke down. Bromadu stood up and shouted at Lotter. Coach Billy shoved Tiro's little brother back down in his seat. Ji-ji didn't know whether Zaini and her boys knew the truth or not. If they did, their acting was as skillful as Coach B's. Sloppy, who stood nearby, caught Ji-ji's eye and nodded as if to say, "I told you so."

Lotter signaled to a guard at the back of the hall, who thrust open the double doors. In marched several dozen armed guards. Though the steaders, most of whom were armed, greatly outnumbered the seeds, the new cropmaster wasn't taking any chances. The guards, dressed in khaki pants, skinny yellow ties, and olive shirts, took up positions along either side of the seed section. Lieutenant Longsby lined up his men a few feet from where Ji-ji stood.

Lotter's voice rang out: "*Bring forth Traitor Tiro Williamsmule!*"

No one stood up. Some of the seeds stared at Ji-ji with pity in their eyes. Others stared at Bad Luck Billy, who peered around the room as if he couldn't imagine where Tiro could be. Billy acted so convincingly that Ji-ji almost believed him.

Just then, another group entered the hall. Two guards dragged a tall, muscular male up the center aisle. A black hood covered his head. It couldn't be. . . .

"As you can see," Lotter informed them, "we have the Toteppi traitor in custody. He was caught trying to run. A loyal seed informed us of his perfidious conduct. Like his traitorous uncle, Tiro Williamsmule is a Friend to those who would do us harm. Bring the traitor before us!"

The guard propelled Tiro up the great hall's long center aisle. He tried to speak, but they must have gagged him. Only grunts and frantic groans came out from under the hood. Ji-ji watched in horror.

A few seeds dared to protest aloud. Guards quieted them with savage blows. The dozen or so seedlings in the hall wept openly. Tiro was popular. He made the seedlings laugh and they adored him. The scarecrow litter followed Tiro—Crow Man carried aloft by two guards. Master-Guard Falrenn brought up the rear of the nightmare procession. The Grim Reaper lay on the black velvet pillow he carried in his outstretched arms. The blade flashed menacingly in the hall's low lighting.

Lotter spoke again. He had received an official supplication from Williams to execute the runaway traitor, who had been caught by the fry-fence attempting to escape. After consultation with their esteemed visitor, he had reached a decision.

Lotter stepped back from the mic. Master-Guard Falrenn approached the platform and presented the Grim Reaper to Williams. The Crow Man litter was laid at Williams' feet, even though the cropmaster usually split the crow. Williams brought down the Grim Reaper and sliced the scarecrow in two. Straw went flying. Lotter stepped back to the mic.

"By the power vested in me by the glorious Father-City of Armistice, the esteemed Lord-Father of Lord-Fathers, and the noble father-men of Planting 437, I, Arundale Duke Lotter, convict you, Tiro Williamsseed, great-nephew to the Toteppi Traitor Dregulahmo, of acts of treason against the Homestead Territories. I hereby sentence you to swing from the penal tree until all breath has been taken from you, and the traitorous poison in your veins is expunged."

Georgie-Porge leapt to his feet in protest. Amid the jeers of steaders, four guards grabbed the fly-boy and dragged him out of the seed section. Four more had to join them before they could haul him away.

Billy stood and yelled "*Have pity, for god's sake!*" over and over again until a guard thrust him back in his seat.

The guards up on the platform with Tiro carried riot gear: high-powered rifles, handguns, jolt sticks, stun staffs, even bad kangaroos. That wouldn't stop her. Ji-ji knew what she had to do. She would aim for Dip's ankle, forcing her to let go of her arm. Out of the corner of her eye, Ji-ji saw her mam trying to squeeze through the guests to reach her. The parrot wouldn't make it in time. No one would be able to catch her before she was up there with Tiro! She would proclaim her love for him and use the one weapon she had left—words. In this hell where all choices were snatched from seeds, she would choose her own death-path.

The guards forced Tiro to his knees. Williams ordered them to remove the hood so he could imprint death-ash onto the traitor's brow.

Ji-ji was about to make her move and rush the platform when Matty Longsby stepped forward, grabbed her arm, and hissed into her ear, "Stay where you are, an' keep your trap shut!" She struggled but he was too strong. How did he know what she planned to do?

As the guards ripped off Tiro's hood, Ji-ji screamed out a single, tortured word: "*TIRO!*"

Williams dropped the Grim Reaper. The blade clattered to the floor.

In a torrent of fury, Williams bent down and ripped off the masking tape covering the traitor's mouth. The fly-boy on the platform cried out, confirming what the seeds already knew.

"Don't lynch me! I been trying to tell you! YOU GOT THE WRONG DAMN MULE!"

IIIIIIIIIIIIII

As Marcus Shadowbrookseed knelt sobbing on the patriarchal platform, a larger-than-life image of his face appeared on the double screens. A split second later, both screens went black.

Dip, giddy with relief, forgot about Ji-ji's tender back and wrapped her arms around her friend. Chaos ensued as the steaders tried to figure out what had happened. Emmeline Shadowbrook rushed up to Lotter to plead her favorite's case.

They weren't out of the woods yet. However calm Lotter looked, he would be seething inside. Marcus could be lynched just cos Lotter needed to save face. Ji-ji glanced over at Coach Billy, who gave her a barely perceptible nod. He must've known all along that Tiro was safe. She looked around for her mam but Silapu had disappeared.

After conferring briefly with Inquisitor Worthy, Lotter strode up to the podium again. He ordered the technicians to turn the screens back on. When his handsome face loomed large over the hall, Lotter spoke. In a tone of righteous indignation, he described how Marcus Shadowbrookseed had been on official business for the diviner yesterday when he had been caught near the fry-fence.

"It is regrettable that this Mule's resemblance to the traitor—in addition to the fly-boy uniform he was wearing—caused the guards to misidentify him as Tiro Williamsmule."

Lotter paused and scanned the dining hall before continuing.

"As *The One True Text* teaches us, 'the Lord droppeth His mercy from heaven.' Inquisitor Worthy, the Lord's true disciple, has decided to show Diviner Shadowbrook's seed . . . mercy." An astonished cheer went up from the seed section. Lotter continued: "I hereby decree that Marcus Shadowbrookseed, who performed well in the flyer trials, will represent Planting 437 as our flyer-battler rep in the Big Race."

The seed section erupted into wild applause. *Let that be all,* Ji-ji thought. *Please, let that be all.*

"Unfortunately," Lotter continued, "this episode sheds light on new conspirators. . . . Coach Billy Brineseed is guilty of treason. I sentence him to twenty years of hard labor in the Rad Region. Guards, *arrest him*!"

Amid vigorous protests from seeds, guards stepped forward and hoisted Billy from his seat.

"It is a sad thing to witness a fall like yours, Coach Brineseed," Lotter told him. "Your association with Traitor Dreg—" Lotter spat on the floor to show how the Tribal had dishonored the Territories. "—should have prompted my predecessor to take action against you. You have been corrupting those in your charge, turning fly-boys into Wild Seeds and Deviants."

Billy's bass voice reverberated through the hall: "Tiro's escaped! Flown the coop! Others will too! Prophet Dregulahmo was right! Heads of midnight! *All* of us! *RISING!*"

"Shut him up! *NOW!*" Lotter boomed.

One of the guards struck Billy in the head with the butt of his rifle. The coach fell to the floor. Lotter looked over at Ji-ji, a slight flicker in his unnaturally blue eyes.

"As for our runner representative, we have a worthy entrant for that part of the race too. . . . I hereby decree that Sloppy Casperseedmate will be this year's runner rep."

Gasps greeted the announcement. Lotter hadn't been looking at Ji-ji after all. He had been looking at Sloppy, who stood directly behind her.

This time, Lotter looked straight at Ji-ji. His ice-blue eyes pried her chest open.

"As for Jellybean Lottermule, my own seed, I have determined that her association with traitors must result in a less elevated role than the one she has heretofore enjoyed. Though I am convinced she was unaware of the fly-boy's treachery, and though his sexual deviancy, like that of his unnatural twin, no doubt means he did not defile her, she nevertheless associated with him, thus proving herself in dire need of reformation. Consequently, I am stripping her of her position as chief kitchen-seed. . . ." Lotter looked down, began reading off his tablet. "I hereby seedmate Jellybean Lottermule to Father-Man Brine, who has long petitioned for her to be a member of his homestead and has agreed to accept a botanical in need of Radical Pruning. I also decree that she is now, and ever shall be, petition-ineligible. She will labor, seedbirth, and die on the 437th, her birth planting."

He went on to remind them that the Propitious Gleaning would take place tomorrow, after the race reps had been given a suitable send-off.

"The Last Supper of the Spring is now over. Congratulations to our two planting reps. May they bring glory to the 437th. Sound the siren, Brother Williams. Master-Guard Falrenn, gather your patrolmen and your search hounds. We have a traitor to catch."

At last Ji-ji knew the real reason why Silapu had wanted to speak to her. She'd known about Brine. Silapu had betrayed her just like she'd betrayed Charra. Luck was a traitor—a parrot that perched itself on your shoulder so it could spy on your dreams.

While trumpets sounded to mark the end of the feast, guests began to file out of the hall. Matty Longsby gripped Ji-ji's arm even tighter. He signaled to a guard to grab her other arm.

In a flash, Longsby performed the Apparel Repudiation, ripping Ji-ji's apron off her body.

"Get your hands off her!" Dip cried. Longsby pushed the Tainted aside.

A small crowd clustered around Sloppy, who called out to Ji-ji as she passed. "Sorry, Jellybean. Guess you thought you were a shoo-in. Wish I could do a kith-n-kin for you after I get to Dream City, I really do. But alas, you're petition-ineligible."

The guards led Ji-ji outside, where Brine waited beside his old jalopy—a restored Chevy sedan older than he was. Silent Pete sat in the driver's seat, revving the engine. Fumes poured from the rusty exhaust. Stinky Brine drew back his hand and slapped Ji-ji's face, hard.

"That's for associating with Deviants," he told her. "Heard you let his pervert brother screw you too—the one Williams tractor-pulled. What a pretty threesome that must've made! Remember, there's plenty more where that came from. I'm known for keeping a tight rein on my seedmates."

"I got orders to accompany you," Lieutenant Longsby told Brine. "Gotta make sure the slut gets delivered safely. This one's slippery. Last thing we need is another runaway."

"I like 'em slippery. 'Sides, I got Silent Pete here to mow the bitch down if she gets flighty," he said, indicating his driver. Longsby didn't budge. Brine muttered, "Suit yourself."

Lieutenant Longsby shoved Ji-ji into the back seat and clambered in after her. Brine tottered round to the front passenger seat. Complaining about his stiff joints, he eased himself into it.

Ji-ji leaned her head against the window and fixed her eyes on the sky. The washed-out disc of a moon stared like the dead. Pain started to hammer at her back, as if her own spine had grown tired of being part of her body and had decided to beat its way out.

Soon, they were hurtling along the narrow, pitted road at thirty miles an hour.

It was dark inside the car. Ji-ji inched her hand toward the door handle. She would fling open the door and leap. It would likely kill her, but that scared her less than the purple path ahead.

Once again, Longsby thwarted her next move. He gripped her wrist in his and yelled a question at Brine. "What time you got, man? My damn watch is on the blink again. Got stuck on the same number. Flashin' on an' off. Drives me nuts. Started actin' up 'bout three weeks ago, round the time o' that filthy traitor's Death Day." Lieutenant Longsby spat out of the window to demonstrate his revulsion toward the traitor. "S'been drivin' me nuts ever since."

"Must be after midnight," Brine shouted back. "Time for bed—right, Jellybean?"

Longsby noticed her watch. "Hey, Mule, gimme that," he demanded. "Hurry up. Ain't got all day. What's a Mule flauntifyin' herself with a wristwatch for anyway?"

Ji-ji undid her watch and handed it to the lieutenant. He held it up to the moonlight and snickered. "This watch is *crap*! What's that damn mouse doing? Looks like one o' them grinnin' minstrel darkies. Strap's okay though." He held it up to his nose and sniffed. "Hmm. Genuine leather. Least the damn thing's not stuck on the same time. Tell you what? I'll let you keep my watch as a seedmating gift cos I'm nothin' if not merciful."

"Mule doesn't need seedmating gifts, Lieutenant," Brine said. "Not when she's got me."

Brine hooted with laughter and Longsby joined in. Silent Pete remained silent, his eyes glued to the light cones ahead. The fugitive siren started up. Its bloody wail snaked across the planting. The young lieutenant removed his watch and tossed it into her lap.

Ji-ji stared at the neon-green numbers, blinked hard, then stared again. She looked over at Matty, who was telling Brine a filthy joke about the pleasures of the seeding bed. She looked at the watch again. There they were, flashing in the dark. The same three numbers she'd heard before, numbers that could mean everything or nothing at all: **9:02 . . . 9:02 . . . 9:02 . . .**

PART TWO
FLIGHT

13 CONFESSIONALS

Ji-ji sat hunched over in the confessional, listening to the scratching of rats and screams of the dead. She knew she was imagining the screams . . . thought she was imagining them . . . prayed she was. . . . Beneath her, the rusted metal bars of the confessional felt like rods of ice.

In the pitch-black, battering-ram darkness of Brine's basement, Ji-ji struggled to cling to her only hope-rope—the numbers nine-zero-two, the person who'd contacted Tiro and met up with Uncle Dreg. Her grip on the hope-rope was loosening. Soon she found it impossible to believe the numbers meant anything at all. Matty wasn't her salvation. He was a lecher like the others. The numbers were a coincidence or some sick joke Lotter had devised to rub salt in the wound. Lotter was testing her, seeing if she would react to the numbers and prove herself a traitor. Her one meager source of light—the numbers on Matty's watch—stopped flashing. The battery must be dead.

Everything on the 437th was a trap, a mockery. The planting itself was laid out like a gigantic wagon wheel, the boundaries between the twelve homesteads its spokes. Seedmating was the worst mockery of all. Tomorrow, Brine would fasten a copper band to her ankle. His name would be engraved on the band in sprawling bold font. Her name would appear underneath his, in small, submissive letters: Mammy Jellybean Brineseedmate.

The truth punched her in the gut. There would be no Rising, no Freedom Miracle. It was nothing more than a dream created by an old man's wishfulness. Uncle Dreg was wrong. Love didn't dream seeds Free; hate caged them.

Longsby had switched off the basement's single light bulb. Though she couldn't see the bulb, she knew it hung by a thin cord from the ceiling in the moldy, dungeonlike basement. She yearned for its circle of pallid light—anything to relieve the nauseating pressure of the dark, anything to silence the scratching and screaming. Rats terrified Ji-ji almost as much as the dark. They nibbled on your body when you were asleep and hunted in hordes. Last year, after Felly Spareseed drank herself into a stupor while on granary duty, rats nibbled off most of her left ear. Ji-ji knew she had to stay awake. But that could be just as bad. Mad Ma Hennypen had been sane, pretty much, before she was locked in a confessional. Nowadays, she ranted about a Dimmer tribe who had visitationed her during her confinement. "The Tribe-Dim revealed to me the terriblest thing of all!" Ma Hennypen would exclaim, in that high-pitched, undulating voice of hers. When you asked her what that was, she'd say, "The Truth the Passengers knew! An' Dimmer-dead don't lie!"

Dip had been confined to a confessional too, by Trip Epson, her first steadermate, who liked to mature seeds "in the cask of the confessional." When the basement flooded, Dip had nearly drowned, caged and alone. Prior to her confinement in the confessional, the steader had plowed her till she'd been so sore down there she'd had to sprint to the steader's ice shed whenever she dared, yank up her skirt, and plop onto one of the ice blocks. After Epson stuffed her in a confessional again for looking at him "sly-eyed," Dip miscarried. By the time she was released, the rats had cleaned away every trace of her deadborn wombling. . . .

Ji-ji shivered. Impossible to believe it was the end of April. In Brine's basement it was winter. She could still feel Longsby's hands ranging over her body. The lieutenant had offered to deep-search her. Brine had opted to observe the process so he could "check its thoroughness."

"Be on the lookout for surprises, Lieutenant," Brine had said, as he stood near the basement stairs, watching. "Botanicals ferret away all kinds of crap. But don't de-hymenize her—that's a father-man's prerogative. Y'hear about the Mule on the 368th? Had a knife slid between her Hottentots. Slit her fathermate's throat while the poor bastard was midplow." Brine had slashed a gnarled finger across his throat. "This one was touted as fallow, but I got my doubts. You seen that Deviant Williamsmule dandy-flying around in my coop? On the last planting I was on we neutered the arrogants. No sense having a stableful of stallions when you got a whole bunch of mares in heat need proper plowing. A good culling's what's needed. Those fly-bucks strut around like they own the place. Came upon Marcus himself the other day dawdling near a restricted area.

You been mixing with Tainteds, Serverseeds, an' Deviants, so you'll need to undergo a thorough cleansing an' sluicing. Tomorrow, after the mating ceremony, you can make me a big batch of those mushroom tarts. Tasty they were. I'm fond of mushrooms."

With Ji-ji locked inside Brine's cramped confessional, the two men had mounted the stairs. Brine had called out in his cheese grater of a voice, "Hope you enjoy the company! Truffie screamed like a stuck pig, but these days she's real quiet an' well behaved." He'd aimed his flashlight at the darkest corner of the basement.

Ji-ji had spotted it then—a skeleton propped up in a confessional. She'd screamed in horror. Both men had roared with laughter.

"Yeah, Mule," Longsby had called back, "time to beg for forgiveness for e Lord is merciful. Let's hope you find His light down here in the dark."

She'd been alone in the dark for an hour . . . longer maybe. The fugi- e siren had gone silent soon after they'd descended into the basement. s it because they'd recaptured Tiro, or was it simply because the stead- lemanded their sleep? She wouldn't be there to meet him at the Salem ost. How long would he wait for her before he gave up? She thought rra, alone with the parrot. When Silapu was tempted to punch out ver's teeth again, who would stop her?

drew her knees to her chest for warmth. Her butt was numb with r fingers weren't much better. The pain in her back was too severe o lie down. From the far corner of the basement, she felt Truffie's ts boring into her. She tried to convince herself the skeleton wasn't d be a trick Brine used to intimidate botanicals. Yet something se and the way its pitiful head rested against the bars convinced eton wasn't a fake. Truffie's gnawed-to-whiteness bones warned it to whatever Brine had in store for her.

e had a candle. There was a bright moon tonight, but there dows in the moldy basement to let the moonlight in. Silapu bout wastefulness whenever Ji-ji burned a candle in her r she'd listened to Luvlydoll draw her last breath (*that rattle, e in her little chest*), Ji-ji couldn't overcome her fear of the less nights, she couldn't fall asleep without some source

pain. One moment she was burning up, the next she was ved it was the metaflu. With luck, she would be dead by d back against the bars as the darkness assaulted her. In her gnawing loneliness, she spoke aloud.

High as a kite—staggering around like some mad cow sufferer. I report it to Shadowy an' what does she do? The old cow tells *me* to bugger off! An' now that drug-sop's the planting flyer rep! . . . Not that the cropmaster's choice was . . . I'm not saying Lord-Father Lotter was wrong to select Marcus or anything like that—"

Longsby had chimed in then. He'd agreed that Marcus was an arrogant sonuvabitch, with his smooth-talking ways and dandified vocabulary. Visibly relieved not to have caused offense, Brine had taken up the steader cause again.

"That Williamsmule—he's even worse. You seen him at the traitor's Culmination? Dandification wings shaved into his scalp!" Brine had spat on the floor to proclaim his disgust for the two traitors. "I reported him. I know insolence when I see it. After I told Drex Williams about them wings he says, 'Don't you worry, Arnie. I got it covered.' Guess tonight proved he did at that." Brine had wheezed out a snicker.

Longsby had said, "Guess you're right, sir. Only . . ."

"Only what, man? Spit it out."

"Only Williams—genius though he is at insolence detection—snagged the wrong Mule. Williamsmule isn't caught yet." Longsby had turned back to face Ji-ji, inserting an eager hand under her shirt. "Dangerous to count your chicks 'fore they're hatched. You never know what's round the corner. Maybe Doomsday's lyin' in wait after all."

"You sound like one o' them Geddonites. All doom an' gloom an' falling sky when it's nothing more than a few bird droppings landing on their heads. Me, I like to think positive. You should too—a good-looking young stud like you. What are you anyway—seventeen? Nineteen at the most? Too young to be pessimizing. That Mule'll be caught before the cock crows, guaranteed. The new crop of search hounds is mean as the devil. An' don't forget that vicious biped's roaming around too. Tore Crate Juniper to pieces. He was muscled too, like you. Dumb as mud like most of them guards from hicksville, but brawny. I ask you, Lieutenant, how stupid do you have to be to venture out beyond the fry-fence to check on a howling mutant? Only thing left of Juniper was a wishbone. The rest was jam an' fleshcrumbs."

Brine had paused to splutter up some phlegm. A moment later he'd begun again.

"She's not near as pretty as her mam, is she? Guess I'll just have to close my eyes an' think of the Territories. Mark my words, Lieutenant, this Mule will bear fruit soon. How's that saying go?

"Plow a Mule and stake your claim
Leave her fallow and she's hell to tame.

"Pruning and plowing—that's what they need. . . . Check her good, Lieutenant. She could be carrying a fucking arsenal under that skirt. Think I want to come down here and get filleted with a fish knife?"

"No, sir," Longsby had replied. "Always better for a fathermate to be bone-in."

Brine had chortled. "I can see why Lotter likes you, Lieutenant. Bone-in . . . very good. . . . Happy to report there's no problem in that regard. Had some duds before couldn't carry to term, but this one looks like a breeder. Anyone ever tell you how much you look like him?"

"Nope," Longsby had replied. "Never."

It had taken Brine several seconds to catch the irony in the guard's voice. He'd chuckled again. "You had me there for a moment. Almost seemed like my funny bone'd been filleted after all."

When Longsby hadn't given any sign that he appreciated Brine's wit, the father-man's mood had swung back to petulance. He'd stomped his feet on the floor in an effort to warm them and complained he was freezing his balls off.

"This blasted homestead's wearing me out. Think the cropmaster'll hold on to Homestead 1 or pass it on to Williams?" (Longsby, deep into the pelvic region of the search, hadn't responded.) "Cos if he passes it on, I'll petition for Homestead 11. By then I'll have seeded this one. I'll be petitioning to demolish that blasted fly-coop too—use the land to start a hog farm. Petrus promised to sell me a few seed hogs to get me up an' running. I attended his seedmate's harvesting. You could tell Danfrith appreciated it. Lydia, her name was . . . or was it Linda? Tiny little thing. Don't know what Petrus saw in her. No tits to speak of. Find anything interesting yet, Lieutenant?"

Longsby had tossed a key ring to Brine.

For the first time since they'd entered his father-house, Brine had addressed Ji-ji directly.

"These your kitchen keys, Mule?" Ji-ji had nodded grimly. Satisfied, he'd switched back to Longsby. "Don't know what her mam was thinking letting her mix with them fly-boys. I'll be tearing down that fly-coop. It's a breeding ground for insurgency. I trust the Lord-Father knows I knew absolutely nothing about Billy's treachery. You'll assure him of that I hope, Lieutenant."

Longsby had glanced over his shoulder to say, "Sure. . . . You been to D.C., sir?"

"Hell no," Brine replied. "You?"

"Yeah, I been. Don't plan on going back to live among them Sodomit
again. You got no idea how bad it is up there. Only thing is, they've
ished that Dream Coop, an' there's a lot o' buzz around those fly-bo
the Dreamfleet, those pros. Rumor has it Wing Commander Cor
lookin' to cultivate a new squadron of flyer-battlers. Rake in b
dough."

"You advising me to hang on to the fly-coop then? Make a
down the road?"

Longsby shrugged. "I don't give a flyin' crap what you do
is an eyesore, if you ask me. Cropmaster Lotter, on the o
a puzzle. Could be he'll be pleased as punch to be rid of
he don't give a rat's ass either way. Or could be he'll h
subtle way he's got, where you don't notice a gun's p
till it's already blasted a hole in your good eye. Gue
cropmaster's unpredictable that way."

While Brine had mulled this over, Longsby h
Ji-ji. When he touched her back, she'd winced
diately demanded to know if the Mule was def
Lotter had been eager to dump her for a mod

"You accusin' the cropmaster o' somethi

Thrown into a tizzy, Brine swore the
him completely. He'd been silent for a wh

During the deep-search, Longsby
Dreg's map hidden in a secret pocket
her seed canal. But he'd lingered at
lecherous fingers under her girlcl
letting, which had come as a surpr
track of time during all the stres
snatched his hand away, sniffed
He'd sworn at her too, said sh

Brine had apologized: "Sc
ful for the warning. I'm n
Still, it'll be the sweeter f

Then, for the second
Brine had addressed Ji
bath tomorrow before

"Where are you, Bonbon? Do you miss me? Is someone looking out for you? I vowed to come an' save you but they've caged me. I can't come rescue you. . . . Tiro, you gotta find a way to rescue Bonbon, for my sake, okay? If you see Charra, tell her I'm proud of her. Promise me."

The pain in Ji-ji's back spread to her shoulders and neck. She steadied her breathing the way she'd trained herself to do when she'd battled injuries as a runner. She tried to keep Brine out of her head but he scurried in. Skunky Brine would be plowing her soon. Then she remembered she was bleeding. She hadn't known it was her time. The rats would smell it. Probably smelled the blood already. She'd been a fool. A fool to believe in her mam's promise of assistance and in Uncle Dreg's magic, a fool to believe in a lecher like Longsby . . . Even now, she could feel his hands deep-searching every crevice, hear the mockery in his voice when he said, "Let's hope you find His light down here in the—"

Ji-ji shot up. Her head struck the rusty metal bars, but she was too excited for the pain to register. *Find His light in the dark. Find His light!*

Ji-ji swiped her hands over the floor of the cage. Bars . . . concrete floor . . . Had she guessed right? *Please, God, please be merciful!*

She tried again, searching every inch of the confessional. No luck!

Defeated, Ji-ji fell back only to feel something small and hard . . . something lodged *inside* her girlcloth. Trembling, she reached up under her skirt, felt the girlcloth, felt the small, cold, alien thing lodged inside it. She pulled out a flat stick, no longer than her thumb. It was wet with her blood. No—it wasn't her blood. It smelled . . . different. Her desperate fingers found a tiny indentation on one side. She pressed it. Nothing. She pressed it again, harder this time.

The world lurched from pitch-darkness into a blessed cone of light!

The tiny flashlight was proof: Lieutenant Longsby was 9-0-2! Matty was a Friend!

Sobbing with relief, she brought the light to her lips and kissed it. As though it were the finger of an angel, she grasped the tiny light and waited for her savior to descend.

IIIIIIIIIIIIII

Ji-ji awoke to pitch darkness! She searched frantically for the light and found it in the folds of her skirt. She pressed the tiny indentation and it came on.

A pair of eyes stared at her! Eyes unlike any she'd ever seen—pupils black holes, irises pulsing white halos! She felt its death-breath, cold as ice and skin-close. She dropped the light and it turned itself off. She was plunged into darkness again!

Quick! Find it! Got it! Switch it on again. You were dreaming. The thing won't be there anymore.

Shaking like a leaf, she found the light, found the indentation, and pressed down hard.

The light came back on. She pointed it in the direction of the ghostly eyes. A few feet away, the Dimmer sat facing her in the confessional, cradling something in its arms.

PrettyBlack is pretty, the Dimmer said. *But he's very quiet. See?*

"Lua? . . . Is that you?"

The Dimmer thrust her deadborn into the air. His limp body slammed into the top of the cage but she didn't seem to notice. Part of the umbilical cord dangled from his navel, as if he were a light bulb that could be hung from the ceiling.

He's dead-dead, the Dimmer said, in an echoey, faraway voice, like someone calling up from the bottom of a deep well. *My angel. My PrettyBlack. Not Dimmer-dead, dead-dead. You can't nurse a dead-dead? A stone don't cry. . . . I pick him from the garbage. See?*

Lua the Dimmer scooted forward toward Ji-ji, her eyes two balls of flame coursing round the two black holes of her pupils. For a moment, the basement felt like it was on fire.

You FORGOT! the Dimmer cried, mad with wrath, reaching to grab her hair.

"No! Let go! I didn't forget you or Silas!"

You forgot everything! The book, the race . . . the boy with a head of wheat!

"No . . . I didn't! But . . . I don't know what they mean. I don't know a boy with a head of . . . Wait! Do you mean Matty? Is he the boy with the head of wheat?"

The Dimmer's flaming irises reverted to white halos spinning round her black pupils. You went blind if you looked in a Dimmer's eyes. Ji-ji tried to look away, but the eyes pulled her back.

I told you. No race till you dream with the dead. You let her kill my PrettyBlack! Why?

Again, Ji-ji tried not to look at the Dimmer's face, couldn't bear to see how much it looked like a bloodless, emaciated version of her Lua. But the strange voice transfixed her, pulling her eyes back to the menacing, white-rimmed pupils.

You let her do it, the Dimmer repeated. *I told you not to let her kill him. . . .*

"Bettieann didn't kill him," Ji-ji said, as forcefully as she could. "Your Silas . . . your PrettyBlack was a deadborn."

Ji-ji watched in horror as Lua opened her mouth like a snake . . . wider and wider till she dislocated her jaw. A shriek began in the bowels of the earth and rose up until the dead formed an earsplitting chorus! Ji-ji tried to cover her ears, but the sound came at her like a hurricane, a blast of mother-rage pushing her farther back into the bars of the confessional.

At last the shrieking died down, though Ji-ji ears still rang with it. The whole planting must've heard it. 9-0-2 must've heard it too. Why didn't he come and save her?

The Dimmer's jaw was still dislocated. It swung on its moorings. A terrible scraping sound as she shoved it back into place. She spat out two molars. They wriggled on the confessional floor like maggots. She picked them up, slotted one tooth back in place, and swallowed the other.

Ji-ji shrank back, appalled. She had to appease this creature—explain what happened.

"It was your pelvis," Ji-ji said. "Too narrow."

The Dimmer spat in her face. The spittle cut her cheek like ice chips.

Fool! You notice nothing! That bitch butchered my PrettyBlack an' you sat an' watched!

Ji-ji tried again. "He was a deadborn."

NO! PrettyBlack was no deadborn! My PrettyBlack was ALIVE!

As the last word bounced off the bars of the confessional, Ji-ji felt like she was falling. Could it be true? Was Silas a liveborn? The thought flayed her. She saw the pretty seedling in the boot box. He'd looked like he was sleeping. . . .

"I thought he was . . . she said he was—"

A lie! You could've saved him but you didn't! An' now look what you've done! Your turn next.

"What do you mean?"

You'll see. You'll see. . . .

The Dimmer rocked her dead-dead deadborn in her arms.

The murdered dead don't sleep! Me neither! Haven't slept in ages! So tired! No race till you dream with the dead!

"I'm . . . I'm dreaming with the dead now—is that what you're trying to tell me?"

This is no dream, dumbass! This is a waking!

Ji-ji almost laughed—would have if she hadn't seen the Dimmer's murderous expression.

Dimmers need appeasing, Silapu used to say. *They come back thirsty for revenge too aggrieved to sleep peacefully in the grave.* She needed to stay calm, think things through. This Dimmer was Lua-Dim, *her* Lua, her best friend.

"I called you a dumbass after he snatched Bonbon. I was scared. I lashed out. Forgive me."

The apology seemed to work. The Dimmer didn't yell at her this time. *Nothing worse than a snatching. You feel it in the long lonely. Leaves a hole inside you big as the grave.*

Pity flooded Ji-ji's chest. "If he was alive, I swear I didn't know it. You were my best friend. I would've run through fire for you. An' for him too."

The Dimmer kept rocking PrettyBlack, but it was no longer the frenzied rocking she'd been doing before. Now, the rocking was gentle. Somehow, as if a light had been switched on in her head, she knew Lua-Dim wouldn't hurt her.

She took a deep breath and asked the question Tiro would have wanted her to ask: "You run into Uncle Dreg-Dim? On your travels? If you, like, travel, I mean. . . ."

Lua-Dim shook her head. Some of her braids sifted down to the floor of the cage in wisps of smoke, as if she were only playing at being a solid thing. It broke Ji-ji's heart to see it.

PrettyBlack an' me are In-Between. I want him to suckle but he won't cos he's a dead-dead. Guess he don't have no rage in him. You need rage to join the Tribe. Or too much love so you gotta come back an' give some away cos over-love's a burden too. I got enough for the both of us but it don't revive him. Here. Lua-Dim offered her deadborn to Ji-ji. *Give PrettyBlack the kiss o' life an' bring him back to me.*

Ji-ji stared at the deadborn. "I can try," she offered. "But I don't think it'll work."

Ji-ji took the deadborn in her arms. He was freezing and light as a feather, as if he were made of air. His skin shone eerily in the dark, like something lit from within. Ji-ji noticed again how much he looked like Bonbon. They could have been brothers—twins almost. And all at once it seemed to her as if he really was Bonbon, returned to her so she could hold him one last time.

She brought his mouth to her mouth without revulsion and breathed into it lightly. Once . . . twice . . . many times. He smelled like nothing she had ever smelled before. A sweet, sad smell that reminded her of Sylvie's purple blossoms. With two fingers, she pressed down on his little chest the way Miss Clobershay had taught her, but he never opened his eyes.

In the end, Ji-ji had to admit it wasn't working. "I'm sorry, Lu. I really am."

My angel's dead-dead. Takes a while to wake from that, don't it, Ji-ji?

"Yes."

It was the first time they had addressed each other by name. Lua-Dim held out her arms. As gently as she could, Ji-ji handed PrettyBlack back to her best friend.

See these holes, Lua-Dim said, and turned him over. Two wounds were visible on his back.

"Bettieann had to use forceps," Ji-ji explained. "Guess they must've punctured his—"

Lua-Dim's eyes flared momentarily: *NO! You gotta pay attention! You gotta wake up!*

Lua-Dim kissed his wounds. When she looked up, her mouth was covered in blood.

"Blood! On your mouth! He's bleeding!"

Lua-Dim nodded. More of her braids sifted down to the floor of the confessional. *You breathed 'em open.* Lua-Dim stared up at a place above their heads. *See the blackbirds climb up inside the spiral-dark an' fly a way home!*

Ji-ji looked up. She couldn't see the spiral-dark or the blackbirds but she dared not admit it. Instead, she asked the other question plaguing her.

"Am I dead?"

You're an angel. Like Silas.

Ji-ji shook her head. "No I'm not. Angels are beautiful."

Yes, you are.

"I'm sorry I was scared when I saw you. It was . . . a shock. Oh Lu, I've missed you so much. I didn't mean to let you down. I didn't know you needed C-sectioning. I was a dumbass."

Lua-Dim, who was tickling her deadborn's stiff toes, didn't seem to hear her.

Ji-ji tried to shift to a more comfortable position, but the tight space made it difficult. Something stabbed her in the back when she moved. She moaned in pain.

Burdens—that's the moaning. Burdens an' old wounds. I got 'em too. My arms hurt from carrying PrettyBlack from In-Between to Nowhere. Had to dig him up with my bare hands.

"I thought you said you found him in the gar— . . . Never mind."

They snatched him. Wouldn't bury us together. You know that?

Ji-ji hesitated. "No."

Lua-Dim stared at her. *Liar. You ain't good at it neither.*

"I didn't know for sure."

But you knew for unsure*. . . . Do you confess it then? Do you confess you didn't save him, even though in your marrowbone you knew?*

Wretched, Ji-ji said, "You're right. I didn't save him. Turns out I need to be saved myself."

PrettyBlack an' me is froze to the marrowbone.

Ji-ji was scared to ask the next thing in case Lua-Dim said yes. But she looked so miserable, and Ji-ji felt so guilty about everything, that she asked it anyway.

"Want me to try an' hold you, Lua-Dim? Keep you warm? PrettyBlack too?"

More'n life, Angel. If only you could.

The black holes of Lua-Dim's pupils seemed to be growing larger. With her weird solar-eclipse eyes, she looked at Ji-ji, who braced herself against the pain in her back and shunted closer. Ji-ji wrapped her arms around them both. It was like snuggling up to ice-cold cotton candy.

"Does this help any?"

Oh yes!

Lua-Dim rested her head on her best friend's shoulder. Ji-ji flinched as a blade of bitter cold cut through her, but she would rather die than push them away. She snuggled even closer.

"Lua-Dim, can I trust the boy with the head of wheat? Is he really a Friend?"

You were my best friend. Don't forget me. Don't forget my angel either.

"Never. I promise."

Ji-ji looked down at Silas-Dim. Apart from the fact that he was dead, he looked real pretty.

"I love you, Lua."

I love you too, Ji-ji Silapu. More'n life.

"Silapu is Mam's name, remember? I'm—"

Ji-ji Silapu.

Ji-ji hesitated. She hated the name Lottermule but her mam was a parrot. She made two decisions. First, assuming she wasn't dead already, she would pick her own damn name. Second, she wouldn't share her decision with Lua-Dim. No need to awaken the wrath of a Dimmer again.

Lua-Dim chanted softly as she rocked her deadborn, her voice different—older, wiser.

Blackbird, pretty bird, take to the sky.
Bye-bye, Blackbird, time to die . . .

Ladybird, Ladybird, fly a way home,
Your tongue is a flame, your offspring all gone.

Rockabye baby on the tree top
When the wind blows, the cradle will rock
When the bough breaks the cradle will fall
And up will rise PrettyBlack, Cradle and all.

Blackbird, pretty bird, take to the sky.
Bye-bye, Blackbird, time to fly . . .

Ji-ji listened more carefully this time, listened for clues the way she'd learned to listen to Afarra.

"Lu, are you talking about Uncle Dreg? About Sylvie's limb breaking at the Culmination? Is that what you mean? Is it a cradle like the one Uncle Dreg made? Or is it the Cradle where he came from?" But Lua-Dim's eyes were growing heavy. In no time at all, she was fast asleep.

Ji-ji snapped off Matty's tiny light. She wasn't alone anymore. No need to fear the dark.

IIIIIIIIIIIIII

What was that shuffling? *Rats!*

"*Shhh!* It's only me."

"Matty? Is that you?"

"Were you expecting someone else?"

It didn't sound like him. Was this a trick? Where was Lua-Dim?

Ji-ji found the light and pressed it. Matty. 9-0-2 kneeling beside the cage, fiddling impatiently with the lock and cussing under his breath.

"Point it over here. Can't see a bloody thing."

Ji-ji aimed the light at the lock. It caught Matty's profile. "I knew you'd come."

"Hold it steady."

"You a Friend?"

"What do you think? Sod it! What the hell is the problem with this damn lock?"

"You're talking weird. Don't sound like you. You got a funny accent."

"So do you."

"No I don't."

"Shut up, and hold the damn light steady."

Her confession slipped out before she could stop it: "I saw Lua. She came back as a Dimmer. You see her too?" What was she thinking? She tried to take it back. If he thought she'd gone mad he could abandon her. Quickly she added, "Could've been dreaming. Could've been those killers I took for pain."

Matty stopped fiddling with the lock and looked at her. "Lua-Dim? Lua, you mean? The Petrus girl who died in childbirth?"

She felt giddy with joy. He'd said *girl* and *childbirth*. More proof he was no steader.

"You're helping me escape, right?"

"Not if this damn padlock won't . . . co . . . oper . . . ate. . . ."

"Think Brine'll hear us?"

"Bastard's out like a light. I slipped a little something extra in his whiskey."

"Why'd you come back for me, Matty?"

"Just following orders."

"From who?"

"Whom."

"What?" She waited for him to say something, but he was too busy fighting with the rusty padlock. She tried again. "They're after me, right? They think I'm a threat."

"Steaders are paranoid as hell. Think Toteppi are out to get them—uppity females, in particular. This lock's a pain . . . in . . . the . . . arse!"

"But you've come to rescue me."

"Friends like to side with underdogs. Never met a Friend who didn't have a Messiah complex. Now let me concentrate. If I can't undo this bloody . . . lock . . . we're both up shit creek without a paddle."

At last, he managed to force the padlock open. He slipped out the bolt and opened the door to the cage.

"Free at last," he said, like someone who'd wanted to make a joke then decided halfway through it was a bad idea. He held out his hand to help her.

Ji-ji could barely move. Her body was a maelstrom of cramps and nerve endings.

"C'mon. We need to get out of here," he said, half dragging her out of the confessional.

"My back. . . . I hurt it."

"In the flying coop, I know. You slammed down hard on that bench."

"You saw us? You were watching? Why didn't you tell us?"

"S'a long story. Think you can walk?"

"I'll try. . . . You coming with me?"

"No. *You're* coming with *me.*"

"Mam's a parrot. She told Lotter about Uncle Dreg."

Ji-ji hadn't meant to blurt that out either, but all her rescuer said was "Yep. I know."

"You do? How? Did Lotter tell you? Does anyone else know? You seen Afarra? I couldn't find her. Did Tiro escape? Is he okay?"

Matty was ordering her to zip it when the floor upended itself and some sadist started hammering nails into her back. Any minute she planned to make him stop. She spied Lua-Dim in the corner, rocking her deadborn. PrettyBlack was suckling at last. Lua-Dim looked up and waved. Ji-ji attempted to wave back, but Lua-Dim and PrettyBlack changed into skeletons and faded away altogether just as something very large keeled over.

Wow, Ji-ji thought to herself. *That large thing is me.*

Darkness. She reached for the light again. This time it was gone for good.

14 A TOWER OF STONE

She lay very, very still. She'd learned to do this as a seedling—check it was safe before she let anyone know she'd woken up. Too late. He'd seen her stirring.

"So . . . you've decided to return to the land of the living," he said.

How long had he been kneeling beside her? She smelled weed and Brine's booze on his breath. He got up and moved a few yards away, sat down, took out a hunting knife, and began sharpening it. The blade glinted in the dim light from a small, battery-powered lamp.

Ji-ji sat up with some difficulty, discovered he'd laid a blanket over her. In the faint light, she could see that they were on some kind of wooden platform with railings and a flight of stairs nearby. She had a tender lump on the right side of her forehead.

She leaned up against the cold stone wall behind her and scanned for an exit. She'd have to slip by him to reach the stairs. Maybe she could trust him? He hadn't sliced her throat. Hadn't raped her yet as far as she knew. At least she'd escaped from Brine's horrifying basement. Had Lua-Dim been real? Was PrettyBlack truly a dead-dead before she'd given him CPR? It had felt so real—realer than real. She pushed it aside. She needed to get her bearings, focus on the here and now.

"Where is this place?" she asked, groggily.

"The shot tower," he replied. His voice was gruff, unfamiliar. "It's fairly soundproof, but we can't take chances so keep your voice down. Greenshirts could be patrolling nearby."

Weird to hear him refer to the guards as "greenshirts" like he wasn't one himself. Although it was too dark to discern color, Ji-ji knew he was wearing a planting guard's olive shirt with the 437th's crest sewn onto the breast pocket. And she knew the skinny tie he wore was yellow. His accent made her wary again. He'd fooled her before, hadn't he? Made them all believe he was from someplace in the Territories. Maybe this was another disguise? She found it impossible to merge his face with his foreign accent. It was like talking to the ventriloquist's dummy the steaders trotted out to entertain seedlings after the Seed Symbol Ceremony. She half expected the old Matty to step out from the darkness and expose the lie.

"But the shot tower's in a restricted zone. S'been boarded up for—"

"Your head hurt? You feel like throwing up?"

"No. Not much."

"Good. Probably don't have a concussion. Your back still sore?"

"No. Not sore like it was before."

He seemed satisfied with that response. "So . . . what's a 'head of feet'?" he asked.

"What?"

"Kept going on about a 'head of feet.' You still seeing ghosts?"

She must have been muttering about a head of wheat. Must've been dreaming about Lua-Dim. "No," she said, more vehemently than she'd intended. "Had a stupid nightmare is all. How long've I been out?"

"About an hour, give or take."

"An hour!"

"Keep your voice down."

"But that's way too long!" She attempted to stand but a wave of nausea came over her. "Dawn's coming," she said weakly. "We gotta get going."

"Sit down. Dawn's always coming. No siren yet, which means they don't know you're not tucked up in Brine's seed box with your little pal."

Ji-ji didn't know if he was referring to Lua-Dim or the skeleton.

"How do we escape? You found a way to turn off the fry-fence?"

Instead of responding, Longsby started rummaging through a large duffel bag, checking its contents. She couldn't identify all the things he pulled out because it was too dark, but she was able to make out a hefty hope-rope coiled up like a snake, some clothes, a flashlight, and something that looked like a screen reader. He'd come prepared.

As she struggled to quell her nausea, Ji-ji rifled through her memory and pulled out things Uncle Dreg had told her about the tower. Hearing his voice in her head calmed her.

Founding Father Bartholemew had transported the seventy-five-foot tower from some place near Austinville and Barren Springs in the Old Commonwealth of Virginia. He'd ordered his followers to reassemble the imposing limestone tower stone by stone. The cropmaster had wanted it to symbolize the steaders' attachment to history and testify to their forefathers' ingenuity. According to Uncle Dreg, once upon a time people had made shot by dropping molten lead through a sieve at the top of the tower into cooling water at the bottom. Bartholemew had the tower reassembled near the Lower Creek so the edifice would look like it actually functioned. As time passed, the seeds and steaders had given it different names. Some of the most popular were Big Dick, Middle Finger, and the Pencil. Ji-ji liked the last name best because both pencils and the tower—formerly, at least—used to house lead. Tiro had shot a hole in that theory when he'd told her graphite was used in pencils, not lead. Nevertheless, Ji-ji liked that name. Whenever they spotted the tower, caged inside barbed wire and half submerged by foliage, she liked to imagine botanicals using it as a secret classroom before a progressive successor to Bartholemew founded Planting 437's legacy school for seeds. She would picture the seedlings sitting in a ring learning about the Cradle, with Uncle Dreg in the middle to guide them. When she was older, Uncle Dreg told her the real story.

After the tower had been resurrected, the seeds who'd labored to build it had been permitted to obtain tower passes and go inside. They could mount the new wooden staircase (the original couldn't be salvaged) and gaze through the window. From there, they could see over the fry-fence into the wilderness beyond.

"Height is a sorceress," the Tribal wizard told Ji-ji and Tiro as they sat beside the crackling fireplace in his cabin. "She begets dreams of flight, which is why the steaders fear her. The seeds who were given passes saw the world laid out below them. As they gazed down upon it, a wild yearning to rise put down roots inside their heads. One night, a construction-seed, one of the stonemasons, climbed the stairs to the top of the tower and stood where the window was located. Then, without permission, he leapt. The next year, another tower laborer did the same. Soon afterward, there was a third Unnatural Leaping. For the planting to survive, soaring had to be caged. Cropmaster Bartholemew boarded up the tower and restricted access to the land surrounding it. These days, in the era of Elevation Prohibitions, the only place where seeds can soar is inside the cage. And that is why the shot tower tells a story of deep yearning written in stone. Its long shadow tells time. But one day, that time will be ours again."

Tonight, Ji-ji felt the truth of that story pulsing around her, as though every seed and every Middle Passenger who had thought about leaping into air or ocean was calling to her to join them. She became one of the seeds compelled to jump, still clutching her tower pass, the slip that would set her Free.

Ji-ji couldn't see the boarded-up opening when she peered up into the gloom, yet she felt the seeds' yearning in her throat and lungs. When Matty spoke again, his voice startled her so much she let out a small scream. Matty, as jumpy as she was, leapt up and drew his gun.

"What's wrong?" he asked. "You hear something?"

"No. Sorry. . . . I was thinking."

"Well don't."

"You mad at me?" she asked.

Her question seemed to surprise him. He holstered his weapon and sat down again.

"Not particularly," he said.

"Who you mad at then?" No response. She tried another tack. "Your voice . . . it's different."

"So you said before you went out like a light."

"You're a Cross-Ponder from the Old Country, right? There's no seeds there, only Freedom."

"Yeah. The Old Country, as steaders like to call it, is paradise all right. Awash in Freedom and bliss. Sounds as if Zyla taught you all kinds of things. No surprise of course. Zyla gets her jollies from taking risks."

"Zyla? Miss Clobershay? You knew her?" Ji-ji put two and two together. "Miss Clobershay is a Friend of Freedom! I *knew* it!"

"Unfortunately, you weren't the only one who discovered that little nugget. And how many times do I have to tell you? Keep your voice down. Want to let Lotter know you're hiding out in Middle Finger?" Still angry, he veered back to Zyla. "Zy was a fool. Bitch almost got herself killed."

"She was good to me—to all of us seeds."

"And guess who had to pay for Zyla's goodness? Her Friends, that's who. Four people died escorting good Miss Clobershay through The Margins."

The lieutenant reached into his bag, pulled out something wrapped in cloth, and tossed it over to her. "Here. Bread and cheese. Eat. You'll need your strength. We've got a long road ahead."

"The Salem Outpost is less than thirty miles east, as the crow flies. We can make it in time for the Freedom Race if we—"

"Shut up and eat."

Matty retrieved some documents from his bag and began rifling through them. When he held them near the lamp, she caught a glimpse of the Territorial seal. Authorization Papers! If he had Papers Proper they could travel through The Margins without fear of Bounty Boys. Was her name on one of them? She was desperate to ask if it was, and if so, how he managed to get hold of the precious documents. But it was clear by now that any inquiry on her part would be greeted with sarcasm or outright hostility. She forced herself to focus on the food instead.

She hadn't thought she was hungry, but as soon as she bit down on the bread and popped the first hunk of cheese into her mouth she realized how wrong she'd been. Too nervous to eat much of anything at the Last Supper, Ji-ji was ravenous. All she'd had since the bread and honey Afarra had left for her yesterday morning was a few spoonfuls of the Last Supper dishes.

Soon, chewing calmed her; the dreadful feeling of suffocation lessened. Feeling stronger, Ji-ji decided to speak again. If it pissed him off so be it.

"We gotta get going," she stated. "Meet up with Tiro in Salem in a couple days for the start of the Freedom Race. Won't get there in time otherwise. Are we heading out soon?"

"We head out when I say so."

He took a wallet from his back pocket and began counting paper money.

"Are those trade dollars? How many you got?"

"Not nearly enough."

His reply scared her. Though his irritation grew with every question, she couldn't be left in the dark again. She'd trained herself to plan everything to the last detail. If she didn't, she could miss something important—a razor blade left near the pit latrine in the outhouse, or a friend's C-sectioning need, or where a fly-boy would run to make his Unnatural Leap. . . . Seeds had to be vigilant, gobble up info and store it for the future. It ambushed you otherwise.

"You think we can make it to Salem in time? It's not far. I can run most of the way."

No response. He didn't even bother to give that callous shrug he'd used around Brine.

She didn't want to admit to herself how much steaderness there was in his treatment of her. She'd always imagined Friends of Freedom as gentle and kind.

"How come you brought me here?"

Matty glanced over at her. "Shot Tower's a layover station. An underground tunnel leads here from the Doom Dell." He couldn't resist taking another jab. "The entrance to the tunnel's only a stone's throw from where you attempted to slit my throat—remember? We came up through a concealed trapdoor in the floor down below. Then I carried you up the stairs to this platform. Don't fancy doing it again either. You're heavier than you look. Finish eating that bread and take a swig of this." He took a long draught from an oversize flask before handing it to her.

"What is it?"

"Nectar. Fruit of the gods. Drink."

She hesitated for a moment, then raised the flask to her lips. The liquid lit up the back of her throat, then put the fire out. She raised it to her lips and drank again.

"Like mother, like daughter," he said, and laughed. Mortified, she handed the flask back to him. He rummaged around in his bag, pulled out a bottle, twisted off the cap, and handed her a pill.

"What is it?"

"An analgesic. Extra-strength painkiller."

"The pain's not bad right now. I don't need—"

"Take it. Your back looks like shit."

How did he know that when he hadn't removed her clothes for the deep-search? Ji-ji suddenly realized that her tan-and-brown-striped kitchen-seed skirt was gone. Her blouse too. While she was out cold, the fairskin must've removed her clothes. She wore a clean seed shift with the customary black-and-white Muleseed symbol. He'd seen everything. Touched everything. And not through her clothes this time. Why not wait till she'd come to and could dress herself?

"You dressed me," she said softly, meaning, *Why did you undress me? You do anything else?*

"Don't get your knickers in a twist. Trust me, you weren't tempting. You were a mess—covered in hog's blood and muck from Brine's confessional."

"Hog's blood? Oh."

He must've faked her bloodletting with hog's blood. Made sure Brine wouldn't want to sample her. For a moment, she was grateful. The moment passed as soon as he spoke again.

"Snarlcats'd smell a treat like you a mile off. Stripers too. Don't worry. I didn't see anything I haven't felt before. Now take the bloody pill."

Ji-ji swallowed the killer down with another swig from the flask because she didn't want to ask for the water canteen, assuming he had one. Didn't want to ask him for anything.

Afterward, they sat without speaking. When she couldn't bear the silence any longer (she kept imagining the whine and stutter of the fugitive siren and the cries of seeds leaping from the window above), she asked him how old he was. She wanted to put him on the defensive, prove he didn't intimidate her.

"Older than you," he said.

"You got family back in . . ." She didn't want to be ridiculed for calling it the Old Country. "You got family back in England?"

"Nope. But luckily I've got thousands of ready-made Friends right here."

"You mad at me?"

"You asked me that already. No wonder you drove your mam to drink."

He took another swig from his flask. He had to tilt it way back. Then he took out a weed stick and lit it with a lighter. Greenshirts were notorious for getting high on duty. They had generous weed rations—a way to get them to remain on plantings in the middle of nowhere and do without the company of fairskin women. Matty pulled long and hard on his pacifier as Ji-ji watched the tiny red embers flare. *Don't let him be too high to get me to Salem,* she thought. She tried again.

"The fry-fence is livid with volts. I don't understand how—"

"No point in telling you what's about to happen if there's a damn good chance it won't."

Ji-ji's heart fell. "How come you're helping me?"

"Told you. I've got orders."

"But you don't seem like—"

"Like what?"

She refused to back down. Steaders had forced her to do that all her life. "Like a Friend."

"You saying I'm a selfish sonuvabitch? Well, the truth of the matter is, I'm not exactly a Friend. I'm an . . . associate—what Friends call a Freelancer."

"What's that?"

"A private contractor."

"You mean . . . fairskins rescue seeds for money?"

"Yeah, shocking, isn't it? Who knew the world wasn't all fairy dust and cupcakes?" The liquor and weed had loosened his tongue: "Okay. I can tell you're not going to let a man smoke in peace, so listen carefully, Jellybean Lottermule, and learn something. Maybe you'll keep your trap shut after this." He took another long drag from his weed stick and washed it down with booze.

"The Friends don't have too many fairskins in their ranks who'll risk a stint on a planting. It's a simple transaction. They reward me upon delivery. Just my luck to draw the short straw—twice, if you can believe it—hence the return of the Prodigal Son to his lookalike Lord-Father. Just when I think my bad luck's about to run out, I was picked to be the backup deliverer of the Friends' Grand Prize."

"Grand Prize?"

"You. The Existential."

Hadn't he said something earlier, before she fell out, about spying on her and Tiro in the fly-coop? For that reason, and because she knew he would enjoy catching her in a lie, she didn't bother pretending she'd never heard that word before.

"So that part was true?" she said. "The steaders believe I'm an existential threat. You wrote that in the note you sent to Tiro. You're not doing any of this cos you believe in Freedom?"

"On the contrary, Jellybean. I believe very much in Freedom. My own, in particular. I'm deeply religious too. I have boundless faith in these." He grabbed a fistful of dollars and waved them in the air. "I'll also admit to harboring an antipathy toward steaders. Your father-man's a case in point. Some of the sick things that bastard's done don't bear repeating. . . . But if you're asking me whether I'd risk torture and death for no reward whatsoever . . ." He cocked his head to one side and pretended to ponder the question for a second. "Answer's no. But I would risk a lot for several thousand SuperState dollars and a one-way ticket to paradise."

Ji-ji was silent for a while. Her fairskin savior was nothing like she thought he would be. Eventually she said, "Are they right about me? Am I an existential threat to the Territories?"

He shrugged. "Apparently, Dreg thought you were. Christ, he had some weird theories about you."

"Like what?"

"Sorry, Jellybean. Already got a half-hysterical seed on my hands. Don't want to exacerbate the situation. Besides, while we're on the 437th, the less you know the better."

"But you said in your note—"

"That was Drex Williams said you were an existential threat, not me. Overheard him and Petrus plotting to get rid of you. Had to let my contact know, 'specially as I was charged with angelship over you."

"Angelship?"

"What the Friends call it. They're corny as hell. Bloody self-righteous too. Lotter interceded—persuaded Herring not to kill you. By then it was too late. I'd already sent the note to my contact. Assumed it was Dreg. Lo and behold, turns out it's your fly-boy. Everyone knew the comm was compromised. Absolute moron."

Ji-ji had forgotten to ask the most important question of all: "Did Tiro escape?" she asked. "Is he safe?" Too late. Matty was done with the conversation.

By now, her eyes had adjusted to the gloom. She studied Matty Longsby to see what she could learn.

He might be two or three years older than she was, but he wasn't two or three years smarter. Couldn't control his anger. Smoked and drank too much. Sounded as bitter as her mam. She kept an eye on his knife so she could grab it and slit his throat if he turned traitor. Could she do that? Kill a man who wasn't exactly a Friend but not exactly a steader either? Seemed like she'd been trying to kill Matty Longsby for months. Maybe the third time would be the charm? But those attempts hadn't been cold-blooded murder; those had been war. She'd never killed anything except a few chickens and a piglet once for a roast. The poor piglet saw her coming and got scared. Fear and her clumsy killing soured the meat—or so Crabstreet claimed. Dip had volunteered to do the kitchen killing after that. Said strangling a chicken or slicing the neck of a goat relieved her of her murder-thirst.

Matty looked at his watch—*her* watch. On his wrist it looked ridiculous. He must've punched another hole in the braided leather strap Uncle Dreg had made—the only thing she had to remember the wizard by. She doubted Matty would give it back to her. "In fifteen minutes we leave," he announced.

A noise down below, in the well of the tower!

In spite of the weed and booze, Matty was on his feet before Ji-ji had time to blink, his gun drawn. Another noise, followed by a shuffling! "*Shit!*" he whispered. "Get under the blanket and stay quiet. If you get the chance, make a run for it. We got someone waiting to switch off the fence."

Someone was waiting for them. A Friend at the fry-fence. But it was too late! They'd been discovered! If she couldn't make a run for it, she knew what she had to do. Climb up to the window, rip the boards off with her bare hands, and leap into the night. Better to fly for an instant than endure what Lotter and Brine would do to her. Then she remembered Matty's hunting knife. She could grab it and help him fight them off. She was Toteppi. She couldn't leave him to fight alone.

A door creaked open. *The trapdoor he talked about? Must be.* Doom clambered up through the tower as Ji-ji readied herself to grab the knife from Matty's bag. The lieutenant cussed under his breath as he gripped his handgun. The steaders would take their time torturing him, burn an *F* onto his cheek, castrate then hang him. Matty's fate would be even worse than hers.

He didn't wait for them to ascend. Keeping his wits about him, he demanded to know who was there: "S'that you, Casper?" he yelled down in his lieutenant's voice. "Lotter send you?"

He strode to the top of the wooden stairs and peered over into the well of the tower. All movement stopped. Three seconds of silence. Four. . . . The silence was broken by a female voice.

"Lucky? Lucky Dyce?"

"What the hell . . . ?" he exclaimed.

Ji-ji knew that voice almost as well as she knew her own. Ignoring the pain in her back, she jumped up, tore over to the stairs, and shoved Matty aside. Before he could stop her, she leapt down the narrow wooden stairs two and three at a time till she stood before the parrot.

"*You betrayed us!*" she cried. She leapt at Silapu, knocking the flashlight from her hand. It clattered to the ground. She grabbed a fistful of hair and pulled.

Two strong hands grasped her from behind and pried her away. While she struggled to Free herself from the lieutenant's grip, she spotted another intruder, climbing up through the trapdoor. The parrot had brought reinforcements!

Matty saw the figure too. He flung Ji-ji to the floor and reached for his handgun.

"*Don't shoot!*" Silapu cried, leaping between the gun and the intruder.

Ji-ji stared into the gloom in amazement. The intruder stared back.

"*Dip!*" Ji-ji exclaimed. "What are you doing here?"

"Wild Seedin' it with you an' Sila."

"But . . . I don't understand . . ." Ji-ji said.

Matty's gun was still aimed at Dip's head. "Keep your voices down! Who's she?"

"She is with me," Silapu told him. "She is coming with us."

"Like hell she is," Matty said, but he lowered his gun.

Silapu approached her daughter and wiped her wet cheeks with her sleeve. She took Ji-ji's face in her hands and kissed her on the forehead.

"I am no parrot," Silapu said. "I am Toteppi. And so are you. And now, we must hurry."

"Who's Lucky?" Ji-ji asked.

"He is," Dip said, nodding over at Matty. "An' so are we. Sila told me, an' Uncle Dreg told her she could trust him."

Silapu turned to Lucky and said, "Dreg told me your name and where to find you and Ji-ji if everything went south. One of the things he decided to tell the truth about, yes? He told me how to find the entrance to the tunnel too. This is my friend Dip. She is coming with us."

Dip stepped forward. "You don't remember me, do you, Lieutenant? Dipthong Spareseed. I helped you hold Ji-ji back when she was on a suicide mission in the dining hall. Used to be a kitchen-seed but I just self-promoted to fugitive status."

The lieutenant said he decided who got promoted and who didn't. Dip was unfazed.

"Seeing as how we're baptizing ourselves, you can call me Donna from now on. Sloppy's picked Delilah for her race name—thinks it's better suited to a runner rep. I decided to pick one too. Don't want to embarrass Delilah in Dream City with a Dipthong."

The lieutenant lit into Silapu: "Dregulahmo told you about this place? The old man wasn't supposed to disclose my name or the layover station. It's a breach of protocol."

"Dreg did not want you to shoot me," Silapu said simply. "You can punish him later."

"You know how close I came to blasting your head off?" He holstered his gun, said, "The Tainted stays behind."

Dip, who was carrying a potato sack filled to bursting, dropped it to the floor. "Well, you gotta shoot me first cos I'm not staying on the 437th, not without Slop. Knew Sila was up to something. Felt it in my bones. Packed my sack an' went to find her. An' there she is on her way out the door! It's destiny."

"You realize you could've been followed?" Matty told Silapu before turning his attention to Dip again. "You're too fat to run. You'll never make it."

"Don't you worry 'bout me, Mr. Lucky. I can keep up with the best of 'em if I got search hounds on my tail."

The lieutenant turned his back on them in disgust and bounded back up the stairs.

"Where's he off to?" Dip asked.

"Probably going to get his bag," Ji-ji replied.

"Hmm," Dip continued, speaking softly so he wouldn't hear her.

"Don't seem like the Friendly type to me. He been drinking? Got that liquor breath. An' some powerful weed too. You smell it, Sila? Seems jumpy. Let's hope we don't got ourselves a dud. Guess we gotta believe the Oz knew what he was doing when he chose him."

Ji-ji addressed her mam: "You're not a parrot then?"

Dip, who always spoke a lot when she was nervous, leapt in: "She *played* parrot all right. But Dreg put her up to it. Told her it was Zaini the steaders was after, only it was Tiro. An' your mam's forgiven the wizard, pretty much—right, Sila? Not cussing him out near as much. Sila's got some shockers to share. Been confidin' in me along the way."

"I tried to catch up with you in the dining hall," Silapu told Ji-ji. "Let you know about Brine and tell you about plan D. Dregulahmo and Billy did not leave anything to chance—is it not so? They anticipated that Billy may be punished after Tiro escaped."

"Plan D," Ji-ji repeated, dumbly. "But . . . how come everyone kept me in the dark?"

The lieutenant was descending the stairs. He paused on the landing to check the contents of his duffel bag again.

"See, I told you," Dip-now-Donna said, glancing over Ji-ji's shoulder and nodding up at the lieutenant. "Luck's perched on your shoulder. Looks like he don't plan to fly off anytime soon." She lowered her voice again and added, "Think I'll ask him about the route. Check he knows what he's doing. He's awful young an' drug-sopped. Don't want to find ourselves in the fire after we just leapt from the fry pan." Dip hurried off to speak to him.

Ji-ji began to apologize to her mam, said she would never have attacked her like that if she'd known. Silapu put a finger on her lips and told her to hush. She would need all the strength she could muster to survive in The Margins. Ji-ji began to suspect her mam had taken some of those uppers she'd gotten from Lotter. She had the glazed look she got when she was high. If she came down from it too fast, her fear could take over and things could get dicey. Ji-ji prayed that wouldn't happen before they made it safely over the fry-fence.

"Think we'll make it over the fence?" Ji-ji whispered. "He said there was someone waiting. Matty—Lucky, I mean—he's not a real Friend. Uncle Dreg tell you that?"

Silapu nodded. "Beggars are not choosers, Ji-ji. And he is real enough for our needs, yes? Dreg chose him for this task himself. He knew his father—or was it his grandfather? Yes, I think it was the grandfather he knew many years ago. Dregulahmo said this Lucky Dyce would rise to the challenge. Even so, it is a gamble—excuse the pun."

Ji-ji nodded. "He doesn't like seeds much."

"He does not need to like us," Silapu said. "Lucky is not for the long haul. All you need him to do is get you to Salem. After that, Dregulahmo said there are Friends among the race monitors."

"Not me. *Us.* You can be a Wild Seed too. Uncle Dreg tell you about that?"

"Yes. Dregulahmo explained this Wild Seed business. It sounds risky."

"You're coming to Salem, Mam. I *can't* lose you again."

Ji-ji paused, scared to ask the next question. After a moment she said, "Did Tiro escape?"

Silapu smiled, and it seemed to Ji-ji that her mother had never looked so exhausted and so powerful at the same time. "What took you so long to ask about your foolish fly-boy? Yes. He escaped. A little bird saw him go."

Ji-ji felt a great weight fall from her shoulders. There was so much hope being pumped into her she was scared she'd balloon up and float clean away. "And Afarra?" Ji-ji asked.

Silapu shook her head. Ji-ji sank back down to earth again.

"The Cloth never returned after the Last Supper. Do not worry. If you still want her, you can petition for her after you win. They will let her go for very little. No one cares about a Cloth."

Ji-ji was about to say she cared very much when the lieutenant interrupted them. He ordered them to stop gossiping and get moving.

"Three gossipy tails. Christ! What did I do to deserve this?"

"You met Dregulahmo," Dip replied.

"Yeah. And wound up with you lot. Aren't I the lucky one?"

Dip barreled right through his sarcasm. "Don't worry. You got me and Sila to help you now. Been thinking 'bout all o' them *D*'s. Dreg was the first. Then there's Delilah, Dip-Donna, Dyce, plan D, Destiny. . . . Strictly speaking, Destiny was first. An' last too. Looks to me like *D* takes the cake as the luckiest letter in the alphabet."

Ji-ji didn't remind Dip that she and her mam weren't *D*'s. Tiro and Afarra weren't either.

"Get a move on, for Christ's sake," Lucky said. "Unless you want the *D* to stand for *Dead.*"

Dip laughed. When he was out of earshot, she whispered to Ji-ji, "He sure does talk funny. Like those missionaries visited the planting last year, remember? Glad I ain't got a accent like that. It's a handicap, if you ask me. Sounds like he's got a mouthful o' hard-boiled eggs."

Ji-ji looked around one last time as she descended through the trapdoor and down the ladder. The planting shot tower, disconcerting though it had been at first, had turned out to be a place of miracles. For the first time it occurred to Ji-ji that Tiro might have taken refuge here recently too. She wished she'd thought of it earlier; it would have made things less spooky and depressing. *Depressing*—another *D* word. Drol too. She pictured the strange creature they'd seen in the Doom Dell (*more* D*'s*). Had he managed to escape?

The four began their journey down the narrow tunnel with only Lucky's and Silapu's flashlights showing them the path ahead.

Dip-now-Donna, barely able to contain herself, said, "Approaching Freedom at last! Bet this tunnel runs all the way to the fry-fence—right, Mr. Lucky?"

"Wrong," he shot back. "Shut up and keep moving. You'll get us all killed with that blabbing tongue."

"Guess he plans to circle back," Ji-ji assured Dip, hoping she was right.

"Hope he knows what he's doing," Dip-now-Donna said, "cos he's the only one in possession of Plan Dreg. If he screws up, it's lights out for all of us."

Ji-ji glanced back down the tunnel. She thought she heard something rolling toward them through the dark. A wailing sound. . . . No, not anymore. It had changed to the sound of paper flapping in the breeze. . . . Feet pounding the earth. . . . No. That wasn't it. At last Ji-ji identified it with certainty. The haunting sound was Sylvie's purple tears as they collided against each other during a storm. "*Ji-ji! . . . Silapu!*" the tears wailed over and over again. She refused to see it as a bad omen. Maybe Sylvie was trying to tell her that Lua-Dim was right, that Ji-ji Silapu *was* her name?

"Come, Ji-ji," Silapu said. "Our littlest blackbird is waiting for us to rescue him. Listen! Can you hear him wail for us? We will find him together, is it not so? Come!"

Silapu took her daughter's hand in hers. *When did Mam's hand become the same size as mine?* Ji-ji thought. She had no answer as the Freedom seekers rushed on through the dark.

15 THAT ONE MERCIFUL THING

You got the sign from the gate lookout tower yet?" Dip-now-Donna asked.

Matty-now-Lucky lowered his binoculars and snapped at her. "How many times are you going to ask me that? We run when I say so and not before."

"It's real late. Dawn'll be here soon."

"You want to climb a live fence? Me neither. Keep quiet and let a man think."

Dip-Donna harrumphed her disapproval but didn't goad him further. Fifteen minutes since they'd first huddled together in the dark, crouched behind an oversize rhododendron bush less than a hundred yards from the perimeter fry-fence. An eternity. Ji-ji looked up. Clouds held the moon hostage. She felt the temperature plummet the way it does before a bad storm.

The tunnel had ended in the Doom Dell like Matty-Lucky said it would. After they'd emerged above ground, they'd followed a series of forbidden footpaths until they were so close to the perimeter fry-fence Ji-ji could hear its menacing buzz. Lucky, who sounded more nervous than before, said no one had given the sign to indicate the fence had been switched off. From what the others could piece together, the sign would come from somewhere close to the Main Gate lookout tower, a quarter mile to the northeast from where they were hunkered down. Donna was desperate to look through Lucky's binoculars, but he swore at her when she asked to use them.

After another ten minutes, Lucky said he was going to move beyond the line of trees to get a better angle on the lookout tower. He ordered them to stay hidden and wait for him to return.

Crouching low and moving like a cat, Lucky crept closer to the fence.

Ji-ji felt a rush of optimism. He might not be a bona fide Friend but he was almost certainly a trained fighter. She followed his silhouette for a few yards before it merged with the darkness.

"Think he knows what he's doing?" Donna whispered. "Boy talks funny. Real graspy with them binoculars too. Why not let us take a peek? I know a thing or two 'bout binoculars. Epson—that steadermate gave me Phyllis an' locked me in that confessional during a flood when I almost drowned, remember? Epson had a pair. I used to peer through 'em when he was out hunting. Keep my eye on things." Ji-ji didn't need to ask Dip for clarification, Phyllis being the name she used instead of the word *syphilis,* so she could talk about it without alarming her listeners.

"You think we can trust him?" Dip-Donna asked, anxiously. "Think the rain's a bad sign?"

"Dregulahmo was close to Lucky's grandfather," Silapu repeated, though this was news to Dip. Perhaps as a way to calm the other two, she added, "When Dreg and the grandfather were in the No Region together, he saved Dreg's life. Dreg insisted the lieutenant escort Ji-ji to safety, if a plan D became necessary. He believed he could be trusted."

A grandfather's heroism didn't guarantee the same on the part of the grandson, yet even so, Ji-ji felt relieved. Uncle Dreg's guidance had gotten them this far. Each time she tamped down one fear, however, another sprouted up in its place. Ji-ji still couldn't figure out if Silapu was high. Downers could explain why Silapu wasn't near as jittery as they were.

"Ji-ji," Silapu said, "stop those teeth from chattering. They are loud enough to wake the dead, is it not so?" Ji-ji clamped her mouth shut. *Guess Mam isn't that high after all,* she thought.

Jerky with nervousness, Ji-ji struggled to keep still. At least her back didn't hurt anymore. No room for pain when fear was flapping around like some rabid bat inside your stomach. Seemed like everything rested on numbers, and numbers had a way of aiding steaders and defeating seeds. She could probably reach the thirty-foot fence in fifteen seconds or less, and thirty strides or so. When Zyla Clobershay had told her scientists could explain the world using the language of mathematics, Ji-ji had asked what the numbers for Freedom were, thinking there was some numerical spell you could recite. Her teacher explained that when it came to Freedom people had to do their own conjuring. Later, when Ji-ji learned a little about equations from her *Intermediate Science* covert, she wondered if the formula could be something basic like *Freedom = Hope × Opportunity squared,* only she couldn't figure out how you squared Opportunity, or how you kept Hope above zero so you could multiply it with something worthwhile.

She leaned to one side and peered at the fry-fence through the bush. The mesh fence topped with barbed wire was over two stories high. She had no idea what they were supposed to do when they reached it. Climbing would be tough even for her. No way to hang on. How would someone Donna's size manage it? She hoped Lucky had a trick up his sleeve. Maybe he planned to use the rope coiled in his bag? He had a tarpaulin too, and a blanket. It would be a treacherous, frantic climb. She wished they could simply unlock the Main Gate and stroll through it, but seeds weren't allowed to stroll through anything on a planting. The area around the Main Gate was fortified, armed with cameras, alarms, and armed guards. The burnt-out carcasses of trucks served as proof that raiders attempting to breach the gates met a fiery end. Ji-ji could see why Lucky (or Uncle Dreg perhaps?) had selected this spot, a hundred yards from the fry-fence and close enough to the lookout that they could spy on it. Soon they would have to scale the fence and climb over its vicious crown of thorns, assuming a Friend shut off the power first. Everything was dependent on that one merciful thing.

The drizzle began tentatively. Three or four minutes of faltering raindrops were followed by a steady precipitation. *Precipitation.* In the old days, Ji-ji had liked the sound of that word, how it rhymed with *nation* and *reunification,* and how it unfurled a world beyond the planting. Zyla Clobershay used to use her yellowed copy of *The American Heritage Dictionary* with an authority only teachers could pull off—as if she had plucked the word from the Tree of Knowledge just so she could bestow it upon her young students in the two-room legacy school. But tonight the word sounded perilous. *Precipitation. Precipice.* The same root? The same tree?

As if the rain were music and they heard their cue, the three females scooted further under the cover of the sprawling bush, which offered scant protection from the rain. Chilly drops plopped onto Ji-ji's head and dribbled down her neck. She tried to make herself believe in rain as a good omen, but it could work both ways: harder for them to be heard over it, but harder for them to hear others. She listened for the lieutenant's footsteps. Why was it taking so long for him to return?

Silapu began to speak in a reassuring tone, reminiscent of Uncle Dreg's storytelling voice. *Time and place are nothing but roads,* her voice implied. *Come walk with me.* Her Toteppi accent soothed Ji-ji's frayed nerves.

"There was a woman once," Silapu said. "Donna knows this story already." Donna nodded. "The woman was not pretty in the dull way men think females are pretty. To most men she was plain; to some she was ugly. Wide, flat nose, small eyes, pox scars on her cheeks and forehead, hair as short as mown grass."

"Like Slop," Donna said. "Her hair's real short too. I like it that way."

"I was young back then," Silapu continued. "A fresh import. I would be dead if not for her. 'Sila,' she would say, 'they want to bury us alive. It is our job to resist.' Soon I had Clay and Charra. She had one seedling only. When he was snatched, it was like an amputation. The part of her that belonged to him was gone forever." (*Precipitation, amputation,* Ji-ji thought.)

"Are you listening to me, Jellybean? This woman found a way to hold on to what remained. The steaders saw her stubbornness as a threat, so they took measures to subdue her. They mashed her right foot. Her sweet toes mashed into mush. When she still refused to hobble like a slave, they stamped her with the planting seal. You could feel the welts on her back when you held her. The sheaf of wheat, the chisel plow . . . always hot to the touch. A vengeance pain, our people call it.

"She was not Toteppi. She was from this ruptured land where you were born, Jellybean—an American African of many generations. But she did not have the certification papers to prove it, so she could not live Free." (*Precipitation, certification.*)

"This female Commonseed was as brave as Uncle Dreg—braver perhaps, because she did not wear a necklace of Seeing Eyes and she could not read, which meant she had no armor. To others, she looked maimed and ordinary. That was her secret. No one—except her son and me—ever understood how much this maimed seed mattered or how beautiful she was.

"And when her offspring's impairments were known, and all the steaders—seeds too—condemned him as a freak, she only loved him more to make up for their stupidity. Then, after the incident in the river, he showed up with his seizure ribbon."

"Who? The son?" Ji-ji asked. "What incident in the river?"

"Not the son," Silapu said, irritated. "Why would the son be wearing a seizure ribbon? Get your head out of the clouds, Jellybean, and pay attention. You overdream like Charra—is it not so?"

Dip-Donna chimed in: "Your mam's right. You gotta listen up, Ji-ji. You're too prone to daydreaming, Slop says."

Ji-ji understood why Dippy Donna got on Lucky's last nerve, but she let it slide because she was desperate to curl up inside her mother's story again.

"Lotter was the culprit," Silapu continued. "He claimed she was too ugly to seed after her maiming. He cast her off and she was happyhappy-happy to keep her body as her own and to share it with me. But then we took one too many chances. Vanguard Casper caught us lovemaking in the night river, the same exact place where you bathe the Cloth. Do not bother to deny it, Jellybean. I was not born yesterday. As punishment, Lotter charged her with thievery because he could. She was his first seedmate. He inherited her from his older brother, Algernon. She was the only one of his seedmates he did not choose. I never told you about the brother because I do not like to have their names in my mouth. Algernon and Arundale. Ridiculous names, yes?

"She was pyred in secret, nine months before you were born. Only Lotter, Casper, and me as witnesses. Lotter wanted to tame me. He seethed with envy. He made me watch her go up in flames. I tell you this so you know what evil is and how it can be clothed in the robes of angels. His love is a lynch rope. He uses it to reel you in just before he chokes you. Do not let him catch you, understand? It will be terrible if you do. Even in Dream City you will not be safe. Arundale Lotter is the Butcher of Dreams, and he has long tentacles."

"Don't worry, Mam. I know what a bastard he is."

"One more thing. This woman who loved me more in a few nights than that devil has loved me in twenty years, this woman was called Elly. But the name her grandmother gave her was—"

Ji-ji was suddenly walking on the same story-path as her mother: "Jellybean! You named me after your best friend."

"No, Jellybean. I named you after my one true love."

Ji-ji forgot the rain, almost forgot the fence. "But you always told me you chose that name because you liked jellybeans."

"Only a fool would believe such crap, is it not so? I knew from the moment I saw you that you were my Elly come back to me—that her spirit had slipped into my womb when Lotter violated me that same evening only two hours after he pyred Elly . . . when he thrust himself into me while I could still smell her melting flesh and hear her screams. I knew each time he said your warrior name he would be invoking her without knowing it.

"You are my warrior child, Jellybean. Whatever happens, never forget that. Charra was brave, yes. But she was not a Try-Again like you. Her temper would flare, and she would burn too hot and too fast, then turn bitter in defeat and wither—like me. You and Elly burn slow." She poked her daughter's chest where the seed symbol was and nodded. "A fire inside others cannot put out. You will burn steady for a long, long time."

"It's not true, Mam. I'm not brave like your Elly. I'm terrified."

"Of course you are terrified! *And* you are here by the fry-fence. Courage without fear is what cowards possess. It is not real so they rely on props. The greenshirts have their guns and zap sticks and grenades; Lotter has his security guards and his fry-fence, yes?"

Silapu tapped her chest while she spoke, her open palm hitting her seed symbol. She used to tell her offspring it was a stroke of evil genius when the steaders herded seeds into different categories and made them sew swatches of fabric onto their clothing. The black-and-white seed symbol for Muleseeds like Ji-ji and her siblings, the solid black one for Tribalseeds like her and Uncle Dreg, the dark brown ones for Commonseeds like Dip and Sloppy, and the broken symbols for outcasts. All these stupid symbols, she said, were designed to sow discontent and fuel resentment. Apart from Serverseeds, all the seeds had three tiny cloth "tears" falling from the symbol to indicate their role as breeders. Serverseeds didn't have any tears falling from their broken seed because cropmasters could have their Cloths neutered or spayed at puberty, depending on how bad the labor shortage was. *The ugly symbols,* Silapu used to say, *are the steaders' way of driving stakes through our hearts.*

In the past, seeing her mam tap her symbol would have made Ji-ji feel a powerless rage. But tonight, as the two women crouched there, they didn't look like seeds nailed to a lower rung by steaders' symbols; they looked like warriors.

"I do not know if Dregulahmo was right about you, Ji-ji," her mam continued. "The Oz said many things, and his words were filled with overdreaming. But I know you and that is enough."

Ji-ji wanted to ask her what exactly Uncle Dreg had said, but before she could, her mam started speaking again.

"You and Elly cannot easily be extinguished. Four times I tried to end you before you—"

"End me? What do you mean?"

"Four times you escaped. My beloved had been pyred. He'd made me watch, and that was why I was determined not to let his demon seed put down roots in my belly. . . . But you were never his, not really. Four times you refused to die. Elly's spirit had come to me again."

"I lied," Donna announced out of the blue. "My four deadborns were liveborns all. Couldn't let 'em live in captivity. Pastor Gillyman would say it's eternal hell for me, which is how come I never told the old fart. Never told a soul 'cept Sloppy. An' now I'm telling you. Cos we're here at the fry-fence an' if things don't pan out this may be our last conversation. Plan to penance myself with four orphans over on the Freedom side. Plan to raise 'em as my own. Me an' Delilah. Two mams. Figure God is sure to forgive me if I do that—assuming he's more reasonable than steaders."

They were silent for a while as they digested what their friend had told them. Then Ji-ji said something she'd wanted to say ever since she'd discovered her mam wasn't a traitor after all.

"Coach B told me you had a chance to escape with Oletto. He said you refused to run without me. I'm grateful, Mam . . . real grateful you didn't leave me behind."

"I knew what Lotter would do to you. He would want me to suffer greatly, so he would never grant my petition for your Freedom. He is a vengeful, petty man filled with passions he cannot control. If his face told his story, he would be a monster."

Ji-ji took a chance and posed her next question. "Mam, is it true you went missing? I remember one time we stayed with Auntie Zaini—me, an' Charra, an' Clay, right?"

As soon as the words escaped her mouth, Ji-ji knew she'd made a terrible mistake. Silapu stiffened, became agitated. She looked around fearfully and pulled on her fingers.

"How *dare* you ask me that!" she cried, as the sky opened up to more rain. "You think I want to remember those violations?" (*Precipitation, violation.*) "You think I don't remember the butchery? Don't smell that slaughterhouse? You think I don't see them in my dreams?"

"I'm sorry, Mam! It's okay. I shouldn't have said anything. It's okay. It's okay."

Silapu began to sob—great, heaving sobs that looked like they ripped her apart. She pulled at her shift and scooted back from the refuge of the rhododendron. The guards would see her if she didn't take cover! She had to calm down!

A voice came at them through a curtain of rain. Lucky had crept back. He startled them. For a split second, Ji-ji thought Lotter had found them.

"Didn't you hear me calling?" he asked. Then he saw Silapu. "What the hell's up with her?"

"Nothing," Donna said. "She's fine. Right, Ji-ji?"

"Yes, Mam's fine. Just scared is all."

Ji-ji placed a hand on her mam's arm. Silapu looked from Ji-ji to Donna to Lucky and seemed to remember where she was. Abruptly, she stopped sobbing and said, "I'm ready."

Lucky didn't look convinced, but there was no time to argue. "Okay," he said. "It's now or never."

"Is it alive?" Ji-ji asked.

Lucky realized what she was referring to. "No. Fence is dead. But not for long. *Follow me!*"

IIIIIIIIIIIIII

Lucky flung his duffel bag on the ground and pulled out some strange devices. Hurriedly, he strapped the clawlike contraptions to his hands and slipped soles of tiny hooked spikes onto his feet. He grabbed a fancy rope ladder too, and some tarpaulin.

"Wait here close to the fence while I climb over," he said. "Got to secure the ladder and lay the tarpaulin over the barbed wire. It's sharp as hell. Jellybean, you climb next when I tell you. Fence could go live at any minute. Sila, you and Dip—"

"Donna."

"*Jesus!* Like it even matters. You steady the ladder while Jellybean climbs. I can loop it over the spikes at the top but you hold it steady down below."

"You sure the bastard's dead?" Donna asked, putting her ear close to the fence. "I think he's still humming."

Lucky slapped his hand up against the fence. "See. Satisfied?"

And then he was climbing, his duffel bag looped crosswise over his shoulder and chest so his hands were Free, his hooked feet and clawed hands allowing him to move swiftly up the fence. At the top, he laid the thick tarpaulin over the barbed wire and carefully climbed over it.

Ji-ji glanced over at her mam, who was on the verge of panic, pacing back and forth and wringing her hands. Why had she asked her that stupid question? She pulled Silapu away from the fence so Lucky couldn't hear them and asked her point blank if she'd taken something. Silapu shook her head. Ji-ji didn't have time to inquire further. Even with the rope ladder, the climb would be tricky in the rain. Ji-ji pulled her mam back to the fence and told her to stay close.

Lucky had looped the rope ladder over the fence, taking advantage of a small gap in the barbed wire. Ji-ji feared he would be immediately attacked by snarlcats and stripers like the steaders always threatened. Turned out, that was another steader lie. On the planting side, the ladder was about three feet off the ground, but on the other side the distance was double that—five or six feet. Numbers lining up to defeat them again. Lucky said he'd be down there on the other side to help them leap the last few feet. The rain intensified. It was becoming harder to hear each other.

Lucky leaned in close to the fence and ordered Ji-ji to climb. She was about to mount the first rung when she realized something. She let go of the ladder.

"You climb first, Donna," she said. "Quick!"

Lucky overheard her. "She climbs last."

Ji-ji drew closer to the fence. Lucky did the same. They were inches away from each other. Nearly a foot taller than she was, Lucky looked down on her through the mesh. His mouth twitched with anger. She caught a glimpse of the gap in his beard where she'd tried to slash his throat.

"I don't trust you!" Ji-ji told him. "You lied to us for years! Donna's my friend. She goes first. Then you can't trick us an' leave her behind."

"S'okay, honey," Donna's voice came to them through the rain. "I don't need to go first."

Ji-ji stared at Lucky; Lucky stared at her. "She goes first," Ji-ji insisted. A standoff. Her heart raced, but she wouldn't let him see how scared she was.

After a few more seconds he said, "Fuck it. What do I care? If the bloody fence goes live after the Tainted hauls her arse over it, don't blame me."

It didn't take long for Ji-ji to realize that Lucky had a point. Donna's climb was excruciatingly slow. After she huffed and puffed her way up, squeals of terror accompanied her way down. It seemed to take an age before she leapt the final half dozen feet to the ground. To Ji-ji's surprise, Lucky stepped forward to break her fall. They both tumbled into the mud, but neither one got hurt.

As soon as Donna righted herself she let out a breathless whoop and waved goodbye to the 437th. "Ain't been on the Freedom side of the fence since they trucked me here. No mutants around either. Guess that crap 'bout ants was lies too. Wait till Slop hears about this. Won't need to petition for me now!"

Donna must know Sloppy better than she let on, Ji-ji thought. *Must've figured she couldn't rely on Slop, even if she made it to the city, to petition for her, which meant she had no choice but to run. No wonder she'd begged Mam to let her come too.*

"Your turn, Mam," Ji-ji said.

"You're joking!" Lucky exclaimed.

Silapu protested even more than Lucky did, insisting Ji-ji go first.

"No, Mam. You're going first." If anything, Ji-ji trusted her mam's word even less than she trusted Lucky's. Silapu knew Lotter wouldn't rest till he captured her again. If she was the last to ascend, the temptation to stay behind so Ji-ji could be safer could prove too great for her to resist.

"Who will hold the ladder when you reach the other side?" Silapu asked her.

"It won't need holding. I can climb real well, Mam. You know that. 'Sides, Lucky doesn't get paid if I don't make it to Salem. We're wasting time. You go first, Mam. If you stay, I stay."

Silapu hesitated. Lucky warned them if they didn't make up their bloody minds he'd leave them both to rot on the prison side.

"You *got* to do this!" Ji-ji cried. "We'll run side by side in the race. You're fast—you know you are. I can't do this without you."

When Silapu grabbed hold of the rope ladder, Ji-ji wanted to weep with relief. She'd stared down the young fairskin and won. Twice. Stared her mam down too. She wouldn't have to do this alone. They would all run together.

Even in a drugged state, Silapu was more athletic than Donna. She reached the top of the fry-fence in seconds.

"See?" Ji-ji said to Lucky as he waited on the other side. "I told you she'd do okay. I'm starting up now. I'm right behind you, Mam," she called.

Silapu had one leg over the tarpaulin at the top of the fence when a voice boomed out through the darkness and jerked back the leash.

"GET DOWN NOW, BITCH, OR I SWEAR TO GOD I'LL SHOOT!"

A stocky figure emerged from the shadows. Baggy carpenter pants, a shirt with the tail hanging out, and a safari hat perched at a jaunty, party-fied angle on its head. Its face got paler as it ambled toward them—gun drawn, a lamp slung round its waist.

Ji-ji's knees almost went out from under her when saw who the clothes were wearing. She'd served it alcohol at the Last Supper. It must've kept partying cos it was rip-roaring drunk.

"How you doing, Mammy Tep? Lotter'll be real disappointed. But then betrayal runs in the family. Felt betrayed myself when your whelp flew the coop. Lotter's had it out for me ever since. I blame you for that shit."

Danfrith Petrus stood before them, his gun pointed at Sila as she straddled the fence.

(*Danfrith,* Ji-ji thought. *The* D *we forgot.*)

"You two sluts want to know what I'm doing here?"

(*He doesn't know about Lucky and Donna, doesn't know Lucky has a gun.*)

"Promised the cropmaster I'd replace the runaway traps after that freaky biped ant uprooted the damn things like they were dandy . . . dandlylions," he slurred. "Lotter likes things done in a timely manner. Didn't want a fine, so I came out here to replant 'em. . . . What do I find? The great escape that wasn't." Petrus roared with laughter. "This'll make up for that ungrateful bitch Charra running off like that."

Silapu must have leapt the last ten feet because suddenly she was down beside her daughter.

She pushed Ji-ji behind her and hissed, "Climb when I give you the signal! Climb the fence!" But Ji-ji had no intention of leaving her mam on the prison side, not when the cavalry was a few feet away. Time contracted into a single point—the whole world balanced on the here and now.

As Petrus moves in closer, the lantern hanging from his belt allows her to see his vicious face. He's wearing those obscene work boots—the ones on PrettyBlack's coffin box.

"You hurt Mam and I'll kill you," Ji-ji warns. "So will Lotter."

Danfrith Petrus steps forward, wavers a little, steadies himself, and orders them not to move a fucking muscle—only he gets tied up on the word *muscle,* which makes him madder than ever.

Ji-ji thinks as fast as fear will let her. *Why hasn't Lucky shot him? Doesn't he know Petrus hasn't seen him yet?* Realization dawns: Lucky can't shoot cos she and her mam are in the way. He's crouching behind them on the Freedom side of the fence—must be. They need to help him get a clean shot without alerting Petrus. Petrus has to take a step back so the angle is right for the kill.

Petrus stands at arm's length from his prey. He reaches out and draws a circle around Silapu's nipple with the barrel of his gun. She's drenched; her blouse clings to her body. "You've always gotten on my nerves with your fancy airs. Can't wait to watch you burn. May get me a little taste first, though. Yeah. . . . I can see why Lotter's nuts about his fudge delight."

"Okay," Ji-ji says. "You win. We'll come quietly—right, Mam?"

Ji-ji tries to ease Silapu away from Petrus. Lucky wouldn't desert her, not now, would he? (*The bastard's moving into position! Shoot, Lucky! Shoot!*)

Petrus chuckles. "Lotter's drunk the Kool-Aid when it comes to your mam. You're right. He'd kill me if I shot her. But I don't think he'll give a fuck if I plug an ugly little Mule like you."

Just before Petrus fires, Silapu leaps. She slams on top of Ji-ji, knocks her down. The earth punches all the wind from Ji-ji's lungs. She's dying! Another shot rings out and something heavy topples beside them. Petrus! Staring at them with open-shut eyes! His work boots are a few feet from Ji-ji's face. The tire treads on the soles of his boots are caked in mud.

Ji-ji rolls out from under her mam. Lucky is beside them. Somehow, he's climbed back over to the prison side in the blink of an eye. He has one claw hand and one gun-toting hand.

Six feet away (*numbers, numbers*), Petrus' eyes are glass. His neck looks like the Italian sub sandwiches Lotter likes her to make him for lunch—split open and stuffed with meat and sauce.

"You killed him," Ji-ji states, looking up from the mud as she lies beside her mam.

"That's the problem," Lucky says, breathing hard. "I don't think it was me shot him. Let's hope it was the Friend near the lookout. . . . But it seemed to come from out there." He points to the line of trees where they hid earlier. His whole arm is shaking.

"We've got to get out of here!" he cries. "Someone could've heard the shots!"

"Mam?" Ji-ji says. "Mam?"

Her mam is lying there in the mud. Her seed symbol is weeping. *We call them weepings,* Ji-ji thinks—or does she say it?—*because of the three "tears" they shed. Sometimes we call ourselves Weepings too.*

In spite of the pouring rain, she can see it: blood seeping from the wound in her mam's chest because Silapu leapt in front of her Last&Only at exactly the wrong moment and saved her.

"I can carry you, Mam, so can Lucky! He carried me for miles."

So dark and used and pretty, Silapu sucks in a fierce gulp of air so she can speak. Ji-ji has to lean way down and bring her ear to her mother's lips to hear her.

"If you see my other angels . . . tell them how much I loved them. Fly, Elly! For all of us!"

She takes another gulp of air. She's drowning! "*Oh!*" she cries, and tries to lift her arm, as if she's spied Clay, Charra, Luvlydoll, and Bonbon hovering in the gusty air above their heads. "My beautiful lost babies!"

Ji-ji uses her body to shield her mother so the rain doesn't lash her like the steaders did.

Someone rushes up. Another male. The two men look at each other. Mirror images.

Lucky's gun is raised; Lotter's is not.

"Drop it," Lucky says. Lotter obeys. Lucky snatches up the gun and pockets it.

"It was you," Lookalike says. "You shot Petrus."

Lotter isn't paying attention. He doesn't behave like a cropmaster or a steader. He sinks to his knees in the mud and pushes Ji-ji away. He gathers his favorite seedmate in his arms and rocks her back and forth. Silapu speaks to him. Ji-ji crawls up beside her mother so she can hear her voice.

"Let her go, Dale," Silapu says. (*Another* D.) "For me. Please. . . . Let our daughter go."

The only part of her mam's body Lotter hasn't claimed are her calves and feet. Ji-ji gathers them up and kisses them, kisses her copper seedmate band on her thin ankle and the ring of worn flesh underneath it, slips off her mam's raggedy shoes and kisses her toes.

Rain is pelting down in buckets as night roars toward dawn, whipping Mam's pretty face. Her eyes are open. She doesn't blink as spears of rain strike them. That's how Ji-ji knows she's dead.

"*NO! Don't leave me!*" Lotter shrieks to the corpse as he rocks her mam in his arms.

Ji-ji tries to touch her mother's face. Lotter bats her hand away, holds Silapu closer. Snarls like a wild animal, then blubbers like a baby.

Lucky has Lotter's gun—Petrus' gun too, maybe. Lucky orders her to climb. Someone's waiting on the other side but Ji-ji can't remember who. She wants to lie down beside her First&Only Mam on the prison side of the fence, cover herself with a blanket of earth, and go to sleep.

"I killed the bastard," Lotter tells Dead Mam. "It was me! I'd never let Petrus hurt you! I came looking for you. Thought you'd do something stupid. Doc Riff'll fix you, Sila. You'll see."

The final violation. Not Mammy Tep. *Sila.* He has her mother's name *in his mouth.*

Ji-ji leaps onto his back and tries to beat the crap out of him. Kicks, punches, mauls, bites, scratches his pretty face. Across his cheek, three nail slashes not deep enough to last.

Lotter tries to punch Ji-ji's teeth out, but he's sobbing too hard and misses. Lucky kicks him in the stomach and pulls Ji-ji off him. Lotter struggles to get the words out.

"Look what you've done, you ugly little bitch! She would never have left me! *Never!* And you!" he screams at Lucky. "You betrayed me, boy! I'll kill you both for this!"

Lucky drags Ji-ji to the fence, hoists her on his back, and climbs. How he manages it with her on his back she doesn't know. Ji-ji hears a man wailing behind her like a mother from the Cradle. His pain her only consolation.

They are scaling the fence when a rumbling sound like thunder—not thunder, something else?—shakes the earth. They nearly fall but Lucky holds on. She knows what the sound is—her heart exploding with sorrow.

The fairskin sets her on her feet on the Freedom side of the fence. The earth sobs beneath them. They don't try to find Dip-now-Donna. She's run off.

The ground rocks again. An explosion like the end of the world. A fireball plumes into the sky. A siren wails across the planting.

"*Bloody hell!*" Lucky cries. "You see that? Murder Mouth! The quake must've caused an explosion! They've got a shitload of toxins in there. C'mon! It's our lucky break. The guards'll be distracted. We can cover a lot of ground before they realize what's happened."

Ji-ji looks back. Mam lies in her jailer's arms. When lightning flashes, Ji-ji glimpses Lua-Dim standing knee-deep in mud on the prison side. PrettyBlack is a limp black doll in her arms. Lua-Dim is only feet from Dead Petrus, Dead Mam, and Live Lotter, but she doesn't seem to notice them.

"Look," Ji-ji says, pointing at Lua-Dim as she raises a skeletal arm. "She's waving."

"Who is?" Lucky asks.

"Death," Ji-ji replies.

The fairskin puts his hands on her (again without permission), picks her up, and throws her over his shoulder where Luck used to perch before it flew away. As the earth convulses under their feet, flames flare up toward heaven. Bouncing along on Lookalike's broad shoulders, Ji-ji knows the seeds' saying is true: earth is the only thing merciful enough to bury a seed's pain for good.

16 RAIN

When Vanguard Casper comes to "check on her" in the horse barn that afternoon, Afarra runs. He's already kept her there too long—cleaning, raking. She sees him from a distance striding toward the barn. Something about his walk tells her he's being the hunter and she's being the rabbit. She knows exactly what he smells like cos he came to her before and the last time Missy Ji chased him away. And Tiro stood outside to keep her safe. She doesn't want to smell him up close again so she runsrunsruns back to her shed, grabs her angel-protector, and slips it over her head.

All Cloths have a hideout plan for emergencies. She will hide in one of the burnt-out trucks near the fry-fence till it's safe to creep to the dining hall and help Ji-ji and the kitchen-seeds with the feast. She will stay mouse-quiet in the burn-trucks. Cropmaster Lotter's 'seer will never find her there in the restricted area. At the feast, even though she is being late, Ji-ji will have scraps for her, wrapped in a special white-white napkin. She will taste each bite as slowly as she can to make it last.

She is leaving her shed with Uncle Dreg's Eyes when a male hand—*Large, Large!*—comes from behind—grabs her and gasps. Hooray! The necklace shocks him. He drops his hold. The one and only reason she is saved. She already knows it's 'Seer Casper (she smelled his stink) so she doesn't turn back to look. She runs to the burn-trucks. Nothing can be touching her now she is wearing the wizard's Eyes, the most powerful Eyes in the world. . . .

She's safe inside the burn-truck. (*Do not be afraid.*) Which is not afire now, flames long gone. The metal is not burning her. It is cool as a cucumber. . . . Dusk. She will be late to the Last Supper. She counts his pretty eye beads, studies them, marvels how they kept her safe. . . .

Until he grabs her from behind again and heaves her out of the burn-truck—tells her to hush, orders her not to scream, whatever happens. Tells her, "Open your eyes an' look at me." He says he has been looking for her. He takes her to the Doom Dell so no one will see them. All the way there she says to herself, *Afarra, do not let go of the safety necklace. It is the one saving you.*

IIIIIIIIIIIII

Ji-ji didn't run, can't run anymore.

Tarpaulin beneath and above. A tent of sorts. Resting. Drums beating like rain, rain beating like drums: "Mam's dead, Mam's dead, Mam's dead!" Then running again—his legs moving, not mine.

A shoulder-to-pelvis pain shunts her in and out of consciousness. *I was shot. No, that was Mam. My fall in the fly-coop set my back afire. The fire this time is bad. Next time it will be worse.* She tries to tell him how much pain she's in but her voice comes out as a moan drowned out by a tempest.

She's read *The Tempest* many times. Hid the play in the heavy folds of her skirt after Miss Clobershay let her borrow it. Snuck it back to the cabin and strapped it under the bed. She'd struggled to decipher the ancient play's strange rhythms and make sense of those funny-looking, unfamiliar words. Too much poetry, she'd said when she brought the play back. Her teacher had laughed and said there could never be too much poetry in the world. Ji-ji didn't like being laughed at, so she tried again. The second time around something clicked. She heard the characters' voices whispering in her ear. She was drawn to the white wizard who reminded her of Uncle Dreg. Like Prospero, Dregulahmo could conjure up tempests. (Was Uncle Dreg the one who had made the earth buck underneath them at the fry-fence? If the Oz was so powerful, why did he take his eyes off the prize when Petrus entered the scene? Why couldn't he save them?) Miranda was a moron. The world wasn't new or brave because fairskin men were in it. The Lookalike, for example. Carrying her to safety. Her protector? Her guardian angel? No. Just a fairskin playing the Good Samaritan for money.

IIIIIIIIIIIII

Under the tarp again. Conscious. He heard something! The tarp thrown back. Gun drawn. The two of them (three if you count the gun) lashed by rain. Did mutants hunt in torrential rain? She couldn't remember. Couldn't remember anything but her mam's face till the rain washed her features away, as if Silapu were a watercolor painting (a condition contrary to fact). Lotter had thrust her aside. "*MINE!*" he'd roared. Silapu would never be Free. The scuff marks Lotter left on her thin body for the past twenty years marked his territory and signaled he'd never let her go.

The Lookalike lifted her up again, eased her over his shoulder. She wanted to tell him to stop, but when she opened her mouth rain snatched her voice away. Young Lotter ran like a dusky through The Margins, steering clear of the Main Toll Road, which ran like the parting in Lotter's hair up through the Old Commonwealth. On one side of the highway Doomsday; on the other Armageddon. Mutants (*call them "ants" like others do so they don't sound scary*)—ants roamed The Margins, where traps that could rip off a foot lay in wait. IEDs, some of them left over from the Civil War Sequel, could rip off even more. Colonies of Virals dwelled here too, victims of resurgent diseases no one could cure. Here, buzzbuzz drones patrolled, and duskies were harvested by pickers and Bounty Boys, or hunted for sport. Seemed like the Freedom side of the fence didn't have much to do with Freedom. It was all about speed. Run for your lives! Run through rivers of water that spiral you down the drain! The Margins were a giant sink with a thirsty navel-mouth, desperate to suck everything down, down. How would they skirt the drain when the going-down was everywhere? She tried to ask that question, but a sack of jostling bones can't speak.

IIIIIIIIIIIIII

I'm under the tarpaulin, she thought, logically. *Protected.*

A dreary sunrise had slunk in from the east, the direction they were headed. Or was it south? A cascade of new *D*'s in her head: Dawn. . . . Dream City. . . . Dimmers. . . . Rain pounding on the tarp, draped over bushes above her. She called out for the Good Samaritan who'd left her there alone to fend for herself. Loneliness morphed into terror. She yearned for his broad shoulders to ride on, no matter the pain it caused her, no matter that he was doing it for money.

She called out his name, but her voice was as silent as a teardrop. Lucky Dyce had Deserted her. *D* = Desolation. *I am the rain,* she thought. *I am a map of all the sorrow in the world.*

IIIIIIIIIIIIII

She opened her eyes. He'd come back! She wanted to thank him but her sore throat and the savage pain in her shoulders wouldn't let her. His hand was behind her head, raising it up. He gave her water and something else, some pill to swallow. She didn't say, *I have already swallowed all the tears in the world.* What good would it do? She simply swallowed more.

The fairskin looked almost as young as she did. In his eyes she glimpsed his fear. He knew what could happen if he kept carrying her, yet he hoisted her up onto his shoulder again and ran. She was so grateful not to be left behind that she became the rain and wept.

IIIIIIIIIIIII

"Thought you'd died on me," he said. "How do you feel?"

She felt the earth lying still beneath them. "It's not sobbing," she told him.

"It's not throbbing? Is that what you said? You've been ranting like some nutcase, but it looks like the fever's broken. The killers're kicking in too. They'll make you woozy."

When she opened her eyes again, he was munching on an apple and cheese.

"Don't want to feed you yet. You could throw up, choke on your own vomit. Not good." *Not good,* she thought. "I think we've rested long enough. We'll go another mile or two. The rain's kept the hounds off our trail but the sky's starting to clear. Not good." *Not good,* she thought again.

"Lotter," she managed to say.

"Yeah. The bastard let us go. With a little encouragement from a weapon or two. Persuasion's always more persuasive when it's armed—the mercenary's motto. Listen. I'll try carrying you in my arms for a while. See if it's less painful. Can't have you screaming like you were earlier—not now the rain's dying down. We're deep inside Bounty country. Got to stay quiet. You're heavier than you look, Jellybean Lottermule."

"Ji-ji," she said weakly, "or Elly." He didn't hear her. "Thank you, Matty," she added.

"It's Lucas Dyson—Lucky Dyce for short. When we're alone, call me by that name, okay? I'm sick to death of the other bloke."

IIIIIIIIIIIII

It was the first time she'd felt close to normal. She sat in front of a weeping willow near a pond. The day had a washed-out paleness to it, as if the sun had turned to goat cheese and some gigantic, careless hand was spreading it from east to west. Earlier, Lucky had spotted snarlcat tracks—a pride of eight or nine. They'd taken a detour round where he suspected they could be hunting, adding several miles to their journey. She stank, so did he. Though they'd run into streams and creeks swollen to bursting after the heavy rains, they didn't hang around for niceties like hygiene after they'd filled the canteens. She'd been awake for some time, watching him as he took a small saucepan out of his bag, filled it from his canteen, and boiled water over a small fire. He opened a packet and poured powdered soup into the water. Afterward, he popped a couple of pills.

"What you taking?" she asked.

Her voice startled him. "Killers," he replied.

"Why?"

"Because carrying you was no picnic. How long've you been spying on me?"

"I wasn't spying. I was just—"

"It's chicken soup like Mother used to make. Makes everything hunky-dory."

He rummaged around again, drew out a mug from his magic bag. He'd changed his clothes, didn't look like a guard anymore. When the soup was ready, he filled the mug and handed it to her.

"Your back still hurt?"

"Not like it did. Where are we?"

"Near the river."

"The one runs the wrong way? Uncle Dreg told me 'bout that. Said people back in the day used to climb inside tires and float downriver." (*Did they know how lucky they were back then, fairskin and dusky playing together in the South? No steaders; no botanicals. Did they know they were living in paradise?*)

"How long we been running?"

"*I've* been running with you on my back like a dead weight for two days."

The pills began to take effect. His body relaxed. Ji-ji didn't think he'd taken killers. Looked like he'd taken something else. Looked like her mam did after she'd taken flukes—only more alert. His tolerance must be good. She resolved to find out as much as she could while he was high.

"How much longer till Salem?" He didn't answer. She sipped on the soup and asked again.

"We're not going to Salem," he replied. "We're heading to Dimmers Wood."

Ji-ji nearly spilled the soup into her lap. Fighting to keep her voice steady, she reminded him that Tiro would be waiting at the Salem

Outpost. "If we don't show he'll be real worried. May come looking for us. May not even compete if I'm not—"

"I doubt that," he interrupted. "Tiro's a fly-boy through and through. He knows which side his bread's buttered. Now listen carefully. I won't be repeating myself. Tiro won't be at the Salem Outpost cos Salem's as dangerous for him as it is for us. The earthquake and the explosion may have given us an extra day or two, but Falrenn's search party'll be in Salem by now, lying in wait. The race monitors from D.C. don't have any jurisdiction beyond the race path. If we're intercepted before we reach it—and we would be—the monitors can't save you, neither can the Friends. Besides, you're in no shape to compete in the first leg."

"But what if—"

"Petrus was a father-man and he's dead. I'd bet good money Lotter's saying *we* killed the bastard. Killing a father-man in the Territories is like offing a cop or sheriff in the SuperStates. Gets you executed on sight. Most people may not have heard about the Wild Seed Rule, but I bet your father-man has. Won't take him any time to realize we're headed to Salem."

"But he let us go."

"Yeah, he did. And now he'll need to prove to everyone it's the last thing in the world he'd do. He's the cropmaster. Unnatural Affiliation's a crime in the Territories or have you forgotten? He can't admit he let his own seed escape or admit he was disarmed by traitors. After we rest up in Dimmers, we've got to get to the second leg in Monticello. You can still enter there as a Wild Seed."

"No! We gotta go to Salem! That's plan D—Dreg's plan."

"Plan D always took Sod's Law into account. If something *can* go wrong it *will* go wrong. Like it did back there at the fence. What a shit show that was! No way we're going anywhere near Salem. We always knew a detour was on the cards. Now eat your soup and stop whinging."

Ji-ji wasn't sure what *whinging* meant but she kept quiet for a while. She felt helpless, vulnerable. She didn't know much of anything. Most of all, she hadn't mastered how to keep breathing after her mam and Lua and Uncle Dreg had stopped.

She gave him time to get over his irritation, took a deep breath, and asked, "Where did you go . . . after you left the planting for the first time, I mean?"

He looked at her oddly, said, "Went on a mission."

"What kind of mission? Were you in Dream City like you told Brine? What's it like?"

"Christ, you're nosey! Oh what the hell. Yep. I was up in NoVA—what seeds call the No Region. Then I visited the City of Dreams, or to be more accurate, the City of Dreams Deferred. That's a reference to Langston Hughes, by the way. His shit's depressing. Makes you think about how long things've been festering. You'd like it."

"Why didn't you tell us who you were at the flying coop when you were spying on us?"

"And what would have happened if I blew my cover there and then? Lotter's known for sending parrots to spy on his parrots. For all I knew we were all being watched—same as at the Doom Dell when you pulled that bloody ridiculous stunt with the paring knife. I'm wielding a fucking assault rifle and you attempt to peel me like a spud! Who does that? A nutter, that's who. Besides, you think you could've kept your cool at the Last Supper if you knew the truth? You would've given me away in a second. . . . Thank god for that tabby. Got a cramp and had to change position. When that fly-boy of yours heard me shifting around, he came within a few feet of where I was hiding. The cat and Ratatouille saved the day. Know who that is? Didn't think so. He's a character in an old cartoon made way back before everything went to hell in a handbasket. You should watch it sometime. And speaking of watches, know who this is?" He pointed to the face of the wristwatch he'd stolen.

"The mouse, you mean?"

"Not just any mouse, Jellybean. This mouse is the king of mouses! This cartoon mouse ruled the roost pre-Sequel. His name was Mickey and he was a god. You heard of Disney? No, I suppose not. Anyhow, there's talk of reviving the theme parks again one day. That's where the god-rodent hung out, mostly. In California and down there in Florida. Not that anyone's dumb enough to resurrect a theme park in the Madlands. Gators'll eat you alive, if malaria doesn't get you first."

Ji-ji's heart turned over. Charra was in the Madlands. "You been to the Madlands?"

"Nope. And I never intend to either. Makes The Margins look like a bloody theme park. That's a joke, by the way. Subtle for an American Territorial, I know, but try to keep up."

"You could've let us know who you were. Tiro an' me could've kept your secret."

"Like hell you could! You're as reckless as he is."

"I'm not reckless."

"Is that so? Then what were all those banned books doing strapped to the underside of your bed? Did they just flock to you one day and strap themselves in?"

Ji-ji's jaw dropped. "My books! Mam didn't snatch them! *You* did!"

"Lotter sent me to spy on Silapu. Mad for her he is . . . was. Don't even want to think about the vengeful shit he'll be pulling now she's gone. Wanted to know where she went, who she saw—crap like that. Dreg told me about your secret stash of books when we met at Blueglass. By the way, as you've no doubt figured out, you being such a world-class sleuth, Silapu was never at Blueglass Lake. Made that up when she parroted to Lotter to implicate Dreg and save Zaini. Except it wasn't Zaini she was saving, of course. It was Mr. Bird, your champion fly-boy. Christ, that boy's *got* to learn to spell! His letter was *pain-ful*! Even spelled 'grammar' wrong. He's allergic to apostrophes too. Zyla would be gutted to see one of her students write a crappy note like that."

"What did you do with my things?"

"Your 'things' could've got you pyred—you know that? Thank you, Lucky, for saving me. You're welcome, I'm sure. . . . I burned 'em."

"Oh. . . . I thought maybe you had them in your . . . I thought you could have . . ."

Everything snatched . . . everything lost! Lotter grasping Mam on the prison side. Lua's seedling not dead at first but dead later cos her best friend was too dumb to put two and two together. She couldn't hold it together any longer.

"Oh for Christ's sake, pull yourself together! They're just books. . . . Don't cry, okay?"

She hadn't meant to lose it. Wave after wave of grief, and terror, and fury overwhelmed her. "She's gone!" Ji-ji wailed. "Mam's gone! We were meant to do this together. Everything's *l-lost*!"

Lucky swore under his breath, said, "Here. I saved these. Now shut up, okay?"

He shoved two folded pieces of paper toward her. She looked at them. Tiro's letter had been crumpled then un-crumpled. Her map looked fine.

"Th-Thank you," she stuttered.

He shrugged in reply, like he had no idea why he'd bothered to save crap like that.

Just before they set off, she asked another question that had plagued her ever since she'd seen the flashing 9-0-2 on his watch: "How do I know I can trust you?"

He shrugged again. "Trust is overrated," he replied.

IIIIIIIIIIIIII

A few hours later, during another break from running, he asked if she could handle a weapon.

"I used a hunting rifle when I was a seedling."

"You strong enough to carry a gun?"

"Yes," she said, adamantly.

She hadn't held a gun for years—not since Lotter stopped taking her on hunting expeditions, which consisted of traveling by car or truck for about fifteen miles along the Main Toll Road, then circling back either on foot or horseback to hunt. They never strayed too far from the road in case they encountered game they couldn't handle and needed to beat a hasty retreat. She'd been a seedling, which explained why she'd enjoyed riding beside Lotter in his red vintage truck, sandwiched between him and 'Seer Casper—who gave her the creeps, but who forced himself to behave like a gentleman around Lotter. She'd been a fairly good shot by age eight, though the rifle bruised her shoulder whenever she fired it. During one hunt, she'd come close to spraying Casper's wide butt with buckshot—something Lotter had chuckled over all the way back to the planting.

Lucky undid his shoulder holster and handed her the gun he'd lifted from Petrus' corpse, reminded her to check the safety. His own gun was still in its holster on his belt. He had Lotter's gun and other weapons in his bag too, she was certain of it. He handed her a couple of magazines.

"Here. Take these. I assume you know how to swap out the mags?"

Ji-ji felt the weight of the weapon in her hand. A fat-barreled semiautomatic. A man's gun. Petrus' gun. The gun that had killed her mam. Lucky sensed her thoughts.

"What's done is done. No point dwelling on it. Think of it like this. Each time you use that sucker, you're getting revenge for what they did to your mum. But don't shoot 'less you have to. Every Bounty Boy and picker within five miles'll hear it if you do. . . . And point the bloody thing over there. I don't intend to pop my clogs today." She looked puzzled. "Kick the bucket, snuff it. You need to learn to speak English." He let out a long sigh and crossed his ankles. "Carrying you was a bitch. I'm knackered. Got to get some shut-eye before we head out again. Your turn to keep watch, Jellybean Lottermule, seeing as how you've returned to the land of the living." He leaned back and tilted his hat down over his eyes. The hat was floppy and wide-brimmed. "I know what you're thinking," he said. "You could run off with that motherfucking gun and take your chances in Salem. You're right. But trust me. You'd be cutting off your nose to spite your face. I know this region—you don't. You wouldn't last ten minutes out here without me."

A few seconds later, Lucky was snoring.

Ji-ji felt the weight of the nine-millimeter in her hand. It was an antique, unlike the unreliable weapons steaders manufactured in the Territories. Petrus, a notorious Scrooge, must have paid a lot of money for it. She wondered if he'd ever pointed it at Charra or threatened Lua with it. Ji-ji felt powerful with the gun in her hand, but she knew she could just as easily shoot herself in the foot as hit a target. For all she knew, a gun that size could recoil on her big-time when she fired. She'd need to be prepared for that. Clasp it with both hands and stand with her feet apart to steady herself. She wasn't much over a hundred pounds and her aim would be lousy. She was grateful for the high-capacity mags. She'd need to get off a slew of rounds to be sure of hitting something.

She raised the gun and took aim at Lucky. He opened one eye lazily, let out a snort of mocking laughter, and closed it again. "Make sure I'm out like a light when you pull the trigger. If you don't get me good and proper, I'll rip your nappy head off." Then he fell asleep.

IIIIIIIIIIIIII

No getting around it. They had to cross it.

They stood on a rocky outcrop and looked down at the swollen river. The rain had become intermittent, the sky threatening. Not many trees nearby, so Lucky said they couldn't stay long, exposed like this. He'd wanted to find a less dangerous place where they could cross.

"We're way behind schedule," Lucky said.

Because he still refused to disclose the schedule, Ji-ji had to take his word for it. She found his nervousness contagious. To calm herself, she went over what she knew about the race. The first leg, between Salem and Monticello, would take runners several days to complete—longer, perhaps, because of all this rain. She still wasn't sure how she and Tiro would make it all the way to Monticello in time, but Lucky was very unhelpful whenever she asked him about it. On the last night, the flyer-battlers had to compete in the coop. It would be the largest coop Tiro had ever set foot inside, but Ji-ji knew no one could beat him. If her back healed up, she could do well herself in the runners' leg, between Monticello and D.C. A big if.

Ji-ji didn't envy the runners. Conditions were terrible. She and Lucky had sloshed their way through the old forest, their shoes so caked in mud Ji-ji had to scrape it off to find out if she still had shoes on. But at least Lucky hadn't had to carry her. Her back didn't hurt nearly as much as before. Earlier that day, she'd even jogged a little. After several unanticipated detours and a much slower pace than expected, Dimmers Wood lay only a few miles to the southeast. But they had to cross the river. Ji-ji had consulted Uncle Dreg's map a hundred times, as if she could will Dimmers Wood closer if she stared at it long enough. Its name still spooked her, but fear fell away when she imagined meeting up with Tiro there.

Lucky glanced down at his map, more detailed than hers, then scowled at the floodwater. He paced back and forth on the rocky ledge, trying to figure out the best way to cross.

Ji-ji moved off to stand under the shade of the only sizable tree in the vicinity—a live oak, with thick branches and a crown that looked to her to be over a hundred feet in diameter. An old soul for sure. Uncle Dreg and Coach B had taught her to think of trees as friends. She touched its rough bark and looked up into its canopy of nearly evergreen leaves. It felt like standing inside a house. She thought of the penal tree that had revenged Uncle Dreg's death, a tree some said had been crossbred, like the wolves and big cats—which made no sense given Sylvie's age. This live oak was magnificent, though her mam would never identify it as an Immaculate, its branches being low enough to tempt lynchers. Even so, it was a thing of majesty. For hundreds of years, it had rooted itself to this place. Bowing her head, she asked for the live oak's protection, the way Uncle Dreg had taught her.

Ji-ji had learned to read Lucky's mood. His anger still upset her, but it wasn't laced with Lotter's extreme vindictiveness. Though the pills Lucky popped made him act like a jerk at times, unlike her morose father-man Lucky didn't seem to have much interest in torturing her. He only demanded that she keep her mouth shut—something she wasn't very good at.

The stronger she'd gotten physically, the more she'd begun to assert herself. They butted heads several times an hour, but more often than not he ignored her. A dozen times since she'd been able to walk, he'd forged ahead up hills and raced down the other side, forgetting that her sore back made it impossible for her to keep up. He had no tolerance for "mopers," even less for "whiners," and none at all for "pillocks." She wasn't sure what pillocks were, but apparently she was one of the biggest. He told her little about himself, guarding his privacy the way a dog guards a bone. Yesterday, seeking shelter from another downpour, they'd crawled into a hollow exhausted. He'd muttered the name "Rachel" in his sleep. Ji-ji had been tempted to ask him who Rachel was, but the question would likely piss him off even more than if she just whinged about something. (At least context had taught her what that word meant.) The only time he became talkative was when he smoked his weed, downed a happy pill, or sucked on his booze flask.

If Lucky was high enough he'd tell one corny joke after another. Most of them were vulgar—the kind of jokes Afarra wouldn't get but would laugh at anyway. The main characters in Lucky's repertoire were toilets, outhouses, farts, boogers, drunks, politics, the clergy, inquisitors, and private parts. Was that what Cross-Ponders always joked about? she wondered. He delivered his jokes in a deadpan voice. She never laughed at any of them, and he took particular delight in this, as if it proved how much his wit surpassed hers. He claimed all Yanks were sorely lacking in the humor department. When she asked him what a Yank was, he told her it was another name for northerners from the States United, which was itself a steader inversion of the correct name and a deliberate nod to states' supremacy. "Say 'States United' in D.C. and they'll know you're a hick."

Once, when he wasn't high but seemed to be a bit less irritated by her than usual, she'd asked him why the SuperStates and Independents didn't go to war with the Territories again to reunite the country. He'd asked her if she knew how many people had died in the Sequel. "Made the first Civil War look like a party. The strife that followed it sucked too. Besides, trade's good right now." "But what they do to us is terrible," she'd pointed out. "Don't the SuperStates and Independents care about what happens to us?" "Not really," he'd said, and walked on. On another occasion, as they toiled up a steep hill, he'd lit into her teacher again. "What she taught you in that legacy school was simplistic crap." When Ji-ji had insisted she'd had a wonderful teacher, Lucky had exploded. His voice cracking, he'd hurled one insult after another at Zyla. "She was a selfish bitch! Should've been expelled from the Friends for the insane stunts she pulled!" From then on, Ji-ji steered clear of the topic of education.

Yet though she was grateful not to be alone, Ji-ji was afraid every moment—a deep-rooted anxiety that lodged itself in her stomach and seemed to aggravate her sore back. She was on the lookout for puffer-puffs—the giant snakes steaders said infested the swampier regions of The Margins. Get bitten and their venom killed you in minutes. In the dark, she'd listen out for the howls of stripers and the roars of snarlcats. Each time they emerged from the forest and the land opened up in front of them, she expected to be confronted by a gang of pickers, a pack of stripers, a pride of snarlcats, or a posse of Bounty Boys. She worried about Dip-now-Donna. How would she fend off mutants without a weapon? How would she make it to Salem on her own? She struggled to numb herself to the current of pain swirling around inside her. Was losing mothers always like that? Did it always feel like your still-beating heart had been plucked from your chest? She realized with shame that she hadn't been compassionate enough when seeds she'd known had lost their mams. She hadn't understood that losing a mother was like losing yourself *and* your past rolled into one. She yearned to share her pain with Tiro, who would gather her in his large arms and comfort her. Or Afarra, who would say in that sweet voice of hers, "No worry time now, Missy Ji."

As Lucky surveyed the landscape yet again, Ji-ji's anxiety grew. She moved out from the tree's shade and went over to join him on the rocky outcrop. "I can swim," she told him, by way of encouragement, as he gazed out over the swirling river, his brows furrowed. Something about the water was freaking him out—anyone could see that. "I mean it. Don't worry. I can swim across," she reassured him.

"You wouldn't make it. Current's too strong. We'll head down that slope. Then I'll tie off the rope on this side and make my way across. Should've done that two hours ago. I'll tie it off again on the far side and you can use it to haul yourself across. It's high-tech hope-rope—a lot of elasticity and almost indestructible." It marked the first time he'd shared his plans with her in advance. Maybe they were beginning to trust each other a little?

"You nervous?" Ji-ji asked.

"What do you think? You know what those bastards do to Friends of Freedom?"

"Thought you weren't a Friend? Thought you were doing this for money."

"Think pickers and Bounty Boys like to split hairs? I'm very fond of my balls. Would like to keep 'em where they belong a while longer, for old times' sake."

She worried about asking the next question, but she did it anyway. "You can swim, right?"

He stopped scouting the area and looked up at the sky. He turned. A look Ji-ji had never seen him wear before clouded his face. "Yes, I can swim," he said. "I swim like a bloody fish."

"Then why are you—"

Suddenly, he was angry. "You want to know why I'm acting like a fucking coward? Want to know why I can't cross the fucking river? Okay, I'll tell you."

He walked to the bank and plopped down like someone too exhausted to talk and stand at the same time. Ji-ji sat down beside him and waited, scared she'd gone too far.

"Last time I crossed water like this was near the No Region. . . . Dad and Mum were Quakers. Very devout. Annoyed the hell out of me. Granddad too. You know about Quakers?"

Ji-ji vaguely remembered something about them from her history text. "Didn't they help the Passengers? Were they fairskins who fought for Emancipation?"

"Yeah, that's right. Quakers call themselves the Religious Society of Friends. Some say it's where the term Friends of Freedom comes from—only most Friends aren't Quakers this time around. I'm not either. Quakers are always trying to save someone—slaves, seeds . . . me. . . . Dreg and Grandad were pals. Fought the good fight together. Grandad used to travel back and forth from the U.K., lobbying for change, helping seeds escape. Tried to get the Wild Seed Rule passed in D.C. ages ago, but it wasn't put in place till after he was dead." He paused. Took out a weed stick and lit it.

"Mum and Dad are dead too. Mum worked in the Rad Region for a while. Died of cancer."

"I'm sorry."

Lucky gave his usual I-don't-give-a-damn shrug. "Shit happens," he said. He pulled on the weed stick, waited a moment, then said, "Dad died escorting Zyla Clobershay to safety."

Ji-ji said the only thing she could say: "I'm real sorry, Lucky."

"Yeah. I'm sorry too. So it was just me and Rachel, my kid sister, after that. Some people are just sweet, you know? Like Afarra. She reminds me of Rachel. Same smile. . . . We had to lead these runaways across floodwater. Get them to Dream Corridor. Friends would take over from there. First time Rachel and I ever worked together. I had ahold of her hand. Honest I did. . . . Then I didn't. Joke's on me, right? For generations, my family's been all about saving people. It's like the family business. All of them were Quakers and Friends except me. I was the black sheep, the one who couldn't be saved. Turns out, I'm the one can't save anyone either."

Ji-ji didn't know what to say. At last she found something. "You're saving me."

Lucky smiled at her. Again, she noticed how startlingly blue his eyes were. Like Lotter's . . . except, now she really looked at them, not like Lotter's at all.

"Let's hope you're right, Jellybean," he said. He snuffed out his weed stick and stuck it in his pocket. "C'mon. Can't sit here sentimentalizing. Not when we've got a river to cross."

They were scrambling to their feet when Lucky thrust out his arm and pushed her to the ground. Ji-ji winced from the pain of the fall. He put his finger to his lips to indicate she should stay quiet. A moment later, he peered over the rock. Ji-ji did the same. The object floating on the water was clearly visible a few feet away.

Ji-ji whispered her question: "Is that a—?"

"Yep."

"What's it doing here?"

She stared at the large corpse bobbing around about twenty feet from where they lay. It was hung up on a half-submerged bush, pinned there while the dark floodwater swirled around it.

"Bounty Boys," Lucky said under his breath. "Probably murdered one of their own. *Shit!*"

She saw it now. The seal on the shirt of the stocky corpse. A lynching tree with a noose around its trunk—the most notorious seal in the Territories. She'd seen the seal up close when the Boys stopped off at the planting for some R & R. Militiamen, like the Bounty Boys and Clansmen, had a constitutional right to be given two nights of shelter anywhere in the Territories. She'd served them food, watched them chew, been privy to their lewd jokes, felt their clammy paws on her. . . .

The corpse was clothed in the Bounty Boys' infamous uniform: black jeans, white shirt, black waistcoat—all designed to conjure up the Old West, or so Miss Clobershay had told her. The small necktie was still wrapped around the Boy's neck. The only things missing were the infamous black Stetson with its lynch-rope chin strap, and the signature black leather, metal-studded jacket. The Bounty Boys—who liked to refer to themselves as the Lord's Limbs—wielded a power only inquisitors and father-men could challenge. They had the authority to lynch paperless botanicals on sight, and they routinely tormented all duskies, even certified Indigenous.

Ji-ji took comfort in the papers she'd seen Lucky pull out of his bag in the tower. Were they official-looking enough to pass? The Bounty Boys, like Lucky, were mercenaries. Unlike him, they were contracted by the father-men and inquisitors to retrieve runaways, employing whatever means necessary to complete their mission. A few Boys worked hand-in-hand with common pickers, who reported to no one in particular and made a living picking up "strays" and shipping them to places where the labor shortage was most severe. Ji-ji couldn't take her eyes off the corpse. The seeds had a saying: "The only good Boy is a dead one." Only this time the dead Boy wasn't good at all.

"You think there are more?" Ji-ji asked, though she already knew the answer.

Lucky looked grimmer than ever. "They travel in packs—a dozen or two. His mates will be close by. Should've crossed earlier when we had the chance. *Damn!*"

"Could be he was killed upriver," Ji-ji said, hopefully. "Could've been floating for ages."

Lucky shook his head. "Body's too fresh. Hunting knife's still lodged in his side. That's a BB knife. Must've bashed his head in for good measure before they threw him in. See that piece of rope round his waist? The Boys don't mess around. Bet there was a fucking stone tied to it. Must've snapped off in the current. His mates'll be close by. We've got to get out of here."

The corpse, twirling like a weathercock in the swift current, remained tangled up in the half-submerged bush. Ji-ji had seen death many times before, but a ritual usually accompanied it—some steader interpretation of what it was supposed to mean. This fairskin's death didn't resemble anything she'd seen—certainly not Cropmaster Herring's. By the time the seeds filed past Herring's coffin for the obligatory Payment of Respects (heads bowed pretending they found the austere cropmaster's death tragic), the late Lord-Father had been composed into a State of Beatitude by the planting's undertaker. There Herring lay, his large, clean hands with their buffed fingernails resting on his breast like the portrait of a saint in the authorized seed version of the Bible. In The Margins there was nothing to stop you from seeing fairskin death the way you saw the deaths of seeds. Their flesh tore like hers did, bled like hers did, turned as gray as oatmeal in rushing water. If Lucky hadn't pulled Ji-ji to her feet, she could have stayed there all day watching the dead Boy stay dead.

But Lucky had heard something: the low rumble of motorcycles in the distance. The rumbling ceased. It was followed by a few seconds of silence, then the whinny of a horse. Then, the most terrifying sound of all: men laughing the way only men with unrestrained power laugh, as if they ruled the world.

Lucky swore and jerked Ji-ji toward the live oak. Moving at lightning speed, he laid the tarp on the ground and placed his flask and a crust of stale bread beside it, picnic style. He lifted the flap on his holster in readiness. He ordered Ji-ji to remove her shoulder holster and hand it to him. Quickly, she undid the strap, removed the gun, and handed him the empty holster.

"Give me the fucking gun!" he ordered. "You know what they'll do to you if you're armed?"

"You know what they'll do to me if I'm not?"

"Shit!" he said.

"Shit!" she mimicked defiantly, as she buried the gun deep in her pocket, its weight threatening to tear a hole in the seams of her bulky shift.

Lucky swore again, but there was no time to argue. "You take your cue from me," he ordered, his breath shallow and fast. "Don't draw 'less it's absolutely necessary . . . or if they've already blown my fucking head off. No fancy words, understand? Keep your bloody mouth shut! Kneel down over there in the shade and look humble."

"I'm not good at that."

Quite unexpectedly, the young lieutenant smiled. "Hell, what's it matter?" he said. "Either way we're screwed. Forget about humble. Just look scared as shit. You can manage that, right?"

"Yeah. I can manage that."

Lucky reached over and pulled hard on the neck of her shift, ripping the fabric. "Got to look the part," he said.

"We can still run."

"We'd be spotted. We hold our ground. Don't panic, for Christ's sake."

He shoved her under the shade of the tree, where she knelt down.

He was right. There wasn't any time to run.

Almost immediately, a group emerged from a wooded area to their right. They entered the clearing. From this distance, it was hard to make out what the group consisted of at first. Then Ji-ji saw why she'd been puzzled. The Bounty Boys—two wheeling motorcycles, two astride horses, and one on foot—were driving a young seed before them, using a whip to propel him forward. He'd been stripped to his boycloth and was loaded down with gear like a pack animal. He wasn't much more than a seedling. Eleven or twelve, perhaps? On his head they'd attached a pair of donkey's ears.

Ji-ji remembered a scene from *A Midsummer Night's Dream.* When she'd read the part where a poor man was transformed into an ass she'd burst into tears, even though Miss Clobershay had assured her it was meant to be funny. "Giddyup, Animule!" one of the Boys cried, brandishing his whip. "C'mon, Mule! Giddyup! The penal tree's gettin' antsy, right fellas?"

Lucky was lounging on the tarpaulin, eating and drinking. After he was certain they'd seen him, he stood up, swaying a little as if he were tipsy, and called out to them: "See you Boys got yourselves a live one!" He was Matton Longsby again, the fairskin guard she couldn't trust.

"Sure do!" the Bounty Boy wielding the bullwhip yelled back. "But not for long. I see you got yourself a live one too! On her knees in readiness, right there under our favorite penal. Could be we'll all wet our beaks at that little trough, eh, boys?" More raucous laughter.

Lucky glanced to his left where Ji-ji was kneeling. He hissed at her too softly for the men to hear: "There's five of them and two of us, and you probably shoot like shit. You draw, we both die. So does the Mule." The Mule. What she never would be again, come hell or high water.

As the fairskin mercenary turned back toward the Boys and smiled broadly, Ji-ji slipped her small brown hand into her pocket.

17 DEAD OR ALIVE

The rope swung back and forth in the breeze. The child in the ass's ears hadn't been lynched yet, so there was no seed on the branch. In spite of this, Ji-ji thought she could hear the live oak groan. Its voice reminded her of recordings of whale song Miss Clobershay had played to them once on an old disc player she'd salvaged from the pray center.

The rope had been slung over the tree limb by a Bounty Boy named Chet, the one who had taken the most delight in driving their prey forward with a bullwhip. Chet leered at Ji-ji, docile and kneeling under the shade of the ancient tree. Claimed he had "a fondness for plain duskies" who were "more appreciative of pettin' than the pretty ones."

Ji-ji stole a glance at Lucky. He wasn't looking at her—didn't seem to have heard Chet's obscene threat. How many times had Lotter's lookalike stood by and watched steaders assault seeds? In her heart, she knew the answer: many times.

Their victim would be hanged with his gray furry ears attached, Chet insisted, because he was a fake Mule with handwritten fake papers, who'd tried to fool them into thinking he was the errander of a father-man. No seed made asses of Bounty Boys and got away with it. Chet, in particular, his black Stetson pushed back on his head, found the ears hilarious—perhaps because his own ears, purple-veined and prominent, must be a source of ridicule. The sight of the ass-eared botanical made Chet laugh so hard he had to take a piss. He unzipped his pants and pulled out his wiener. He directed his stream onto the roots of the live oak. Ji-ji heard whale song rumble beneath her feet. Louder this time. Doom-laden.

She tried again to catch Lucky's eye to get some indication of a plan, but her escort kept his eyes on the Bounty Boys. Lucky wobbled unsteadily on his feet, as if he'd had one drink too many. While Chet relieved himself, a heavyset, red-haired Bounty Boy stood nearby. Another sat astride his horse a few yards away. Standing off to one side were the last two of the five, the only ones not under the shade of the tree. Every one of them was armed. It would take a miracle to kill them all.

Ji-ji remained kneeling because no one had ordered her to rise. Rising without an express command would be viewed as an affront, especially if a female seed initiated the rising. Her right hand stayed hidden in her pocket. She fingered the gun, realized she couldn't remember if she'd turned the safety on or off. *Think, Ji-ji. Think!* A crazy idea leapt into her head. Maybe, even if the safety was off, the gun wouldn't fire. Maybe a father-man's weapon would resist a Wild Seed, like one of those ornery Cradle objects Uncle Dreg used to tell stories about. Charra wouldn't have hesitated to fire Petrus' weapon. Her sister would certainly have known whether the safety was on or off. But wasn't she, Ji-ji, half Toteppi too? One of the last members of a doomed tribe of warriors? Drawing her gun would be suicide, but it would be worth it to see the Boys' faces when she pulled a bigass semiautomatic from her seed shift and started shooting. She would kill one of them, at least—two maybe. Or—more likely—they'd shoot her before she had the chance to fire. But at least the poor seed in mule ears would know that someone in this blighted world gave a damn.

She cursed herself. Stupidly, she hadn't thought to attach one of the thirty-round mags. She had about a dozen rounds, if that. She'd have to scramble for cover behind the tree while shooting. It would be impossible for her to brace herself and fire with both hands; her aim would be pathetic. Hopefully, Lucky would draw his weapon and provide cover. He would do that, right? *Forget it,* Ji-ji thought. *It's not about Lucky Dyce anymore. I can only control what I do.*

She rehearsed her attack. She had the element of surprise. She would aim for Chet first. He'd stuffed a fat wad of tobacco into his mouth after he'd zipped himself up and was masticating like a cow. He wouldn't be looking for an attack from a seed, and a female seed at that. Next, she'd take out the Bounty Boy on the aged sorrel mare, the one who laughed the loudest at Chet's jokes. She'd have a decent chance of hitting either him or the mare. Hitting him would be the best option, but if she hit the horse instead, it would rear up or crumple. Either way, the Bounty Boy would be vulnerable at that moment, unable (Ji-ji hoped) to draw his gun. It didn't seem right to shoot an innocent; Ji-ji hoped the mare would forgive her. Next, she'd take out the heavyset Bounty Boy a few feet to Chet's right, the red-haired Boy they called Daryl. She couldn't decide which one to aim for after that. Only two left: the black moustache who kept himself to himself and didn't laugh at any of Chet's jokes, and a man who must've been at least seventy-five, with long gray whiskers to match his long gray beard. The elderly Boy held an axe in his hand with a shaft as long as his leg. Out of all of the Boys, the two off to the side worried her the most.

The noose dangled in front of the victim's face. Whenever the breeze kicked up it slapped his ass's ears. He looked over at her and mumbled something incoherent. Could've been "please." Could've been "help." Could've been "coward." She couldn't blame him if it was. His fake ears were vibrating like the tuning fork Old Patrick the Younger used when he tuned the piano in the pray center. The boy was having difficulty swallowing, and he was breathing real shallow, like she'd seen other seeds do during panic attacks and executions. His eyes bugged out, and he was so terrified he could barely stand upright—like a goat when it sees the butchery knife. Although he didn't know she had a gun, his big brown eyes begged her to save him. It made sense. Between the two of them, she was the lucky one only scheduled for a gang rape. As long as she remained submissive, she stood a chance of getting out alive. If only he hadn't been wearing those ears. That was what did it. The ass's ears roused in her a fury she couldn't suppress.

"Well?" Chet said. "We don't got all day, Blondie. Let's see them papers."

Lucky handed them over. Chet shuffled through them. He spat. A large brown glob of spittle landed so close to Lucky's feet he had to dodge to avoid it. (*One point to Chet.*)

"Nick Resolute," Chet said, reading from the papers with some difficulty. "That your real name? You one o' them preacherly types. Sounds like one o' them Geddonite names. You a Niter? Think Doomsday's on the horizon—that it?"

"Hell no! Ma liked to properfy her children. Didn't want me takin' a common appellation."

The Boys laughed on account of the fancy word he'd used and the way he'd said it—mimicking his mother in a cheeky, belligerent way. (*One point to Lucky.*)

"Hey," Lucky said, playing tipsy and throwing the dice. "How 'bout I take the Muleseed off your hands? Could use me a Mule like that. Lookin' to find some good supplemental labor."

"This one's not a genuine Mule," Chet informed him. "Not a ounce of father-man in him. That's how come we got him costumed up. This dusky's a Commonseed from the 368th."

The 368th. The planting Ji-ji and other seeds had been leased to during the harvest a few years back. She pictured the female seeds in their black "modesty hoods," recalled the paltry list of words seeds were allowed to utter. Brine had mentioned the 368th too—the story of the brave seedmate who had a knife lodged between her buttocks. She looked at their prey's emaciated, trembling legs and felt a pity so intense it nearly choked her.

"They want this one back dead or alive," Chet continued, "with the emphasis on the former, eh, boys? Lied about where he come from. If you wasn't so fuckin' drunk, Nick, you'd've heard me read the Runaway Sentence." Chet held up his comm device. "Got a notification 'bout Donkey here before the comm went down. Been on his trail ever since. Got slowed down by Mother Nature. Man, that quake a few days ago was a doozy! Never felt anythin' like it. You feel it too?"

Lucky acted like someone whose memory had been muddied by alcohol. Then he acted like he suddenly remembered the quake. Said it was how come he'd wound up in this predicament, without his cousin Lance, transporting a goddam ugly seed down to the Triad alone.

Chet interrupted him: "Yeah, yeah. Cry me a river. This dusky here had a weapon on him. A butchery knife. That's a hangin' offense."

"Sure is," Lucky agreed. Then he added, "By the way, speakin' of knives, there's a stiff bathin' in the floodwaters back there. Got all tangled up in the weeds. He belong to you?"

The Boys seemed taken aback by this news. Ji-ji figured it was on account of the rock they'd likely tied him to. Hadn't expected such a swift rising. (*Another point to Lucky.*)

"That'll be Jimbo," Chet said, recovering his composure, "Daryl's older brother. Jimbo always was clumsy. Had an accident, right, Daryl?"

Daryl spoke up. His voice was much higher than you'd expect, given his size: "He still got my favorite huntin' knife lodged in his gut?" (*A point to Daryl.*)

"Yep," Lucky replied, cool as a cuke. "Still got one side of his head mashed in too. Guess the healin' waters ain't workin' this afternoon." The boys laughed at that too. (*Point to Lucky.*)

Daryl piped up again: "Guess I'll go retrieve that knife after the entertainment's over. Special knife that. Extra sharp. Would hate to lose it.

Never know when you'll need to de-ball some motherfucker you run into in The Margins." The Boys laughed again. (*More points to Daryl.*)

"So?" Lucky said. "How 'bout I give you five hundred to take this Commonseed off your hands?"

Ji-ji held her breath. He'd done it. The fake steader was risking everything for a fake Mule.

There was a long pause. (*Points dripping off Lucky like beads of sweat.*)

"How much we want for him, Daryl?" Chet asked.

Daryl rubbed his beard while he pondered the question. "A thousand," he said at last. "Trade dollars or Independents'll do. None o' that virtual shit those swindlers use in the fuckin' SuperStates. How you meant to trade with somethin' you can't grasp ahold of? None o' that Territorial crap neither. Steader currency's in the toilet. Hate to say this—an' I'm not bein' unpatriotic, s'just the god's honest truth—only use we got for Territorial dollars is for butt wipin'."

"I'll give you six hundred trade dollars," Lucky said. "The dusky's lame."

The Boy on the old mare was offended: "That's a lie! He stubbed his toe is all."

"You got that kind o' lucre on you?" Chet asked. "Let's see it." (*A cascade of points to Chet.*)

Lucky laughed like he didn't have a care in the world. "Not till we got ourselves a deal. . . . But I guess I can sweeten the deal with a few o' these." Slowly, so they wouldn't think he was going for a gun, Lucky eased a small red tin from his shirt pocket and shook it.

"What the hell're they?" Chet asked. He took a step back and waved his hand in front of him as if he were warding off a ghost. (*Point to Lucky.*)

"They call 'em sunsets," Lucky replied. "Or blots. They're real popular in the Independents. It's like an upper fornicated with a downer and crapped out these little darlin's. I swear, it's the best high I ever rode. Lightnin' fast too. Here, try one."

"*Hell* no!" Chet said, as if the pills were poison. "Know how many years it took me to get shit like that outta my system? Daryl, you up for a tryout?"

"Sure," the big man said. He approached Lucky and held out his hand. "You sure this is safe? Cos if not I'll gut you, Blondie. Gut you *real* slow with a knife I'll borrow from my brother."

Lucky smiled. "How 'bout we swallow at the same time? I could use a hit. Whiskey's not doin' the trick, and it's been a pretty crappy day so far."

The two men counted backward: "Three . . . two . . . one." They popped the pills at the same time. A few seconds later, Daryl said he needed to sit down. He plopped to the ground, high as a kite, and started giggling. (*One down, four to go. A slew of points for Lucky!*)

Chet, hot with suspicion, demanded to know from Nick why he was still standing.

"I got a high tolerance," Lucky-Nick replied. "But believe me, Chet, I'm buzzin' right now. You got giant purple earrings on—you know that? Real pretty they are. Tinklin' in the breeze."

It was a risky move. But the other Boys, none of whom seemed especially fond of Chet, roared with laughter as Chet's gigantic ears turned a deeper shade of purple. He looked like he was thinking of drawing his gun when the man with the moustache who'd stood off to the side called out to him. "Hold up there, Chet," the man said. "No need to take offense."

The man strode up to Lucky and stood facing him. The way the others turned to watch him told Ji-ji Chet wasn't their leader, neither was Daryl or Mare-man. Moustache was.

"Name's Zinc Shokovsky," he said, offering his hand to Lucky as if he were his best friend in the whole wide world. "Let's act like the gentlemen we are and do things right this time."

Lucky shook his hand. "Nick Resolute."

Apart from his thick black moustache, Zinc Shokovsky was as clean-shaven as an inquisitor, his chiseled jaw notable among the group of bearded steaders. He had the same vindictive good looks Lotter had, though his hair was as dark as midnight and cropped shorter than was customary in steader country. He held the rim of his Stetson loosely in his hand. The hat's lynch-rope strap dangled to the ground. Zinc was the only one whose necktie was neatly tied and whose shirt was spotless. He'd ridden in on the other horse—a magnificent black stallion of seventeen hands or more. The horse's reins were being held by the old guy with the axe. Every so often, the stallion stomped his hoof impatiently, as if he sensed what was about to go down. Ji-ji hadn't expected to see a horse like that in The Margins. She didn't want to shoot it any more than she wanted to shoot the aged mare. She didn't even know if she could. . . .

"Pleased to meet you, Nick," Zinc said. A northerner for sure. Must be one of the large army of fairskin northerners who'd emigrated from the SuperStates to join the steader cause. Some said there were as many fairskin northerners in the Territories now as there were southerners.

"Please ignore my posse," Zinc said. "They get overeager just before a Retribution. You're real young, kid. What are you? Eighteen? Nineteen?"

"Twenty-one."

"Is that so? Twenty-one. You must've imbibed from the Fountain of Youth."

The Boys roared with laughter, especially Daryl, who giggled so much he wound up splayed out on the ground like an ant offering. "And how old is she?" Zinc asked.

Lucky shrugged convincingly. Belched. "Gotta peruse her papers. Jog my memory. Fifteen going on sixteen, I think. Or could be sixteen going on seventeen. Want me to take a look?"

"Nah, don't trouble yourself," Zinc said. "We don't give a damn."

The conversation was between the two of them now. It wasn't about points anymore. Ji-ji noted how close Zinc's hand was to the gun in his holster. Out of the corner of her eye, she saw the Boy on the mare ease himself onto the ground and set himself down in front of the horse's head. The blast would likely go right through him and hit the mare. *Damn.*

"Course, anyone can falsify a few papers," Zinc said, "right, boys?" They grunted in agreement. "So why is a pretty young fella like you out here in the middle of nowhere on foot? And why are you so keen on purchasing Ears over there? You some kinda Deviant?"

"Not last I checked," Lucky said, giggling tipsily. "As for how we wound up here—we were on horseback till yesterday. Planned to head on down to the Triad. Got a buyer for this breeder here." He nodded in Ji-ji's direction. "Horses got spooked by the quake. Reared up an' threw us. Took off like rockets." Lucky's tone became sodden with emotion. "Cousin Lance stepped on a trap. Ripped his fuckin' foot off! Ripped it right off at the ankle!" Lucky was so choked up he couldn't speak. Swaying too. Ji-ji didn't know if it was an act or if the sunset had gotten to him. Lucky swiped his forearm over his eyes and sniffed hard.

Chet turned to the others and made a face as if to say, "This Nick Resolute fella is a total wimp." Then he turned back and addressed Lucky. "You need to toughen up, kid. You don't see Daryl whimperin', do you? Even though he lost his own brother." The others hooted at Chet's wit.

Zinc looked over at Ji-ji. "We'll sell you the fake Mule for six hundred. Trades or Independents'll be fine." Lucky held out his hand to shake on it, but Zinc wasn't done yet. "You throw in the hinny as a loaner, just so we can relieve ourselves. Won't take us long. Then the three of you can be on your way. Tell you what, we'll throw in his ears too, to sweeten the deal."

Lucky seemed to consider it, at one point steadying himself against the effects of the fake booze, his fake grief, and the sunset. Ji-ji held her breath. She was a Mule. A hinny. Sellable. Rape-able. Lucky glanced at her over his shoulder and shrugged the way he did to show he didn't give a damn. But then he shook his head.

"'Fraid I can't do it, sir. Wish to god I could. But my client's real particular. He don't want a de-hymenized Mule. Gotta be intact else I don't get a dime."

"Understood," Zinc said. "But there's more than one way to skin a cat. I mean, the mulatto's kneeling already, after all."

Ji-ji held her breath again as Lucky gave that lazy shrug of his and shook his head once more.

"Wish I could oblige, Zinc, I really do. I can see you Boys're deservin' of relief. But my client's real strict about the purity of his seeds. Don't want problems in the oral vicinity either. Not that you boys would be infected, of course." No one laughed.

Chet stepped toward Lucky. "Show some respect to the Lord's Limbs," Chet said. "You know who you're speakin' to? Master Shokovsky ain't no common BB. He's none other than—"

Zinc told Chet to keep his mouth shut. Said if he didn't, he'd shut it for him. Chastened, Chet glared at the ground.

"Tell you what, kid," Zinc said. "How about you give us the six hundred as a toll, and as compensation for refusing to allow five upright Territorialers to indulge in the wares you're escorting? And how about, in addition, you do the honors with Ears here—just to put my mind at ease that your allegiance to the blessed Territories is genuine. Cos it seems to me—and I admit I was raised in the Eastern Super, so what do I know?—but it seems to me there's a lack of Territorial fervor in you. A laid-back quality that makes me suspect you may not be a true believer. And I'm not even gonna count the fact that you're acting drunk and disorderly in a public place and thereby disrespecting Jimbo Spiers, a nearby dead hero—God rest his soul. There's a price to be paid for that too. So whaddya say, young fella? We got a deal?"

"I got a choice?" Lucky asked.

Chet chimed in this time: "No, Blondie. You ain't."

"Fair enough," Lucky said.

Zinc nodded over toward the noose. "Do the honors, Nick Resolute," he commanded.

Chet, clearly disappointed that his executioner's role had been usurped, seemed to contemplate a protest but thought better of it. He scowled and kicked the tree trunk.

The boy who was not a Mule screamed as Lucky, under Zinc's watchful eye, eased the noose over his ears. The sound the boy made was a cross between a whimper and a shriek. He tried to slip his head Free but Chet came up and grabbed him. Lucky grasped hold of the rope and pulled. The boy rose a few feet off the ground and swung there like a seizure. Lucky tied off the rope as instructed. The Bounty Boys were so focused on the risen seed they didn't notice Ji-ji rise too.

IIIIIIIIIIIIII

But Lucky did. "*Gotta barf!*" he cried. To roars of mocking laughter, he staggered over to the boulder where he'd left his bag. He'd given her cover!

Ji-ji sprinted behind the low-hanging tree limb farthest from the boys and steadied Petrus' gun on one of the oak's low, spreading limbs. It was exactly the right height for her to balance her arm on it and shoot, thick enough to shield most of her body. No one had seen her move to her new position; she was invisible.

She fired. And missed.

But before the Boys could tell where the first shot came from, Lucky dived behind the boulder and began firing too.

The Boys scattered like roaches. Daryl, still high, crawled desperately toward the motorcycles for cover. Chet seemed to think Lucky was the only one shooting. He turned and began to run, heading straight for Ji-ji. The tree's limb kept her hand steady as she braced herself more firmly against the recoil. She adjusted her aim and pointed the gun at Chet's head.

She missed his head. Hit his heart instead. Chet's burly chest erupted.

Lucky lobbed two grenades—one at Zinc, the other at Daryl, who hadn't been able to crawl to cover fast enough. (Why didn't he tell her he had grenades? What else did he have in that bag of his?) One grenade exploded, the other didn't. It took Ji-ji a moment to figure out that the top half of Daryl was gone, pretty much. Zinc kicked the unexploded grenade away and aimed his gun at Lucky. He fired. Lucky fell back behind a boulder. He'd been hit!

The boy was still swinging from the lynch rope, twitching every now and then, but Ji-ji couldn't get over to him. They'd shoot them both if she did.

The stallion, terrified by the explosion, bolted. The mare ran in circles. Ji-ji took aim at Mare-man running for cover. She pulled the trigger.

Hit him in the leg. He went down. Another shot to Mare-man's head. Not her gun—Lucky's! Lucky was still alive!

Ji-ji turned in time to see the old man with the axe behind her, arms raised. *Bang, bang, bang!* In spite of the lousy angle Lucky had, a bullet whizzed past Ji-ji and tore into Axe-man's jaw, leaving him with a bloody scream for a mouth. He was dead before he hit the ground.

Four down, one to go! Zinc crouched behind one of the motorcycles, shooting at Lucky, still tucked behind the small boulder. Ji-ji fired at Zinc, but her hands shook wildly. She missed. She fired four more rounds. Missed again. Then Lucky fired too, but not at Zinc. He fired at the cans of fuel in the other bike's sidecar. Why hadn't she seen those?

An explosion! Another! Both bikes went up in flames!

Suddenly, Black Moustache was hiding behind nothing, his arm and leg on fire! He dropped and rolled, picked himself up before he was extinguished, and ran toward the panicked mare.

Lucky took aim. Shot Zinc in the back! Zinc's arms flung out as if he attempted to embrace the world before he slammed into the ground. Ji-ji rushed up to Zinc, gun drawn, afraid he would rise from the dead. He didn't. Zinc Shokovsky was as dead as a dodo.

"*Grab the damn horse!*" Lucky called out. Too late! The mare took off like a bullet.

Ji-ji tore over to Lucky's bag, grabbed a knife, and dashed over to the boy. With quivering hands, she cut the rope Lucky had tied off.

The child fell from the tree. He lay on the ground, not moving, not twitching.

She turned him over, tried to give him CPR. But she knew before she began it was useless. His neck was broken, like the baby birds you find who have fallen from the nest. She'd taken too long to get to him. Unforgivable.

With the utmost tenderness, Ji-ji removed his ears. It was only then that she noticed the rain.

When she got back, Lucky sat propped up against the boulder, blood seeping from a wound in his shoulder and another in his side. "Fake Mule's dead, right?" he asked.

"Yeah."

"Get me to the tree," he told her. "It'll give me some protection."

It took a while for them to get there because she had to half drag him most of the way. After Lucky settled against the trunk, he ordered her to gather the Boys' weapons and ammo and pile them up next to him. He instructed her to gather anything else she thought would be useful. Asked her to get Zinc's wallet and any papers the Boys had. She did all these things, trying not to look at the ruined bodies around her. Seemed like most of their possessions had been in the sidecars and were blown to kingdom come, but she found weapons, ID on Chet and the axe man, some trade dollars, and a few other valuables. Lucky instructed her to take some of the loot for herself.

When she asked him what their plan was, he said, "*My* plan is to stay here and give 'em hell. *Your* plan is to get to Dimmers. If you come across one of the horses, take it. Maybe you can ride part of the way. The edge of Dimmers is about eleven miles from here." She started to argue.

"You want to die here with me, Jellybean? No. Didn't think so. Even if we grabbed the horse, don't think I could've mounted her. I swear, eighteen never felt so bloody old. Yeah. I'm eighteen going on nineteen. So now you know. . . . Take the first-aid kit from my bag and leave that with me. Take a handful of killers too. You'll find another knife, flashlights, mags, a little food, hope-rope, and papers. Give me the whiskey flask." She found the flask and handed it to him. He took a couple of long gulps. He didn't have to play at not being sober anymore. Laughing grimly, he said, "'A horse, a horse, my kingdom for a bloody horse!' If I had a kingdom . . . which I don't."

"Why did you save us?"

"I didn't," he pointed out, slurring his words a little, gulping down more whiskey. "See Donkey Kong over there. Didn't do so well with that one, did I?"

"Who's Donkey Kong?"

"And that's your most important question?"

She couldn't read him—couldn't tell if he liked her or despised her.

"Listen up, cos I'm drunk and getting higher by the second. If you don't fancy hanging around for some knock-knock jokes, take the compass from my shirt pocket and head directly east then southeast. Cross at the safest point. Tie off the rope and keep a hold of it so you don't get swept away. Water's swifter than it looks. Boys'll be arriving soon. I'll hold them off long as I can. Don't wimp out on me. You get all scaredy-cat and this Jesus stunt will mean nothing."

He tried to ease himself into a more comfortable position, then spoke again. "If you run into trouble, tell them Nick Resolute, the steader who was taking you to the Triad, got killed by snarlcats. Those papers'll let them know you're on the up and up. Go by Faith Planterseed from now on. You're a Muleseed from the 497th. That's what your papers say, but don't let on you can read. If you get transported to the Triad, a one-eyed fairskin Friend posing as . . ." He paused, couldn't seem to find the name. "Posing as . . . Lee Stapleson—that's it . . . I think? Or is it Mike? He'll be on the lookout for you at the auctionmart. He'll have a patch over his left eye. Or is it the right?"

Lucky winced again. Ji-ji tried to stanch the blood at his shoulder but he pushed her away.

"No time. Only an hour or less of daylight left. You got Dreg's map? This rain won't slow them down much. Take mine too. Soon every BB within ten miles will be making a beeline for this place. . . . Head east, then southeast. Did I tell you that? When you get to the warning signs for Viral Colony Four, ignore them and keep on going. . . . And keep that ridge over there at your back. Reach into my bag and get my caller. It's in a hidden compartment at the bottom of the bag."

She reached in and eventually found the secret pocket. She pulled out a small caller.

"Comm's been down for two days," he said. "But it could've been worse. No APBs. . . . The Boys weren't on the lookout for us. Couldn't call for help. Man Cryday'll be searching for you."

"Who?"

"Cryday. Push that button there and enter the code 9-0-2. It's red now—see? If it turns amber the signal's iffy. If it's green, it's a go. Keep checking. Cryday'll be doing the same."

"I gotta bury him," she said, looking over at the lynched boy.

"Like hell you do! Listen to me. *Listen!* The kid wouldn't want that. He'd want you to live. God knows he's better off dead than on the 368th. Time to strike out on your own, Jellybean."

"Ji-ji."

"Who gives a crap? Go on. Get out of here."

She bit her lip as she struggled to say what she meant: "Thank you, Lucky . . . for saving my life."

"Yeah. *De nada* and all that crap. A word of advice. If some ashy-kneed wizard asks you to do him a favor, tell him to bugger off. You owe me, Jellybean Lottermule."

"Yeah. I know."

Ji-ji finished sorting out what she would take and what she would leave. She left him almost all the weapons, but she took Petrus' gun and the mags. The tree's enormous canopy kept Lucky fairly dry, but she insisted on leaving the tarp with him and arranging it so he would have some protection. She left him the blanket too, ignoring his order that she take it.

He took off the watch he'd taken from her. "Here," he said. "Trade you. Don't think I'll need this anymore." He handed her the watch. She cried when he did that. She wanted to tell him that Uncle Dreg had braided the watchstrap for her himself when the strap it came with had broken. She wanted him to understand what it meant to her to have it back. But her stomach was caving in and the words wouldn't come.

"Don't go all blubbery on me, for Christ's sake. If you get waylaid before you can reach Dimmers, don't tell anyone your mum was Toteppi, and for god's sake don't mention the wizard. Even if they don't know you're the runaway from the 437th, they'll target you. Tiro was right about one thing. Some of the steaders want to cleanse the Territories of every last Toteppi, understand? You're a Commonseed, that's all. You got that?"

"I don't want to leave you! Maybe I can go search for the horse an' then we can—"

"No. It's over. S'okay. I'm not scared. Should be I know, but I'm not. Nothing much to keep me here now. . . . Don't forget, Ji-ji. Head directly east-southeast. Dimmers is big. Can't miss it."

He'd called her by her name. She was on the verge of losing it completely, so she hoisted his duffel bag onto her shoulder, turned, and began to walk away. He called after her. She looked back.

"Hey! You weren't bad with that gun. Don't lose it. I think it'll be lucky for you. Did a hell of a lot better with it than you did with a knife and fork. Cutlery's not your specialty. Stick to semiautomatics, okay?" She managed a nod. He seemed satisfied.

The young lieutenant sat only a few feet from the lynched boy. It looked like they were having some crazy, waterlogged picnic under the tree. She thought he might have smiled at her when he said the part about the cutlery, but she couldn't say for sure cos pelting rain obscured her view. Under her breath, she asked the live oak to look after the dead boy and her dying friend. She called him that in her head—her friend. She didn't look back again. Couldn't. Instead, she walked on.

Unraped.

Alive.

Lucky.

18 A MURMURATION OF TREES

Waves of intense pain brought Ji-ji to her knees. She couldn't move, could hardly see. The pain radiated from her spine—its roots down at her tailbone, its branches burning a trail across her shoulders.

Seeds called some types of physical pain "ugly." Ugly pain was usually unexpected but short-lived. You could recover from pain like that. Seeds called grieving pain and other forms of emotional pain "purple." The seedlings' nursery rhyme that began

Purple pain is prince again
Rain tears, and wince again

was an attempt to make light of a pain born of deep sorrow. Pain strong enough to kill you was given another name to signify its power: "vengeful." Vengeance pain was worse than the other two because it had an agenda; it *wanted* to make its victims suffer. Vengeance pain was what seeds felt after a lashing, an assault, or a lopping. Seeds who suffered from this type of pain had to be watched. Every seed knew that a lopping wasn't limited to physical amputations; it could also be the lopping off of a loved one from your life. Seeds said victims of vengeance pain, if it went on for too long, could *become* their pain and be eaten up by a thirst for vengeance themselves.

Ji-ji refused to give in to it. It didn't make sense that the pain was so capricious. Increasingly, a suspicion had grown in her that the pain was psychosomatic. As a volunteer at the seed clinic, she'd heard Doc Riff explain what a psychosomatic illness was when he'd examined Felly Spareseed, who felt ghost pain in her right ear, even though rats had gnawed off her left one when she'd fallen into a drunken stupor in the granary. Ji-ji had seen the ailment again when Lizzie Marshallseedmate, who'd seedbirthed twelve deadborns, came in with a bloated belly and an empty womb. Though Doc Riff had diagnosed her condition as psychosomatic, Bettieann had sworn up and down it was one of her twelve deadborns come back as a wraith to purge her womb and prep it for reseeding.

A wave of nausea thrust Ji-ji's face down into the earth. It was as if the vengeance pain were trying to bury her alive. Desperate, she pawed through the duffel bag until she found painkillers. She grabbed her canteen of water. Her hands shook so badly she nearly spilled the contents of the pill bottle. She willed her hand steady and downed both of Lucky's killers in a single gulp. . . . *Lucky's killers*—the terrible phrase she mustn't focus on now. She fought against the killers as they tried to force her to vomit them up again.

Guilt choked her. She'd abandoned the fairskin who had saved her. If their roles had been reversed, Lucky would never have left her to die alone. He would have hoisted her onto his broad shoulders and taken his chances. Sure, he would have bitched about it afterward, but he would still have done the right thing. He'd proven his loyalty and his courage repeatedly. When had she proven hers? He'd played the hero, so what did that make her? A coward. Wasn't that what the poor boy in the ass's ears said? She'd agreed too quickly to leave Lucky there alone. Maybe together they could have fended off an attack? They had enough weapons. . . . But they only had two pairs of hands—one and a half, in fact. Lucky's wounded arm was useless.

Ji-ji gazed around her. For the first time in her life, she was alone in the wilderness. It was near dusk—a cloudy night without a lot of moonlight. Even if it weren't cloudy, the forest wouldn't permit much light to penetrate. She had a flashlight in the bag and spare batteries. Would that be enough for her to keep her bearings? The forest bore down on her, brooding and hostile. She could hear the river rushing by in the distance. The sound reminded her that she'd strayed too far from it. She needed to cross it before darkness enveloped her. She heard a distant roar—an eerie howl in response. Snarlcats? Stripers?

The mutants weren't the only wild things in The Margins. There were stories of wild hogs as big as goats, snakes as fat as boa constrictors, armies of cat-sized rats. She didn't know what was fact and what was fiction. All she knew was that she'd witnessed a snarlcat tear a seed to pieces on one of her hunts with Lotter. She'd seen how fast an ant could move. If a pride of snarlcats attacked her, she would never get a shot off in time. Stripers hunted in packs too. Bred for savagery, the oversize, hyena-like stripers had proved to be untrainable. And then there was Drol—the bloodthirsty biped that tore Cray Juniper to shreds. Juniper was the only other half-decent guard on the planting. Could be more of those bipeds roaming around. Even if she could get off a shot, she would be announcing her whereabouts to every Bounty Boy within a radius of several miles. If she couldn't come to grips with the pain, her choice boiled down to this: die quick or die slow.

The killers kicked in at last. She felt light-headed, but the sharp edges of pain had been filed down. She checked her Mickey-the-Godmouse watch. She'd lingered for more than twenty-five minutes! Way too long. The rain had eased up; the going should be easier.

Groaning in pain, Ji-ji stood. She shouldered Lucky's bag but cried out when the straps made contact with her back. She'd have to carry the bag in her arms like a baby or drag it behind her. She opted for the former and started to walk toward the sound of water.

To take her mind off the pain, Ji-ji went over her revised plans for the race. Lucky hadn't revealed much of anything. Had gotten mad whenever she'd asked him for details. She wasn't even sure exactly how long she'd been traveling. She'd been barely conscious for the early miles. Thank god for the layover after the first leg. There was still a chance they could get there in time. At Monticello, they would be ratified as Wild Seeds. Tiro would battle in the Jefferson Coop and compete in the flyer-battler sprint before competing in the city's famed Dream Coop. She'd have to race to D.C. The race monitors and inquisitors would determine exactly how long the run would be and finalize the route. From what Coach B had told her, a lot would depend on prevailing conditions, how many guards were available to man the route, and how hard the inquisitors pushed for a longer, tougher run. If it was true the runners were sabotaged last year, she had to be prepared for an exhausting race. Before her injury, a run like that would have been doable. She could sleep at the rest stations along the race route. They even gave competitors real running shoes. She'd never had a genuine pair of running shoes before. But how could she run with a back like this?

Last night, she'd asked Lucky if the Friends could sneak her into the city if she couldn't compete, or if she could petition for asylum when she reached the city gates. He'd told her the odds: 99.9 percent of refugees were denied entry, the handful who made it through granted transitional status only, which meant they could be deported at any time. Worse still, the D.C. Congress had already threatened to dismantle the refugee tent city of KingTown. If that happened, thousands of former seeds who'd camped at the feet of the Dreamer King would be trucked back to the No Region or The Margins. "Is that what you want?" Lucky had asked her. "To be trucked back?" "NoVA couldn't be worse than the 437th," she'd argued. "Yeah it could," he'd replied. "Trust me." She didn't remind him he'd said trust was overrated.

Thinking about the race only reminded her she'd left Lucky behind. She would give almost anything to have him yell at her again or accuse her of being hopelessly naïve. She needed to find something happy to focus on. Then she remembered Doc Riff's *Book of Beasts and Birds.*

When they were seedlings, she and Tiro used to play a game where they tried to list the crazy names people had come up with in the old days for groups of animals. Ji-ji had discovered them in the book the doc had loaned her. Tiro wasn't in love with words the way she was, but he'd enjoyed flipping through the book with her. Jam-packed with pictures of exotic animals they'd never seen (and probably never would now that people had poisoned so much of the world), the book listed crazy names for groups of birds and beasts: a parliament of owls, a zeal of zebras, a murmuration of starlings, an obstinacy of buffaloes, a murder of crows, a clowder of cats. Doc Riff, always sensitive to the feelings of seeds, had blacked out "a barren of mules," but they'd still been able to make it out. "Guess they got Muleseeds muddled up with Serverseeds," Ji-ji had joked too young to know any better. "I can litter a whole bunch of seedlings cos I'm not a Cloth." Tiro had asked her how many seedlings she wanted. "Four," she'd replied at once. Luvlydoll was still healthy, and Charra and Clay still lived on the planting too, so four seemed like a perfect number. Tiro accepted her logic about the other names, but joked that if a herd of cats was a clowder, he was a bowl of chowder. He'd doubled up with laughter. She'd laughed too. When Tiro laughed, it was impossible not to join in. Back then, a "barren of mules" wasn't personal; it was just a name that tickled their funny bones.

She heard it before she saw it. Something very large . . . snorting. *A snarlcat!*

She threw down the duffel bag and drew Petrus' gun from the shoulder holster. A giant form was ambling through the shadows toward her! She raised the gun unsteadily, planted her feet, took aim. With a sudden intake of breath, she lowered her weapon.

Zinc Shokovsky's black stallion looked at her in terror and began to back away.

Ji-ji thought fast. There was an apple in Lucky's bag. She retrieved it, coaxing the horse to stay put while she did so. She extended her arm as she approached the magnificent animal. *Careful! No sudden moves! If I startle him he'll bolt.* Without thinking about it consciously, she mimicked the way Afarra spoke to animals on the planting, making the trilling, clucking sound in the back of her throat like Afarra did.

It worked! The stallion trotted up to her, inclined his regal head, and plucked the apple from her outstretched hand. She clucked to him some more and stroked his beautiful ears as he chewed. As soon as she dared, she grabbed her bag and moved round to his side. She lowered the left stirrup and slid her foot into it. Grasping the horn of the saddle, she pulled herself up, up, up!

She couldn't believe how tall he was. Had it not been for the saddle, she didn't know how she would have gotten onto his back. With some difficulty, she readjusted the stirrups to fit her better and settled back into the generous seat. She secured Lucky's bag to the saddle. If she lost it, she'd be toast. The cantle cradled her tender back, and the reins slipped easily between her fingers. Zinc Shokovsky must've been rich as the devil to afford a mount like this one.

Normally, Ji-ji would have been nervous to ride a stallion, but tonight being high up gave her confidence. Pain slid off her body like snakeskin. She couldn't avoid the truth any longer: the pain was all in her head—a sign she was going nuts. But it also meant that if she conquered the pain she could compete in the Freedom Race. She was Silapu's daughter. She could do this.

The horse felt warm beneath her. Her days riding as a seedling came flooding back. Before she'd been old enough to be subject to the Elevation Prohibitions on female botanicals, she had ridden with Lotter during hunts, whenever the flood rains made the roads impassable for the hunt trucks, and whenever there wasn't gas to spare on the planting. When she turned nine, Lotter let her ride a mount of her own—a gangly mare with a loping gait and flatulence, the main reason why no one else wanted to ride her. Ji-ji called the mare Tara because it rhymed with Charra. After Lotter told her on her eleventh birthday she was too old to accompany him anymore, Ji-ji hadn't wept for the loss of the hunt or for the loss of her father-man's company. Instead, she'd wept because she knew there was a good chance she would never again experience the feeling of elevation she got on the back of Tara. Ji-ji couldn't help but suspect that Uncle Dreg's wizardry had brought the amazing stallion to her just when she needed him. It made no sense to have a valuable horse like this in The Margins, not when it could fetch more than what a prize juvi could fetch at the auctionmart.

She unbuckled the flap of Zinc's saddlebag and peered inside. Encased in a plastic bag she found a photo of a fairskin woman holding an infant in each arm. Zinc's wife? Was Zinc the father of twins? The photo looked old. Was it Zinc as an infant? Was that his mother and his twin? Depressing to think there could be two Shokovsky bastards in this world. She also found a copy of *The One True Text,* a knife in its sheath, and a caller. She had two callers now, for what it was worth.

She checked Lucky's caller again. Still red—no signal. She thought about trying Zinc's, but she'd picked up a lot of useful information observing Lotter in his role as the planting security chief. For all she knew, the caller was linked exclusively to the Bounty Boys' network. Or it could have a tracking device, like the kind Lotter used on the hunt. Safer to toss it. She was tempted to stomp on it first but that would mean she'd have to dismount. Way too risky with the horse still jumpy. He could easily bolt and leave her. She opted to hurl Zinc's caller as far as she could into the forest. It sailed off like a wingless plastic bird into the dusk.

She reached down into the saddlebag again to check she hadn't missed anything and found a letter tucked away in a hidden side pocket. Like the photo, it was inside a sealed plastic bag. She pulled it out and glanced over it. The handwriting was abnormally neat. The letter opened with the word "Brother" and went on to mention something about the city. She assumed it was Dream City at first, but then she suspected it was Armistice. She peered at the handwriting in the failing light. Something about being late for something. A line about "the sins of the father." Ji-ji turned to the last of the three pages to find the signature. It was signed "Fester." So Zinc's brother—his twin, most likely—was called Fester. Fairskins had the weirdest names.

The horse stomped his hoof on the ground restlessly. "Okay, boy," she said. "I don't like this place either." She needed to get going. She could read it later. She folded the letter, slipped it back into the plastic bag, and returned it to the saddlebag's hidden pocket. She didn't want it to get wet, so she decided to put the photo in there too.

And now she was faced with a dilemma. She had a horse, which meant she could go back, find Lucky. She could help him mount the stallion and the three could journey to Dimmers together.

She leaned forward onto the horse's neck and rested her head there, thinking. She heard the horse snort, heard—or thought she did—his great heart beating: *ba-BOOM, ba-BOOM, ba-BOOM!* Once again, she needed to admit the truth to herself.

A few minutes after she'd left Lucky, she'd heard a burst of gunfire over the pelting rain. She'd taken off running, headed in the wrong direction because, in her panic, she'd forgotten to look at the compass. All this time, she'd been telling herself maybe it wasn't gunfire, maybe it was something else. She'd been lying. If she turned back now, she would find another corpse under the live oak. Maybe find a mischief of Bounty Boys as well. No. Turning back wasn't an option.

She pressed her heels into the stallion's flanks and said, "Giddyup, boy!" He began walking. They had a river to cross. Tiro waited for her on the other side. At least she didn't have to cross it alone.

IIIIIIIIIIIIII

Dusk was almost over before she found a place to cross. At a section of the river where the bank didn't seem too steep, she eased the reluctant horse down toward the water. The mud was deep. She spoke to him reassuringly, gave him a name. "C'mon, Black Majestic," she coaxed. She'd named him that because he was the closest thing she'd ever seen to royalty—or to what she pictured royalty looking like anyway. As they descended the bank, she didn't let him know how terrified she was. Horses—stallions especially—were high-strung. They could sense when riders were scared. She gripped his body with her thighs and knees, pressed her heels down in the stirrups like Lotter had taught her, and leaned way back in the saddle so she didn't topple over his head during the treacherous descent. No way to get a clear view of what awaited them on the other side of the river—too dark. Maybe over there the bank was too steep to ascend? No point worrying about that when the swift water would likely push them downriver anyway. She prayed that the stallion's weight and strength would prevent them from veering too far off course.

Lucky had instructed her to tie off the hope-rope and use it to haul herself back to safety, if necessary. But she reasoned they could get tangled up in it. For the umpteenth time, she wished Lucky hadn't been so scared of the water. If he hadn't been, he would have crossed with her hours before. She said a quick prayer for him and for herself. The river was moving fast and this was the narrowest place she could find to cross before night overtook them completely. She forged ahead.

It took ages to persuade the stallion to enter the water. Sensibly, he balked at first. She urged him on: "*C'mon, boy! It's not far. You can do this!*" Finally, with a shake of his head (as if he knew how dumb this idea was) he ventured in. It was already too dark to see much of anything.

After only a few tentative steps, the riverbed fell away. They plunged into the frigid water! As Ji-ji hung on for dear life, the stallion thrashed back up to the surface. Once there, he raised his head so his nostrils weren't submerged. Terrified that the extra weight was too much for him, Ji-ji leapt off into the water, keeping a tight hold on the saddle and reins. Dismounting was a lousy idea. The horse was even more spooked without her on his back. Sputtering and shivering, she heaved herself back up onto the saddle and urged him to keep going.

The deeper they got, the more the current picked up. She stopped urging the horse on and let him take the lead. He seemed calmer after she did that. She rested her head on his withers and spoke to him the way Afarra would have. It seemed to help until something barreled toward them. A small tree! It struck the horse's rump and he spun around in terror. She managed to turn him toward the far bank again but he was tiring. Abruptly, he stopped paddling and began to sink. She kicked hard with her heels. "*No, boy! NO! Don't give up now! We're almost there!*"

Black Majestic mined strength from somewhere and started swimming again more frantically than before. They were only feet from safety! They were going to make it!

When the stallion's hooves touched the bottom again, Ji-ji yelped with joy.

She'd rejoiced too soon. Just as it was on the other side, the riverbed was steep and uneven. The horse lost his balance and stumbled back into the murky water, landing on top of her! In her distress, pinned as she was beneath his great weight, she sucked in the river water and began to choke. The stallion rolled off her and pitched away into the gloom, flailing and kicking as he frantically sought the surface. His hooves missed her head by a hair.

Swallowing all that water punched the breath from her lungs. She must get to the surface! *Blow out some air! Follow the bubbles!* It didn't help. She had a few seconds of air left!

Something caught her eye. A light—very faint. Desperately, she clawed her way up toward it.

she realized it was only the wind whistling through the trees. She looked up and saw the swaying branches. "A murmuration of trees," she whispered.

Years after she'd discovered the word in Doc Riff's book, she'd looked up *murmuration* and found out that it referred not only to the group name for starlings but also to their synchronized movements, the breathtaking aerial ballet she'd observed while laboring in the fields. Numerous bird species had been driven to extinction, but Uncle Dreg said some species were coming back stronger than ever now that communities were less industrial and therefore less adept at poisoning themselves and others. The week after he'd told her that, she'd seen a murmuration of starlings overhead at sunset. When she'd told him about it, he'd said, "Flight is prayer, little one." When she thought about how she'd felt when she'd seen the flock concertina in the sky above her, she knew the wizard was right. Even there on the 437th, amid so much suffering, beauty found a way in.

Ji-ji closed her eyes, listened again to the leaves, and took a deep breath. A cleansing. None of the foul odor of Petrus' pig farm; none of the planting's factory stench. She thought about stopping to rest but a seed on a stallion would be easy prey. Better to keep going. It could be wishful thinking, but it seemed as though Black Majestic knew this area. He'd found a trail of sorts, and they'd been walking along it with more confidence. She decided to trust him.

When she was little, her mam used to tell her stories about animal "mask wearers" who came back clothed in the spirits of dead ancestors. Could Zinc's stallion be one of these? She decided to change his name to Oz Majestic, in honor of Uncle Dreg the Oziadhee. "Do you like your new name, Oz?" she asked. He snorted a yes, or at least she decided to believe in that translation.

A short while later, she almost missed it. Luminous letters graced a large sign ahead. At the top of the sign, above the wording, a hastily drawn skull and crossbones. Ji-ji read the warning:

VIRAL COLONY IV

Pathogens: Active

Access Restricted by order of

District Judge, the Honorable Ellis Boyle, Jr.

ENTER AT YOUR OWN RISK!!!

Re-entry into the Homestead Territories is at the discretion of the Territorial Border Patrol & the HTQB.

She surfaced, gasping. The clouds must have parted in the r
The moon's reflection had been just enough to save her. She sw
lower water and peered through the gloom. She spotted his fra
ette on the moonlit water! He was downriver. She scrambled
water and ran along the bank shouting his name. "*Black Majestic!*
He didn't hear her. He was going to drown!

She hesitated for a moment, then plunged back into the wa
the aid of the current, she swam toward the stallion. It was o
most reckless things she'd ever done. But she'd left Lucky and M
refused to leave this innocent, petrified animal.

At last, she caught up with him. She grabbed hold of his bit an
his head back toward her with as much authority as she could
"This way!" She only half expected him to follow her, but as soo
heard her voice he calmed down. "Come on, boy . . . that's it
That's it! This way!"

Not long afterward, she led the exhausted stallion up the bank.
top, he collapsed onto his side, almost squashing her. She only lau
They'd made it. They'd crossed the river together. She hadn't aban
him.

She laid her head on the stallion's neck, and wept with grief
gratitude.

IIIIIIIIIIIII

The sodden saddle squeaked and squelched under her weight. It wo
take hours for it to dry out completely. It was a mild night but she w
soaked and shivering. Thankfully, she hadn't lost the compass in the riv
and she'd thought to tie Lucky's duffel bag to the saddle, so she had th
too. Uncle Dreg's map, which had been in her pocket, was soaked, bu
he must've used permanent ink, so it was still okay, as long as the pa
per didn't disintegrate. For the life of her, she couldn't find Lucky's map
Must've lost it in the river. Lucky's caller was okay, however—snug and
dry inside Lucky's bag. She took it out and turned it on. A little red light
shone in the dark . . . flickered . . . turned to amber. . . . *Amber!* Not
green, but maybe she could still get through?

She entered Lucky's number: 9-0-2. "Man Cryday? It's me. Ji-ji . . .
Jellybean. Silapu's daughter. . . . I'm Uncle Dreg's—" She hesitated.
"—friend," she added. Static. She tried again. Useless!

A half mile farther on she tried once more and got a similar result,
though she thought she heard voices murmuring on the other end before

Judge Boyle's signature followed, accompanied by the official seal of the Homestead Territories' Quarantine Board. At least, that's what Ji-ji assumed, though the serpents and wings on the seal's caduceus were so badly drawn it was hard to say for sure.

Oz Majestic refused to budge. Ji-ji suspected he'd been trained to come to a halt whenever he saw a skull and crossbones. When she urged him forward, he neighed in protest.

"It's okay," she told him. "Don't be scared. Man Cryday is waiting for us. So is Tiro."

At last, she convinced the stallion to obey. He took off at a canter, moving past the sign in a wide arc, as if the skull and crossbones were a ferocious mutant.

Soon afterward, the trail came to an abrupt end. The canopy cover was thicker here; moonlight could barely penetrate it. The inhospitable landscape reminded her of the planting's Doom Dell: trees she couldn't identify, a strong smell of mold. She tried the caller again. "Man Cryday, where are you?"

The ground became pitted with deep potholes and strewn with sharp rocks. It wasn't safe to ride anymore, so she dismounted and led Oz along the trail. She heard running water. A stream—a few yards to her right, sounded like. She was tempted to stop and let Oz drink, and fill her canteen too, but decided against it. She'd noticed something strange: there was a stiff breeze but the trees emitted no sound. She stopped to examine one and caught her breath when she saw it up close in the flashlight's glare. The leaves weren't green, they were a deep red. She reached out and touched one. They were hard and waxy, like the leaves of a holly bush. "*Ow!*" It felt as though she had been stung by a bee! She shook her hand, but it did nothing to lessen the pain. She stuffed her fingers in her mouth and sucked while she examined the leaves more closely. They had tiny thorns on their edges. Oz began chomping on mushrooms clustered around the foot of the same tree. She pulled him away. For all they knew, the 'shrooms were poisonous.

They walked on to a clearing filled with moonlight. The ground had leveled off. For the first time, she heard the leaves whisper in the breeze, and then she heard a tinkling sound. Wind chimes! Someone must have hung them in the trees! "It's a sign, Oz! We must be near Dimmers Wood!" In high spirits, she climbed back into the saddle and kicked lightly with her heels to urge the horse forward. He obeyed, his gait more relaxed than before. Oz liked this place.

Ji-ji could hardly believe her eyes when the clearing led to a wide avenue of perfectly spaced live oak trees, which had obviously been planted by someone many years before. Over time, they had joined limbs across the avenue to form a stunning arch. A large wooden sign hung from one of the trees. In white glow-in-the-dark paint, someone had written the words ***Dimmers Wood Straight Ahead.*** All the fears Ji-ji had about the name left her. This place was beautiful!

Sadly, the grand avenue of oaks didn't last. The oaks disappeared, and the avenue shrank to a footpath. Soon Ji-ji found herself in a grove of densely clustered trees. The sound of the chimes grew louder. She looked up. Teardrop-shaped buds shimmered in the moonlight.

All of a sudden, a burning pain in her back. She tried to breathe through it. A female voice said something like, "Alice Volatpro pray us," or was she imagining it? It was coming from Lucky's caller! She snatched it up.

"Who is this? I need to speak to Man Cryday. This is Ji-ji. Lucky's friend."

The voice again: "*Alice Volatpro pray us.*"

What did it mean? Was someone asking this Alice person to pray for them?

Ji-ji shouted into the caller: "It's not Alice. It's Ji-ji . . . Uncle Dreg's friend." No response.

The sound overhead had changed. It wasn't melodic anymore; it was harsh . . . jangling. . . . She smelled a stench she couldn't identify. She looked up again at the droplets. What was this place?

She trained the flashlight up into the trees. The stallion shuffled backward, startled. These weren't wind chimes. These trees were hung with what looked like glass tears! She looked more closely. The tears—yes she was sure of it now—the tears were purple. The trees gave off a sickly odor, the tinkling sound of wind chimes replaced by a discordant, nearly deafening clamor. Oz whinnied in terror. Ji-ji tried to calm him, but he spun in frenzied circles.

Suddenly, out of nowhere, a sack of meal slammed into her head! It swayed there in front of them, dangling from a vine. No. Not a sack of meal. A maggot-infested corpse!

She flung it away from them, rotting flesh sliding off bones into her hands!

Oz reared in terror. Somehow, Ji-ji managed not to be thrown. All around them more corpses dropped from the trees like ghastly blossoms.

Some fell to the ground with a thud; others dangled by their necks. A lynching wood! They hadn't entered a place of harmony at all. They'd entered a grove of slaughter!

Ji-ji screamed for Man Cryday, for Tiro, *anyone*! A mob of maggots spilled from the corpses' eye sockets. As they exited their hosts, the maggots turned into flies and formed a black, undulating mass, a mad swarm of buzzing! They changed again. This time into flocks of demented birds that swirled and dipped around them. Oz reared up, then tore off through the wood, crashing into the trees' strange fruit as he ran. Ji-ji attempted to pull on the reins, but he didn't even seem to know she was riding him.

As suddenly as he'd taken off, the stallion slid to a halt. He reared up again and screeched in terror. She had never heard a sound like that come from a horse before. It sounded human—the sounds made by the condemned when they were pyred. It turned her blood to ice. She looked down.

The ground opened up around them! Gaping holes, filled with bones!

The stallion reared again. This time, Ji-ji couldn't hold on. Oz tossed her into the wet earth. She landed on her back at the edge of one of the openmouthed graves as birds corkscrewed a black shroud around her body! Oz raced into the darkness. A hulking shadow took off after him. One of the Dimmer-dead. Must be.

"*RUN, OZ!*" Ji-ji cried.

The noise had become unbearable. A dreadful moaning joined by jarring chimes. Thousands of people shrieking in pain! Ji-ji covered her ears. Black-hole mouths sucked her down into the earth! She couldn't see . . . couldn't breathe!

The branch of a tree reached down, turned itself into a gnarled hand, and grabbed her by the shoulder. Where the tree's hand touched her, tributaries of pain bubbled and burned all across her back! A voice invaded her head. *Death is always lucky in the end,* it told her. *There's no escape. No race till you dream with the dead.* Lua's words! *No race till you dream . . .*

She yearned for one thing only—suicide. She wanted to bury herself alive! Wanted to do exactly what the voice told her and dream with the dead. She had to resist! She covered her ears. "*SHUT UP!*" she screamed. With her last ounce of strength, she forced herself to her feet.

Almost immediately, she was knocked back to the ground. A pair of eyes shone in the dark, a wet nose snuffled near her head. Oz had returned to save her!

Then she glimpsed the black-and-white bars on the beast's misshapen body and wondered for a split second why Oz was inside a cage. No . . . not the stallion. *A striper!*

As the vicious mutant lunged for her throat, Ji-ji screamed. Out of her mouth flew a pandemonium of maggots, a maelstrom of flies, and a vast black murder of crows.

19 THE MUTANT

She woke to the smell of herbs. The hand of the tree rested on her hand. She snatched hers away and moaned. Her back was aflame as she tumbled back into the grave. . . .

She woke. The hands of the tree were kneading dough. She watched them work, gnarled and beautiful. In the open doorway, flooded with sunlight, a monster. His hunched back was a rug of black-and-white stripes. The mutant. The savage striper. She tried to warn the hands, but the quiet earth was a cradle rocking her to sleep. . . .

She woke. The hands of the tree offered her water. *Thank you,* she didn't say, because those who are buried alive have no voices. The grave was impatient; she had to go. . . .

She woke. The hands were connected to arms and shoulders, a neck and a face. *Who are you?* she didn't say, but the face told her anyway. "Man Cryday." *You're . . . female!* The tree witch laughed—her falling-all-over-each-other teeth familiar. *Am I dead?* "Not yet." *I thought you were the hands of the tree.* "And that is what I am, child. The hands who remember the trees' sorrow. . . ." Another voice silhouetted in the doorway. It took her other hand. It had come to escort her from the grave. The voice belonged to Tiro Dregulahmo. She could rest peacefully now. She didn't need another thing.

||||||||||||||

"Good. You have finally decided to resurrect yourself. How do you feel?"

"Okay. . . . Tired."

"That is to be expected after a purple exhumation. Your strength is return—"

Ji-ji interrupted: "I thought I saw Tiro."

"Flight Boy arrived two days before you did. Lie back down."

"Tiro's here? Where is he?"

"He has gone on a hunt with the others. Do not fuss. He will be back soon."

It made sense they would need food, but why go now? Alarmed, Ji-ji sat up and said, "There's no time for hunting. The Freedom Race! We have to leave now!"

"Lie back. You are not yet ripe for travel. How is your back today?"

"Sore. But it's been worse. I injured it, in the fly-coop. . . . Or it could be psychosomatic."

The old woman looked disgusted. "Riff taught you this word. That young man has spent too long away from his land and his people. He speaks as though body and mind are distant cousins. What is anything if not an idea?"

This was too deep for Ji-ji in her weakened state. She settled for, "You know Doc Riff?"

"I taught him much of what he obviously does not remember."

"So you don't think the pain's in my head then?" Ji-ji asked, unsure of which option would be better, real or imagined.

The old woman pulled her leaf-green head-tie down further onto her wide forehead. "The pain is real," she said. Ji-ji was relieved. A diagnosis from a female healer-philosopher who had taught Doc Riff must count for something.

"Is it a broken bone, or a pulled muscle, or—I don't know—a slipped disc or something?"

"Yes."

"Which one?"

"The last one."

"A slipped disc?"

"No. An 'or something.'"

Ji-ji couldn't tell if the woman was trying to be funny. She didn't want to push her luck to find out. Tiro would return soon from the hunt. She would find out more about her condition then.

"Are you Man Cryday?"

"That is my trickster-name. It is not safe for people like us to say who we really are."

Ji-ji understood. Man Cryday's accent and features identified her as Toteppi. No wonder she used a fake name. No Toteppi was safe in the Territories anymore. For the first time, Ji-ji noticed the wall hangings in the cozy cabin. The batik and kente cloth her mam used to speak of showcased a menagerie of animals, circles, squares, ovals, and half-moons, eyes white and ghostly, and eyes that could see, and forests of jubilant greens.

Story-cloths hung from the walls too. Unlike the faded ones Uncle Dreg kept hidden in the treasure hole he'd dug under his bed, these could have been painted yesterday. Shown in painful detail were depictions of the Long Warming, the Water Wars, the canes, the floods, and the Sequel; seeds loaded into planes and onto cargo freighters heading from the Cradle to the Territories, while soldiers with guns stood guard and one tribe betrayed another. Corpses swinging from penal trees, women pyred. . . . In others, the depictions were much older: Middle Passengers being loaded into sailing ships; Passengers toiling in cotton and tobacco fields while a few lucky ones took to the air, arms outstretched as, wingless, they flew home.

One story-cloth reminded Ji-ji of Uncle Dreg's Origin Story, though it had none of the fuzzy gentleness she remembered. In the beginning according to Man Cryday's version, the One was a blind white eye glowering down from on high. When One became Two, the bifurcation rent the story-cloth itself in two. When Two became Three, a woman lay screaming while something—Ji-ji wasn't sure what—escaped from between her bloody legs. Some of the fishfolk and earthfolk lived in harmony, but others slaughtered each other. In the next scene they aimed their bloodthirst at the Bird tribe, the massacre so real she could hear the birdfolk's screams. The chief's wives who didn't want to help the birdfolk murdered some of those who did, and the few maimed birdfolk who took refuge in the mountains were shadows of who they once were.

"Why is the First Story so . . ." Ji-ji said, searching for the right word, "so violent?"

"You think beginnings are easy?" the woman replied, angrily. "You think Dregulahmo's pretty pictures portray the world? We who know suffering must see the past with clear eyes or it will blind us to the future." The woman's ire surprised Ji-ji, who didn't dare say how much she loved Uncle Dreg's hopeful story-cloths.

"Is this Dimmers?" Ji-ji asked when she felt confident Man Cryday had calmed down.

"Dimmers Wood is close by. This place we call Memoria. It is located deep within Viral Colony Four. It is well protected. The entrance can only be accessed through a maze of caves and tunnels. No enemy has found it. You are safe here."

"In Dimmers Wood I saw terrible things." Ji-ji didn't reveal that some of the most disturbing story-cloths reminded her of the dreadful corpses she'd seen in the wood.

"You saw the things you have known, the things you know now, and the things you dread for the future. In Dimmers, time flows forward and backward. Of course it was terrible."

Man Cryday ordered Ji-ji to turn over and raise her T-shirt so she could apply a cooling balm to her back. Ji-ji realized someone had dressed her in a pale yellow T-shirt and light blue shorts—pastel colors she wasn't permitted to wear. No black-and-white seed symbol on her chest either. It felt weird. Good, but weird. Her body had never belonged to her that way before.

"Their filthy stain is gone," Man Cryday said. "We do not wear such desecrations in Memoria. The steaders work very hard to screw with our minds, yes?"

"Yes, they do. All the time."

Her response seemed to please Man Cryday, who smiled more warmly than before and said, "Dreg was as right about some things as he was wrong about others. You will do. Yes, you will do."

As Man Cryday applied the balm in sweeping spirals of coolness, Ji-ji knew she'd died and gone to heaven. The balm smelled of rosemary, mint, and a floral fragrance Ji-ji couldn't identify. As she massaged Ji-ji's back, Man Cryday answered questions Ji-ji was afraid to ask.

"Chemists would explain away Dimmers Wood. They would say there are hallucinogens in the leaves and mushrooms. Gaseous emissions too. They would not be wrong. Psychologists would sermonize about the power of the subconscious. Priests would insist that you believe they have the power to mediate between you and the Wood of the Immaculates. And storytellers would tell you a tale of unbearable violence and suffering."

Ji-ji thought for a moment before saying, "An' what would *you* tell me, Man Cryday?"

"At last a sensible question. I would tell you to seek out all ways of seeing, child, and then to find your own way. Your mind should be open to new paths. A learned belief can be as stultifying as ignorance. Wisdom follows the blossoming, is it not so?"

Ji-ji deduced that *blossoming* was Man Cryday's term for bloodletting. She didn't want to admit that no wisdom at all had come with her periods, only blood and discomfort. She was relieved when Man Cryday changed the subject and asked her what else she remembered.

Ji-ji told her what had happened—the escape from the planting, Mam's death (would it always shred her heart when she talked about it?), Lotter's arrival at the fence, the Bounty Boys, the poor fake Mule in furry ass's ears, Lucky's courage, the river crossing. She described how she'd abandoned Lucky but not the stallion—kept circling back to Lucky, filled with guilt because she hadn't stayed with him, wretched because she'd left her mam behind, cradled in her jailer's arms.

"Be careful, Jellybean," Man Cryday warned. "Excessive regret curdles to self-pity, yes? You were right to continue alone. You would be dead otherwise."

In a tone gentler than before, Man Cryday explained that a search party of Friends had found the scant remains of Lucky's mutilated body near a live oak. There had been little left. It looked as though the group had been attacked by hungry snarlcats before another posse of Bounty Boys came across them. "Friends buried his remains under the protection of the great oak, alongside the remains of the poor lynched child."

Though she'd been certain Lucky was dead, the news devastated Ji-ji. She burst into tears.

"Do not weep for him. Far better to be finished off by cats than Bounty Boys. Cats kill cleanly, without vengeance. It is the kind of death all of us should desire—is it not so? Hush, hush. Lucas went on this mission with his eyes open. He knew how dangerous it was when he volunteered."

"He d-didn't volunteer. He drew the short straw—t-twice."

"Is that so? You think people tell you who they are? Of course not. They show you. You think a mercenary would sacrifice himself like that? When I found Lucas he was a mess, but he was not a coward. And before you accuse yourself of cowardice for leaving him, remember that is exactly what the steaders want us to do—paralyze ourselves with self-doubt. You must not follow Silapu's path. Your mind must be your friend. If it becomes your enemy it will sabotage you over and over again—is it not so? There, the ointment will numb your back for a while."

"So Lucky wasn't a mercenary?"

"Of course he was! But he volunteered for the assignment to the 437th. Twice. Peter Dyson, his grandfather, and Dregulahmo were like brothers. I was close to Peter too. It was I who arranged for Lucas to go to Planting 437. Dregulahmo did not know Lucas was 9-0-2 until they met up at Blueglass Lake. I should have let Dreg know earlier and then perhaps . . ." Her voice trailed off. "See? Regret is not helpful. I must practice what I preach, yes?

"When Dregulahmo met up with Lucas, he discovered he was Peter's grandson and asked him to be your escort if it became necessary. Though he did not know the boy, he bet on the notion that the fruit had not fallen far from the tree. He was right. Lucas Dyson had his grandfather's courage, is it not so?"

"So you hired Lucky?"

"Yes. I hired him. I needed clear eyes on the 437th. Dregulahmo did not always see the trees for the forest. His quest was peace and brotherhood."

"What's your quest?"

"Another good question. My quest is justice."

As Man Cryday spoke, something stirred in Ji-ji. "Do I know you?" she asked.

"You met me once, when you were a little girl. I wanted to see you. I needed to know if Dregulahmo's suspicions were right."

"But how did you get on and off the planting?"

"I do not venture onto plantings unless it is to raid them. You were with Lotter at the Salem Outpost. You stopped there during a hunt. You bought—"

"—one of your bonbons!" Ji-ji exclaimed.

"So. You remember."

She'd bought five bonbons. One for her, one for Mam, one for Charra, one for Clay, one for Luvlydoll—even though Luvlydoll had been too young to do much except suck on it.

"I called the bonbons angel turds."

"Yes, you did. And Lotter laughed. I considered slitting his throat then, but I thought it may cause a disturbance so I restrained myself. I am still not sure if that was a grave error."

Again, Ji-ji couldn't say whether Man Cryday was joking or not, but she thought it best not to inquire further. Instead she said, "I called my little brother Bonbon."

"Yes. I know. Dregulahmo told me."

Ji-ji had never tasted anything sweeter in her life than those bonbons. They'd sat in a circle and eaten them slowly—all except Clay, who'd stuffed the whole thing into his mouth cos he could never wait for anything. Years later, the word sprang to her lips again when her brother slipped out from between her mam's legs. By that time, all her other siblings were gone. The evening of bonbons abided in her memory as a time of pure happiness.

"Were the bonbons magic?" she asked.

"What a ridiculous thing to say! They were bonbons. Dregulahmo has created a cult of nincompoops." Man Cryday sounded a lot like Silapu.

The old woman got up briskly, walked over to the window, and looked out. "The black stallion has been caught. He is in a pen in the far clearing. He is not happy, of course. What Free Spirit would be happy locked inside a fence? But he cannot roam alone in The Margins. It is too dangerous for a creature as splendid as he—is it not so? I have your saddlebag and Lucky's bag, with your book, your map, and Flight Boy's letter. The boy's spelling is appalling. What was he doing in that legacy school? Getting high? Zyla would be heartbroken if she saw it."

"The stallion an' the saddlebag—they're not mine. I stole them."

"Another ridiculous statement. The stallion stole you. The saddlebag is his gift. Hasn't the poor beast been carrying it all this time?"

Ji-ji liked that idea. "You knew Uncle Dreg?"

"Yes. I knew him for as long as he lived. Dregulahmo was my brother."

Ji-ji stared at Man Cryday. She saw it now, not only the resemblance between the two—same proud dark skin, same mischievous black eyes, same broad nose and generous nostrils—but the way she spoke, as though her words could nourish or scold you back to health. All those years ago, when she was only six years old, it must have been this resemblance to Uncle Dreg that had subconsciously drawn Ji-ji to her at the market in the Salem Outpost. And now it was as if Uncle Dreg had come back to her. Ji-ji felt a deep contentment, but her mood changed abruptly when she saw a shadow in the doorway. The striper from Dimmers Wood!

"Do not be afraid," Man Cryday said. "Musa is a Friend. Stripers are underappreciated. Their distinct odor should not be a catalyst for prejudice."

The mutant plopped down on its behind and scratched its flea-bitten coat of dirty stripes. A cloud of dander flew into the air and sifted down in the sunshine.

"Come, Musa," Man Cryday added. "Introduce yourself to your sister."

Ji-ji tried not to be offended by the term *sister.* Like most people who managed to survive into old age, Man Cryday was very eccentric.

The striper heaved itself to its feet and loped across the cabin. When it approached the bed, Ji-ji shied away from it in revulsion. Over four feet at its hunched shoulder, it was almost as large as a snarlcat, and by far the ugliest creature she'd ever seen. It stank—a nose-accosting odor of boiled eggs and manure. Hard not to be prejudiced under the circumstances.

"It's real . . . big," Ji-ji said, searching for an adjective that wouldn't be offensive.

"*He* is a full-grown striper! What do you expect? A Pomeranian?"

Man Cryday reached up and stroked the mutant's head, warning Ji-ji to avoid the antennae that adorned his skull like coral polyps. "He likes you. See? He licks your fingers. Be grateful. Musa does not like everyone. Sometimes he gnaws on them instead. We found Musa as a cub, half dead inside a box trap. We brought him back here and reared him. Other trapped or abandoned cubs we have found and reared too. Eight stripers live with us now. They guard Dimmers Wood and the entrances to the caves; they accompany us on hunts. Two of them—Kuru and Amay—are with Tiro and the others. . . . Now it is time to rest. If you wake with a nightmare and I am not here, you may pet Musa. But remember, do not touch his tiara. It is very sensitive."

IIIIIIIIIIIIII

When Ji-ji woke again, it was evening. Man Cryday rocked back and forth in a wooden rocker. Ji-ji didn't need to ask who'd braided the twigs into a chair fit for a queen. Only Uncle Dreg was skilled enough. Man Cryday didn't look up, but she must have heard Ji-ji stir.

"Is he—" Ji-ji began to ask.

"No. He is not back yet."

"Do you think—"

"No. I do *not* think the Bounty Boys have ambushed him. He is with Bently and Germaine, two of our most experienced hunters. Kuru and Amay are with them too, as I said. It is not possible for humans to ambush stripers. Tiro will return. With luck, he will not be empty-handed."

The concern in Man Cryday's voice indicated how short of food they must be. Ji-ji resolved to eat only small portions of whatever food was offered. Less than an hour later, after Ji-ji had eaten her first real meal in days (a scrumptious vegetable stew with thick slices of warm bread that forced her to abandon her vow not to eat much), Ji-ji heard the sound she'd been dying to hear: Tiro's voice calling her name. Man Cryday caught her arm in a ferocious grip to prevent her from rising to greet him as Tiro burst into the room like a tornado. He whooped with delight when he saw that Ji-ji was fully awake, rushed over to the bed, and hugged her.

"Stupid boy! Watch her back!" Man Cryday told him. "I told you it would be very delicate. You remember nothing."

"Sorry," Tiro said.

Man Cryday raised her eyes to heaven and said she had to step out but would be back soon.

Ji-ji felt as if she would burst with happiness. After so much pain and so many trials, they had finally dreaminated themselves on the path to Freedom, just like Uncle Dreg said they would.

They talked and laughed and told each other their stories. Tiro said how sorry he was to hear about her mother. A Friend embedded on the 437th had got a message to them saying Silapu hadn't made it over the fence. Tiro refused to reveal the Friend's identity but said he was sad to hear about Lucky too, especially after he learned how much he'd done for Ji-ji.

"Never liked the guy," he admitted. "Looked way too much like Lotter. But if he really did all those things you said, he was a hero in the end, I guess."

Tiro explained how he'd hidden out in Shot Tower until the Last Supper was underway, which meant he'd only been a few hours ahead of her. Ji-ji explained how Lucky had carried her much of the way, so it had taken longer than anticipated.

"We'd almost given up on you," Tiro said. "Man Cryday said you must've crossed the river on that stallion out there?" She nodded. "*Damn,* Ji! Impressive."

He told her about Memoria, said there were upward of three dozen Friends who called the place home—a dozen more who used it as a layover as they made their way through The Margins. Some Friends slept in cabins, some in tents, some in huts, and some in tree houses. Most of the Friends were black or Latin like Germaine Judd, and about half a dozen others were white. He warned her not to use the words *dusky* or *fairskin* around the Friends. Some of them had been botanicals once and they were real sensitive about it. Others had come all the way over from the Cradle or the Caribbean to serve in the resistance, while a few of the Spanish-speaking Friends had traveled on foot from below the southern border. "There's lot of Indigenous in the resistance, 'specially African Americans. That's what they call themselves. No hyphen neither. They're real sensitive 'bout that too. You can say *black* and *brown* but not *dusky.* An' it's *white,* not *fairskin.* Don't forget. They have a hissy fit if you get it wrong. . . . Man Cryday said anything to you yet?"

"'Bout what?"

"Oh nothing. I swear, she's the angriest female I ever met. You noticed. Doesn't like me much. Feeling's mutual. Says some crap 'bout Uncle Dreg too. Accuses him of being an idealized."

"An idealist?"

"Yeah, that too."

"She told me she's his sister."

"Yeah, she is." Tiro checked to make sure Musa was their only witness. "Uncle Dreg didn't like her very much. . . . Well, maybe he didn't *hate* her or nothing, but they weren't real close. Thinks she knows everything. So you feel okay then? You look good."

"I feel great. Just tired is all. Oh Tiro, we made it!"

"Course we did. Ben—he's one of the Friends—Ben says the Dreamfleet'll likely snap me up. Folks in the city, they already heard o' me! Can you believe it, Ji? Heard of Uncle Dreg too. They got copies of that speech he gave at the Circle. Those scouts—the ones from the Dreamfleet who visited the planting way back when, remember?—seems like they spread the word after they saw me fly. Got the fleet owners excited. They want to see Bad Luck Billy's protégé—that's what Ben says. I was born for this. So were you, Ji. It's destiny."

He veered back to Dimmers. Told her how the elders there saw themselves as guardians of the wood, how they hung purple tears on the trees for every seed who'd been killed or tortured. "Man Cryday is an arborist like Coach B. Prefers trees to people. No surprise there. Favors mutants too." He looked over at Musa, who hadn't left his guard post. "Go figure. Germaine says Man Cryday's an ant whisperer. S'how she domesticated the mutants. Only don't call 'em *mutants.* An' don't say she trained or domesticated 'em either. They're stripers or Friends, *not* mutants. An' they're 'companioned,' not trained. She's my grandmother's sister. Not that I ever knew Grammy. That makes her my great-aunt. But she's none too fond of me. You see how she gives me the stink eye when she looks at me? Seems like she blames me for what happened to Uncle Dreg. Like I don't feel bad enough about it already. Jesus! She bitches nonstop 'bout everything. You noticed?"

Ji-ji felt uneasy talking that way about their host, so she asked Tiro if the place really was a Viral Colony. He said it was originally, but that now it was an ideal hideout cos most people avoided it like the Janglarian plague—which was what the first so-called Virals, or Janglers, as they were also commonly known, suffered from. "Germaine says steaders freak out if they see a Jangler heading toward 'em. An' don't call 'em *Janglers* or *Virals* or *Ebolans,* for god's sake. They're *Hoods* here, cos of their hooded cloaks. Or sometimes they're called *Bells* cos of the string of warning bells they wear round their necks. I tell you, Ji. They got a name for everything and everyone. Folks here say if you got your own name for something it can't be snatched like it can be if you don't—or something like that."

Tiro had barely paused to take a breath. His jitteriness began to make her nervous. He looked and sounded like her mam. She confronted him outright. "You taken something, Tiro?"

"Me? No! Don't look at me like that. Okay, yeah. But don't go all freaky on me. It's not like that crap your mam used to snort with Lotter. There are these 'shrooms in Dimmers. You gotta try one. Ben showed me. They're harmless. They pull everything close up—like you don't just *see* color, you can *step inside* it. You gotta try it."

"So that's why you're acting so wound up?"

"I'm acting wound up cos I'm so damn happy to see you! We get to race together, just like we dreaminated it with Uncle Dreg. We'll be Wild Seeds. You can watch me fly to glory in the coop, an' I can watch you take the runner prize. Day after tomorrow, we'll be hopping a train to Monticello. They call it the Liberty, but it's nothing fancy. Just a string o' freight cars. Still . . . it's a *train.* You know how fast a train goes? Me neither. But it's fast. I was scared you wouldn't make it, but you're out of the woods at last. Guess we know where that saying came from." He chuckled, became serious. "You were real sick when you got here. Delirious. Didn't recognize me. You kept saying Man Cryday was a damn tree! She's nothing like Uncle Dreg. Wouldn't believe they were brother an' sister if Uncle hadn't told me himself. . . . She hasn't exactly taken a shine to me," he repeated, "but she's cured you with her witchery herbs so I can put up with her bad-mouthing."

"Dimmers Wood was real bad for me," Ji-ji confessed. "Saw all these corpses an' stuff. You see 'em too?"

"Yeah. I saw 'em. Heard Father-Man Williams laughing in my ear, an' heard Mother weeping, an' saw her with Amadee that day . . . an' saw Uncle Dreg all strung up too. They said things. . . ."

"Who?"

"The trees. The Dimmers. Man Cryday. Who the hell knows? Said it shoulda been me got tractor-pulled. Said Amadee was the one could fly. Said he was the one worth saving."

"You're a great flyer, Tiro. Best I've ever seen."

"Amadee was tons better. But what's the point saying all that crap now? What's done is done. Guess they'll all have to settle for second best."

"You're not second—"

He interrupted her. "You been awake long?"

"A while. Was afraid something bad happened to you. I mean, how long does it take to hunt game in a place like this?"

"She hasn't told you then?"

"Told me what?"

"What we were hunting for."

"Food, right?"

"Wait here, Ji. I got a big surprise for you. Should be all cleaned up by now."

"Don't leave again, Tiro. You only just—"

"S'okay, Ji. Trust me. Be back in two shakes of Musa's tail."

He cupped his hand to the side of his mouth. In a fake whisper he said, "Don't tell him, but that striper's butt ugly." He looked at the striper and shook his head. "Sorry, fella, but it's true. Butt ugly. You stink too—'less it's you, Ji." Musa raised his head and yawned. Tiro took off.

Ji-ji quashed the uneasiness she felt. What did it matter if he'd sampled a 'shroom or two? His jitteriness was nothing like her mam's. She could relax. The day after tomorrow they would set out for Monticello on the Liberty Train. She was among Friends. She listened to the sounds coming from outside. People bustled around. Someone was humming, someone else was chopping wood. No one had ever found this place. She was safe. She dozed off again.

Ji-ji woke to see Tiro standing in the doorway, flanked by two strangers. The man was a male dusky—a black man. The woman was a female fairskin—a white woman. Or did Tiro say she was Latin?

"Ji, meet Bently Turner and Germaine Judd."

Bently bowed low and doffed an invisible cap. Germaine curtsied. Ji-ji laughed.

"This is how come the hunt took a while."

Pheebs stepped out from behind Ben. All four foot six of her.

"*Pheebs!*" Ji-ji cried in amazement. "You escaped! How?"

It was a huge relief to see that Pheebs had made it out alive. After Lotter decreed Coach B a traitor, Pheebs would be in danger too. But she wasn't the only surprise. The other one couldn't wait for her cue. She leapt out from behind Tiro and ran full tilt toward Ji-ji.

"I *knew* we find you with the Dimmers!" Afarra cried. "I tell it over and over!" She twirled around like a spinning top and flung herself on the bed.

Amid the celebration, Tiro explained how he'd promised Uncle Dreg he would try not to leave Afarra or Pheebs behind if it looked like they were in danger. Pheebs had been working with Afarra in the fields that morning of the Last Supper. She'd seen Casper follow her back to her sleeping shed. "Had a knife," Pheebs said. "Planned to use it. But Uncle Dreg's Eyes surprise Casper an' he backs off. I follow Afarra to the burnt-outs. Then, later, Tiro an' me snatch her up."

"Only then we got separated—a long story," Tiro said. "But Pheebs here saved the day, an' here they are. We found 'em down near the river. Guided 'em back here."

The entire time Tiro was speaking, Ji-ji had been too overwhelmed to say anything. Afarra climbed into bed, put her arms around Ji-ji, and refused to let go. Man Cryday returned and ordered Afarra out of Ji-ji's healing bed. She wouldn't budge. Evidently, there were some battles even Man Cryday couldn't win. She told the others to let Jellybean get some rest. Afarra could remain.

The last thing Ji-ji heard before she fell asleep was Afarra prattling on about what they would do in Dream City. Afarra would be entered as a Wild Seed. It would be tough for her to keep up. But whatever happened, Ji-ji wouldn't abandon her little sister. Even if she had to carry her, they would cross the finish line together.

As she was dozing off, Ji-ji said, sleepily, "Where did you find the necklace?"

"I am not finding him. *He* is finding *me*. With his Seeing Eyes. He is leaving them in my sleep shed. It is very thoughtful. When I see him on the next time I will say thank you."

Ji-ji couldn't imagine who'd left them there in the shed. Pheebs? Coach B before they arrested him? Tiro? How could so many dreams come true at once? Smiling, she toppled into sleep.

IIIIIIIIIIIIII

Ji-ji awoke. Morning. Birds sang outside, and a wide slab of sunlight had slithered under the door. She must've slept all afternoon and all night. Man Cryday slept in her rocker while Afarra was curled up like a baby at the foot of the bed. Round her neck she wore Uncle Dreg's Seeing Eyes. On a chair nearby, Tiro slept as well. The scene was so peaceful Ji-ji didn't want to wake them, but she desperately wanted a drink of water. She had a strange, musty taste in her mouth, and a revolting smell permeated the cabin—like a skunk had found his way into the crawl space underneath them. The culprit dozed a few feet away, his huge head resting on his paws. He felt her eyes on him and lifted his head expectantly. Ji-ji called out to Man Cryday, who jerked herself awake. Moving with an agility that would have been impressive in someone half her age, she hurried over to the bed.

"How do you feel?" Man Cryday asked. She sounded anxious. "You came down with a fever last night. Afarra alerted us."

Ji-ji tried to sit up but the pain was too intense. "Feels like Oz kicked me in the back."

Man Cryday felt her forehead and cheeks. "The fever is broken," she said.

Afarra woke up. She cheered when she saw Ji-ji. "I am saying you will break! And here it is!"

The commotion woke Tiro. He leapt up from the chair with a wild expression on his face and said, "Does she know?"

"Know what?" Ji-ji asked. She attempted to shift onto her back, but Tiro yelled at her not to move. Something in his voice put the fear of god into her. "Why? What is it?" she asked.

Ji-ji followed Tiro's eyes and saw something wriggle out from underneath her T-shirt! Musa rushed at the bed, growling. During the night, a transparent worm almost as long as her arm had crawled into bed with her! It nosed itself farther out from beneath her T-shirt! *Oh my god!* There were *two* of them!

Hysterical, Ji-ji sat bolt upright and tried to slap them away. Instead of helping her, Tiro grabbed one of her arms and Man Cryday the other. She was having a nightmare. Any second she'd wake up. Like leeches, the giant worms latched on to her shoulders. She could feel them undulating there. She had never felt anything more repulsive in her life.

Tiro was crying. He looked terrified. "Ji, they're not what you think they are! They're—"

Man Cryday interrupted. "They are sproutings. With luck, the blossoming will follow."

She was still feverish, still dreaming. That was it. The aftereffect of Dimmers, that's all.

"The stink worms are not for harming," Afarra said. "They are for hope. They are for us."

Ji-ji looked from one to the other. This wasn't a dream. This was *real*!

She steadied her voice, enunciated every syllable: "I . . . want . . . to . . . see . . . my . . . back! *NOW!*"

Man Cryday spoke sternly. "I will let go as long as you promise not to rip them out. If you do, you die, understand?" Ji-ji nodded. She was shaking so hard the bed was trembling.

Satisfied, the old woman hurried over to a cupboard, opened it up, and pulled out two large mirrors. Tiro, his hands shaking, held one mirror in front of Ji-ji while Man Cryday positioned another behind her. On Man Cryday's signal, Afarra slowly lifted Ji-ji's shirt.

Ji-ji stared at her reflection in horror. Two protrusions, like an old person's wrinkled knees, had attached themselves to her shoulder blades. The deformity continued in a bony ridge across her shoulders. Two intestine-like appendages grew out of the knobby protrusions—feelers that hung down past her waist but that could also contract back into her body and disappear, like lizard's tongues. The stench they gave off made her want to gag. All across her back, from her shoulders to her ass, like the roots of an ancient tree, was a network of what looked like keloid scars.

She was the ugliest creature she'd ever seen.

"What have you done to me? You put a curse on me, witch! A voodoo!"

"Oh child." Man Cryday put the mirror down and cupped Ji-ji's face in her hands. "This is no curse. It is a translation. You have survived the first phase."

"The first phase of *what*? I can feel them *writhing*! Get them off me! *Cut them out!*"

"This is not a curse, child. It could be a miracle." Ji-ji reached back to rip them off. "No! Do *not* pull on them!" Man Cryday warned. "Your blood is theirs. You will bleed to death if you damage them. They are a part of you now, like your arms and legs. You are a chrysalis, a metamorphic. If my brother was right, one day these sproutings could translate themselves into wings. *Wings,* child! Like your ancestors. Like the Bird tribe from the—"

Ji-ji almost spat at her. "*Wings! These?* Look at them! These aren't wings! They're . . . *maggots*!"

"The sproutings have not yet evolved," Man Cryday said. "It will take time but—"

"Shut up, you stupid old witch! This is *my* body, not yours! I hate you!"

Ji-ji buried her head in her hands. She was a freak, a mutant. Man Cryday had called her Musa's sister. The witch had known all along about the horror waiting to ambush her. This was why they'd brought her here, to live among the mutants, Virals, and Dimmers. They'd all known she would never be able to leave. Even Tiro. He'd known too. Why hadn't he warned her?

She was lying on her side with her back to them. Tiro reached out and tried to touch her shoulders. One of the feelers latched on to his wrist. He cried out and yanked his hand away.

"Get out!" Ji-ji cried. "*All* of you! *GO! Please!*"

Tiro couldn't get out of there fast enough. Man Cryday wanted to stay, but when Ji-ji threatened to scream herself hoarse if she did, the old woman agreed to go, instructing Musa to stay behind and keep guard.

Apart from the striper, only Afarra remained. She climbed back onto the bed, wrapped her arms around Ji-ji's trembling legs, and didn't let go. Every so often, she rubbed the Seeing Eyes and asked Uncle Dreg to help them. But Ji-ji knew the truth: no one could help her now.

She closed her eyes. One by one, she buried her dreams.

20 STORIES OLD AND NEW

An infestation writhed on her back. Ji-ji felt the maggots convulse and struggled to resist the urge to rip them off. Musa lay a few feet away. She and the mutant were kin. For the third or fourth time, she threw up. Afarra held a bowl under her chin and wiped her mouth with a cloth. The vomit stank, though not as much as her back. Rage coursed like lava inside her. For a brief time, her body had been hers. No seed symbol, no plowing peril. And where the hell was Tiro? Scared off by a pair of feelers! If their roles had been reversed, she would have stayed by his side—smothered the horrible things, if necessary, just to keep them quiet so he could rest.

"Do not be scared, Missy Ji. I am staying with you all the time."

"I'm not scared. . . . Okay, I am. And don't call me Missy Ji. You're not a Cloth anymore."

"Okay. I call you Elly, yes? Like Jellybean who was brave on the pyre."

Accustomed to Afarra knowing things she shouldn't be able to know, Ji-ji didn't ask how she'd found out about her namesake.

After a while, Afarra said, "Tiro is saying we ride the Liberty Train."

"I won't be riding anything. Not with these."

"Your wings are being very shy. That is what they are saying."

"*Shy?* Are you *insane*! Look at them!"

Ji-ji had discarded her T-shirt earlier. Confining the feelers made them even more antsy. She turned over so Afarra could see them writhe on her back. "These look shy to you? No. Not to me either. So shut up about it. An' don't call these filthy goddam worms wings."

"Uncle Dreg is saying wings. He is looking inside the window."

Ji-ji glanced at the cabin window, half expecting Uncle Dreg-Dim to be peering through it. "You mean the Window-of-What's-to-Come," she stated, bitterly.

"Yes. That one. The big one. The Eyes are seeing you in the sky. It is very uplifting."

"No one can fly with these!"

"They will grow. Like a caterpillar-butterfly. It is almost a sure thing."

Ji-ji wanted to scream. Afarra's dogged hopefulness felt like an accusation, like she hadn't tried hard enough to look on the bright side or see the glass half full. How do you do that when your back is a nest of snakes? Ji-ji couldn't say all these things to Afarra—couldn't say them to anyone. All she said was "Why are you always so hopeful?" She really wanted to know.

"Cos I am being here with you. With you is always hopeful. It is true, Elly. The Eyes are agreeing. Listen." Afarra held the Seeing Eyes up to Ji-ji's ear. "They are saying, 'When you fly, you carry us with you please.' And they are clapping very loud."

Ji-ji batted the necklace away. Afarra was nuts. The wizard's necklace was as silent as the grave. And yet . . .

. . . something happened when Afarra said those three impossible words. *When you fly,* Ji-ji thought. The trinity of words took root inside her head. Not a dream yet—too soon for that. Merely the seeds of a dream. Planted. Dormant. Thirsty for rain.

IIIIIIIIIIIIII

It was afternoon when Ji-ji sent Afarra with a message for Man Cryday, apologizing for her earlier behavior. She wasn't really sorry, but she had a mountain of questions and no one else to turn to. She put on her T-shirt and endeavored to look calm. Question marks littered the path ahead. Ant traps that could rip off her foot. She'd always found solace in being able to anticipate what was on the horizon. She could bear almost anything as long as it didn't ambush her.

The old woman arrived thirty minutes later with a pot of stew and a steaming loaf of bread. She greeted Ji-ji as if nothing unusual had happened: "Well, daughter of Silapu? I am glad to see you looking better. Are you ready to talk now?"

"I guess," Ji-ji replied.

Afarra made herself comfortable on the bed next to Ji-ji, and soon they were both eating the stew and the fresh-baked bread. Ji-ji was shocked to see how ravenous she was.

"They keep writhing like snakes," Ji-ji said bitterly, between mouthfuls. "They itch too."

"What good is a pair of petrified sproutings? They are vivacious. That is what we want."

What you want you mean, Ji-ji thought, infuriated again by the tree witch's know-it-all attitude.

Man Cryday ordered Ji-ji to turn over. She lifted her T-shirt and sniffed at her back. "Hmm. Your sproutings are less pungent. Another good sign. Now eat the rest of the stew."

Ji-ji finished the stew and the last hunk of bread. Mad at herself for not turning her nose up at the food to punish her host, she struggled to remain composed. God, she was angry. Fortunately, she'd rehearsed her most urgent questions. She would trot them out one after the other.

"You knew all along I was a mutant, didn't you? So did Uncle Dreg."

"That filthy word is not used here. 'Ant' is acceptable. For now, you are an In-Between."

Lua had used the same word, only she'd said it about a place. *My arms hurt from carrying PrettyBlack from In-Between to Nowhere.* Ji-ji kept that to herself. She wouldn't tell the tree witch anything unless she felt more confident she could trust her.

"How long will I be an In-Between?" Ji-ji asked, dreading the answer.

"Gestation periods vary. It is possible you will remain a Wingchild In-Between."

"You mean . . . I could be like this forever? But I thought . . ."

"The idea of wings is growing on you, is it not so? Of course we must hope for a full flowering. But for now we focus on other things."

"Yes," Afarra affirmed. "The Seeing Eyes are saying to listen to the story now."

"It is very fortunate, Afarra," Man Cryday said, dryly, "that my brother's Eyes so often see what you most desire."

Afarra ignored her and continued to whisper to the necklace in unintelligible, singsong language. Her fixation on the necklace reminded Ji-ji of a group of fairskin nuns who used to visit the planting. The black-robed women fingered their rosary beads, praying for miracles and forgiveness. One of their visits had come soon after Bonbon had been snatched. Ji-ji had been tempted to tell them their prayers were worthless. Didn't the silly women realize the only thing steaders paid attention to was brute force? Months later, however, Ji-ji learned from Zaini that the nuns belonged to a radical group called the Sisters' Alliance. While they'd been handing out leaflets about the importance of patience and submission they'd also been providing Doc Riff with desperately needed antibiotics and other medicine. "A nun can hide a lot of things in those black robes," Zaini had said. The memory chastened Ji-ji. She'd been wrong about the nuns. Maybe she was wrong about other things as well?

"Why didn't you tell me I was a—" She'd been about to say *mutant.* "—I was different?"

"I was not certain you would progress to the next phase. It is a story written in air not stone. There have been others whose wings were ingrown. It was not clear whether yours would be an extracorporeal liberation or an ingrown colonization."

Ji-ji had no idea what that meant but she swallowed her irritation. "You've seen this before?"

"I have seen it and heard about it too. Sadly, the outcome has always been . . . unfortunate."

"Then I really am alone."

"Only if you fail to pay attention—a skill for which you have a prodigious talent. Listen, child. You are part of something large. Look at these story-cloths. No, not like that. Do not look to glance over—look to *see.* Are you ready to hear the rest?"

Ji-ji nodded gloomily. What did she have to lose? Musa placed his shaggy head on Man Cryday's lap as she began to speak.

As it turned out, the story was very similar to the one Uncle Dreg had told Ji-ji when she was a seedling—the Origin Story about the Bird tribe. Ji-ji traveled back in time to Uncle Dreg's cabin. It wasn't just a memory. She was with the wizard, in his cabin with Tiro gazing at the ancient story-cloth. Man Cryday spoke of the breaking-apart, but she interspersed the telling with her own commentary, which was more scientific than the wizard's had been. The One breaking apart was similar to what scientists called the Big Bang. She compared the making of Two to the division of cells, and the subsequent diversity of creatures to the evolutionary journey Darwin described. Man Cryday ended the story with the same words Uncle Dreg had used.

"In Totepp, *to* means 'bird,' and *teppi* means 'to remember.' And though there has not been a full-fledged Wingchild in so long that even our elders' elders' elders do not recall exactly what they look like, the story has not lost its power. Stories are the wings of dreamers, and that is why some of the Passengers found their way back home to the tribe of birds whose songs filled their dreams. This story belongs to us and to the Passengers before us, and to those from the many kidnapped tribes. After so much abuse, we, like our brothers and sisters all over the world who have been persecuted, should be extinct. Yet we survive and multiply. We rise again. Why? Because we remember the truth the Passengers knew: the living can heal the dead and the dead can heal the living."

Where had she heard words like that before? Ji-ji couldn't remember—didn't want to. The story had not filled her with the same delight she'd felt as a seedling. A story was only a story.

"So, what are you saying? Am I a Wingchild from some lost tribe of birds?"

"Dregulahmo thought you may be. He saw it in his vision-dreams. My brother was a storykeeper, a griot for the Toteppi. I am one still—a task handed down for generations. Wherever those from the Cradle have taken root, griots reside to tell our stories using words, music, dance, art, and song. We work with storykeepers everywhere to Free our oppressed brothers and sisters—the Dark Diasporans in the Americas, the New Maroons in Jamaica, the Liberators in Liberia . . ."

"Why do steaders care about our stories? Why are they so scared of us?"

"All stories mate with other stories. When some in the Territories heard the story of a Bird tribe, they looked to their own *One True Text* and found a story written by one of their prophets, who spoke of the coming of a winged scourge that could lay waste to the plantings. Some say it is why the Lord-Father of Lord-Fathers (a snippet of a man with lofty ambitions, not unlike the jealous chief in the Origin Story, remember?) is building an army of drones to defend the Territories and fight against the flying horde who would topple it. Some say he hopes to engineer an army of the enslaved who can embrace flight. Still others point to avian biology—hollow bones, the strength-to-size ratio, and so on, and say humans are incapable of rising. The Passengers never rose like birds, they say, and they will never rise again."

Why couldn't the old witch simply tell her what she was? Frustrated, Ji-ji asked, "So why do they think *I'm* an existential threat? I'm not the only female Toteppi on a planting."

"It wasn't only you. As I said before, there have been others."

"Who? And for god's sake, don't tell me some riddle-story."

Man Cryday smiled and said, "I know this is hard, Jellybean. You are scared, angry. Of course you are. You have been kept in the dark. I told my brother to share some of this with you earlier. I feared otherwise it would be too much of a shock. But Dregulahmo was as stubborn as an animule. You want answers, only some of which I can give you in the brief time we have. So I will try to tell you what I can."

"Don't talk down to us," Ji-ji warned her. "We won't listen if you do."

"Is that what I have been doing?"

"*Yes!*" Ji-ji and Afarra exclaimed in unison. Like many growns Ji-ji knew, whose tongues were sharp enough to gut you, Man Cryday had decided what your words meant before you uttered them.

She hadn't expected Man Cryday to laugh.

"*Ha!* It is true—I admit it. I have seen many decades, you have not. It is natural for me to talk down to you from the impressive height of my years. But I see why this could be extremely annoying. All right then. Let us begin again. On a more equal footing this time, yes? And do not complain if the truth is hard to stomach. You remember when Silapu went missing?"

"Yeah . . . no. I didn't remember at first when Tiro told me, but then I asked Mam about it when we got to the fry-fence . . ." Afarra placed her hand on Ji-ji's and patted it. "Mam got hysterical. Said she didn't want to remember a violation like that. Talked about a slaughterhouse."

"I am not surprised by this," Man Cryday said. "Her addiction began then—after she disappeared the first time. She came back drug-sopped and raving. Dreg and your mother used to be very close—like father and daughter. When she arrived at the 437th, Zaini took your mother under her wing. They were sisters in all but blood. Silapu used to tell Zaini my brother was the only male who ever showed her true kindness. No agenda, no demands."

"Mam hinted at something like that when we talked one time. But then Uncle Dreg encouraged Charra to run away, an' Mam couldn't forgive him."

"It wasn't only that. For years he tried to recruit Silapu to join the Friends because he believed she knew what was going on in that arsenal. That's where he thought they took her. He also suspected Lotter had told her more than she let on. Dreg wanted her to become a voice for the Freedom cause—a Root Voice, we call it, because it enables other voices to grow. Silapu refused, swore she could not remember what happened, would barely admit the steaders had done anything to her. Not long after Oletto was born she changed her mind. Something happened—we're not sure what—and she'd had enough. Pledged to flee to the city and record her whole story. Your mother was a beautiful woman of keen intelligence. She would have attracted many to our cause."

"Coach B told me she had a chance to run. With Bonbon—Oletto. Only she didn't cos she couldn't take me with her."

"No one could find you in time. Apparently you were off somewhere with Flight Boy, and then the opportunity was gone. Silapu never forgave Tiro for that. Who can blame her? Someone parroted to Lotter about Silapu's plans, so he punished her by taking her lastborn."

"But I still don't understand why Father-Man Williams an' some of the others think I'm a threat when they didn't even know about all this blossoming-flowering stuff."

"Yes, that is a puzzle. We are still not sure if Father-Man Williams' antipathy against you was personal. Maybe Williams is just so damn *mean* he used you to get at Tiro. That is Flight Boy's theory. No surprise that it revolves around him. In light of your blossoming, however, it may be that they knew this metamorphosis was a possibility. It helps explain why Lotter kept you close. Dregulahmo always believed that you, Afarra here, and Tiro too had special roles to play. Two out of three isn't bad, yes?" Man Cryday had made a joke. Ji-ji declined to laugh.

"Why do steaders hate Toteppi so much? Is it just cos of those words in their book?"

"It is complicated. We make the mistake of seeing steaders the way steaders see us and think they are all the same. But there are many kinds of steaders, and the two types holding sway right now call themselves Literalists and Futurists. Literalists believe every word of *The One True Text* and think Toteppi pose an existential threat to the Territories. Futurists—they christened themselves, obviously—think steaders are poised to shape the future in ways never seen before. They want to harness science, which puts them in direct conflict with steaders who blame technology for the world's woes. The Futurists may be more dangerous. They want to turn the Toteppi threat into an asset. They don't simply want to own us; they want to own flight itself in all its many forms."

Ji-ji felt even more overwhelmed than she had that day in the flying coop when Tiro had piled one revelation on top of another. How could she make sense of it all? She came back to the one concept that made her feel, if not hopeful, a little less miserable.

"Am I a Wingchild like in the story? Do you believe I am?"

"It should not matter what *I* believe. You are you and I am I."

It must have been obvious to Man Cryday that her answer wasn't what Ji-ji had hoped for, because she looked at her long and hard and tried again. "We Friends have many theories about what is truly going on, but this we know for certain. During the Age of Plenty, before the steaders' Necessary Reversal, there were few limits on scientific experimentation. Scientists had already mapped the human genome. Did Zyla at least tell you what that is?"

"She gave me a science book. It was in there."

"Good. I'm glad to hear she wasn't completely useless. Scientists found ways to mutate humans into states of . . . how should I put it? States of genetic otherness. Though that type of experimentation is banned now, and though the world has been preoccupied with trying to survive the onslaught of natural and man-made disasters, some say the mutation quest was never abandoned. They say it continues in the Father-City of Armistice and on select plantings in the Territories. We believe the arsenal on Planting 437 is one of these mutation sites."

"Are you saying the steaders mutated me?"

"We do not know exactly what they did. But we do know that they were experimenting with embryos, fetuses, and insemination. In these mutation sites, we suspect they treat so-called botanicals—not just Toteppi either—like lab rats. Not since World War Two have such heinous acts been perpetrated against a people under the cloak of the victims' inhumanity. As soon as reclassification occurred, the rest was inevitable. Like Jewish people, who were forced to wear a Star of David, our people have been forced to wear a seed symbol. Classification and genocide are cellmates. Perhaps some steaders believe that Toteppi genes are the most receptive to manipulation? We hoped to learn more from Silapu and from others too, about what goes on in those disgusting facilities. But Friends of Freedom are not steaders. We do not force people to do our bidding."

Ji-ji, who had been silent for a while, resurrected something long buried.

"I was still a seedling," she said, quilting a memory together. "Mam took my hand and half dragged me to a place near Murder Mouth, the arsenal. On a forbidden path in the Doom Dell."

"The Dell is very doomy," Afarra interjected. "Slimy toes!"

"It was very late," Ji-ji continued. "Mam said she had to warn me. Made me promise to resist if they tried to take me there. I didn't understand what she meant. I was scared."

"Do you recall what else she said? *Think,* Jellybean. It could be important."

Ji-ji shook her head. "I don't remember. She was crying so hard she could hardly speak. An' she was drunk or high. Both maybe. But I think . . . I saw Casper, Lotter's overseer. Yes, I *did* see him! Digging . . . burying something! A body! A seedling! No. . . . More than one! I saw him bury a whole bunch of them!"

All these years, each time she saw Vanguard Casper Ji-ji thought of shovels. At last she knew why. "How could I forget something like that?"

"Like all who have been damaged," Man Cryday told her, "there are things you must forget if you want to survive. More proof of another Tuskegee. Did Zyla teach you about that disgraceful experiment?" Ji-ji shook her head. "Then she was negligent. My brother believed the steaders' unnatural experiments would doom them to the very fate they were seeking to avoid. Sometimes I wish Sylvie could have restrained herself. Sending that bullet back to its source gave the Toteppi haters the proof they wanted."

Ji-ji was tempted to inquire further about the penal tree's actions but decided against it. Man Cryday was a tree witch. Tiro had told her that one of Man Cryday's official titles was "the Gardener of Tears." It wasn't likely she could be objective about anything related to trees.

Man Cryday had continued speaking: ". . . so that is why my brother's death proved to some steaders that Toteppi pose an imminent threat. Many on the Territorial Council are under the spell of one of the masterminds of this experiment. A grand inquisitor by the name of—"

"—Fightgood Worthy!" Ji-ji exclaimed. "He was at the Last Supper as Lotter's guest."

Man Cryday exploded: "And that stupid Flight Boy did not think this was worth mentioning? The boy is an ass!"

"Don't *ever* call him that!" Ji-ji cried.

Afarra raised her fists in readiness.

"I apologize," the old woman said when she saw how upset they were. "I should not have let my anger get the better of me, and I should not have used that word. But your Flight Boy is a danger to himself and others. The boy is oblivious to everything that does not immediately relate to him. How could he not think to tell me the Lord-Secretary attended the Last Supper?"

Afarra answered her: "Because Tiro is not being at the feast. He is with me and Pheebs in the tower. Then the fry-fence is not humming and we are climbing it."

Man Cryday, clearly flustered by having wrongfully accused her great-nephew, pursed her lips and drummed her fingers on the arm of the rocker. In the pause that followed, Ji-ji didn't mention Inquisitor Tryton's assault, or repeat what the Lord-Secretary had said to her. For all she knew, the old woman would find a way to blame Tiro for that too. Besides, there were some trespasses—especially sexual ones—that seeds learned to keep to themselves.

Man Cryday seemed to let her guard down. She dropped her air of superiority and confessed to them that things were going badly. "The fact is, these are trying times. We are losing the fight for liberation. Our allies in the SuperStates grow weary of how long it is taking. Some of them have bought the steaders' assertion that beneficent patronage is preferable to chaos in the Territories. Now that the new trade treaties are in place—another of Inquisitor Worthy's triumphs—the SuperStates are increasingly indebted to the Territories for raw materials and food. Silapu's story could have convinced some of them to help us, especially if she'd agreed to be examined. . . . So much tragedy because she was too afraid to—"

"Mam was brave! She did her best."

"You are right. She was very brave at times. But at other times, fear paralyzed her. You must not let that happen to you, Jellybean. For all our sakes, you must stay focused on the path ahead." Man Cryday leaned back and rocked back and forth. "I do not always share my brother's optimism. But even I suspect he may have been right about the special roles you and this little one could play."

Ji-ji pondered what she'd learned. Eventually she said, "If I'm some kind of experiment, does that mean the others were too—the ones like me?"

"It is possible," Man Cryday replied.

"So I'm not part of a lost tribe then?"

"That is also a possibility. It does not matter what engendered this metamorphosis."

"Does to me. I'm the one being engendered."

"Then you must not let it matter," Man Cryday said sternly. "All of us have a choice to make in this life. We can let others make us, or we can make ourselves. Which will you choose?"

Ji-ji shrugged. "Don't know yet." She came back to her most pressing request: "Tell me about the others like me."

"I know of a handful. Some had only a drop of Toteppi blood, if that; others had more. The steaders transported many tribes to this foreign land and we have all intermingled. We do not know how many they experimented on."

Ji-ji remembered something else: "Chaff Man—the planting executioner—threatened to reveal what was going on at the arsenal. And he refused to lynch Uncle Dreg."

"Yes. The executioner owed his life to Dregulahmo. Years ago, Cherub Holleran was a child living among a group of white Indentures, mostly imported from Europe. A holdover from the earlier system of contractual labor. Their subservience was grandfathered in—a way to mask the real nature of the Necessary Reversal and persuade the SuperStates not to interfere. These white Indentures had none of the rights and privileges of today's white Liberty Laborers. They were botanicals in all but name. Dregulahmo helped a group of them escape from a planting in Ole Mississip and seek asylum in D.C."

"But Chaff Man wound up as an executioner?"

"As I said, we can make ourselves or let others make us. Cherub's father was an egotistical idiot and a bully—the worst combination. Cherub followed in his father's bloody footsteps. I warned Dreg that risking everything to save those with a tainted heritage defied common sense. I told him that the other white Indentures would soon forget their indebtedness and turn on us. That is exactly what happened. But my brother saw the world he wanted to see."

Ji-ji had never imagined that Chaff Man had a story. To her, he'd always been a hooded executioner, the embodiment of evil on the 437th. Hard to imagine him as a freckled, redheaded boy who needed to be saved. Harder still to imagine him executing so many seeds after his own experience should have made him compassionate. At least he'd balked at lynching Uncle Dreg. Granted, he'd changed his mind when his Pomeranian was threatened. *Guess we all got our limits,* Ji-ji thought. "Who are these other In-Betweens?" she asked.

"You and Afarra encountered one of them on Death Day. Is that not so, Afarra? He is not a Wingchild In-Between, he is . . . It is not clear exactly what he is or whether his metamorphosis is complete. Dreg helped him flee from the arsenal when he was in retreat from his own escape."

"Drol is in Memoria," Afarra stated, as if it were the most natural thing in the world. "He is the one catching the black horse for you."

"That's impossible!" Ji-ji exclaimed.

Man Cryday bristled: "Is he so unlike you that you cannot imagine him performing an act of kindness? As far as we know, Drol is singular, tribeless. His 'keepers' called him Lord Mutant because he was fastidious for a 'monster.' When his intelligence intimidated them, they inverted his name from Lord to Drol. Names can be cudgels. Is that not so, Kitchen-Seed Lottermule?"

"Drol is not for killing," Afarra said, defensively. "He is for living. He is for Free."

"No one here is going to hurt Drol, little one," Man Cryday said. "His speech is hard to understand. His language, like Afarra's, is self-taught. It has . . . peculiarities. Some concepts he has no words for yet. It would be good if Afarra and Drol could spend more time together. You are better than I am, little one, at communicating with him. Right now, however, time is our biggest enemy."

"You will be liking Drol," Afarra told Ji-ji. "He is very likable."

Ji-ji was tempted to respond with sarcasm, but when she saw the look on Afarra's face, her desire to lash out deserted her. "You like him, so I will too," Ji-ji said, which prompted Man Cryday to nod her approval.

"You and Uncle Dreg are not the only ones to say Afarra is an ant whisperer," Ji-ji said. "Coach B and Pheebs thought so too."

"Of course Afarra is an ant whisperer! Has she not been whispering to you for years?"

It could have been a cruel joke, but the way Man Cryday said it made Ji-ji smile, something she'd doubted she would ever be able to do again.

She readied herself for disappointment and asked, "Will I ever be able to fly?"

"I know of one adult case where the sproutings flowered. Someone Germaine knew—a fly-boy. She says his wingspan was wider than this cabin. But try as he might, he could not fly. A few weeks after his flowering, he came down with a fever. They performed a wexcision—a wing amputation. Tragically, by that time it was too late."

"An' there are others like me?"

"Yes. There have been a few others."

"But how come no one's seen them? Wouldn't we know if that was true?"

"Who says no one has seen them? Did you realize it when you saw one yourself?"

"No," Ji-ji had to admit. "Drol looked more like an ape or bear than a human—"

Man Cryday interrupted. "Not Drol. A Wingchild. You saw one emerge."

"When?"

"Think back to births you witnessed."

"Bonbon wasn't a Wingchild. He was—" Ji-ji slapped a hand over her mouth in surprise and sat bolt upright. "Lotter! When he came to see Bonbon for the first time I thought he was trying to rub the color off cos Bonbon was so dark. He rubbed an' rubbed where his sproutings would be. And then he laughed like he'd never been more relieved in his life."

Man Cryday grabbed Ji-ji's wrist. "Are you sure Lotter examined his back?" Ji-ji nodded. Man Cryday looked stricken. "Did you tell Dregulahmo about this?"

"No. It didn't seem important."

The old woman let go of Ji-ji's wrist and sank back down in her rocker. "I need to think. . . . If Lotter suspected Oletto he will suspect you too. Explains why he wanted to keep you close. All this time we thought his snatching was about vengeance. It may have been much more than that."

Ji-ji looked at Man Cryday as understanding dawned. "You weren't talking about Bonbon. You didn't know Lotter suspected he could be a Wingchild. Who then?"

Ji-ji could hear her own heart beating. The sproutings pulsed like twin hearts on her back.

"*Silas!*" Ji-ji cried. "That's who you mean. Lua called him her angel-boy. . . . Afarra did too. Bettieann wrapped him up so fast I didn't see anything. Silas was a *Wingchild*!"

In spite of the pain it gave her, Ji-ji made herself picture the deathbed scene all over again: Bettieann's anger when she'd taken the lid off the boot box; the strange, scissorlike instrument she'd used during the birth; Lua imploring her not to let Bettieann hurt Silas. How had she missed all these clues? Lua knew what Bettieann planned to do. Lua-Dim in the confessional, the two wounds in Silas' back. Lua-Dim had invoked blackbirds too: *You're an angel,* she'd said. *Like Silas.*

"Bettieann cut them off!" Ji-ji exclaimed in horror. "She cut off little Silas' wings!"

"Bettieann Plowman has lost her way," Man Cryday said. "After Sidney died—did you know the American African lost her only son?" Ji-ji shook her head. "After that loss, a purple pain took her. A vengeance pain followed, which choked off motherhood. She will never escape what she has done. Guilt will hound her into her grave."

Ji-ji remembered what Lua-Dim had told her. She hardly dared ask the next question. "When she cut them off, was Lua's seedling—her baby, I mean—was Silas already dead?"

"We do not know the answer to that. Bettie confided in someone she trusted, not knowing that person is a Friend, but she did not tell them everything. Even before then we suspected she was a collaborator. If Lua's infant was liveborn, the wexcision would kill him. Was there much blood?"

Ji-ji recalled the blood-soaked boot box, how saturated his swaddling clothes had been, the cabin floor slippery with it. She nodded. Lua-Dim and Live Lua had told her the truth.

"Lua was right. I wasn't paying attention. She begged me during the seedbirth to save him. Threatened to Dimmer Bettieann if she went through with it. I could have done something. I just sat there while that bitch murdered him."

"Hush now. Marcie was there too. It was her responsibility to look out for her offspring, not yours. You would be a purple tear yourself if you had tried. You are lucky you were able to escape before your sprouting became visible, is it not so? I have told you. Wasting energy on regret is foolish. I have spent too many years doing that." Absentmindedly, Man Cryday tapped the arm of her rocker as she pondered what Ji-ji had told her. Eventually she said, "We have been searching for Oletto ever since he was taken, but now I see I sent Lucas to all the wrong places."

"What do you mean? Was Lucky searching for him?"

"Yes. Did he not tell you? It is why he left the planting after Oletto was snatched. I asked him to follow the infant, retrieve him if he could. But what you've told me explains why none of the server camps yielded any fruit. Lucas had to abandon the search and go to the No Region to assist in another mission. If the steaders suspected Oletto could undergo transformation they would never send him to a camp. He would be shipped off to Armistice instead."

"Why Armistice?"

"They have a facility there they call the Decipula. It means 'the trap' or 'the cage.' Drol was there for a time, we believe. As far as we can tell, it is where the steaders conduct most of their experiments."

"Then I must go save him!" Ji-ji cried.

"I go too," Afarra declared. "I do not meet Bonbon yet. This is my opportunity. I am the consolation bow. Missy Silapu did not like. It is nothing personal, Uncle Dreg is saying."

"Silapu regretted her cruelty toward you, Afarra," Man Cryday said. "She was sick. She could not help what she did. Do you understand, little one?"

Afarra nodded.

Man Cryday turned to Ji-ji and said, "As for you, Jellybean, how can you save your brother before you have saved yourself? You have a Freedom Race to run and a Freedom race to save. It is not one or the other. It is both."

"Are you saying *we're* the Freedom race? The seeds?"

"I am saying the race must survive, and for us who remember, flight *is* survival. Again and again we return to this refrain. The race is more than a question of winning; it is a quest to *be*. This is your path, child." She looked at Afarra. "I believe it is the little one's path too."

"Yes," Afarra said. "I am seeing him fly now. Very high in the sky."

Clearly affected by Afarra's words, Man Cryday said, "You see my brother?"

Afarra closed her eyes and said, "He is smiling and he is nodding like this." Afarra nodded her head up and down, looking uncannily like Uncle Dreg used to look. "He goes now. He is saying 'Bye-bye, Blackbirds' to the midnight."

Man Cryday was overcome for a moment. She turned her face away from them. "We need to prepare you for the race," she mumbled at last, and brushed her cheek with her hand.

"But how can I run like this?" Ji-ji asked.

"Do you feel weak? Are you in pain?"

Ji-ji thought for a moment. Apart from the strange sensation of the sproutings, she felt stronger than she'd ever felt before. "No! The pain's gone!"

"You are riding the Wake of the Spring. With luck, this renewal period will last for the duration of the race. Had your sprouting been a few days after this you could not have competed."

"But they'll see the growths on my back. And the steaders will be looking for me."

"The sproutings retract—disappear almost. You must learn to control them. We do not want them to announce themselves to the inquisitors, or even to the race monitors, who are not accustomed to seeing such things."

Who is? Ji-ji thought. "Your sproutings can be bound up and hidden under clothing," Man Cryday continued. "There is some good news. We intercepted a comm. A posse of Bounty Boys reported your death. We suspect Lucas sent an earlier message over the comm to that effect, knowing the enemy would intercept it. They will not be looking for you—not for a while, at least—because of Lucas' quick thinking."

Ji-ji felt grateful for this new information, but she soon lit upon another obstacle: "Sloppy's the runner rep from our planting, an' Marcus is the flyer rep. They'll recognize us. Marcus won't parrot but Sloppy will in a heartbeat."

"If all goes well that will not matter. As soon as you pass through Hemingsgate at the Monticello border you will be under Jeffersonian patronage and the race monitors' protection. You can declare who you are and no one can stop you from competing. But you *must* pass under Hemingsgate. Neither of you will be safe till then."

"Do you think there's a chance I'll find Bonbon? Think he'll have his own sproutings by then? Looks like this wing business runs in the family."

Man Cryday opened her mouth to speak, then closed it again. She puffed out her cheeks and closed her eyes briefly. When she opened them, they were filled with sorrow. "There was another who experienced the sprouting," she said. "But she is damaged. Dreg brought her here pregnant. Her child was born with wings perfectly formed. Like gossamer, but strong, unbreakable almost. The infant came three months early. I could not save him."

"But you saved the mother? She's still alive?"

"In a way. I had to amputate. If we had known how the wexcision would affect her, we may not have gone through with it . . . I don't know. But her sproutings were gangrenous. The choice was amputation or death."

"Where is this person now? I must find her."

"No! Finding her would be a terrible mistake! Dregulahmo was wrong to suggest it. She is damaged beyond repair. She is what we would call *malaika aliyeanguka*. She is fallen."

"What are you talking about? Who cares if she's 'fallen' or not? Who is she?"

"She is your sister, Ji-ji. The one you knew as Charra."

21 ALIS VOLAT PROPRIIS

They heard the Liberty Train before they saw it. The din terrified Afarra, who clung to Musa's craggy head like someone drowning. The thunderous *CHUG-chug-chug, CHUG-chug-chug* of the engine didn't scare Ji-ji. She knew how risky it was to hop a freight train, especially one carrying a cohort of heavily armed guards. In spite of this, she felt dizzy with exhilaration.

When the metal serpent came to a screeching halt at the timber-loading station, Ji-ji wanted to cheer. All her life she had fretted over what would slam into her next. The future invoked dread because it was indeed dreadful and beyond her control. "I betroth myself to my own future," Ji-ji whispered as she prepared to race toward the train. "I will never be meek again in the face of it."

As soon as they spotted a man in uniform sliding open the rusty door of the boxcar and signaling to them to rush out from their hiding place in the woods, Ji-ji knew they would make it all the way to Monticello. They would not be caught, *couldn't* be caught, because it had already happened in her mind and now they were just reliving it. She couldn't pinpoint the reason for her courage. It could be her sproutings, or the fact that Charra had been a Wingchild too. Or maybe it was simply the sight of the salvaged train, which seemed to gather up all the tenses of her life and slingshot her from a traumatic past, through a stupefying present, into a future that could be anything at all. She was certain of only one thing: her future would be *hers*. She would write it herself in bold font. Whatever dangers lurked inside the train's belly, and whatever horrors waited for her in the next place, she would not permit them to erase her.

She was Silapu's daughter, Charra's sister, and Lua's best friend. She was Toteppi, from the tribe who remembered flight. She had known Uncle Dreg and witnessed his sermon at the Circle. She had been tended by his sister, a.k.a. the Gardener of Tears, and she loved his descendant who flew Free in the cage. She was with her adopted little sister. Whatever the cost, she would thrust herself into her aching dreams and live there. She had gumption. She had purpose. She had (almost!) wings.

IIIIIIIIIIIII

They only had a few minutes to make it across the field before the train would depart from the loading station. Ji-ji was grateful the three of them would not be traveling unaccompanied. Germaine Judd and Bently Turner, selected by Man Cryday to serve as their escorts, were pros.

Tiro and Ji-ji grabbed hold of Afarra's hands while Germaine and Bently ran ahead, guns drawn. Musa, also accompanying them, bounded along in the rear. If they were spotted they were done for. The railway men and security contingent were farther down the track loading timber onto the train. All the freight hoppers had to do was slip into the boxcar and slide the door closed.

Under the cover of early-morning darkness, the group sprinted forward. Ji-ji's disobedient sproutings had been bandaged into submission by Man Cryday, who'd been as merciless with them as Silapu had been with her hair on the morning of Lua's harvesting. Her back was still tender, but at least her sproutings didn't bounce around when she ran like her breasts did in her ill-fitting bra. She carried Zinc's saddlebag. Ben had gone through it hurriedly before they'd set out and determined what she should keep. He hadn't found the letter or the photo. He surmised they must have been lost during the river crossing. Ben called the tooled saddlebag "exceptionally high quality" and advised her to hang on to it.

The fairskin rail guard who hurried them onto the train was nothing like Ji-ji expected. In a hoarse whisper, he cursed them for moving too slow and told them to haul their lazy butts into the boxcar before someone spotted them. When he saw the striper, he drew back in consternation. "Hold up!" he said in a furious whisper. "No way you're bringing that stinkin' mutant on board!"

Musa was in agreement. He bared his teeth and started to back away.

The man pulled nervously on his full beard: "Morons, all of you! No one tames a striper! That filthy ant belongs in a cage like the other one." He gestured to a dark corner of the car. They realized the train hadn't spooked Musa. Something else had.

There among the crates, in a cage taking up a third of the boxcar, lay a sleeping snarlcat, his mane forming a shaggy halo around his head. It was too dark for Ji-ji to see his dagger-length canines or lethal claws, but she remembered from the attack she'd witnessed on a hunt with Lotter how easily they could rip someone to shreds. Snarlcats weighed even more than stripers. With their huge, leonine jaws and lightning-fast speed, these superpredators could make quick work of almost any foe. As Ben pointed out, Musa, with his hunched, hyena-like back and piercing yellow eyes, could intimidate the crap out of anyone, yet even he shrank back when faced with a snarlcat. The creature was sedated, but Musa seemed to think he was faking it, and the others didn't trust he would stay asleep either.

The guard insisted this boxcar was their only option: "Train's packed to the gills with coal, grain, an' timber. Everyone's scared shitless of the cat, so no one'll bother you. Tell the ant to get lost before someone catches us!" But Afarra had no intention of riding the serpent without her friend. As the man continued to abuse them, she coaxed the striper up into the car with a stick of candy one of the Friends had given her.

The railman, muttering something about never doing another favor for that black bitch even if she put a hex on him, leapt down from the boxcar. Speaking fast and addressing Germaine, he told her to tell the dusky witch Reggie's debt was paid in full and then some. He reminded them they would only have a couple of minutes to disembark when they reached Monticello, unless of course they wanted their heads blown off, which it looked like they did cos only morons traveled in a boxcar with an unchained striper. "This car's at the back so you should be able to sneak off okay. But the area around Monticello's swarming with Bounty Boys. Some bigwig's been murdered."

"Who?" Ben asked.

"How should I know, boy?" Ben's eyes flickered in anger at the word *boy.*

Railman Reggie turned his attention to Tiro. "There's a reward out for you. Saw your face flash across the Wanted screen 'fore the whole damn system messed up cos of that quake a few days ago. Man, that was a doozy! Must be drillin' for gas round here again or somethin'. You from the 437th, ain't you, Mule?" The man took his silence as a yes. "Thought so. They're lookin' for you."

Reggie said to Germaine, "NoVA's the next stop after Monticello. Every car's inspected then. Disembark before then or you can say sayonara to liberty. You'll be toast, understand?"

Afarra, who still didn't seem to understand what the phrase meant, repeated what she'd said to Ji-ji after she'd lost the map: "We can be toast together."

Reggie looked Afarra up and down. "I guess you can," he said, "but I wouldn't advise it." He turned back to Germaine. "Dusky's a Cloth, right? Pretty. Not like the other one. What is she? Eleven? Twelve?" He looked down the track toward the loading dock. "Looks like we could be here a while. She available for a quickie? I ain't particular when it comes to pussy. Won't take a second."

As Germaine pretended she was considering his offer, Ji-ji grabbed hold of Afarra's arm and held on tight, Tiro moved his hand closer to his gun, and Ben took hold of Tiro's arm and whispered, "Easy, T. Germy can handle it."

"How can we trust this jerk?" Tiro whispered back.

"Beggars can't be choosers," Ben replied.

Germaine and Reggie kept talking. "Yeah. That sounds like a decent price for a quickie," she said, all smiles and accommodation. "Only one drawback. Wherever she goes, he goes too." She patted Musa's tiara. "They come as a pair. Still interested?"

Railman Reggie backed away so fast he nearly stumbled on the gravel. "Take me for a fuckin' pervert?" he hissed. "You tell that witch to leave me alone, y'hear? Tell her if she don't I'll have somethin' to say about it." Even Reggie seemed to know how pathetic his threat sounded. He spat on the ground in disgust and slid the door closed, leaving them in the dark with the snarlcat.

Tiro holstered his weapon. "Think the bastard knew how close he came to having his fuckin' balls blowed off?"

"Easy, fly-boy," Ben said. "You go chasing after every insult an' you'll be dead before we reach Monticello. An' no swearing in front of the ladies. Germaine here ain't used to vulgarity, are you, darlin'?" Germaine raised her eyes to heaven. "Now let's make ourselves comfy."

In the confined space, the stench of snarlcat excrement and urine was so strong it burned Ji-ji's sinuses. Musa's odor didn't help either. Ji-ji was thankful her sproutings no longer stank. As long as she wasn't the cause, she could put up with almost anything.

A few minutes later, just when they were breathing sighs of relief, they heard other men approaching, calling out as they came.

"Hey! Reggie boy!" Two men. Maybe three. . . . No, four!

Musa started to growl. "Keep him *quiet*!" Ben hissed.

Afarra mumbled entreaties to Musa, who stopped growling and lay down on his belly. Germaine and Ben drew their weapons. Tiro wasn't far behind. Ji-ji dug her hand into Zinc's saddlebag and withdrew Petrus' semiautomatic as the group of men strode closer to the boxcar, their heavy work boots crunching on gravel. They could be heard clearly through the warped metal door. One of them told Reggie plans had changed. The entire train would be inspected by inquisitors in Monticello. It would be up to Reggie to make sure the snarlcat behaved himself.

"Thought we didn't get inspected till we hit NoVA," Reggie said.

"You deaf or just plain dumb?" another man asked. "If Tate here says cars get inspected in Monticello, that's what happens. It's an inquisitorial inspection too. You know what those cardinals do if you keep 'em waiting. Am I right, Tate?"

"It's not pretty," Tate replied. His accent made Ji-ji think Tate was from the Midwest Territories. "Cards like their victims to squeal. 'Specially fond of newbies. How's Pussykins? I gotta hand it to you, Reggie boy, you're a natural. Could be the Dreamfleet'll be willing to let you keep the cat company. Bet Kitty would enjoy nibbling on a coupla fresh Rocky Mountain oysters. That's if you got any. Hear tell you're one of them hick Deviants they got a whole bunch of down here in the boonies. Is it true you fellas got a preference for bitches of the four-legged variety?"

The men howled with laughter. Ji-ji thought of Zinc and Chet and Daryl. The laughter was the same—thirsty, menacing. . . . She aimed the gun at the door and held it steady.

"How 'bout we check on the cat?" a voice—Tate's?—suggested. "He still out like a light? Al, get that door. Let's have us some fun with Reggie an' his little friend."

They heard Al attempt to slide the door open. It stuck.

Musa leapt to all fours. His tiara stood up straight on his head. Ben put his hand to his lips to signal quiet. They'd have a second or two before the men saw them hiding in the shadows.

Al jerked on the door again. Harder this time. It slid partway open!

"*JESUS!*" Al yelled, as he reeled back and covered his nose.

Quick as a flash, Reggie grabbed the handle and yanked the door closed. "Sorry, Al," Reggie said. "Guess I should've warned you. Kitty pooped. He's a big fella. Don't do nothin' small scale."

There was a long pause. The tension was broken by a voice yelling in the distance—an order to the railmen to get their butts on the train. Tate cussed Reggie out, promised he'd pay him back later. The men scurried off, their voices melting into the distance. A few seconds later, they heard Reggie walk away.

When Ben was sure they'd gone, he holstered his weapon and said,

"Well, how 'bout that? Guess we're indebted to Pussykins for pooping." He inhaled more deeply than was wise. "This place smells a whole bunch sweeter'n it did earlier. It surely does."

Ji-ji slipped Petrus' gun back into Zinc's saddlebag. They weren't toast yet.

IIIIIIIIIIIIII

After the Liberty Train got underway, Musa didn't seem bothered by the snarlcat in the cage. For Ji-ji, it wasn't so easy. Squeezed between crates, she could hear the wild creature breathing and snuffling a few feet away. Ben had said it was safe to have a mini light on a dim setting so they could keep an eye on their fellow traveler. If Ji-ji leaned forward a little, she could make out the outline of the snarlcat's enormous back, which rose and fell with each drugged snore. The smell got worse, if that was possible. Afarra offered to reach into the cage, scoop up the mountain of poop, and toss it out of the car, but Tiro said Musa, who was extremely protective of Afarra, would go nuts if she went anywhere near the snarlcat. "The cat is not for killing," Afarra insisted. "He see us but he is very sleepy." "I don't care if he's dead," Tiro told her. "You're not sticking your hand in that cage. He could swallow you in one gulp an' he wouldn't even belch afterward." Unwisely, Ben happened to mention that if the cat woke before they disembarked, he would go berserk when he realized he was in an enclosed space with a striper. Ben said they'd be forced to shoot him if he made a ruckus. Afarra got so upset that Tiro told her Ben had a gun with "special sleeping bullets." He'd use that one. It took some convincing, but at last Afarra seemed to buy it.

Ji-ji wondered aloud why the Dreamfleet needed a snarlcat. Germaine said the fleet was assembling "a menagerie of exotics" to go along with their state-of-the-art fly-coop. The owners of the Dreamfleet's flyer-battlers would pay a lot for a full-grown male. It was rumored that, come fall, the flyers would fight in the coop's upper tiers while ants prowled in the ring below. "The truce has been in place for a while now," Germaine said, "which means there's money to be made. The Dreamfleet used to serve as guards to the D.C. Congress when it re-formed itself as an Independent. But the flyer-battler wing is all about entertainment—keeping the public occupied so they don't see how screwed up things are. Distract people enough an' they forget what they were objecting to in the first place. Fans'll pay good money to see a few privileged flyer-battlers get mauled . . . or worse."

"No way I'm climbing in the coop with that," Tiro asserted.

Ben feigned surprise: "Don't tell me the great Tiro Dregulahmo's afraid of a little pussy."

"You bet I am. S'why I still got my Rocky Mountains. How'd you lose yours, Ben?"

Ben gave Tiro a friendly swipe on the back. "The fans're gonna lap you up, man. Kitty over there'll be first in line. Ignore Germaine the Judgmental. Got kicked out of the fleet. Been bitter ever since—right, Germ?"

"You better not call me that, Bennyboy. Not when I got a loaded gun on me."

"She loves me somethin' awful," Ben boasted. "S'why she hates me so much." Ben blew her a kiss, which Germaine batted away in contempt. Ji-ji had never witnessed a black male acting like that before with a female who looked white. On a planting, a seed could be Tilled to death for less than that.

Tiro and Ben were soon in a deep, 'shroom-laced conversation about the pros and cons of the equipment in flying coops. Ben spoke about his experience as a pro wistfully, describing the daredevil moves of flyer-battlers like X-Clamation and his female partner Re-Router. Excitement stirred inside Ji-ji. Not a single Elevation Prohibition against female flyers in Dream City. Maybe she would be the first flyer-battler in history to soar unassisted in the coop.

Ji-ji could see why Man Cryday had picked Ben to serve as one of their escorts. The confident black man dismissed Germaine's concern about the APB out on Tiro. As long as they kept out of sight till they reached the walls of the Monticello Protectorate they'd be fine, he said. Compact and stocky, with a weightlifter's build and strength, Ben had a rich brown complexion. If he'd been born in the Territories, he would have been on a slightly darker color arc than Ji-ji, but he had never been a botanical. Bently Turner had been born "New England Free," as he put it. His knowledge of fly-coops surpassed even Coach B's. Not surprisingly, Tiro pummeled him with questions. Joining the race at the second leg, Ben said, meant Tiro would have only two opportunities in the coop to score high marks, cos neither of his scores could be dropped. He had to do well in the Jefferson Coop, meet the qualifying time in the sprint segment, and do well in the Dream Coop too. "That's where the rubber hits the road. Corcoran'll be there watching."

Ji-ji wished Pheebs had decided to enter the race. Between the two of them, they could have helped Afarra make it to the finish line. Wild

Seeds had no age limit on them, and though she was probably in her fifties, Pheebs was fit as a fiddle. But no one had been able to persuade her to join them. She'd promised Billy she would escort Afarra to safety, if it proved necessary. Having completed her task, she was heading for the Rad Region to rescue her friend and mentor. "Are you nuts, Pheebs?" Tiro had exclaimed. "That's the last thing Coach B would want. He'd kill me if he found out I let you—" "*Let* me!" Pheebs had shot back. "No one *let* me do nothing, fly-boy! Not you an' not the beards on the 437th. Billy save me. Taught me to read an' write. Never let 'em hurt me. My turn to save him. I forget no one." Ji-ji wondered whether Tiro would give up his dream to fly with the Dreamfleet to search for her. If she'd asked herself that question a few days ago, her answer would have been yes. Looking at him now, however, she doubted it.

Before she'd taken off, Pheebs had put her arm around Afarra. "Look after this one like gold," she'd said. "She small like me—but she grow two inches since we leave. See how she tower above me now? Why? Cos she Free to grow in outer air an' cos she stay in the tower an' stretch to the sky at last. No need for hiding small anymore."

Pheebs' logic sounded iffy to Ji-ji. Hard to imagine that the old shot tower caused Afarra's growth spurt. Besides, anyone looked tall next to Coach B's tiny assistant. . . . On the other hand, Ji-ji had to admit Afarra had shot up uncannily fast in just a few days.

Pheebs had snuck off during the night, leaving a brief note behind in a sprawling hand.

> ***To say Goodby is bad. I Can not do it Afarra. Musa protect you now. And Jiji too. And Tiro. He is not so dumb for a fly boy sometimes. Love Pheebee. (NOT Cloth-34b) XOX***

After Pheebs' departure, Afarra had been so cut up that Man Cryday agreed to ask Musa if he wanted to go with them. He couldn't enter the Monticello Protectorate—they shot stripers on sight—but he could travel with them until then. Presumably, Musa had agreed to Man Cryday's request, because there he was, serving as Afarra's pillow.

If there had been any doubt that Afarra could communicate across species, doubt dissolved that morning when Afarra began talking to the striper in a hodgepodge language even Man Cryday had difficulty following. She'd detected a mixture of English, patois, Creole, Swahili, sign language, baby talk, and Afarra's own invented language. A spattering of

Totepp too, words she must have picked up from Uncle Dreg. She had the same uncanny ability to converse with the stallion, who would stop fretting in his pen whenever Afarra approached. She could also communicate with Drol. Ji-ji had witnessed it herself.

Late yesterday evening before they went to bed, Man Cryday had invited Drol to her cabin so he could converse with Afarra. When she saw him, Afarra ran to the door, grasped his huge hairy index finger, and pulled him inside. Outfitted in a Jangler costume with a large cow bell and a series of smaller bells in a chain around his neck (so people would know a Viral was approaching and beat a hasty retreat), Drol proved to be a bashful giant. At over seven feet, he made Afarra look like a toddler. He'd been caged for so long, Man Cryday said, his back had forgotten how to straighten itself. She estimated him to be a few years older than Ji-ji, though his stooped posture aged him.

Ji-ji had prepared herself to see Drol's face, having only seen it in shadow before. But when he slid back his hood she couldn't stifle a gasp. More ape than bear, and more beast than man, his hairy face and skull were grievously misshapen. His distorted mouth exposed his gums and made his speech—closer to grunting than speaking—almost impossible to decipher. His eyes and many of his facial features were decidedly human, and his fingers and toes, though misshapen, looked human too. His prominent forehead, tiny ears, and thick body hair alarmed Ji-ji until she reminded herself they had a lot in common. *I'm like this creature now. When Tiro looks at me he sees what I saw when I looked at Drol for the first time.*

Afarra had served as an enthusiastic translator, though Ji-ji couldn't say for certain how much Drol actually told her and how much she made up. In the end, however, they learned that a guard named either One Monty or Juan Monteverdi (the latter being Man Cryday's adaptation of Afarra's translation of Drol's indecipherable speech) had shown him kindness, joining him in his cage to tutor him whenever he could get away with it. Drol didn't know when he'd been transferred to the 437th, but it had taken him days to make the journey in the back of a covered truck. The most surprising part of the conversation related to how he'd escaped from the arsenal. He'd been held there for days, in transit to somewhere else, if Afarra's interpretation was accurate. Apparently, on Death Day morning, Uncle Dreg had been hurrying past the arsenal on his way back to PenPen when he'd heard Drol's moans through an open vent on the outer wall of the building. Casting his own sorrow aside, the wizard had ripped off the vent cover, climbed down into the shaft (at least, that was how Afarra translated it), found Drol, and unbolted his cage. After she heard this, Ji-ji understood why Drol uttered the wizard's name with a reverence usually reserved for God.

Man Cryday did her best to elicit as much information from Drol as possible about his time in captivity. Unfortunately, he hadn't been able to tell them much about the first cage where he'd spent his younger years, or the last one on the 437th. Each time Man Cryday asked him about it he screamed and wailed. Eventually, Afarra realized that Drol remembered very little apart from the other prisoners' screams and wails, which explained why all he could do was scream and wail when they questioned him about it. He'd been kept in solitary confinement for much of the time, and his weak eyesight made it difficult for him to see much of anything. His heartbreaking revelations prompted Ji-ji to leap up from the bed and spontaneously embrace him. (A reckless thing to do because he'd returned the embrace with gusto and almost crushed her wing sprouts.)

In the swinging hammock of the train, Afarra the Ant Whisperer soon slept as peacefully as a baby. She looked so comfortable snuggled on Musa's belly she could have been one of his cubs. His odor didn't bother her. Ji-ji had always assumed Afarra was about three or four years younger than she was. The more time she spent with her, however, the more she questioned that assumption. Afarra had an ancient quality. Each time she wore Uncle Dreg's Seeing Eyes, she seemed to age a little more. Her language was evolving into more complex structures. Her stubbornness, on the other hand, hadn't changed at all.

Man Cryday had given Afarra a pair of shoes—the first real shoes she'd ever had—yet she adamantly refused to wear them. Her toes had told her they didn't like being "cooped up," so Afarra tied the laces together and hung the sneakers around her neck, a substitute for the Seeing Eyes she carried in her bag. Tiro had warned her that the wizard's necklace would attract attention if she wore it in public. "Folks'll freak out if they see weird stuff like that," he said. As Ji-ji recalled his words, she felt her sproutings struggle against their restraints.

Ji-ji struggled to adjust to her new body. In the past, her body had obeyed her. She told it to run fast and it ran fast. She told it to eat and it ate, to piss and it complied. But her wayward sproutings did whatever they felt like. Once, when they were seedlings of seven and nearly nine, Ji-ji heard one of the field-seeds say his penis had a mind of its own. She'd demanded to know if this was true and asked to take a look at Tiro's to see its brain. He'd been reluctant at first, but she'd kept pestering him and eventually he'd pulled down his boycloth. She was disappointed. His penis looked like a small, undercooked sausage; she couldn't imagine what it must be like to have one of those things slapping around down there, nor could she figure out where its brain was. She'd laughed when she'd seen it, and he'd gotten angry and stormed off—a reaction she hadn't anticipated. Why wasn't his fat little sausage funny? Now, for the first time, she realized what a liability it was to have appendages with wills of their own, and how sensitive you could be about them.

Tiro caught her looking at him and smiled before turning back to talk to Ben. He had new friends now who were older and wiser than she was. Ben and Germaine spoke with authority but they didn't talk down to their young companions. Ben had an easy confidence that could charm the pants off most people, while Germaine's earnestness told you to listen carefully to what she had to say cos you'd almost certainly learn something. Ben had a SuperState passport that granted him the inalienable Right to Roam Free. In theory, as long as he didn't break the law in the Territories (which he did regularly, he said, as this situation demonstrated), the steaders couldn't touch him.

"Your timing couldn't be better," Ben told Tiro. "With a pedigree like yours they'll want to interview you for the D.C. sports channel. Uncle Dreg's a hero after his Culmination Speech. Everyone's talking about it. Just give 'em that big sappy grin an' say you're humbled by all the fuss. Fans don't take kindly to an uppity Mule." The two flyers laughed. Ji-ji felt her wing sprouts stir again underneath the bandages.

Germaine, who had spent three years as one of only a handful of female flyer-battlers, eased herself down next to Ji-ji.

"Benny romanticizes the coop," she said. "But most flyers are black and brown for a reason. Takes desperation to risk your neck like that."

"Man Cryday says things aren't going well," Ji-ji said.

"She's right. S'been rough lately. Uprooting the planting system's tougher than the reunionists anticipated. It staked its claim to a third of the country before most people realized how quickly it was spreading—states writing their own Declarations of Independence after the Sequel, disgruntled whites from the north an' west pledging themselves to the Territories and the Found Cause. Chaos, rationing, riots. . . . Law and order's tempting, 'specially after you seen chaos up close. So you trade justice for peace, an' avert your eyes when the disease metastasizes. . . . Thing is, Ji-ji, the Friends need a symbol—something to raise 'em up, give 'em hope. Man Cryday says you could be the one to do that."

"But I'm not a symbol. I'm a—" Ji-ji stopped herself. She'd nearly said she was a Muleseed. "I'm just . . . me."

"Maybe," Germaine replied. "But the Oziadhee thought there could be more to it than that. Sounded pretty certain about it too. We all gotta dream, kid. And we all gotta find someone to help carry that dream to the mountaintop. S'what leaders do."

"I'm no leader. I guess I was pretty good at public speaking but I hated it."

Germaine smiled and patted Ji-ji's knee. "I don't think public speaking will be something you gotta worry about yet, kid. You'll likely have a few other things to tackle first."

Ji-ji nodded. Her sproutings were itching like crazy. She wanted to rip off her T-shirt, tear off her bandages, and scratch herself raw. Man Cryday had shown Germaine how to apply the ointment, and Germaine had done it without flinching, but it hadn't had the same effect. Germaine had been worried about hurting her, so she hadn't massaged it in as deep as it needed to go. No one had a touch like Man Cryday. Ji-ji had underestimated how hard it would be to part ways with the Gardener of Tears.

When they'd said goodbye, Man Cryday had kissed Ji-ji on the cheek and said, "*Alis volat propriis,*" and Ji-ji recognized the words as ones she'd heard through the caller. She'd asked who Alice was. Man Cryday had smiled and said, "Each congregation of Friends has its own saying. Some have been transplanted from the old state mottoes. The phrase is Latin. It means 'She flies with her own wings'—or 'his own wings,' some say. I like 'her' better, yes?" Then she'd held her close like a grandmother. Ji-ji had wanted to ask if the phrase was just coincidence, but it had seemed like a vain question, the kind that would result in a flauntification fine on the 437th.

Ji-ji shifted her position. Man Cryday had bound her sproutings so tight it was like wearing one of those ridiculous corsets fairskin women in the Territories had to wear. Unaccustomed to restrictive clothing, Ji-ji found it impossible to take a deep breath. There was no way she could run for miles bound up like this. Luckily, one of the Friends—a Cradle recruit named Kofi—had been tasked by Man Cryday to make her a runner's short-cape. In the early days of the Freedom Race, everyone wore these mini capes that ended just below the waist. Man Cryday said a few runners usually paid tribute to this tradition by wearing short-capes themselves. The clothing was treated with the same respect afforded to

military uniforms. With any luck, therefore, Ji-ji wouldn't be required to remove it. Man Cryday gave Ji-ji strict instructions not to do so in public unless she could retract her sproutings and keep them retracted. Until then, she had to keep them bound under her short-cape, which should make them hard to detect as long as they didn't act up too much.

The train slowed down to take a curve, then sped up again. Prior to the train ride, Ji-ji hadn't experienced speed often, apart from the occasional ride in an automobile. Like height, speed was something female botanicals were prohibited from indulging in "to excess." If her wings flowered, would she be able to match the speed of a horse, or a truck, or a train? What would it feel like to rise into the air and see things fall away, as if the force of gravity were little more than a cape?

The train jolted noisily along the tracks. At times, it lurched abruptly to the right or left. Ji-ji wondered if it felt like this sailing on the ocean. How frightened the Passengers must have been if it did—lying in filth among strangers in the dark belly of a wooden beast as the ship rocked them farther and farther away from home. The motion, though it made her companions drowsy, made her pensive. She welcomed having time to reflect on the past few days.

Zinc's saddlebag lay beside her. Into it she'd transferred many of the items from Lucky's duffel bag—Tiro's letter, her watch, and her map among them. Man Cryday had added a change of clothes, and a book called *The Dreamer King*, about the civil rights struggle. Books were pre- cious. Few were printed anymore and new ones cost a small fortune. Ji- felt rich. She would have to surrender her bag to Germaine before she e tered the race, but she knew she could trust her to return it when (if?) s made it to the city. Aside from shoes and a change of clothes, competit weren't permitted to bring anything with them.

Carrying so much wealth had a sobering effect. She'd never had thing of real value to leave to someone else. If she didn't make i if Tiro and Afarra didn't either, she'd instructed Germaine to lo Dipthong Spareseed, who would probably be going by Donna, a the bag to her. Ji-ji knew chances were slim Dip had made it ou Margins alive, yet it made her happy to imagine her generous frie City of Dreams. She pictured the long-suffering kitchen-seed li pily inside the city walls, reading excerpts from the Dreamer' to the four orphans she'd adopted. No contamination cross c to shame her cos her days as a Tainted were over.

Ji-ji knew how fortunate they'd been. If the train hadn't b

the snarlcat, there wouldn't have been room for them. Following the latest trade treaty, the steaders had salvaged and returned to service more of the trains built in the Age of Plenty. Lotter often complained that spotty maintenance and the labor shortage made these trains notoriously unreliable. In addition, unrest in the Territories and recent floods forced them to take circuitous routes. Their journey to Monticello, not very far as the crow flies, would take several hours. They should arrive at the second checkpoint before dawn. After they disembarked and passed under Hemingsgate, Tiro would battle in the Jefferson Coop. The morning after that, assuming they'd been ratified as Wild Seeds, she and Afarra would set out on their marathon to the city. If the monitors were kind, they would bus the runners part of the way and the race would be a fifty- or sixty-miler. If the inquisitors had their way, the runners would have to cover the entire distance—110 miles over some rough, hilly terrain, right through the heart of wild country. Ji-ji looked at Afarra. How would she run that far?

Germaine woke for a moment and felt instinctively for her gun before dozing off again. Earlier, she'd told Ji-ji her real name was Maria Mya Alexander Santos, but she'd said that name could be tricky in a region filled with first-class morons, so Ji-ji shouldn't use it till they met up again in the city, if then. Germaine's father was a white Texican, her mother "Mexican through and through." As a child, Germaine had traveled up with her mother and two sisters in search of the man who'd left one day when he'd gotten bored. "Mom searched for my dad her whole life," Germaine had explained, "even after she found him. He didn't give a crap about her or us. Mom refused to believe that. Never believed anything she didn't want to believe. She was a bitter romantic. Beware of that, kid. It's a lethal blend."

Germaine had described how they'd been hoisted up over the Weeping Wall on the southern border. Her mom hadn't a clue where to go and they'd wound up smack-dab in the middle of the Rad Region. Germaine said she probably had the same type of cancer that killed her mom. "I check my boobs every morning an' wait for lumps to appear. It's depressing. But it's spurred me on to do more with my life, y'know? Don't want to look back and discover I never made a difference. . . . Mom had PTSD real bad. Made her crazy mean. I got the scars to prove it. Mom was carrying too much crap around and only a fraction of it was hers. Ate her up in the end, along with the cancer. But I was a teenager by then. Could take

care of myself. Like you." Ji-ji had nodded sympathetically and instructed herself to look up PTSD when she got her own dictionary in the city.

Germaine had said she'd heard there were hardly any white women on plantings anymore. Said the more the SuperStates and Independents got their act together, the more wives were hightailing it off the plantings to seek a better life for themselves. "Who wants to see your husband screwing around with girls young enough to be his granddaughters, even if it's all a grand sacrifice to seed the Territories? Figure the Wives-Proper are the steaders' Achilles' heel. They're the ones we gotta persuade. S'why Man Cryday was pinning her hopes on your mam. From what I hear, she had a classiness all her own. Wanted her to appeal to other women. Tell 'em why all females had to band together and fight for liberation. Were there many white women on the 437th?"

"Only Old Shadowy, the planting diviner," Ji-ji had told her. "An' a few Liberty Laborers' wives. Miss Zyla Clobershay used to live there too, but she was fired. You know her?"

"You kidding? Everyone knows Zy. She's amazing. . . . She also happens to be batshit crazy. Takes chances no sane person would dream of taking. But if you're in a tight spot, it's Zy you want fighting next to you over and above everyone else in the Friends—'cept Lucky, of course."

When Ji-ji had made the mistake of pointing out that Lucky hadn't officially been a Friend, Germaine's temper had flared. "What the hell do you know, kid? Lucky Dyce was the bravest friend I've ever known!" Then, to Ji-ji's surprise, Germaine had burst into tears.

IIIIIIIIIIIIII

The Liberty Train chugged along through the night. Everyone except Ji-ji had been rocked to sleep. The snarlcat, thank god, was still out cold. The notion that she'd forgotten something important gnawed at Ji-ji, but then it always did. The revelations about Silas, Bonbon, and Charra highlighted how blind she'd been. From now on, she would do better.

Tiro moaned, softly at first, then louder. He was dreaming. Probably one of his recurring nightmares about his brother. Sometimes Amadee appeared whole; at other times, he'd been tractor-pulled and Tiro had to gather up the pieces and put him back together like a puzzle. Tiro said that was the worst cos he knew how futile it was but he had to keep doing it, otherwise he'd have to show his mother what happened to her son. Which made no sense either cos she was the one who'd rocked Amadee in her arms that morning, so wouldn't she know about it already? Tiro had discovered them like that. Pushed his way through a crowd of gawking seeds. He still didn't know why he'd been drawn to the cornfield behind Williams' father-house where he'd found his mother with what was left of Amadee.

Tiro moaned again, tried to speak. His nightmare must be getting worse. Ji-ji didn't feel she could go over to where he lay and comfort him, not when her back disgusted him so much. While they waited for the Liberty Train, Ji-ji had told Tiro about Charra's double amputation and he'd gotten excited. "They got a bunch of surgeons in the city. Got a new hospital up an' running at full strength, pretty much, in the city's Elevated Zone. The doctors got loads of experience with the terror and disaster victims. Ben says they got a special wing devoted to the Dreamfleet battlers an' their kith-n-kin." Ji-ji had attempted to make light of it by saying, "So you want me to have my wings amputated in a special wing?" Tiro had looked at her like she'd gone mad. Though she'd never wanted to chain him to her, it still felt like she'd lost her conjoined twin—like she'd woken up after surgery to see him standing there in front of her, separate and distinct. She wished she could be sensible and admit that he was he and she was she and that was that.

If only Charra were here. Her warrior sister would never be intimidated by a couple of wing stubs. Charra had been right about so many things. Steaders being scared of Toteppi for one. She must have been pregnant when Ji-ji had stopped by Petrus' seed quarters to see her. Truth was, Ji-ji had been too young and dumb to notice anything. (*Another time when I wasn't paying attention.*) All she'd noticed was Charra's beat-up face as she stood there, beaten by Petrus . . . the steader who'd seeded both Lua's and Charra's offspring . . . the bastard who'd killed Mam in cold blood. Could it be coincidence that Petrus seeded both Wingchildren? *Maybe he didn't,* Ji-ji thought. *Maybe Charra an' Lua were taken to the arsenal and inseminated like the Tuskegees? Does that mean Lotter may not be my father-man either?* She had to think this through. Her mam had said Lotter forced himself on her a few hours after he'd pyred Elly, but maybe something else got her pregnant? The idea that Lotter wasn't her father-man should have made her glad, in a way. Yet she felt suddenly adrift, as if she wasn't tethered to anything real at all. Who was she? More to the point, *what* was she? She needed consolation. She reached into the saddlebag and took out the book Man Cryday had given her.

Most seeds had heard of the Dreamer but few had an opportunity to read his words. She trained Lucky's flashlight onto the pages as closely as she could so the bright cone of light didn't disturb the others. She'd heard the Reverend's words before. Uncle Dreg had played them to her and Tiro on his old gramophone. The wizard had to turn the volume way down so no one else would hear the Dreamer's impassioned pleas. His voice had stayed with Ji-ji all these years. Like Uncle Dreg's, it was filled with so much yearning it inspired you to do something to make things better. Man Cryday had inserted a bloodred leaf from an Immaculate tree into one of the pages that featured excerpts from the Dreamer's letter, the one written on April 16th, when he was confined to a jail cell. Ji-ji began to read. It seemed to her like the Dreamer was worried the dream would fly away. A chill ran down her spine. *I'll be in jail one day,* she thought. *A caged bird.*

She looked over at the snarlcat's cage and saw herself inside a cage, her wings broken and useless. A six- or seven-year-old Bonbon lay bleeding beside her, his wings ripped from his back. Someone had mounted them to the bars of the cage! She heard the *drip, drip, drip* of wing blood as it hit the floor. She reached out to comfort her brother. Her touch engulfed him in flames!

She was back in the boxcar. The snarlcat still snored. She must have dozed off, had a nightmare. Yes, that must be it. The memory of her time in the confessional haunted her; so did the Dreamer's letter. What she'd learned about those awful mutation sites haunted her too. She must have mixed it all together in her head.

Afarra woke. "You are shaking like a leaf, Elly," she said. Afarra reached into her bag, pulled out the Seeing Eyes, and hung them round her neck.

Afarra's voice changed: "'Read the letter,' he is saying. 'Read the letter now.'"

It seemed like good advice. Uncle Dreg knew the Dreamer's words could heal her.

Ji-ji turned again to the book, which had fallen to the floor. She picked it up, found the page with the letter again. The excerpts moved her—certain sentences in particular, the rage and the tears and the weariness all mixed together. Though the Dreamer felt compelled to keep going, Ji-ji sensed he yearned to lay his burden down. She understood why so many refugees flocked to the City of Dreams to set up their tents and cardboard hovels at the foot of the Reverend's statue in the flood-prone part of the city. There he was in the photo—a small black man, preaching in front of a monument to another assassinated leader, who would understand his burden the way others couldn't.

Afarra moved her head from Musa's belly to Ji-ji's lap. "The sproutings are sad?" she asked. "They are hurting?"

"No," Ji-ji replied. "Nothing hurts as bad as it did before."

"Do not concern. We will see him. I will pass the exam and race the way home."

Tiro said he'd gone over the questions on the Race Eligibility Exam with Afarra during their journey through The Margins, before they'd gotten separated. He and Pheebs had both concluded that Afarra's answers were beyond peculiar, so Man Cryday had sent word to Friends in Monticello that Afarra needed to be quizzed by a race monitor who would appreciate her unique point of view. Tiro had told Afarra that as long as she didn't wind up being quizzed by an asshole she'd be fine. Afarra had asked him how many assholes there were in Monticello. When Tiro, pulling a number out of his ass, had told her there were seven altogether but none of them would be working on the day they arrived, Afarra had been visibly relieved.

Ji-ji put her arms around Afarra and held her close, tried again to dismiss the gnawing sense that she'd forgotten something important.

Their companions soon began to stir. They needed to disembark while darkness was still their friend. The train began to slow down.

Ben jumped up and eased the door open a little. He peered into the dark.

"Okay," Ben said. "You ready? I can see the lights of Monticello way off in the distance. We gotta jump when we slow down an' hit this next curve."

"Jump?" Ji-ji cried. "From the *train*? While it's *moving*?"

"Don't you remember?" Germaine told her. "There's an inquisitor inspection in Monticello. No way we can risk riding this thing all the way. Last person you want to tussle with is a cardinal."

"If we ride all the way we are toast," Afarra declared, rubbing sleep from her eyes.

Oh crap! Ji-ji thought. *Does everyone know this but me? Please let this be the only important thing I missed.*

The train slowed a little more; then it slowed more than that. Ji-ji grabbed her saddlebag.

"You ready?" Ben yelled to Tiro above the clatter of the train.

"Yeah, I'm ready," Tiro yelled back.

Ben slid the door open further. "You first, fly-boy!" he cried.

At least I won't be the first to jump, Ji-ji thought, grateful for small mercies. Wrong again.

Before she could protest, Tiro grabbed her hand and pulled her down with him into the rushing dark.

22 DECLARATIONS

Apart from the Salem Outpost, the Monticello Protectorate was the only place in The Margins where botanicals had the right to petition for status as Wild Seeds. Zyla Clobershay had told Ji-ji about Monticello, how it served as an important symbol for the various governing bodies in the fractured nation. The homesteader secessionists saw Jefferson as a model patriarch, a beneficent owner of botanicals who believed in his God-given superiority, owned hundreds of seeds, and sowed his own seed among them. The reunionists in the Eastern and Western SuperStates were equally loyal to the founding father, viewing him as the man whose lofty principles made impossible unions possible. The Independents admired him too, because of his bold arguments for liberty. Ji-ji had told her teacher it proved that you could please all of the people all of the time after all. Zyla Clobershay had warned her not to share her ironic assessment with her father-man or any other steader, reminding her that seeds could be whipped for heresy if they mocked a patriarch.

Uncle Dreg used to say that Jefferson gave the nation the ability to gaze down from the mountaintop, but he'd neglected to teach it how to climb a hill. Ji-ji still wasn't exactly sure what the wizard meant by that. But she did know that the words Jefferson had written, words she'd memorized in legacy school, still thrilled her. His Declaration of Independence had put down roots in her head like a poem or a prayer. Even after she realized that the fairskin father-men who'd signed it had failed to see how many of their flock were cooped up in the nation's cages, Jefferson's words made her heart soar. She would like to meet Thomas. She would ask the father-man if his Dimmer-seeds—his kin, especially—slipped into his afterlife to haunt him. She suspected they did, and that even his beautiful words were not enough to appease them.

IIIIIIIIIIIIII

Ji-ji couldn't believe she hadn't been hurt when they leapt from the train. Miraculously, the same was true for everyone except Tiro, who'd twisted his left foot. Tiro had been focused on protecting her. As a result, she believed, he'd fallen awkwardly. During the arduous trek from the train, he winced if he put too much weight on it. When she asked if he was okay, he told her not to fuss. Because they'd disembarked much farther from Monticello than they'd planned, they had to maintain a furious pace. Several times during their journey, they caught sight of members of the Supreme Council's security contingent—highly trained, red-jacketed forces who reported directly to the inquisitors. With Musa's invaluable assistance (he sensed their proximity long before they did), they had avoided detection.

About halfway to Monticello, they stumbled across an abandoned Bounty Boy camp. The Boys had tacked a Wanted poster onto a tree. It announced the search for the killer of "Selfless Patriot Zebadiah Moss." The Supreme Territorial Council was offering a reward of fifty thousand Armistice dollars to anyone who captured Zeb's killer. This must be the murdered bigwig Railman Reggie told them about. Instead of the usual sketch or mug shot, the poster featured the outline of a face shaded in black. Ji-ji noticed the authorization signature: *Lord-Secretary Fightgood Worthy.* It brought back the episode in the storeroom in all its lurid detail. She pictured the grand inquisitor's creepy smile at the Last Supper, the enigmatic way he'd looked at her when he'd come upon her in the storeroom with Inquisitor Tryton. She couldn't figure out why the Lord-Secretary was there. Did he suspect she was a Wingchild? Did Lotter suspect her too?

Ben said Zebadiah went by a host of different names. A notorious drug lord who delighted in torturing his victims, he siphoned drug money to Central Command in Armistice. Ben suspected the killer must've gotten away with either a huge stash of illicit drugs or a load of cash. "Won't be easy for the council to recover from this," he said. "Won't be easy for us either," Germaine pointed out. "Not with dozens of cardinals and red jackets flocking to the area. The killer's timing was lousy."

They reached Monticello at midafternoon, later than they'd hoped. There it sat at the crest of the hill: Thomas Jefferson's father-house.

Ji-ji could just make out the cabins along Mulberry Row where seed entrants stayed during the layover. The quaint photos of a tranquil planting in Zyla's history book must have been taken a long time ago because post-Sequel Monticello looked nothing like the photos. Cozying up to Jefferson's domed, porticoed father-house were a motley collection of houses and cabins, interspersed with makeshift shacks and tents, ramshackle stores, and the odd assembly hall. The place had a claustrophobic, cobbled-together appearance; apart from the father-house, nothing looked level or plumb. Ji-ji never expected the walled protectorate to look as muddy and run-down as Brine's seed quarters. Yet, in spite of its shabby appearance, Ji-ji's heart skipped a beat when she saw it. All they had to do was pass under the Hemingsgate. After that, the steaders couldn't touch them.

While they waited for a group of racers to approach so they could merge with them undetected, Germaine told Ji-ji about the protectorate, impressing upon her how carefully they needed to tread while they were there.

Monticello's residents, commonly known as Cellists, didn't take kindly to "outside agitators," and some of them viewed all the Freedom Race entrants in that light. A pioneer, gun-slinging atmosphere prevailed inside the walls of the overcrowded protectorate. Though fairskins could enjoy the rights of citizenship, duskies could not. Monticello regulations prohibited non-white Freemen from the SuperStates or Independents from staying in Monticello longer than seven nights without a special dispensation from Monticello's governor. The non-white Liberty Laborers and Indigenous workers, restricted to sleeping in the flimsy prefabs or tents (brutal during the winter), had few rights to speak of. If the population exceeded capacity by more than a thousand, certain groups—Blacks, Latins, Asians, dusky Liberty Laborers, internationals from non-European nations, and Green Cards—could be chased out of the protectorate and forced to set up camp beyond the settlement walls. Clansmen, militiamen, pickers, and Bounty Boys congregated here to get liquored up, visit the drug dens, and relieve themselves in the *miscegenations,* the protectorate's notorious interracial brothels. Ji-ji commented on the stench wafting toward them. Germaine said Monticello smelled positively fragrant in the spring. Much better than it did in the summer months when its open sewers made the place almost uninhabitable.

The two entry gates could be seen from where they hid. To the right was the Jefferson Arch, which served as the "Freemen Only" entrance. To the left was Hemingsgate, the entrance for "Botanicals and Miscellaneous"—a wrought-iron double-hung gate about twenty feet wide. The Hemingsgate's original name was the Gate of Principles—a useless fact Ji-ji knew because occasionally Doc Riff allowed her to research the Freedom Race on the seed clinic's refurbished computer. At both entrances, militiamen in navy-blue uniforms stood to attention.

On the top of the limestone wall that marked the boundary of the protectorate were statues of the Six Noble Historians, honored for raising the alarm when insurgents attacked Monticello. All six had perished defending the old house until reinforcements arrived. On top of the imposing Jefferson Arch, wide enough for six Monticello horse guards to pass through at once, was a bronze statue of Jefferson, seated at a writing desk, pen poised over his Declaration. The flag of the Homestead Territories displaying the familiar Territorial seal—a steader rifleman straddling a planting—flew on the right of the arch, while the flag of the Monticello Protectorate—an image of Jefferson's father-house, alone on a grassy hill—flew on its left. The Territorial flag was at half-mast. "Must be in honor of that butcher Zebadiah," Ben said.

Ben pointed to an enormous pavilion, located inside the wall and up the hill a ways. "That's where you're set to make your big debut tonight, man," he told Tiro. The Jefferson Coop, with its white-domed tribute to the father-house, looked nothing like the dilapidated old fly-coop on the planting. "The other battlers'll be in there now practicing," Ben added. "They'll have formed alliances during the battle in the Salem Coop. Don't let 'em draw you into a trap."

So far, they'd spied only a handful of exhausted runners dragging themselves along the wide race path. Had the rest of the runners arrived already? As if in answer to the question, a runner burst from the woods and sprinted onto the race route. She must have been running off-route for a while, even though protection for the runners ended as soon as they stepped off the official path. The lone runner wore her hair in elaborate braids. Her strong, even stride carried her speedily to the Jefferson Arch. The smattering of spectators shouted warnings, but the runner didn't hear them. As soon as she reached the arch, two Monticello militiamen in navy uniforms marched up to her and punched her to the ground. They swore at her for trying to enter through the Freemen Only entrance and kicked her viciously in the stomach. Germaine moved to intervene. Ben grabbed her arm, insisting it would only make things worse. The runner, clutching her ribs, blood dripping from her mouth, struggled to her feet and stumbled toward the Hemingsgate.

"What'll happen to her?" Ji-ji asked.

"If there's a race monitor on duty, nothing much, I hope," Ben replied. "But if there's some inquisitor in charge, she could have her race ratification revoked. Trying to obtain entry at a forbidden entrance constitutes a cardinal offense in Monticello—an' believe me the cardinals enforce it. . . . Stick close to Afarra. Make sure she doesn't make the same mistake. An' don't forget—go through with her first. With an APB out on Tiro, it could get hairy when he declares himself. Thanks to Lucky, you're presumed dead, which means you should've been erased from the planting databases. Plantings don't bother to make a record of their Serverseeds, so Afarra should be okay too. . . . Remember, we've got Friends on the inside. They likely won't identify themselves, but they'll be doing whatever they can to assist you."

Germaine pulled her gaze from the lone runner, who had just staggered through the Hemingsgate. "Don't forget what I told you," she urged. "Wild Seed status can be revoked if seeds lie about their identity and planting affiliation. Watch your back, Ji-ji—pun intended. When the steaders hear you're resurrected, they're likely to try to— Hey! You listening to me?"

Ji-ji tried to look like she was paying attention, but she couldn't bear it any longer. "Scratch 'em, for god's sake! It's *agony*! You gotta scratch 'em—*now*!"

"Keep it down!" Germaine said. "Man Cryday said you should try not to scratch—"

"Scratch the damn things! Quick!"

"Okay! I'm scratching!" Germaine scratched and scolded at the same time. Ji-ji almost wept with gratitude. "There. Is that better?" Germaine said. "How come you didn't speak up earlier? I wish there was time to apply some salve. You still got that jar in your cape pocket, and those extra bandages?" Ji-ji said she had. "Good. You're gonna need 'em. Afarra, apply plenty of ointment to her back tonight an' rub it in real good, okay? Don't let anyone see."

"They will not be seeing nothing," Afarra assured her. "I see in the dark. Like the moon."

Ben instructed Ji-ji to give her saddlebag to Germaine. He stuffed Afarra's bag and Tiro's backpack into his larger bag and left them each with the few possessions they were permitted to take with them. Afarra had resisted putting on her sneakers, but they'd convinced her it would be impossible to run with shoes flapping about around her neck. Ji-ji felt vulnerable without the bag and without any weapon to protect herself, but she'd never be granted entry if she showed up with murder victim Danfrith Petrus' gun and murder victim Zinc Shokovsky's saddlebag.

"They don't allow much contact between racers and non-racers," Germaine told them. "An' we got to make sure the Friends're ready for your arrival. But we'll see you in the coop tonight."

"Wouldn't miss it for the world," Ben said. "Don't forget. Steer clear of inquisitors an' militiamen an' look for a sympathetic monitor. You do that an' they won't be able to touch you."

"No touching," Afarra said softly.

"Tiro and me won't let anyone touch you," Ji-ji promised.

Ben pointed to the race route: "Look! Runners! A whole bunch o' them! That's your cue."

They'd been absurdly fortunate. They hadn't expected to see a sizable group of runners at this late stage, as most of them would have arrived days ago. They could merge with this group and gain precious seconds in their wild dash to the Hemingsgate.

With no time to waste, Tiro grabbed Afarra's right hand and Ji-ji pried her left from Musa's neck and grabbed it herself. The three of them rushed out from their hiding place in the trees. A convoy of trucks rolled by as they approached. The trio of Wild Seeds stepped onto the race route and merged with a dozen runners.

Focused on the convoy, neither the few spectators nor the guards noticed them at first. Soon, however, people pointed at Tiro, who was taller than the others, all of whom were female. Ji-ji kept her eyes on the backs of the competitors ahead of them, where large bibs of fabric with the runners' numbers were pinned. Above the numbers she saw the Freedom Race logo: a solitary figure on a white winding path, flanked by a black *F* and a black *R*.

"What . . . you . . . doing?" one of the runners asked, between pants. She looked like hell. Blood seeped from her running shoes and she had a large gash on her cheek.

"We're chasin' after Freedom!" Tiro declared.

"Are you *crazy*!" another weary runner cried, gasping for breath. "The Long Leg's . . . only for females. 'Sides, everyone . . . got . . . to start . . . in Salem!"

"Not if they're Wild!" Tiro yelled back.

He grabbed Afarra's hand again and the three friends sprinted past the group of stunned, exhausted runners. In her peripheral vision, Ji-ji saw a guard chasing them, shouting at them to stop. The gate was a few yards away, but her sproutings were a torment, the desire to scratch unbearable. Could she stop herself from tearing off her cape and ripping off her bandages? She looked over at her friends. Tiro had a pronounced limp but he refused to let it slow him down. Afarra looked terrified—like someone who was about to be given an oral exam by a mad dentist. In spite of her fear, Afarra's mouth was set in that stubborn line Ji-ji had seen many times before. Yes. They would make it. They had to. Willing her back quiet, Ji-ji kept running, her eyes fixed on the prize.

IIIIIIIIIIIIII

The monitor seated at the table stared up at them. In the hot sun, wearing his dark green academic robes and a matching eight-sided velvet tam, he sweated profusely. He kept batting aside the tam's gold tassel as if he couldn't imagine who'd been dumb enough to put it there. He squinted at them through the weighty lenses of his glasses, which doubled the size of his eyes.

"Wild Seeds, you say?"

"That's right, sir," Ji-ji replied, "her an' me. She an' me, I mean." Repeating words she'd rehearsed with Germaine, she took a deep breath and said, "We hereby officially declare ourselves to be Wild Seeds. As such, we seek the protection of the race monitors, an' petition for the rights an' privileges afforded us under the Wild Seed Rule."

The monitor's glasses steamed up in the humidity. He took them off and wiped them on the wide sleeve of his robe. "No such thing as a Wild Seed. No such thing as a Wild Seed Rule either."

"There *is* a Wild Seed Rule, sir," Ji-ji insisted. "Only most people don't know about it."

She glanced toward the Jefferson Arch for help, but Germaine and Ben, who'd been standing in line earlier, were nowhere to be seen. The "Freemen Only" line moved much faster. They must have entered the protectorate already.

Meanwhile, the other runners had caught up and were dragging themselves through the Hemingsgate, bruised, battered, and utterly exhausted. Ji-ji saw fear and trauma on their faces too. It must have been a race from hell if it had taken some of them this long to reach Monticello. Ji-ji saw the runners looking at her resentfully. One gave her the finger; another spat in her direction.

In a desperate effort to get the attention of the monitors at the recording table, Ji-ji raised her voice and said, "There really is a Wild Seed Rule!"

The race monitor slipped his glasses back on. "Don't shout at me, dusky. I'm not deaf."

"Sorry, sir. What I'm trying to say is any seed can join the race at either Salem, or here at Monticello, and request the protection of the race monitors."

"We are not in the protection business," the monitor informed her.

Tiro couldn't take it anymore. He stepped forward and stated, "It's under Section F, Rule 28. The FRC, the Freedom Race Council—"

"I know what the FRC is!" the monitor said, reddening with irritation.

"Sorry, sir. Course you do. The FRC passed the rule years ago. It was endorsed in a joint agreement by the D.C. Congress an' the Territories' Supreme Council."

"Who are you?" the monitor asked. "And why is a *male* running in the *female* Long Leg?"

Tiro hesitated, looked at Ji-ji. He'd remembered too late the uproar it would likely cause when he gave his name. She and Afarra needed to get processed first. He stepped back and murmured softly, "Sorry, Ji." He moderated his voice, tried and failed to sound submissive.

"All I'm sayin', sir, is that she's right. The Wild Seed Rule *is* in the FRC rule book." He pointed to a sun-bleached book with a worn green cover lying open on the table. "On page forty-one."

The monitor was astounded: "How on earth would a seed know what's inside the FRC's rule book? Access to that text is restricted."

A Monticello militiaman who'd been lounging against the wall watching the scene play out stepped forward, his hand resting suggestively on his holster. Ji-ji couldn't tell if it was the same man who'd kicked the runner earlier, but she sensed immediately that he would be happy to oblige should the need arise. The militiaman seemed to take personal offense at Tiro's height, which exceeded his by several inches. He moved in closer to Tiro until they were only inches apart.

The monitor, his voice spiked with panic, pleaded with the militiaman: "I assure you I have the situation in hand, Officer Webster. No need for trouble. Everything's under control."

The militiaman ignored him. "You a Mule or a Common?" he asked. Officer Webster was a spit talker. A glob of spittle landed on Tiro's cheek.

It sat there, winking in the sun. *Don't wipe it off,* Ji-ji prayed. *He'll beat you bloody if you do! Look down, Tiro! For my sake, for Afarra's—please look down!*

Tiro cast his eyes down at his feet. "Sorry, sir. All but deaf in one ear. I'm a Muleseed, sir."

"S'what I thought," the officer said. His voice was educated—refined almost. "Another dandified fly-boy come to perch in our coop. This one decided to run with the females. You sure are pretty enough. Or p'raps you're one of those randy duskies? I hope for your sake it's the former. Deviants need a good lashing, but sexual predators are worse. You heard of Till from way back? Know what happened to him? You looking to be Tilled, Mule?" Tiro shook his head. Webster moved in closer. "Good. Because—and you should trust me when I tell you this—there's a thousand fellas in Monticello itching to teach a lesson to fly-boys like you."

Webster took a step back from Tiro and looked at the monitor. "Seems like we've got ourselves a reader here, eh, Miller? A reading Mule's like a piano-playing monkey, that's what I—"

A deep bass voice rang out: "Monitor Miller, what's going on?"

A gray-haired, balding man in a monitor's green robe strode to the Hemingsgate from the direction of the Jefferson Arch. Tall and heavyset, he looked to be in his late sixties, a generation older than Miller. He wore a large silver chain, which glinted expensively in the bright sun. His robe had discreet silver piping around the collar and sleeves.

Miller shoved his chair back so fast it toppled over with a clatter. He stood up. "First Monitor Schultz," he said, bowing his head and sounding relieved. "These three botanicals thought they could enter the race in Monticello, which of course they can't. They're attempting to invoke some Wild Seed Rule that doesn't exist and—"

Monitor Schultz interrupted him: "Ah yes, the rarely invoked Wild Seed Rule. Section F, Rule 28."

Monitor Miller's magnified eyes widened in disbelief behind his glasses. He sputtered out a protest. "But, sir . . . there's no such rule!" He grabbed the rule book and opened it up, found the page he was looking for. "See. Here's Section F, and it ends with Rule 27, the Prohibition on Seed-to-Seed Fraternization during the race. There's no Rule 28 . . . sir."

The First Monitor retrieved a rule book from his ample sleeve. Like Monitor Miller's copy, it was green, but the cover looked new.

"Ah, now I understand your confusion, Mandely," he said.

"*My* confusion, sir?"

First Monitor Schultz opened his copy and showed the rule to the monitor. "You have an old edition. Fortunately for these petitioners, I have a newer one."

Race Monitor Mandely Miller turned as purple as an eggplant. From behind her, Ji-ji felt resentment radiating off the bonfire of Officer Webster's body.

"I never heard of this Wild Seed Rule," Webster said.

The First Monitor spoke to the militiaman the way a tolerant father speaks to his young son. He explained that the rule was one both parties had agreed not to publicize—steaders feared it would result in an exodus of seeds from plantings, Districters feared it could result in an influx of refugees to a chronically overcrowded city.

"How come this dandified dusky knows about it then?"

"It's not a secret, Officer . . . er. . . . I'm sorry, what did you say your name was?"

"I didn't. And it's Webster."

"Ah. Like the great Noah Webster, the Father of American Education."

The militiaman muttered something about patronizing Jewish dusky lovers. The First Monitor chose not to acknowledge the insult and simply smiled. Webster vowed he would be reporting the incident to Inquisitor Pious.

"By all means," Schultz said, affably. "If you prefer, I can do it myself when he and I enjoy a drink before the match."

Animosity radiated from Officer Webster as he looked at Monitor Schultz. Schultz kept right on smiling as though the homicidal man before him were a buddy of his. Thwarted by the monitor's rank, connections, and immunity when it came to bullying, Webster had no choice but to retreat.

Ji-ji wanted to cheer almost as much as she wanted to scratch. She signaled her desperation to Afarra, who slid a merciful hand under her friend's short-cape and began scratching.

After Webster left, Schultz helped Miller right his chair and offered to assist him with the paperwork. The young monitor, mortified by the implication that he was incapable of doing his job, begged to be allowed to complete the paperwork himself. "My error entirely," he insisted. "I should have known. . . . I apologize. It was inexcusable."

Schultz patted the younger man on the shoulder. "There are many things in this world that are inexcusable, Mandely. Your ignorance of the Wild Seed Rule isn't one of them."

With the First Monitor's assistance, Miller located a form they could adapt for Wild Seed ratification. Ji-ji removed Afarra's hand from her back, afraid the monitor would assume she was vermin-infested, or worse. Miller, his pen poised in the air, addressed her.

"Name?"

"Jellybean Lottermule." Her sproutings writhed and tickled.

The monitor wrote it down in an elaborate hand. It took forever.

"Affiliation?" he asked, after he'd stopped scratching his pen across the paper.

"Planting 437." Ji-ji held her breath while she waited for his reaction. Nothing.

While First Monitor Schultz walked over to the recording table to confer with the monitors there, Miller consulted his screen but couldn't locate her records. "Are you sure you're not a Cloth?"

"I'm sure," Ji-ji said.

"This is highly irregular," Miller said.

At a pace that made her want to scream, he filled in her planting designation. The process was repeated for Afarra. Miller started to look up her records, but Schultz returned and told him not to bother. Serverseeds weren't included in the databases, he said.

"An outcast," Miller said, anxiously. "It's rare we have an outcast among the runners. The steaders will object, to say nothing of the cards. Excuse me, Monitor. The inquisitors was what I meant to say."

"You have a point, Mandely," Schultz said. "But it would be a shame—would it not?—if we, who represent the great City of Dreams on the very site where our Founding Forefather opined on the nature of liberty, were to exhibit small-minded prejudice?"

Flustered and shiny with sweat, Miller blinked several times. He removed his glasses, cleaned them, and slipped them on again. "I assure you, I meant no harm when I—"

"Of course you didn't, Mandely! And now, all we need to do is administer the entrance exam." He turned to a group of monitors who'd gathered nearby. He called a female monitor over: "Ah, Monitor Carson. Please escort these two Wild Seeds to the holding yard and administer the standard entrance exam."

Schultz nodded at Tiro to indicate it was his turn to speak. As Ji-ji and Afarra were led away, Tiro petitioned to enter the race as a Wild Seed.

"My name is Tiro Dregulahmo," he declared in a clear, loud voice. "I'm from the 437th."

Monitor Miller stood up so fast he slammed his knee into the table. "*Ooo! Ow!* He's the one they're looking for!" he declared.

First Monitor Schultz looked at Tiro aghast. "This seed's the one who killed Patriot Zebadiah Moss? I will notify Inquisitor Pious at once!"

"*No, no!* Not *that* one, sir! I meant he's the *Deviant*! That wizard murderer, that Tribal they're all talking about—the one who murdered the planting cropmaster with black magic! This Mule's his kin! His name's not Druguleemo, or whatever he said. It's . . . I forget. But he's wanted. For *treason*!"

"All runaways are wanted," Schultz said. "It comes with the territory. Race rules clearly state that seeds who seek sanctuary, as long as they declare themselves honestly and pass the entrance exam, must be accommodated." The First Monitor turned again to Tiro. "How about we stick with your planting name? If you're not a regular seed, you can hardly petition to be a wild one, can you?"

To her relief, Ji-ji heard Tiro say, "No, sir. Sorry, sir. . . . My name is Tiro Williamsmule."

As they walked to the holding yard, Afarra whispered to Ji-ji, "Tiro is Wild too, isn't it?"

"He's wild all right," Ji-ji whispered back. "He'll get himself killed if he's not careful."

IIIIIIIIIIIIII

While Afarra waited outside, Ji-ji was ushered into a tiny prefabricated building no larger than a prison cell. Monitor Carson sat down in the only chair in the dimly lit, stuffy room and opened up her notebook. *You scratch an' you're toast,* Ji-ji told herself.

The questions turned out to be much easier than she'd anticipated: What were the three main causes of the Sequel? Quote the opening of the Declaration of Independence. Define Trifurcation. Ji-ji realized she was absurdly overprepared.

After she'd recited her answers, Monitor Carson closed her notebook. "I have one last question," she said. Her voice was soft; Ji-ji had to lean forward to hear her. She had an accent. Irish maybe? "Answer truthfully. What is a quote you live by, and why is it meaningful to you?"

The question was a kick in the gut. Ji-ji looked at the monitor in horror as her sproutings pulsed on her back. For years she'd trained herself to give the answers fairskins wanted, taking into account how screwed up they were. But she was totally unprepared for an open-ended question like this. She thought about pulling something from Thomas' Declaration, but she'd been asked to quote from it earlier. Besides, it had flown out of her head. She stood in front of the green-eyed, fair-skinned, narrow-nosed, thin-lipped woman who would determine whether or not the rest of her life would be worth living and felt tricked.

Then something strange happened: her sproutings urged her to say something bold. There, in the tiny, hot, dim-lit hut in the holding yard behind the Hemingsgate, she saw a black man in a cage with a pen in his hand and knew she had to declare it, even though, for seeds like her, declarations like the one she was about to make were nooses. Of her own Free will, Ji-ji Silapu slipped the noose over her head and pulled it tight around her neck.

"My quote is this: 'Injustice anywhere is a threat to justice everywhere. We are caught in an inescapable network of mutuality, bound in a single quilt of destiny. Whatever affects *one* directly, affects *all* indirectly.'" She took a deep breath and added, "I have the audacity to believe this is true!"

There was a long pause before the woman said, "Send in the Cloth and wait outside."

The moment Ji-ji stepped into daylight, the full extent of her recklessness hit her. She thought of a hundred different quotes she could have chosen. Why had she felt the need *at that pivotal moment* to butcher her own dreams?

A few agonizing minutes later, Monitor Carson emerged with Afarra in tow. Without saying a word, she led them back to the Hemingsgate and to Schultz, who waited for them next to the recording table.

"Well, Monitor Carson," Schultz said, "how did they do?"

Monitor Carson looked from Ji-ji to Afarra. As blond as Lotter, she wore a neat bun under her tam. Ji-ji was about to throw herself on the First Monitor's mercy when the woman said, "They both passed with flying colors, First Monitor."

"Excellent!" Schultz declared. "Now we can ratify their papers."

Schultz picked up the seal and stamped their paperwork with the runner logo. The rickety recording table wobbled under the force of his stamp. Ji-ji thought it was the most beautiful table she'd ever seen. First Monitor Schultz handed their documents to them, along with their number bibs, a pair of running shoes, a belt to which they could clip two water bottles, meal tickets for each of them, and a pouch through which they could thread their belts, in which they could store their new legitimizing documents, and upon which was stamped the official seal of the Freedom Race.

He smiled at them both and said, "The race for the female runners begins promptly at eight o'clock in the morning here at Hemingsgate. The inquisitors are insisting that all hundred and ten miles be undertaken by the runners for this second leg. And before you ask—yes, the wayward seed is ratified too. Beware of wandering around this place alone. It's not safe, especially not for some. Monitor Carson, will you escort these Wild Seeds to Mulberry Row? Let's hope they don't take their designation too literally. Goodness knows we have enough wildness in the protectorate already."

As they made the steep trek up the hill, through crooked alleys and bustling streets the likes of which they'd never seen, Afarra whispered, "We make it. We run in the Big Race, yes?"

"Yes," Ji-ji whispered back, stunned. "We made it! So did Tiro!"

Before Monitor Carson handed them over to one of the volunteers at Mulberry Row, she asked Ji-ji why she'd changed the words of the quote. Ji-ji said she didn't know she had.

"It should be 'tied in a single garment of destiny,'" Monitor Carson told her. "You said 'bound in a quilt of destiny.'" For a moment Ji-ji was afraid her Wild Seed status would be revoked, but all the woman said was "When you reach the City of Dreams, go and see your quote."

"You can *see* it?" Ji-ji said.

"It's etched in stone, there in the heart of the City of Dreams. So we won't forget."

It felt right to share something else with her: "My mam had a quilt. So I could look at something pretty when . . . whenever I wanted. Three blackbirds in a giant tree. Other birds taking off from it like fireworks. I used to look at it an'—"

"And what?" the woman asked.

"Wonder what it must be like to be a bird in a tree an' not a bird in a cage."

The woman bent down and whispered in her ear: "*Alis volat propriis!*"

Monitor Carson turned and walked away, leaving the faint scent of roses in her wake.

IIIIIIIIIIIIII

They were ushered to a long narrow building erected between two cabins by a Liberty Laborer named Salome, who said she hailed from the

Caribbean. The structure served as the female dorm. She said it had been built after the Sequel in the old style, only "stretched out like a wiener dog, so the beds fit. We call it Sally's House. It sleeps the female flyers."

"We are not being flyers," Afarra corrected her. "We are runners. On the ground."

"Is that so?" Salome replied. "Sure look like flyers to me."

Ji-ji tried to figure out if she was being sarcastic; it was impossible to tell.

Salome told them where the bathhouse was and pointed to their beds. On every pillow was a towel with the runner logo and a bar of soap.

Ji-ji counted fewer than two dozen girls in the dorm. She asked where the others were.

"Ten at the bathhouse. Two watching the fly-boys practice in the coop. Thirty-six made it so far, out of two hundred."

"What happened to the others?"

"What always happens. Look after that one," she said to Ji-ji. Afarra sat on her bed and touched her bar of soap as if it were a wonder. "She's different . . . special."

"I know. I will."

Ji-ji wanted her to keep talking, but Salome was called away by a monitor. After she'd gone, Ji-ji left Afarra admiring the soap and walked to the far end of the dorm where three runners clustered around a bed. She needed to find out what to expect tomorrow. "Hi," she began, "I'm—"

The group parted, and Ji-ji saw another runner sprawled on the bed, winding a bandage around her grotesquely swollen big toe. The runner screamed as if she'd seen a ghost.

"Jellybean Lottermule! You almost gave me an embolism!"

She stood up, slipped her bad foot into a slipper, and hobbled to embrace her. Accustomed to pain, she didn't let any show on her face. "Heard you kicked the bucket," she said. "How'd you get here? You seen Dip? She with you?"

"'Fraid not," Ji-ji replied.

Sloppy spotted Afarra at the other end of the room chatting with the soap. "Jesus Christ Almighty! Don't tell me you brought Loony Cloth!"

"Shut your mouth, Sloppy," Ji-ji said.

"Who's Sloppy?" one of the runners asked. "Thought she was Delilah Moon."

Sloppy looked at Ji-ji with unmitigated hatred.

The runner Ji-ji saw earlier with the nasty gash in her cheek pointed to

Ji-ji and said, "She's one of them cheaters. She an' the male an' the Cloth barged past us on the final leg like they was entitled."

"S'okay, Sookie," Sloppy said. "Jellybean's a friend. She's with me."

Ji-ji stared at Sloppy in surprise as she asked the three runners to give her a moment; they obeyed at once. Clearly, she had established herself as the leader of that particular group. Why was she being so friendly? After they'd left, Sloppy kicked off her slippers, sank down on the bed again, and grasped her horribly swollen toe. She rubbed it and moaned.

"You got no idea what it's like to have a digit that's acting up like this." She tapped the mattress, inviting Ji-ji to join her. "Take the weight off or you'll wish to Christ you had when we race tomorrow." Warily, Ji-ji sat down. Sloppy continued, punctuating the conversation with groans of pain. "The bastards delayed the start of the race, then all kinds of mischief awaited us on the road. *Ooo, that hurts!* How'd you get ratified anyway? Lotter change his mind? You could always twist that bastard round your pinky." The statement was so ridiculous Ji-ji didn't bother to respond to it. When she explained how they'd entered as Wild Seeds, Sloppy stared at her in disbelief.

"Well isn't that fucking peachy! A Wild Seed Rule for those in the know. How come no one else heard of it?"

"The steaders like to keep it quiet."

"Yeah, I bet they do. So. . . . How did Shitcloth over there manage to pass the oral? Guess I got a pretty good idea how—it being an oral exam. Casper got himself serviced by that filth once or twice. She plays all sweet an' innocent but it's a lie. Cloths got no shame. Could've infected Casper with Phyllis an' then I'd get it too. Wind up a Tainted like Dip. Selfish little bitch."

"If you don't shut up about her, I'll slap you into next week," Ji-ji said. Sloppy stared at her openmouthed, as though she'd already done it.

"Keep your hair on, chief. If someone seduced your steadermate, how would you feel?"

"*Seduced?* Are you nuts?"

Even Sloppy seemed to realize the absurdity of her claim. "Okay. Maybe that's not how it happened. That Cloth rubs me the wrong way. . . . You sure Dipthong's not Wild Seeded herself too? You know what she said to me once? Said, 'You're a lousy kitchen-seed, Slop. Only one I ever known who's regularly defeated by a ham sandwich.' I almost hit her till I had to admit she had a point. Remember when I burned the boiled eggs? You sure Dip's not with you?"

"I swear I don't know where she is," Ji-ji replied. "You got any news about the 437th?"

"Only that the arsenal got blowed up. Part of it anyway. That quake did it. Seeds're saying it was Uncle Dreg who was the culprit—that his Dimmer-dead were on the rise an' that's why the earth shifted. What a load of bullshit! Superstition keeps seeds down even more'n steaders. Your father-man went nuts after that lieutenant shot your mam."

"The lieutenant didn't shoot her," Ji-ji said, leaping to Lucky's defense. "Petrus did."

"You sure? Everyone thinks Longsby's guilty. Lotter said Longsby shot Petrus too. Said you an' the lieutenant were in cahoots. Swore he'd get revenge for what you did. Father-Man Williams picked up the slack when Lotter went all to pieces. That's about all I heard 'fore I had to take off with Marcus for Salem. We nearly missed the race start cos everything was in a pandemonium cos of you an' your mam, an' the explosion. We had to ride to Salem on horseback. Both of us on *one* horse unaccompanied. No car ride, no celebration, no cake, nothing. I was looking forward to that send-off. You spoiled it. Had to ride this farty old mare." Sloppy did an excellent impersonation of the horse farts. "Clop-*fart*-clop-*fart*-clop-*fart*-clop-*fart*!"

"Did you really think I'd run with someone who shot Mam?"

Sloppy shrugged. "How should I know? Could be you got the hots for him. People do things you don't expect 'em to do. Do things they don't expect neither."

"I told you. Lucky didn't kill her. Petrus did."

"Who's Lucky?"

"Longsby. I said Longsby."

To Ji-ji's relief, Sloppy moved on. "Guess I'm not surprised Lotter was lying through his pearly whites. Suspected his story had holes in it from the start. That Unnatural Affiliation he had with your mam would sink any other father-man but not Arundale I'm-So-Damn-Handsome Lotter. Your father-man's got friends in high places from what I hear. Got followers too—you heard about them? They call Lotter 'the Twelfth'—like being 437's twelfth cropmaster is some kind o' feat on his part. Twelve's just a random number. Folks'll look for meaning anywhere if you give 'em enough rope. Steaders're as superstitious as seeds. . . . Bet that male Wild Seed Sookie saw was Tiro, right?"

"Yeah. He's competing tonight in the coop."

"Hope he's well rested. There's this Tribalseed took first place in the Salem Coop. Huge motherfucker! Hands the size of dinner plates. Much bigger an' faster than Georgie-Porge. Could tie Tiro in a double bow if the fancy took him. My money's on him."

Ji-ji felt sick. With his injured foot, how would Tiro defend himself? "Tiro doesn't have to come first. He only has to do okay tonight, complete the sprint, and do well in the Dream Coop."

"Yeah, an' I'm sure the other fly-boys'll be rooting for him. I'm sure they'll be tickled to see his skinny, well-rested ass in the coop after they've already competed in Salem and ran a sprint too."

Sloppy's words hit home. Every one of the other fly-boys would be gunning for Tiro. Ji-ji pinned her hopes on Marcus. Surely Tiro's flying buddy would have his back?

After she'd let her words sink in, Sloppy spoke again: "Dip proposed to me. Gave me a ring she stole from her first steadermate—the bastard Trip Epson that gave her Phyllis an' locked her in that confessional. Guess you knew she was a Deviant? Personally, I don't blame her. Who fancies cock after abuse like that? Heard she jumped the fence. That true? She didn't think I'd petition for her but I would have. I told her that. Tainted didn't listen."

Ji-ji was tempted to tell Sloppy that Dip ran off at the fry-fence—that maybe she made it to safety. But trusting Sloppy was like wrapping your arms round a boa constrictor. It might seem like she just wanted to snuggle, but forget she was a snake and you were screwed.

"Sorry about the Delilah Moon thing. I forgot Dip said Delilah was your race name. . . . Dip changed her name too. To Donna."

"Since when did she tell you our secrets?"

Quickly, Ji-ji came up with a plausible explanation. "When we were prepping for the Last Supper. We went down to the storeroom for another killer. She told me then."

Sloppy shrugged like someone who didn't care much either way. "Donna's a good name," she said. "A lot better'n a Dipthong. I used to think Dipthong was obscene underwear 'fore I asked your Miss Clobershay, an' she tells me it's two vowels butted up against each other. Spelled a bit different, with a extra 'h.' Bet you knew that already. You were always the teacher's pet. You been spoiled all your life, you an' your snooty mam. An' the shame of it is you don't even know it. . . . *Ooo!* This toe's giving me *fits*! Dip had this way of massaging it better. You sure she's not here with you?"

Ji-ji shook her head. An exceptionally tall runner walked by the bed. "That's the one came in first," Sloppy whispered. "Faster'n a snarlcat she is. Keeps to herself. Snooty, like your mam. You won't beat that one. Not in a million years. She's ten times faster'n you."

Tired of Sloppy's snide remarks, Ji-ji got up to leave.

Sloppy grabbed her hand. "Don't go! I'm sorry for those things I said.

Guess Casper beat all the sociableness out of me." Ji-ji pulled her hand away. "Wait!" Sloppy said. She sounded desperate. "How 'bout we turn the page an' start over? You didn't run the first leg. Those cards made us do nearly a hundred miles! Only three rest stations the whole route! Some of us only got here yesterday, an' you saw some only got here today. I had to run at night just to keep up." Her expression darkened. "Know what it's like to run alone at night through The Margins? You ever done it?"

"No."

"Don't. Just don't. It's . . . not good. . . . Makes you desperate. How 'bout we help each other?"

"What do you mean?"

"The Cloth doesn't have the strength to—"

"Her name's Afarra."

"Fair enough. You call me Delilah an' I'll call her Afarra. She can't make it to the city without help. You know I'm right. How 'bout I scratch your back if you scratch mine?"

You have no idea how tempting that offer is right now, Ji-ji thought.

"Don't give me the stink eye, Ji-ji. I mean it."

"You got a bum toe. You'll be lucky if you can keep up yourself, never mind helping her."

"You ever once in your whole entire life seen me give up?" Sloppy-Delilah asked.

Ji-ji pondered the question. "No," she admitted.

"Well then. You think I'll give up now when Freedom's on the line? We work together an' we make it through those city gates. We can do this. Who cares if we hate each other's guts?"

"I don't hate your guts. I never have."

"Well, I guess that makes one of us. Could be we'll need to take a few shortcuts."

"We gotta stay on the race route. It's guarded. We're safe there."

"Yeah, an' I'm Cleopatra. Know how many guards we saw after we got out of Salem? Six. Know how many runners were picked off along the way? Dozens. All of 'em obedient little seeds like you who stuck to the race route. Why'd you think it took so long to get here? If we work together, we can get all the way to the corridor, sprint the final miles to the city gates an' wow the crowds. I like your cape, by the way. A few of the other runners were wearing 'em too, only most got picked. I hear there's collectors that collect race paraphernalia in the city. In case you're flummoxed by my vocab, paraphernalia is like the accoutrements of the race. You got a spare cape for me? Wouldn't want to be picker meat so I wouldn't wear it till we got to the corridor, I'm not a moron. Fans'd get a real kick out of it if we both wore short-capes an' crossed the finish line together—holding hands maybe? Think that's too much? You gotta have a gimmick to get fans interested otherwise they don't give a damn about female duskies. What about it, Jellybean? We in this race together or not?"

IIIIIIIIIIIIII

It took a while for Ji-ji to explain to Afarra why they would be running alongside Sloppy. For now, at least, it seemed better to have someone like Slop as an ally. They sat together on Afarra's bed. All the other runners were either sleeping, at the bathhouse, or at the flying coop, so they could talk without fear of being overheard. While Ji-ji spoke, Afarra didn't take her eyes off the bar of soap. The smell of lavender reminded Ji-ji of Lotter's lavender-citrus aftershave, but at least it was real soap with none of the waxy, faintly rancid smell of soap on the planting. Ji-ji realized that seeing Sloppy had upset Afarra more than she realized. She changed the subject.

"Did Monitor Carson ask you for a quote you live by?" Afarra nodded. "What did you say?"

"I say to dream with the dead."

That's what Lua said, Ji-ji thought. *"No race till you dream with the dead."* Ji-ji asked who she was quoting.

"I am quoting me. *I* say it. Just now. You got to pay attention."

Ain't that the truth, Ji-ji thought. She asked why she'd chosen it.

"Cos it is the true I live by. That was the question. This soap smell delicious. Can I take it?"

"Yes, it's yours. . . . Afarra, does Uncle Dreg really speak to you?"

"Oh yes. In and out. To burn away the lonely. But sometimes, Elly . . . sometimes . . ." Afarra rocked back and forth on the bed and muttered to herself.

"What is it? Are you sad about Musa? Is it Sloppy? Don't pay her any mind, okay?"

Afarra stopped rocking and sat up straight as a rod. "Dregulahmo must not battle-fly!" she said, her voice deep and guttural. "He must not fly in the white cloud! He will be falling a long time!"

"Dregulahmo? Do you mean Tiro?" Ji-ji knew enough to take Afarra's prophecy seriously. She stood up. "C'mon, Afarra. No time to waste. Grab your soap and towel. We'll wash up real quick an' head down to the coop. You an' me got a friend to save."

23 BROTHERS, SISTERS, FRIENDS

Ji-ji and Afarra eased their way past Cellists, dogs, horses, soldiers, militiamen, monitors, and racers. They stepped over horse manure, dog poop, and drug-sops passed out in the street. They dodged two street fights and a brawl that involved at least a dozen drunk steaders. Sleepy-eyed males, and the occasional female, lounged inside drug dens—shacks or lean-tos that had been erected on almost every corner, or attached to bars and miscegenations. The sewer system, such as it was, was backed up, but the Cellists had placed enormous clay pots with what looked like giant incense sticks at regular intervals to mask the stench. Most of Monticello's roads were little more than muddy footpaths. On a few of the streets, a raised wooden walkway made the going a little easier, but Ji-ji and Afarra soon discovered that duskies were expected to give way to fairskins. Walking on the wooden walkway for more than a few yards at a time proved impossible.

The unruly throng made Ji-ji nervous. Every time someone brushed up against her back she feared her sproutings would betray her. Afarra was enchanted by the tattoo parlors, street vendors, bakeries, gambling places, and currency exchanges. She stood rooted to the spot when they came to a ramshackle building with a railed balcony perched over a falling-down portico—a nod to Monticello's famous architect. Afarra asked if the building was a palace.

"No," Ji-ji replied. "Definitely not a palace."

Two bearded steaders entered the building. Through the open doorway, an aroma of weed, cigarette smoke, and whiskey wafted into the street. Several bare-breasted females from the duskier arcs of the Color Wheel leaned seductively on the balcony railing. Afarra couldn't take her eyes off them. "They are Free?" she asked.

A group of fairskin men passed by and shouted up obscenities to the women. One of them promised to show them "a real good time tonight."

"No," Ji-ji replied, hurrying Afarra past the men. "They're not Free. Not even close."

Afarra stumbled several times because she kept looking back over her shoulder to catch a glimpse of "the most beautiful, not-Free nakeds."

They were about to turn down a street that looked as though it led to the coop when Ji-ji stopped dead in her tracks in front of a newspaper stand. She stood staring at it. An impressively large woman with a mahogany complexion sat in a ratty leather armchair next to the stand, an ID brooch pinned to her breast pocket to indicate she was a Liberty Laborer.

"How much?" Ji-ji asked, pointing to the Monticello paper.

The woman recited the price: "Two-fifty in SuperState dollars, eight-fifty in Armistice dollars, and twenty in cellos. You got SuperStates, hon? We call 'em rebels or trade dollars round here."

When Ji-ji nodded, the woman cranked her mouth into a smile. "Tell you what, just cos I like the look of your cute little friend, I'll give you a deal. Two SuperState dollars even. Genuine SuperStates. None of that counterfeit crap the beards've been passing off as genuine."

Ji-ji reached under her cape, careful to extract two dollars exactly. The woman's hand went out at lightning speed and snatched up the money. She held the dollars up to the sunlight, licked the corner of each to determine its authenticity, then handed Ji-ji the paper.

"Don't see many seeds buying a paper," she said pointedly. "May want to read it in private."

Ji-ji was grateful for the warning, but it proved difficult to find a place where she could sit and read without being spotted. At last she came across a quiet alley, deserted except for a tabby cat.

"We go to the coop now, Elly?" Afarra asked.

"I need to read this first." She sat down on an empty crate. Afarra sat beside her.

Ji-ji stared at the front page of the *Monticello Sentinel.* There he was staring back at her. She skimmed the article. "I don't believe it!"

"What?" Afarra asked.

Ji-ji folded the paper in two. "We gotta find Germaine an' Ben."

"We are saving Tiro. He is flying in the—"

"Yeah, we will. I promise. First, we gotta find the others."

Finding the Friends in the throng of people was all but impossible.

Ji-ji had almost given up when it hit her where Ben would be. The flying coop—their original destination. They hurried on down the hill. As they got closer, they passed more and more betting booths and souvenir stalls. At last, she saw the entrance. The coop's canvas entry flaps had been pulled back to accommodate an enormous oscillating fan, jerry-rigged to the biggest generator Ji-ji had ever seen. As they were about to step inside, Ji-ji spotted Germaine at a nearby barbecue stall. Faint with relief, she hurried over, dragging Afarra with her. She tapped the Friend on the shoulder.

"I need to speak with you. Something awful's happened."

Germaine got up in her face. "Listen, dusky," she snapped, "I don't appreciate havin' you trailin' after me. Is it Max? Is he fightin' again?" Ji-ji knew enough to nod. "That's it! I've had it!"

Germaine turned to the fairskin Liberty Laborer serving the barbecue, handed him some money, and asked him to wrap the pork. Peeved, she said, "Why do I put up with it?"

The laborer shrugged. "Love is love," he told her. "Can't fight nature."

"Nature's 'bout the only thing my goddam fool of a husband hasn't picked a fight with!"

With that, she grabbed the barbecue and propelled Ji-ji and Afarra unceremoniously up the street, cussing as she went. She herded them down a side street and into a back alley, halting in front of a sturdy wooden door she proceeded to unlock. She checked they hadn't been followed before pushing them through it and stepping inside herself. She closed and locked it behind them.

The room was dark and stuffy, with only a trickle of sunlight entering through a thin slit of skylight above. Germaine flicked on a battery-powered lamp, which gave off a drab, melancholy light. The only furnishings in the room were two wooden chairs, a small circular table, a lumpy double bed, and a cupboard. Germaine unlocked the back door and peered out into a tiny, enclosed yard. Ji-ji caught a glimpse of a water pump and outhouse.

Satisfied the yard was empty, Germaine locked the back door again. Only then did she turn and speak to them. "What the hell, Ji-ji! There are spies everywhere! You address me in that panicky, familiar way and every Cellist with ears'll be wondering what—"

"I *had* to speak to you. *Look!*"

Ji-ji held up the paper so Germaine could see the front page.

"So?" Germaine said.

"It's *him*!" Ji-ji told her.

The three of them whipped around to face the door at the same time.

Someone was fiddling with the locks. They'd been followed! Quick as a flash, Germaine positioned herself in front of her visitors and pulled out a knife. The door opened and a man stepped inside. . . .

"Don't gut me, woman! Not till I've had a bite o' barbecue!" Ben pleaded.

"Idiot," Germaine replied, sheathing her knife.

Ben closed the door and locked it. Said he'd just come from the coop when he saw Germaine tearing up the hill like a cat with its tail on fire. "What's up, Cat Lady?" he said. He turned to Ji-ji and Afarra: "What are you two doing here? You aiming to blow our cover?"

"It's *him,*" Ji-ji insisted again, pointing to the paper.

"What's she talking about, Germ?" Ben asked.

"Zebadiah Moss," Germaine told him. "An' don't call me that. But, Ji-ji, I don't see why—"

Ben saw how upset Ji-ji was: "Take a deep breath an' tell us what Zebadiah Moss has got to do with you."

"He *wasn't* Zebadiah Moss. That's how come I didn't know till I saw the photo!"

"What the hell's she talking about?" Ben asked.

Ji-ji lowered her voice. "I know who his killers are."

"Let me get this straight," Germaine said. "You know who killed Zebadiah Moss?"

Ji-ji nodded. She looked so miserable that Afarra reached up and began to stroke her hair.

"Okay," Ben said. "Don't leave us in suspense. Who killed the bastard?"

"Lucky an' me," Ji-ji said. "We're the killers they're looking for."

IIIIIIIIIIIIII

Apart from Afarra, no one believed Zinc Shokovsky was Zebadiah Moss.

"Granted, they both begin with Z," Ben offered.

"Hardly an airtight case, Sherlock," Germaine quipped.

In an effort to prove she was right, Ji-ji summarized the article for them. Zebadiah and his "aides" had been ambushed not far from Slim Pickins. Five bodies. Three were shot ("That was Chet, the axe man, an' the man on the mare," Ji-ji said); one of the others was blown in half ("that was Daryl who was high on sunsets"); and one was shot and charred ("that was Zinc—Zebadiah").

Ben whistled in surprise. "Wow! You an' Lucky didn't mess around, did you? Remind me to stay on your good side."

Ji-ji didn't laugh. She could see the murder scene: the boy in the ass's ears, pleading with his eyes; Daryl's bloody torso; Axeman coming at her (*I should've grabbed Axeman's axe soon as Lucky shot him. Maybe then I could've cut the boy down in time?*); Chet's face as he realized he'd been running toward doom and not away from it—exactly how she'd felt in the Doom Dell, how she felt right now.

"Let me get this straight," Germaine said, "you're saying you an' Lucky killed these guys?"

"Lucky was a lot better at it than me," Ji-ji confessed. "I'm lousy with a gun. My hand shakes. He killed most of 'em cos they made him lynch the boy an' they . . . threatened to . . ."

"S'okay, kid," Germaine said. "We get the picture. Let's think this through together. Lucky reported you were dead, right?"

"But don't you see? I'm *not* dead. They'll figure it out. They'll know I did it."

"Hang on," Ben argued. "If they knew it was you, they'd say it on the poster or in the paper. Or if they didn't know it when this stuff was printed, they'd have come for you by now cos you're registered for the race, which means you're in the system. Racers get immunity from anything committed on their plantings, but crimes in The Margins are prosecutable."

"Ben's right, Ji-ji," Germaine said.

Ben continued: "If all this is true—I'm not saying you're lying, but you've been under a lot of stress lately—if we assume you an' Lucky rid the world of five scumbags, it seems likely that the ones who came upon Lucky after you left weren't aligned with the council. Could've been Clansmen, or pickers . . . anyone."

Germaine nodded. "Ben's right. Bottom line: even if all this is true, they don't know it was you and Lucky. To be honest, I'm still not convinced it—"

Ji-ji remembered something. "Where's my saddlebag?"

"Calm down," Germaine said, "it's right here."

She went over to the small cupboard, unlocked it, and pulled out the saddlebag.

"That's Zinc's saddlebag," Ji-ji told them. "An' the stallion Drol caught—that was Zinc's too. Zebadiah's, I mean. Only I lost the letter an' photo. Don't know how."

"That was a mighty fine horse, Germ," Ben admitted. "Worth a small fortune. Never seen a horse like that in The Margins before, have you?"

"No," Germaine agreed. "Let's take this step by step. What do we know? We know Zebadiah was well connected. The Jester won't take kindly to having his brother—"

"Who's the Jester?" Ji-ji asked.

Ben explained: "They call him that cos he rarely cracks a smile. An' cos of his name, of course. Zebadiah was his brother. His twin, some say, but that's up for debate."

Ji-ji looked at the newspaper again. In her head, she shaved off Zebadiah's moustache. It wasn't that they looked identical, far from it. It was something about the eyes. . . . She felt her blood run cold. "What's the Jester's real name?" she asked.

"Fester," Ben said. "Fester the Jester. But he's better known as—"

"—Lord-Secretary Fightgood Worthy!" Ji-ji said.

"Bingo," Ben said, taken aback. "How'd you know that?"

"He was Lotter's guest at the Last Supper," Ji-ji told them. "He smiled at me."

"Fightgood Worthy smiled at a seed!" Ben exclaimed. "A female seed at that! Wonders never cease. Guess our noble Lord-Secretary can perform miracles after all. Hope you got a photo."

"I did," Ji-ji replied, reaching into the saddlebag. "Along with the letter. You sure they weren't in the saddlebag?"

Ben took offense. "I went through it already. You think I would've overlooked a thing like that? No photo, no letter. Sorry, Ji-ji."

"Let me look," Ji-ji said.

"Suit yourself," Ben said, obviously annoyed that she didn't trust him.

"Did you check that pocket down at the side?" Ji-ji asked. "The one you have to pry open?"

"What pocket?" Ben replied.

Ji-ji slipped her hand down inside a small slit in the leather bag and pulled out two plastic bags. Inside, clearly visible, the letter and photo.

Ben's face fell. "Oh shit!" he said. "I missed it."

IIIIIIIIIIIIII

Germaine read the first page of Fester's letter aloud. It opened with the word *Brother* and went on to mention a city Germaine immediately identified as Armistice.

"That doesn't sound too bad," Ben said. "Sounds like a typical bro letter—assuming your bro's a psychopath an' you are too."

"Don't count your chickens," Germaine warned him. "Did you read the whole letter, Ji-ji?"

"There wasn't time," Ji-ji said defensively. "It was late. I had to cross the river. Why didn't I check the bag? Something kept gnawing at me but I didn't know what it was."

"I am telling you, Elly, read the letter," Afarra said.

"When?" Ji-ji asked her.

"On the Liberty snake."

"What are you talking about? You didn't tell me—" Ji-ji suddenly recalled Afarra's words on the train. "I thought you meant the Dreamer's letter. Why the hell didn't you say you were talking about this one?" Afarra's bottom lip began to tremble. "S'okay," Ji-ji said, reining in her annoyance. "I'm not mad at you. I wasn't paying enough attention, that's all. What else does he say?"

Germaine read on in silence. "Hey, here's something else. 'Unanticipated delays have made us late. We must never forget the sins of the father.'"

"That could mean anything," Ben said.

Germaine skim-read the rest of the page. "Not much of interest on page one. Let's look at page two." She read in silence for a while. "Here's more: 'Don't forget to burn this after you've read it, brother. I have taken the usual precautions. The censor will detect treachery if our carrier got nosey.'"

Ben snatched the letter away. "Could be a censor embedded in the paper, coded to Zeb's fingerprints. If it's still live it can track us. The cards could be on their way right now!"

Germaine snatched the letter back. She ran her hands across the paper and held it up to the lamplight. "S'been removed. See this nick in the corner and that little bump? Seems like Zebadiah didn't want Fester peering over his shoulder any more than we do. Looks like it gets interesting further down the page. Listen to this:

"'The DLs won't see us coming. Our allies are in place in C. No one trusts anyone in the city. The Ds are so busy screwing each other over they can't see the forest for the trees. The S's are preoccupied with our rosy little fish.'"

"What the hell's a 'rosy little fish'?" Ben asked.

"A red herring," Ji-ji said. They all looked at her in surprise. "I could be wrong," she added.

Germaine continued: "'I am more convinced than ever that the T are the key to the puzzle. She has been studying the Truth as it is written. She is certain now they are a bona fide threat.' There's a bunch more personal stuff," Germaine said, turning the page, "then the interesting stuff starts up again."

> *I found a photo of the three of us without him. Keep it secret, keep it safe, as the old grey wizard says. After the city is redeemed, we pick the T from every planting and escort them to their new nests. If we run out of mice, we find more (DC). There is much to learn. Keep searching for a way in. Yes. A Viral Colony could be a good disguise. Search further, search harder, search deeper. You're closing in. Root out the tree huggers. Leave no one to tell tales.*
>
> *Dr. N is still pleased with how things are progressing. We must also turn our attention to 368 and the others, not forgetting 4-MPH. Our man is in place but he's greedy. He'll need funding. Our woman too. C-man is ours, turning on the spit. We're depending on you, brother. If you keep up the good work, all should be ready soon after the season begins in the fall. We will move under the cover of plain sight. Trust no one.*
>
> *She still suffers from visions, one after another. She saw you bathed in flames. I told her that is the light of Truth burning within you. She was comforted. She sends her love and kisses. You always were her favorite. Luckily, you were always my favorite too. No brother comes close to being as beloved as you, Zebadiah.*
>
> *I am thee and you are me. Yours in fraternity for eternity,*
>
> *—Fester*

Germaine looked shaken. "Are you thinking what I'm thinking, Ben?"

"Yeah. Sounds like they're homing in on Dimmers."

"But Memoria is safe, right?" Ji-ji asked. "No one has ever found it."

Germaine shook her head. "Lucky and you weren't far from Dimmers when you ran into them. An' Zebadiah's no Bounty Boy. The stallion never made sense. No Bounty Boy has a horse like that in The Margins. My guess is the Bounty Boy business was a diversion—for Zeb anyway."

"Who are the *DL*'s?" Ji-ji asked.

"Not sure," Germaine said. "But it could stand for Dusky Lovers."

"*C* could stand for the D.C. Congress in the city," Ben conjectured. "The *D*'s could be the Districters, *S*'s the SuperStates."

"Or *D* could stand for Dreamers," Germaine proposed. "The Dreamer Coalition is gathering strength in the city, gaining power in the D.C. Congress too."

Germaine was puzzled by the reference to four miles per hour till Ji-ji said, "Could it be the 437th? There's no date on the letter, but the former cropmaster's name was Michael Prinshum Herring—MPH."

"Clever girl!" Germaine said. "Obviously, the *T* stands for—" She broke off awkwardly.

"It stands for Toteppi," Ji-ji said. "They plan to exterminate us."

"I don't know," Germaine replied. "Seems like they have other plans in mind. Relocation maybe. They're prepared to get some from D.C. too, sounds like. Who's this '*she*'?"

"Their mom," Ben told her. "The woman in the photo. Sounds like Fester an' Zebadiah are Mommy's boys through an' through. Listen, Ji-ji. I'm real sorry. I messed up big-time."

"S'okay," Ji-ji replied. "I did too. How did she know Zebadiah would go up in flames?"

"Maternal instinct?" Ben suggested. "Right now, that's not our main problem. We got to warn Man Cryday. Warn the city too."

"How?" Germaine asked. "They got people on the inside, sounds like. We don't know who to trust. C-man could be anyone."

"No. I think I know who that is," Ben said. "If there was one person you'd want to turn traitor in D.C. who would it be?"

Germaine's eyes grew wide: "Not Commander Corcoran? But he's the Dreamfleet commander. He knew Uncle Dreg and sympathized with our cause! Ben, if it's him we're screwed. He's privy to our plans for the next set of raids. He may even know how to enter Memoria."

While they stared at Fester's pathologically neat handwriting searching for clues, Afarra retrieved Uncle Dreg's Seeing Eyes from the bag they were taking care of for her and slipped them on. "Doomy Dell," she murmured. "Doomy Dell, he is saying."

"What do you think, Ben?" Germaine asked. "Think we should call in the troops?"

Ben looked from Ji-ji to Afarra and back again. "Yep," he said. "An' I reckon it's time to add a couple of extra ones. Don't you agree, Germ?"

IIIIIIIIIIIII

The two recruits placed a hand over their hearts and swore allegiance to the glorious cause of Freedom. Afarra placed one hand over her heart and the other on Ji-ji's back. Germaine looked over at Ben and said, "What did I tell you? They're sisters now. They'll protect each other."

The two repeated the Friends' motto after Germaine: "*Dum spiro spero:* While I breathe, I hope." Afterward, Ji-ji knew she'd never think of herself in the same way again. Linking arms with others, she and Afarra had become part of an unbreakable notion.

Uncle Dreg, who'd served as the Friends' senior advisor, had recommended their induction into the Friends of Freedom. Though the Friends had planned to invite the two to join after they arrived in the city, the explosive contents of the letter meant they were now privy to information even the most senior Friends didn't possess.

Ben had been hesitant about inducting Afarra, concerned she would be unable to keep a secret. Afarra had tried to prove herself trustworthy by disclosing secrets she'd kept in the past—where Silapu hid her stash of whiskey, how often she, Afarra, had swiped food from the dining hall kitchen or snuck into Ji-ji's bed—none of which eased his mind. But Germaine reminded him that Man Cryday had also recommended that Afarra be inducted. Subsequently, Ben and Germaine, in the company of half a dozen other veterans whom they summoned, had proceeded with the short induction ceremony.

By this time, Ji-ji understood the true nature of Germaine and Ben's relationship. They were lovers—married perhaps? Uncle Dreg said interracial marriage was permissible in the SuperStates and most of the Independents too, including D.C. The Friends of Freedom must have entered into a consensual relationship, without copper seedmate bands or ownership claims, without a seed-price or an obligation to seed the Territories. Germaine was fiercely proud of her Mexican heritage; she didn't think of herself as white. Yet she looked white to Ji-ji, with her straight black hair and green eyes, and Ben was definitely black. On the planting, a union like that would be an abhorrence. If caught, the couple would be accused of Unnatural Affiliation by Inquisitor Tryton. Ben would be lynched or lopped; Germaine—assuming the steaders classified her as a fairskin—would be bundled off to Armistice and "cleansed" in an inquisitorial conversion asylum.

The coded messages sent via callers had summoned Friends in Monticello to the lodging. Five Friends had crowded into the small room. All five were black or brown. Three wore Liberty Laborer or Indigenous brooches; two—those without brooch IDs—Ji-ji assumed had SuperState passports. When they'd knocked on the door, they'd murmured the phrase "Live Free or die." Each time she heard it, some of Ji-ji's anxiety fell away. When the sixth Friend showed up—the only fairskin Friend in the group—Ji-ji and Afarra hadn't recognized him at first because he wasn't wearing his planting guard's uniform, his formerly brown hair was dyed black, and he'd shaved off his steader's beard in favor of extra-long sideburns. He wore glasses too. When he introduced himself as "the guard formerly known as Crayton Juniper," they were shocked.

"They said you were dead," Ji-ji told him.

"Hear they said the same about you," Crate replied.

"Lotter said you'd been viciously attacked when you strayed beyond the fence. Brine said you were 'jam an' fleshcrumbs.'"

"*Eew!* Brine must've salivated over that—nasty old goat. Turned out that vicious biped decided against snacking on me. Drol and me left a nice little trail for the steaders to follow."

Afarra felt vindicated: "See, Elly? Drol is not for killing."

Ji-ji looked around the cramped, stuffy, badly lit room. They were friends among Friends.

She and Afarra weren't alone. Not even close.

IIIIIIIIIIIIII

A few hours later, Ji-ji sat in the seed section with several hundred spectators gathered to watch the flyer-battlers fight it out in the impressive Jefferson Coop. Runners could watch without paying as long as they showed their papers. Only a handful of runners watched with them; the others needed to rest up before the second leg of the race commenced tomorrow, especially those who'd only made it to Monticello today.

Ji-ji left Afarra in the bleachers and went in search of Tiro. Not unexpectedly, Tiro didn't seem too concerned about either Afarra's premonition or Sloppy's warning. Said his foot was a tad sore but it wasn't a problem now he had it bandaged up, and a race medic had given him a shot or two of industrial-strength killers. "Can't hardly feel it, Ji." She begged him to keep his safety harness on. "If it's safer to have it on an' do what I need to do I'll keep it on, I swear." Ji-ji knew it wouldn't do any good to argue with him.

She hadn't said anything to Tiro about Zebadiah or the letter, hadn't wanted to distract him. She did have to tell him, however, that Ben couldn't make it—that he'd been called away on a mission at the last moment. Tiro was disappointed, she could tell. When he heard Germaine had taken off too, he realized something was going down. She pulled him over behind the bleachers to a secluded part of the coop and asked him to meet up with her at midnight at the lodging used by Ben and Germaine. All the Friends had keys. She needed to talk with him.

"*Dum spiro spero,*" she said softly.

"So, you made it. That's great, Ji. Afarra too?" Ji-ji nodded. "Uncle Dreg an' me both thought it was a good idea. Glad that happened before the race. Could come in useful. Sorry 'bout the way I been acting. I'm a dumb fly-boy with a lot on my mind, that's all. Gotta get Mother an' the boys off the planting. They're not safe with that bastard Williams sniffing around." Ji-ji knew it wasn't just his anxiety over his family that had caused the rift between them, but his apology still meant something to her. "It's okay," she said. "Don't worry about it. Fly well, okay?"

The wings shaved into Tiro's hair were all the proof she needed that Marcus had made it through the first leg. Good. She liked Old Shadowy's favorite seed. With a practice partner's pride, Tiro said Marcus had earned second place after the Salem battle and the first sprint. He owed Marcus a great debt, he said. "Impersonating me when he knew how risky it was. . . . You don't find many friends like that. Not unless you're real lucky."

"We've both been lucky with our friends," Ji-ji agreed.

Ji-ji slipped back into her seat next to Afarra and watched the spectators file into the coop—fairskins in certain sections of the bleachers, duskies in others. She went over what she'd need to tell Tiro. Neither Ben nor Germaine had thought it safe to use the comm to convey such sensitive information, and finding a working copier in Monticello would be both extremely difficult and very risky. Knowing time was of the essence, Germaine had scrawled the most important parts of Fester's letter onto some paper and given it to Ben so he could share it with Man Cryday. Germaine would take the original to the Friends headquarters in D.C. She took Zinc's saddlebag and Petrus' gun too. She and Crate Juniper, who went by Greg O'Leery now, would travel by truck on the Main Toll Road from Monticello to the city, an arduous journey with numerous checkpoints, but less risky than Ben's horseback ride through The Margins. Germaine hypothesized that the Friends at headquarters would share the letter with Edelmann and Lowenstein at the *D.C. Independent*. If the city's esteemed paper authenticated the letter and published excerpts, Districters would know what the Territories were planning and ensure it never occurred, she said. Ben wasn't so sure. "The city's doing a lively trade with the Territories," he cautioned. "Residents are nervous about the flood of refugees. We could be in for a bumpy ride."

Ji-ji's anxiety grew as the beginning of the battle drew closer. Some of the other fly-boys clearly weren't happy to see the famous Wild Seed. Tiro would be a target, but with Marcus flying with him in the coop he wouldn't have to go it alone. How would she break it to Tiro that his dream of being a flyer-battler in the Dreamfleet might be an impossible one? Without a contract from the fleet, he would never have the funds he needed to get Zaini and the boys off the planting.

Ji-ji happened to look over to her right. The runner beaten up by the guards at the Jefferson Arch sat by herself a couple of rows back. She had a black eye and swollen lip, yet her braids looked as neat as ever, wound in a splendid coronet on her head. Ji-ji gestured at her to join them. Thinking Ji-ji beckoned to someone else, the runner looked over her shoulder, realized there was no one behind her, and stared back incredulously. She moved over to join them. In no time, the girls warmed to each other.

The runner's name was Tulip Rogersseed. She'd grown up as a Muleseed on Planting 871. She and the flyer rep from her planting had traveled hundreds of miles southeast in the back of a truck to get down to the Salem Outpost. Hers was a semi-progressive planting, she said, so a few seeds (Mules of senior father-men, mostly) learned to read and could serve in low-level clerical positions on the planting. The planting had a system for naming seeds too. They named female Muleseeds and most Commonseeds after flowers, plants, and herbs, and males after animals, fish, or birds. "I'm grateful," Tulip said. "A female Commonseed I know had to make do with the name Mustardseed Custardseed. And a male on the planting had to answer to Cod Ettamule. Tulip Rogersseed don't seem bad when you look at it that way." Tulip said when she made it to the City of Dreams she planned to keep her first name and find herself a new last name. But after what happened during the first leg, she wasn't sure any of them had a chance of making it to the city.

"If a miracle happens an' I do make it, I'll be petitioning for Mam soon as I get to the city. An' my little twin siblings, Rosemary an' Thyme. The twins' names was Mam's idea. Father-Man went along with it cos he don't give a hoot 'bout much of anything. He's near eighty an' senile. Mam'll have to switch to Gumption, his brother, after he kicks the bucket. Gumption's only seventy-three, but he's a lively one so he'll want to mess with Mam's tits big-time. I plan to get her out before then, cos Mam's thirty-one an' spunky. Spunky can get a seedmate killed on a planting—a tongue lopping, at least."

Ji-ji asked Tulip if she had any other siblings. Tulip said yes, she did—a male sibling named Clownfish. But if she never saw him again it would be too soon. "I hate him," she added, unnecessarily. "Gotta get Rosemary an' Thyme outta there. That's what I think of when I get scared an' don't think I can keep on running. Them two. Only six years old. In our cabin. With Clownfish."

Afarra took Tulip's hand and stroked it tenderly. "You a Cloth?" Tulip asked her. Afarra started to withdraw her hand, but Tulip wouldn't allow it. "Don't worry. I don't got no issue with Cloths. Never believed that crap they fed us about disease an' black witchery." Tulip leaned in and whispered to them both: "Truth is, steaders talk out of their butt holes most of the time. That's what Mam says when there's no parrots around."

Tulip described the first leg of the race. Said on account of the fact she was a lagger (trying to conserve her strength so she could sprint the last few miles), she hadn't reached the rest station in time to spend the night there. Had to bed down in the open. Said it was terrifying out there alone. But afterward, when she arrived at the rest station the next morning, she knew how lucky she'd been. "They'd been taken. The others. Every last one o' them. Pickers most likely."

"On the race route?" Ji-ji said. "I thought the rest stations and the route were protected?"

"They did too," Tulip replied. "But nowhere's protected for females. It's all a wildness."

At that moment, Grant Thadduck, coop ringmaster, outfitted in dandified black boots, jodhpurs, top hat, and sequin-edged tails, strode into the lower ring to announce the battle would commence. He brandished his riding whip a few times. He reminded Ji-ji of Overseer Crabstreet. Coopmaster Thadduck acknowledged the VIPs, who sat in a cordoned-off section of the bleachers on the opposite side from the seeds. He went on to apologize profusely for the lack of projection on the big screen and assured everyone that technicians were working furiously to restore it.

The bleachers for VIPs rose pretty high up inside the coop, so they had a good view of the entire cage, whereas the seats for seeds were low down, which gave seeds a skewed angle on the main action. Ji-ji peered across the coop and thought she caught a glimpse of First Monitor Schultz sitting next to an inquisitor—Pious, probably. By the time the battle began, word had spread about the new flyer. Word of the Tribalseed's strength also ginned up the crowd. At least two hundred more spectators had forked over the entry fee and taken their places in the bleachers. The goal for this match was simple: score points, be one of the last battlers standing, and don't get injured. Tiro wasn't limping when he walked into the sawdust ring with the other forty or so flyer-battlers who'd survived the first leg uninjured. So far, so good.

The flyers had one minute to select their weapon of choice from the weapon warren and choose a spot in the cage from which to begin. Almost all the battlers chose long staffs, but both Tiro and Marcus chose coop swords. Though not sharp enough to slice into an opponent, the swords could still do serious damage and were much easier to wield and fly with than long staffs.

At the start of battle, most fly-boys didn't position themselves any higher than the center platform ring, a.k.a. "the donut." The hollow ring had almost the same circumference as the ground ring where the coopmaster sat in his fancy hutch. According to programs given out to spectators at the start of the match, the donut platform, positioned directly above the safety net, stood exactly thirty-six feet above the ground. As long as they fell into the hole, they'd land in the net. Every battler knew how lethal it could be to fall backward, away from the hole. The sizable gap between the net and the sides of the cage would result in serious injury or even death. Fly-boys with any sense wore a harness. Having listened to Coach Billy, Ji-ji knew that the plan of attack favored by traditionalists involved beginning close to ground level and working your way up from one level to the next slowly and steadily till you reached the dome. A sensible battler maintained a height advantage over his opponents and avoided doing anything too risky early. If a battler fell before accruing enough points it could spell disaster.

From the outset, Marcus and Tiro embraced the element of risk, much to the delight of the fans. As soon as Coopmaster Thadduck lashed his whip to signal the start of the battle, Marcus climbed to the top of a Jacob's Ladder, which put him at nearly twice the height of the battlers on the donut platform. Tiro climbed even farther, shimmying up the center hope-rope at lightning speed and swinging himself onto the rim of the Jimmy Crow's Nest, where he drew applause from spectators when he balanced on his one good foot like a flamingo and surveyed his prey. Then, to make things even more dramatic, he removed his harness. Marcus followed suit. *Great,* Ji-ji thought.

As it turned out, it wasn't as dumb as it looked. The harnesses severely limited the movements of the battlers. Tiro and Marcus could fly unhampered through the cage, taking advantage of all the equipment, even things like the King-spins and Plessy Pulleys, which could easily get tangled up in a harness. The flying partners made sure their riskiest moves were centered over the safety net. After making a few passes and racking up an impressive score, they put their harnesses back on. They even timed their movements so they secured themselves with a flourish at the same moment. Ji-ji looked around. Some members of the crowd were starting to fall in love.

Tiro swooped down from the nest on a zip line, slashing as he went, coordinating his attack with Marcus. Together, they sent one opponent after the other into the net, or left them dangling from their harnesses so they could be winched to the ground. Spectators urged the fly-boys to remove their harnesses again. Coopmaster Thadduck preached recklessness too, strutting around in the sawdust ground ring, reminding battlers there were far more points to be had for seeds who dared to "fly Free" than there were for cowards.

One of the flyers who'd taken the coopmaster's advice and disengaged himself from his harness crept up behind the flyer-battler Sloppy had told Ji-ji about, a giant named Laughing Tree. Introduced by Thadduck as a Tribalseed from the 215th, Laughing Tree, although he didn't laugh much, lived up to his last name. He'd won the first leg in the Salem Coop. (Marcus had been awarded more points, but the huge battler had been the last one left standing.)

Laughing Tree looked to be in his thirties—considerably older than many of the contenders. Thadduck said the giant had been "plucked from the Dark Continent" and had only been flying in the coop for a couple of years. Ji-ji figured he outweighed Georgie-Porge, the largest flyer she knew, by a hundred pounds or more. Thadduck's fake concern echoed around the coop: "This is the big man's chance to make it big and live the American Dream!" Tulip was crazy about Laughing Tree. Said she'd bet a man that size could choke Clownfish with one hand tied behind his back.

The big battler had spent much of his time gauging his competitors and deciding when to make a move. Given his size, he had to conserve his energy, be strategic. But the small flyer named Ink Wrayseed had a strategy too, or so it seemed to Ji-ji. His plan was to sneak up behind Laughing Tree, knock him into the donut hole with his long staff, and get a slew of valuable points.

Ink drew back his long staff and tried to knock the giant off the platform and into the hole. The staff barely made contact before Laughing Tree batted his frail opponent through the donut hole with such force that Ink bounced out of the net and sailed into the side of the cage to land in front of where the three were sitting. The seed section fell silent.

The cleanup crew loaded Ink onto a stretcher and carried him off. Both his legs pivoted bizarrely from his knees. "*Kill me, please!*" the fly-boy begged. A few minutes later, the coopmaster, his voice awash in phony commiseration, said poor Ink Wrayseed had sustained two badly broken legs. Ji-ji knew what awaited him—Tiro had told her what happened to fly-boys injured in the race. Ink would be patched up and shipped back to his planting. If he was lucky, he would be put to work as a "Damaged," unless someone took pity on him and purchased him from the race's Damaged Roster before then. Ji-ji felt even worse when Thadduck said he was from the 368th, of all places. Did Ink know the boy in the ass's ears? Were they friends? No wonder Ink was begging them to kill him. Ji-ji realized that Fester's letter had mentioned the 368th too, along with her own planting, assuming she'd guessed right about 4-MPH. Why did the 368th keep returning to haunt her?

Ji-ji looked up and saw Laughing Tree staring down into the well of the cage.

"He did not mean to hurt the Ink," Afarra said. "Purple Tree is not laughing."

The stunned battler remained in that position for a while, ignoring the battles around him. Then he let out an anguished cry and smashed his long staff against the bars of the cage. He slumped down onto the donut ring and buried his head in his hands. Fans booed and threw projectiles at him. The coopmaster threatened him with expulsion if he didn't "get a grip and start playing by the damn rules." The big man began fighting again, but he was so leery of hurting his opponents that two of them almost managed to defeat him.

It wasn't long before most of the fly-boys had been injured too severely to continue. They fell into the net or hobbled down Jacob's Ladders. Tiro and Marcus swung down from the nest and picked off two more in synchronized attacks, swinging from one of the two giant hamster wheels, to Plessy Pulleys, zip lines, hope-ropes, trampolines, and King-spins. She shouldn't have worried. The pair was unbeatable.

Another flyer tried his luck and attacked Marcus. He leapt from a trapeze, to a three-tiered sycamore copter, to a hope-rope. His timing was off. During the ambitious maneuver, he missed the hope-rope altogether and crashed into a King-spin. His harness got tangled up and snapped. The crowd watched him plummet to the ground. At first, it looked like he'd be caught by the net, but he landed a foot shy of it. No more than twelve inches between him and survival. Small like Ink, not much older than the boy Ji-ji had cut down (*too late too late*) from the tree, he lay there not moving, his thin neck broken. Afarra wept. Tulip started praying. Too incensed to do either, Ji-ji looked up at the flyers who had halted their battles in sympathy.

Coopmaster Thadduck signaled for a two-minute time-out, but some of the Cellists got impatient. They stomped their feet till the bleachers shook, and demanded that the battle resume. Someone threw an orange and knocked off Thadduck's top hat. Another threw eggs. One threw a brick. The coopmaster ducked just in time. Two minutes became a mere minute and five seconds as Thadduck, pale as a ghost, acceded to the mob's demands and ordered the flyers to take up arms again. A few of the flyer-battlers, including Tiro, Marcus, and Laughing Tree, paid their respects by placing their hands over their hearts and bowing their heads.

As the match drew to a close, five of the eight fly-boys remaining—all except Marcus and Laughing Tree—ganged up on Tiro. Tiro, obviously limping badly now, headed up to the welkin staging platform, the highest platform in the cage. Somehow, he fended off two battlers who came at him together. Just then, the giant screen at one end of the coop flickered on. Those fans sober enough to notice that the screen had lit up cheered. Now everyone had a bird's-eye view of the action high up near the dome.

Each time Tiro got away from one battler, another took over. The tag-team approach was as rehearsed as Tiro's and Marcus' coordinated attack had been. The predominantly fairskin crowd, some of whom felt sorry for the underdog, began to shout in Tiro's favor. A few who'd been following the fleet's scouting reports had placed bets on the nephew of the traitor-wizard. They railed against his opponents and called them cheats. They cussed out the twelve black-robed judges on the judging bench. "*Tiro the Pterodactyl flies!*" someone yelled. Chants from the seed section: "*Long live Dregulahmo!*" "*FLY, BOY, FLY!*"

In spite of it being two-on-one, Tiro held his own till he stepped back heavily onto his bad foot. It couldn't bear his weight! Afarra hid her face in Ji-ji's shoulder. One of his attackers tripped him with a long staff. Tiro toppled from the platform. Somehow, like a high diver, he twisted his torso toward one of the cables that attached the platform to the side of the cage, grabbed it, and held on. But now he dangled from the welkin platform! *He'll be okay,* Ji-ji told herself. *He's in a harness.*

At that moment, his harness cable snapped! Spectators screamed. If he fell he would die!

Tiro tried desperately to signal his surrender. His opponents didn't care. One of them raised his staff to smash Tiro's hands from the cable! Ji-ji leapt up from her seat.

Out of nowhere, Marcus came flying on a hope-rope toward Tiro, yelling, "*Grab the rope, bro! Grab the rope!*" Just before his opponent's staff came down, Tiro leapt toward the hope-rope, caught it cleanly, and swung away from danger to wild applause.

"*He is not falling!*" Afarra cried. "*He is being saved!*"

The crowd went nuts.

Marcus and Tiro made their way to the center platform ring, where Laughing Tree waited for them. Instead of attacking each other, the three fought as a team, picking off their five opponents one by one. They saved the best for last: the fly-boy who'd shown Tiro no mercy. To roars of "*KILL! KILL! KILL!*" from spectators, Laughing Tree shoved him into the donut hole. He fell to safety in the net before Marcus, still seething over what happened earlier, could get to him. Ji-ji honestly didn't know what Old Shadowy's favorite would have done if he'd gotten there first.

Laughing Tree raised Marcus' and Tiro's arms in triumph. Coopmaster Thadduck tried to goad them into battling each other, but most of the crowd, thrilled by their teamwork, jeered at him when he did so. Thadduck hurried from his hutch, consulted with the twelve judges on the bench, and returned to declare a three-way tie.

Laughing Tree, Marcus, and Tiro shimmied down the hope-ropes. When they reached the ground, Laughing Tree and Marcus hoisted Tiro into the air. With a fervor that both thrilled and terrified Ji-ji, the seeds and a good number of fairskins chanted one word over and over again: "*Dreg-u-lah-mo! Dreg-u-lah-mo! Dreg-u-lah-mo!*"

Inquisitor Pious stood up abruptly and exited the coop. The twelve judges followed suit.

Ji-ji left Tiro surrounded by fans. He'd made it through his first major battle, thank god.

She decided to escort Afarra and Tulip to Sally's House, then go to the Friends' lodging to tell Tiro what she'd learned. They left arm in arm, as if they'd known each other for years.

The three girlfriends were laughing when they turned onto Mulberry Row and ran into a group of six fairskin men. Ji-ji could tell at once that the laughter they had shared didn't sit right with the group. Experience had taught her that unbridled laughter from seeds often carried a penalty. The three females lowered their heads and stepped meekly to one side to let the men pass.

"Hey, I know you," one of the men said to Ji-ji. "You were with that traitor from the 437th. The dandified one in the coop."

Officer Webster stood before them, legs astride, as if Mulberry Row were a horse he could ride whenever he wanted. He and his friends carried weapons. The silver badges of Monticello militiamen blinked in the lone streetlight near Sally's House.

"I'm speaking to you, Mule."

"Yessir," Ji-ji said, raising her eyes but not her head so as not to cause offense.

There was a pause of several seconds. All seeds knew that, at times like these, the desire to inflict harm lurked inside that pause, an interval that had endured over the centuries and been passed down from one bully to another. A birthright of sorts. The men were armed. The men were Monticello militiamen. They could drag the three females behind Sally's House and rape them one by one. They could kill them and claim self-defense, or thievery, or express the opinion that the duskies were reaching for weapons.

The roots on Ji-ji's back remained silent. Not a timid silence, a silence that precedes ambush. She didn't know what she planned to do, but she did know she would do *something*. She was calm, as if she'd anticipated this encounter all along.

"Hey, fellas," Officer Webster said. "How's about we take the ugly Mule and have ourselves a bit of fun?" He reached out and grabbed Ji-ji's arm. Tulip screamed.

Afarra leapt between them, breaking his hold on her. "*NO TOUCHING!*" she cried.

Five of the men laughed. Webster didn't. He grabbed Afarra by the neck and shoved her against the wall of one of the cabins. Ji-ji touched his arm. He whirled around and swore at her.

"Leave her an' take me!" Ji-ji pleaded. "She didn't mean to cause offense."

"*Yes!*" Afarra mumbled through the choke hold. "I am . . . *meaning* . . . it!"

"*Shut up!*" Ji-ji told her. "She doesn't know what she's saying! She's nuts. Always has been."

A female voice from the islands rang out: "Racers? You out there? Can't see a damn thing without my glasses!" Salome stood fifty yards away at the door of Sally's House and peered out into the night. "You got some o' them fly-boys with you? You get your butts inside right this minute! We got notice of an inquisitorial inspection. Lord Pious himself! You want Lord Pious to see what sluts you are?"

Webster's mouth twitched. He waited a full five seconds before letting go of Afarra's neck.

The officer turned to Ji-ji and said, "Think you'll be safe on that race route? Think again. We got some nice surprises for you runners. Tell that fly-boy we got our eyes on him too. Tell him Toteppi don't get to fly in our coops anymore." He bent down and murmured in Ji-ji's ear: "No way he'll be safe in D.C. Not even close."

Webster pinched Ji-ji's nipple hard, then reached over and squeezed Tulip's breast. Because he could. He nodded to his men and they strolled off into the night.

Salome came running. "How many times I got to call you? You come with me right now!"

Ji-ji thought she glimpsed a gun in Salome's hands, though she couldn't swear to it.

The three girls held each other as Salome propelled them into the bunkhouse.

"Monticello ain't safe in the dark," Salome said, shakily. "You get tucked in an' stay there."

A short while later, the other runners were sleeping when Ji-ji crept past them, past Salome's sleeping alcove in the hallway, and out into the night. She had to tell Tiro she was one of the killers they were searching for; she had to warn him about Webster's threat; and she had to tell him that the Lord-Secretary's letter told an all-too-familiar story. Some in the City of Dreams had decided who their friends were and which dreams they wanted to invest in. And the dreams weren't theirs, after all. Not even close.

24 RUN!

Ji-ji had been sitting on the bed in the Friends' lodging room for more than thirty minutes when she heard the key turn in the lock. She'd taken off her short-cape due to the room's sweltering heat. Now she wished she'd kept it on. Her sproutings could play up, and she didn't relish Tiro's reaction if they did. She rose when he entered.

"Hey, Ji!" he said, sounding as thrilled to see her as he did in the old days. He locked the door and stood awkwardly in the center of the room, the flush of triumph clearly visible on his face mixed with . . . what? Nervousness? Dread?

"Sorry I'm late," he told her sheepishly. "Couldn't find this place. Ben gave me directions just in case, but everything looks different in the dark. You been waiting long?"

"No. Not long."

"So what's this mission Ben an' Germaine went on?"

"Sit down, Tiro. I got a lot to tell you."

At the foot of the wobbly double bed, Tiro perched on the edge of the mattress. Ji-ji didn't want to make him uncomfortable, so she sat down at the other end.

"Okay," she began, "we should probably keep our voices down, just in case. You remember Zinc an' Chet an' the others?"

"Yeah, you an' Germaine filled me in. How could I forget?"

"Well, turns out his real name wasn't Zinc Shokovsky. It was Zebadiah Moss."

It took a moment for this to register. "Ji! Are you saying you killed Zebadiah Moss?"

"*Sssh!* Keep it down. Don't know how soundproof this place is."

He lowered his voice. "Are you telling me you're the one the cardinals're looking for? You know who he was, right? The Lord-Secretary's brother!"

"I didn't actually kill him. Lucky did. I tried but I kept missing."

"Not sure that'll work real good as a defense, Ji."

"I guess they're looking for both of us—me an' Lucky. Only Lucky's dead, so it's just me."

"This one of Ben's practical jokes? Germaine says he loves playing pranks on people. They hiding out somewhere cracking up?" He actually bent down and looked under the bed.

"I wish it was a joke," she told him. "Been trying to wrap my head around it too. Germaine an' Ben called a meeting. Old Harlan came—said he an' Uncle Dreg were close. Mad Cleo, Lyla Cotton, Otumbo Jehovah, Terence Pham, Cray Juniper, they were all here too."

"Juniper? A Friend? You're kidding! So how come nobody invited me to this meeting?"

"It was spur-of-the-moment. No one wanted to distract you before the match."

Tiro shook his head. "Should've been here, Ji. You an' Afarra—you're my responsibility."

Ji-ji bristled. "Afarra an' me look out for each other. Sloppy's helping us too. We'll be running together." Using Sloppy as an example might not have been the best way to convince Tiro she knew what she was doing. "We'll be running with Tulip Rogersseed too," she added, to strengthen her case. She knew she was babbling but she couldn't stop. "Tulip's a Muleseed from the 800s. Wants to murder Clownfish her brother cos he's scum."

"I wouldn't trust Sloppy far as I can throw her. She's no friend to you, Ji. Believe me."

"You're not telling me anything I don't know already. Seems to me instead of worrying 'bout us, you should do a better job looking after yourself."

"I promised Uncle Dreg I'd look out for you an' Afarra both."

She'd been sharp with him; she felt ashamed for overreacting. "Sorry. This stuff's real bad, Tiro. An' you haven't heard the half of it yet."

"So fill me in. Whatever it is we'll face it together, like always."

Speaking so fast she could barely take a breath, Ji-ji described how she'd found out about Zinc being Zebadiah, described how she'd discovered she had his letter and photo after all. "They'd been there in the saddlebag the whole time! The letter's got this terrible stuff in it. Stuff about Toteppi—leastwise we think that's what he means, an' even about Dimmers Wood, maybe. An' the Dreamfleet too. Looks like he's turned Commander Corcoran into a spy for the steaders—if that's who he's talking about. He used initials so it's hard to know for certain. But it's bad, Tiro, real bad. An' you can't fly in the coop anymore cos Webster's itching to kill you."

"Webster? That militiaman? What's he got to do with anything?"

"He and his men ran into us when we were headed back to Mulberry Row. They tried to . . ."

"To what?"

"Doesn't matter. The letter's more important."

Tiro didn't look satisfied with her answer but he let it go. "So why did Zinc write this letter?"

"Zinc didn't write it. Fester wrote it. The Lord-Secretary."

Tiro shook his head as if to clear it. "Hold on, Ji. I'm confused. Start over. Go slower this time, okay? Give a weary fly-boy a chance to catch up."

Ji-ji took a deep breath and began again from the beginning. She remembered key phrases from Fester's letter and was able to quote them to him almost verbatim.

After she reached the end of her account, Tiro sat very still for a while. She could see his mind churning the way hers had when she'd tried to come to grips with the implications of all this. Her mind raced again too. They might not know she and Lucky had killed them, but the letter, the photo, and the saddlebag served as evidence, to say nothing of the stallion. She didn't know how newspapers worked in the city, but the twelve planting censors had to approve every word in the planting newsletter. Would those newspaper folks in D.C. reveal she was the killer? As if that weren't bad enough, Sloppy confirmed Lotter had implicated her in her mam's and Petrus' deaths. She and Lucky looked like serial killers.

She didn't tell Tiro she feared Fester the Jester would never rest till he'd avenged his brother; she didn't tell him what she'd seen in the Lord-Secretary's eyes the night of the Last Supper after he'd come upon Inquisitor Tryton attempting to rape her. Or was the Lord-Secretary himself behind the attack? Did he suspect there was an existential threat under her blouse? Had he sent Tryton to deep-search her? She shivered as she recalled the sinister way Fightgood Worthy had looked at her, as if he were trying to decide if he would enjoy torturing her, or if it would bore him. She still hadn't told anyone about the incident and she didn't plan to, if she could help it. "Keep it secret," Worthy-Fester had said in his letter, "keep it safe," and even though he'd been referring to something else, it felt like he'd been speaking directly to her.

"Don't cry, Ji," Tiro said, and scooted up to the head of the bed. She hadn't realized she was.

"It's the sproutings," she said, between sniffs. "They mess with my emotions, my hormones. Like I'm menopausal."

"Like you're what?"

"Forget it."

"We'll get through this, Ji. As I see it, they don't know you had anything to do with Zebadiah's death. If you think about it, finding the letter was a stroke of luck. We know they're coming for us now. Ben'll get word to Man Cryday, an' Germaine'll tell Friends in the city."

He put his arm around her. She felt the pity in his touch and pulled away. "My back," she told him, by way of explanation. "Those feeler-things could grab ahold of you again."

He smiled. "Just let 'em try." He rested his hand on hers. This time, she didn't pull away.

"If it's true Corcoran's allied with the Territories, you can't enlist. An' Webster threatened you too tonight. Said they don't want you flying in their coops. You'll be in real danger if you do."

"What you think I was in tonight? Marcus checked my harness before an' after the match. Been tampered with. It's how come it snapped in two like that. An' those two thugs on that welkin platform—no one has a clue who they were. Marcus says they ain't registered as flyer-battlers. No seed's safe, Ji."

"But enlisting could be futile. Father-Man Williams has got it in for you. No amount of lucre'll convince him to part with—"

Tiro's temper flared. He pulled his hand from hers. "Think I don't know that? What do you want me to do, Ji? Who's next in line for tractor-pulling? Bromadu? Eeyatho? They're eight an' six, an' that bastard's got 'em both! An' Mother too! I *got* to get 'em out. 'Specially now if Toteppi are in danger like the letter said."

Tiro quickly shed his anger. He sounded worn out. "Uncle Dreg told Williams he'd put a hex on him if he touched Mother. Said, 'Impotence would be irreversible.' Said if he touched the boys, he'd die within the week. Problem is, Williams probably don't give a crap 'bout some Tribal wizard's curse. Wouldn't have been so keen on lynching me if he did. Hey, it's getting real late an' you got the race in—what?—less than eight hours. If you don't rest up you'll never make it to the city."

"Don't need rest. Wouldn't sleep anyway. . . . You still planning to enlist in the Dreamfleet?"

"Figure I got no choice. All these years I been thinking how Free we'd be if we made it to the city. Guess I never understood how big the cage is."

"Don't say that. Things'll get better. You'll see."

"Growns've been feeding us that fairy-tale dream for years. I know what the coop is, what it does to flyers, what it's trying to tamp down an' distract from. I know most of the fans'll cheer for me when I'm flying and spit on me when I'm not. But for an hour or two during a match, they're all looking up at us an' holding their breath, living to see our next move. It's the only time seeds like us matter. An' if that means I been duped—'co-opted,' Marcus calls it cos he loves them fancy words—if I been duped so be it. If you can think of another way to get 'em out I'm all ears."

"I *can* think of another way," Ji-ji said. They were talking the way they used to. She could risk sharing this dream with him. "We could find Charra an' ask her to raid the 437th an' Free the—"

"For Christ's sake, Ji! What planet you living on? Know how long it'd take to find Charra in the Madlands? Bribing Williams is the only option."

Ji-ji opened her mouth to argue with him, but he looked so distressed she couldn't think of anything convincing to say. She searched for a kinder subject and lit upon one.

"I'm glad Marcus made it through the first leg. Is he a Friend of Freedom too?"

"I wish! Been trying to recruit that fly-boy for months. Emmeline tried too."

"Wait a minute. Emmeline Shadowbrook? Old Shadowy? The diviner's a Friend?"

"You think Marcus could get away with shit like that if she wasn't? Shadowy was the one come up with the idea of Marcus impersonating me. Knew the guards couldn't tell the difference."

"Did Marcus know he was a decoy?"

"Course he did. Had to be his choice. I bet Emmeline turned off the fry-fence for you an' Lucky like she did for us. Silent Pete's a Friend too. Helped Uncle Dreg. Helps Emmeline too. He was one of the others assigned to keep an eye on you. Pete an' Shadowy may look old as the hills but they're pretty formidable as a team. You should see some of Emmeline's moves. Talk about sneaky."

"Silent Pete never let on he was a—"

"Course he didn't. . . . Him an' Emmeline were devastated when Uncle died. Can't believe the steaders haven't caught on to her yet. Lotter won't be as dumb as Herring. He'll figure it out, an' then poor Emmeline'll be pyred. . . . Marcus says he's not a joiner, but what he really means is he don't approve of the Friends cos they let anyone in. Says you can't know what it's like to be a seed if you never been one. Says fairskin suffering's not near as bad as ours."

"Emmeline may disagree with him if she's pyred. Bet Lucky would have had something to say about Marcus' theory too."

"There's holes in my fly-boy's argument. But you know Marcus. Stubborn as an animule."

Guilt welled up again inside Ji-ji. "I messed up," she said. "Ben says it's his fault but it was me didn't remember the letter. How do you forget something like that?"

"You got a lot going on, Ji. It's not every day a seed gets inducted into the Bird tribe. 'Sides, second-guessing's a fool's game. It's what I did on account of Uncle Dreg, an' it's what Tree's doing now—beating himself up. Wasn't Tree's fault Ink crept up behind him. Marcus says the fly-coop net's a tragedy masquerading as a mercy. Says we didn't make this mess; we just inherited it."

Ji-ji had to agree that made sense. "How's your foot? I forgot to ask."

"Fine. Got killers, an' they'll pump me up with more shots if it gets bad. They got four docs assigned to the flyer-battlers. The owners of the Dreamfleet Flyers're hoping the race'll generate a good crop this year. They need a boatload of us to fly in that new Dream Coop. Plus I got close to three days to recover 'fore they truck us to the corridor. Don't seem fair you gotta run so far. Flyers used to run the full distance an' battle too, only they were too wiped to put on a decent show in the coop, so they kept shortening the run portion for the flyers." He paused. She could tell he wanted to ask her something. "Can you feel 'em? They hurt?"

"Not anymore. They itch like crazy. It's like they're tied to my emotions. When I get scared or stressed they act up. Can't wait to remove the binding during the race an' just wear my cape."

"Think that's safe?"

"Can't run a hundred miles in a damn corset."

"So. Sometimes playing it safe don't matter? Interesting." They laughed.

"Sorry I reacted that way when I saw your back before. Guess it was a shock."

"Don't worry about it. Was a shock to me too."

Tiro stopped looking at her and directed his words to the uneven, wood-plank floor.

"It's like I'm hanging on to this hope-rope, Ji, only all of a sudden it's not a hope-rope. Been fooling me all along. It's a lynch rope. I'm swinging from a penal tree with Uncle Dreg an' Amadee, an' I don't know how the hope-rope got switched. But I gotta keep hanging on . . . to you, an' Mother an' Bromadu an' Eeyatho. . . . Only I miss Uncle Dreg. . . . I miss Amadee even more. . . . It's different with a twin. It's like you miss yourself. Like most of you is dead too. Keep hoping I'll see Amadee, like you told me you saw Lua in Brine's confessional. Wouldn't care what he said or if he looked all ghouly. Wouldn't care if he lectured me nonstop like he used to. Always on my case like he was ten years older'n me instead of ten minutes. . . . Amadee was wild for nature—I ever tell you that? Went on about the Appalachian Trail an' stupid shit like that. Said it used to be paradise. When he talked about it he got so excited you almost believed one day folks like us would live Free in The Margins again—hike, savor nature, camp out just for the hell of it. . . . Crazy, huh? You remember the things he could do in that cage? Was like magic."

They sat in silence. She wanted to tell him he was every bit as good as Amadee because it was true. Before she'd had a chance to come up with a response, Tiro spoke again.

"You noticed Afarra's growth spurt?"

"Thought Pheebs was exaggerating at first but she wasn't. Afarra was right about tonight."

"I didn't fall."

"You would have if Super Marcus hadn't swooped in."

He groaned. "Don't rub it in. My man Marcus'll never let me live it down. . . . Ji?"

"Yeah."

"Can I see 'em again?"

"You're kidding, right?"

"No."

"They're still the same, Tiro. Worse maybe."

"S'okay. Figure I gotta start getting used to 'em. Could be around for a long time."

"Oh god, I hope not." She thought for a moment. "Okay," she said. "You can see 'em. But you gotta help me unwrap the bandages. They could latch on to you again. You okay with that?"

"You forget, Ji. I'm a fearless champion."

"Who almost got his ass kicked an' had to be rescued."

"Yep, that's the one."

Ji-ji took off her shirt. Together, they unwound the bandages constricting her sproutings.

"Well? What's the verdict?" she asked, nervously. She sat with her naked back facing him and thought about the first time she'd done that in Brine's fly-coop. So much had happened since.

"They're so damn *weird*! No—don't cover 'em up. I don't mean it like that. I mean, it's like your back's on the way to being . . . something else. Will it hurt if I touch 'em?"

"You can touch."

"They feel like . . . nothing I ever felt before. . . . Sorry. Did I hurt you?"

"No, it's not that. They're sensitive is all."

"Good sensitive?"

"Yeah. Good sensitive."

"Think these feeler-things'll ever blossom into wings?" he asked.

"Don't know. But whatever happens, I don't want you to let 'em amputate, okay?"

"I can't promise, Ji."

"You *got* to. It would kill me if they took 'em now. I know it would. Man Cryday said Charra was never the same after they took hers. You know 'bout that?"

"Yeah. Ben an' Germaine been filling me in."

"Are those two married?"

"Yeah. Coming up on their five-year anniversary. Ben's stumped 'bout what to get her. . . . I hate to say it, Ji, but these feeler-things don't look nothing like wings."

"Ain't that the truth," Ji-ji said. "But you still gotta promise you won't let 'em amputate."

"Hope I won't live to regret this. . . . Okay, I promise. . . . An' now I got a duty to escort the Existential back to Sally's House. But first . . . you got that ointment? Want me to slather some on?" She nodded in amazement.

He applied the salve with tenderness and only flinched once or twice. Then he helped her bandage them. His way of asking for forgiveness.

Afterward, he escorted her back to Mulberry Row. When they said goodbye at the entrance to Sally's House, he promised to join up with them when they reached Dream Corridor.

Ji-ji shook her head. "May not make it by the deadline if we wait for you fly-boys. Bet we'll be miles ahead of you by then."

"You've always been miles ahead of me, Ji. S'what your mam was scared of. Still hoping you'll wait for me to catch up. We got Friends posted along the route. Not many but some. They'll do what they can to protect you. Be real careful, okay?" She nodded.

Tiro turned and walked back along Mulberry Row. A fairskin called out from a nearby miscegenation: "Hey, Dregulahmo! That you? Sure was some sweet flyin' you an' the others did in the Jefferson tonight. Buy you a drink for the road?" Tiro asked for a rain check, said he had to practice. "At this time! What are you? Some kinda masochistic night owl?" Tiro said he wasn't a night owl, he was an early riser. "Fair enough," the man replied. "The early bird catches the worm."

From the doorway of Sally's House, Ji-ji watched Tiro make his way back down the hill. He happened to pass under one of a handful of streetlights in Monticello. She caught sight of the flyer logo on the back of his T-shirt: a black bird on a white background inside a cage. The wide-open door of the cage looked small. Too small for the bird to escape. For all their sakes, Ji-ji hoped she was wrong.

IIIIIIIIIIIIII

The race path, which had been wide and accommodating when they left Monticello, and asphalted, for the most part, shrank to a dirt footpath as the morning progressed. When running four abreast became difficult, Ji-ji took the lead. Afarra, Tulip, and Sloppy followed.

When they'd set out, the thirty-six runners were tightly grouped together. A few minutes in, about fourteen runners had shot out ahead of everyone. Ji-ji's group came next. Behind them came the remaining runners, eighteen in that last group. They'd maintained the same order ever since.

The hole Sloppy had cut in her running shoe to make room for her grotesquely swollen toe seemed to help a little, but she often flinched in pain. Before they set out, Ji-ji had come upon Sloppy near the outhouses behind Sally's House, injecting her toe with something. Without waiting for a question, Sloppy told her to keep her nose out of other people's business. Since the race began, after checking to see if any guards were around, Sloppy had taken out a weed stick and smoked it down to a nub while she ran. At one point, Ji-ji overheard Sloppy, who always insisted someone go between her and Afarra, ask how Tulip could bear to run beside a Cloth. "You'll get Janglers," Sloppy said, panting as they ran uphill. "Outcasts are carriers. Your nose'll drop off one night. There one second, gone the next. Those fancy braids won't compensate for noselessness. I'd steer clear of the Cloth if I was you . . . were you." In response, Tulip had stuck even closer to Afarra.

Somehow, Sloppy had managed to wind up in fifteenth position after the Salem-to-Monticello leg. Ji-ji still couldn't figure out how she'd made it through the first leg. Her story about running through the night didn't seem plausible, especially not for a runner with a bum toe. When she fell behind again so she could get relief from her weed stick, Afarra summed up the sentiments of all three: "Sloppy is a very excellent cheat. That is how she does it."

The distance between the three groups widened steadily as the day went on. "Think we should try an' catch up with the others?" Tulip asked. Her face was swollen from the beating and her ribs were very sore. Even so, like Sloppy, she kept up a decent pace.

Ji-ji shook her head. "Let's keep the pace easy for now." What she worried about more than the pace was what Tulip and Sloppy had told her about pickers snatching runners during the first leg. The lead pack of runners would probably be the first to encounter trouble, which would give those who followed time to react. Not a great plan but better than nothing.

Ji-ji felt comfortable as she ran. Her steady pace allowed her to sprint for a while then pull back when needed. During training runs, bursts of pure, raw energy would propel her forward till her feet became a blur—or, at least it seemed like they did. Her legs were wheels, turning in endless cycles, pistons, pumping her forward. She'd read on the Grubby Pipe that people could run hundreds of miles without sleep. Uncle Dreg, an impressive long-distance runner himself, used to tell her they ran like that in the Cradle. He claimed Toteppi feet "beat the drum of the earth."

At intervals, they encountered guards stationed along the route. Some were Monticello militiamen. Ji-ji, anxious in case Webster and his cronies ambushed them, had felt relieved when they'd left the place behind, even though she feared what lay ahead. Bored militiamen along the race route sat in front of wooden booths, playing cards and smoking weed. Some of them yelled lewd comments as the runners passed by; a few wished them good luck; most didn't bother to look up. They passed a smattering of D.C. patrollers too, whose navy caps featured an image of the Capitol Building. Every time Ji-ji saw the white dome of the Capitol, her spirits rose. What did it matter if the female runners enjoyed none of the fanfare that accompanied the male flyer-battlers?

Only a few spectators had watched them leave from Hemingsgate. Tiro had been there with Marcus, cheering them on. She'd caught sight of Laughing Tree too, and been grateful hardly anyone else showed up. The last thing she needed was attention.

To First Monitor Schultz's vocal objections, Inquisitor Pious' assistant, who'd shot the starter pistol, had informed the runners they had to reach the city by 6:00 P.M. of the third day to be eligible for admission to D.C. That meant getting to Dream Corridor not long after midday. Running at night was madness, so they'd need to run until dusk that day and start out at dawn on each of the two days following. Even then, admission was at the discretion of the Freedom Race Council, made up of race monitors from D.C. and inquisitors from the Territories. Runners could be ruled ineligible for entry into the city if their times placed them in the bottom third, especially if the inquisitors got their way.

Ji-ji's strategy was simple: catch up with the lead group on the second day and, on the morning of the third as they approached Dream Corridor, surge to the front of the pack. Their time should be good enough for them to gain entry, even without the benefit of the Salem-to-Monticello leg. As long as they ran steadily, they could handle around thirty-plus miles a day over fairly challenging terrain. If the race route was real windy or muddy, of course, it would take them longer. She'd need to make sure she didn't push Afarra and Tulip too hard. She'd need to keep an eye on Sloppy too, for all kinds of reasons. Nor could she forget about something else she'd learned. That morning at breakfast, Salome had pulled Ji-ji aside and said, "Two truckloads of pickers showed up at the miscegenations last night, fresh off their success on the first leg, an' eager for new picks. If you spy them vultures, run like the wind."

"Want to stop so you can take off your cape?" Tulip asked, after they'd been running for hours over hilly terrain. "You can stuff it in your backpack. It's awful hot."

"No," Ji-ji replied. "I don't feel the heat. . . . S'my lucky cape, that's why."

She hoped Tulip and Sloppy wouldn't notice how much she was sweating. At least she'd removed the corset bandage a few hours previously when she'd gone into the bushes to pee. She'd stuffed her bandages into her backpack to wear again when they neared Dream Corridor.

As they ran, the intervals between guards increased. By noon, the guards supposedly lining the route had all but disappeared. By midafternoon, they hadn't seen a guard for hours. *We're on our own now,* Ji-ji thought. *God help us.*

Because Sloppy had fallen way back—the farthest she'd been behind since they started out—Ji-ji felt comfortable removing her backpack, which irritated her sproutings. She looped it round her neck and secured it over her chest. She called back to Tulip to ask how long she'd been offroad on the first leg.

"Miles," Tulip called back, drawing closer so she wouldn't need to shout. She was breathing heavily from the run, and Ji-ji could tell her ribs hurt her. In spite of this, she maintained the steady pace of an athlete. "Why you asking, Ji-ji?" Tulip added, nervously.

"Just got a feeling, I guess."

Tulip stopped running so abruptly that Afarra crashed into her.

Alarmed, Ji-ji turned back to face them. "What is it?" she cried.

Tulip raised a trembling arm and pointed straight ahead. "I saw something *move*!"

"Where?" Ji-ji said, spinning around to survey their surroundings. Had a snarlcat crept up behind her?

"*There!*" Tulip cried. "On your *back*!"

"Oh shit," Ji-ji muttered under her breath.

"Oh shit," Afarra echoed, the Cellists having given her a new appreciation for swearing.

"It's nothing," Ji-ji said, in a desperate effort to quiet her sproutings. "You're exhausted, Tulip. No wonder you're seeing things. We'll take another break soon."

They commenced their run. Ji-ji ransacked her brain for a good lie and came up with some whoppers. She could tell Tulip she suffered from an aggressive form of spinal cancer, which explained why she'd been desperate to compete, cos doctors in D.C. could remove her growths—a lie that hit too close to home. Problem was, no tumor she'd ever seen looked anything like the pulsing roots on her back. Or she could tell Tulip her sproutings were fake, that she'd had them grafted to her back to make sure no one would rape her. She had to dismiss that lie too. Her sproutings looked way too real to be fake. In the end, she settled for the truth cos she couldn't come up with a good lie or with a good enough reason for lying. Tulip had shared things seeds didn't share unless they believed they could trust their listeners absolutely. Something else also convinced her to tell Tulip the truth. Last night, Tiro hadn't run when she'd shown him her back.

Ji-ji checked that Sloppy was still a long way back and pulled Tulip into the woods that flanked the path. Afarra followed.

"I need to tell you a secret. You gotta swear you won't repeat it. Sloppy can't know."

"Don't worry," Tulip assured her. "No way I'm telling that bitch nothing. Reminds me of Clownfish. You hear what she said about Afarra?"

Without wasting any time, Ji-ji explained that her back was deformed. A famous healer, she said, an expert arborist, had told her the sproutings could turn out to be . . . Ji-ji hesitated.

"Turn out to be what?" Tulip asked.

"Wings!" Afarra declared. "They are being wings! One day soon."

Tulip looked at them both incredulously, said she wanted to see these "sproutings" with her own eyes. The term seemed to have confused Tulip, who asked if they looked more like brussels sprouts or cauliflower florets. Ji-ji prayed their new friend wouldn't go into hysterics when she saw how thoroughly inedible and peculiar her feelers looked.

Ji-ji removed her cape and raised her T-shirt. Tulip gasped and took several steps backward. A second later, however, she crept toward them.

"They don't look like nothing human. When they get to be wings?" Tulip asked.

"Maybe tomorrow," Afarra told her. "Or in the fall at flowering time. Or next year."

"It's already flowering time," Tulip pointed out.

Afarra corrected her. "April and May is blossoming time. Too early for flowering."

"We don't know when it'll happen," Ji-ji said. "Sometimes they never change."

Tulip's eyes, even her swollen black eye, looked like they'd pop out if she opened them any wider. "Other seeds've got these sprouts too?"

Ji-ji was tempted to lie. *No. Better stick to the truth.* "A few. None we know of has 'em now though. You gotta keep it a secret. Steaders'll kill me if they find out cos I'm so different."

"You saying these sprouts could kill you?" Tulip asked, full of concern.

"These are not for killing," Afarra told her. "These are for flying."

Tulip asked if she could touch them. Ji-ji told her she could help Afarra put some ointment on them, if she wanted, cos running chafed them so much, but they had to move fast. The salve felt wonderful, but, to Ji-ji's dismay, one of the feelers latched on to Tulip's wrist. She was taken aback at first, but recovered quickly.

"It's like Moose," Tulip said, "a caterpillar Rosemary an' Thyme found. Was Thyme's idea to call him that. She gets all the animals mixed up cos she was stuck in Mam's seed canal too long an' it left an impression. They were waiting for Moose to turn into a butterfly, only he ain't the butterfly type. Just a caterpillar. When Moose died we had us a big funeral. That was Rosemary's idea. But your sprouts're way bigger, an' they look—" She broke off.

"Look what?" Ji-ji asked. "S'okay, Tulip. Tell me."

"They look . . . *rude.*"

"That's what I think. Gave me a whole new appreciation for the shit males gotta deal with."

"They don't gotta deal with nothing much," Tulip countered. After a moment or two she added, "You think you could whip 'em out in an emergency an' use 'em to throttle Clownfish?"

"Oh yes," Afarra told her, before Ji-ji had a chance to respond. "They are very good for that."

"They're amazing," Tulip concluded. "Think there's a chance you could get me a pair?"

IIIIIIIIIIIIII

They came upon it unexpectedly. One moment the forest was there, then they crested a hill and it disappeared. Tulip said the place looked like the stricken forest she'd seen when she'd been leased to Planting 804. Ji-ji recalled what Lotter said about the epidemic of forest fires they'd endured on plantings due to the Long Warming. "Fires on a scale like that don't take prisoners," he'd told her. "They're tidal waves of flame." And it certainly looked like tidal waves of flame had torn through acre after acre of trees and bushes, leaving behind little more than blackened stumps on a charred forest floor. No birds and no insects to speak of. Dead land.

Sloppy was still struggling to keep up. Ji-ji thought about how it would feel jogging through that desolate landscape alone. "Hold up," she said. "How 'bout we walk for a while? Give Slop a chance to catch us." Reluctantly, Afarra and Tulip agreed.

Many things terrified Ji-ji, but fire had a special menace to it. She always covered her eyes when they had pyreings on the planting. She would smell the burning flesh and wish it didn't remind her of the roast venison she would prepare for the steaders cos that only made it worse. Apart from those they convicted of being Practicing Deviants, they didn't pyre males on her planting, or on other plantings as far as she knew. It was a form of execution reserved almost exclusively for females. Auntie Zaini said it was because they burned witches at the stake in the old days. All witches were females, which was how the practice of pyreing females got started in the Territories. Ji-ji suspected there was another reason. A female's high-pitched shrieks were more haunting than a male's low-pitched ones, and therefore more likely to instill terror in seeds in the viewing coops. She blamed Lotter for making her think of something as manipulative as that. Because of what Lotter and the other steaders had put them through, a part of her brain looked like the ravaged, fire-plagued wasteland they walked in, a wretched place of desolation and despair.

Ji-ji thought of Bonbon's beautiful cradle of braided twigs and how, in her despair, she'd fed it to the flames. She thought of how Zinc-Zebadiah looked when half his body was on fire. His mother had foreseen her son's fiery demise but her foresight hadn't saved him. Ji-ji recalled how Lotter hadn't thought twice about pyreing Jellybean, her mam's one true love. If he were fed to the flames, would he remain silent, or would her father-man shriek like a girl? It scared her how much she wanted to know the answer to that question.

IIIIIIIIIIIIII

The next morning, having made it through the stricken forest, and having found an abandoned hunting hut to sleep in, the four runners huddled together near the race path. Rather than being grateful for them giving her time to catch up, Sloppy seemed to think they'd done it to humiliate her. Ji-ji had learned her lesson: nothing she could do would ever satisfy the former kitchen-seed. Sloppy's resentment ran too wide and way too deep.

They'd stopped to eat one of the energy bars the monitors had given them when they heard the rumble of trucks. Making their way up the hill through dense undergrowth, they discovered they weren't far from a gravel back road that paralleled the race route. Ji-ji told the others to get down low so they wouldn't be seen. They duckwalked forward to the crest of the hill and peered down onto the road below as two large trucks rumbled past.

"Pickers!" Tulip said. "Heading south. Saw two like that the night they took the others!"

"There are too many," Afarra murmured.

"Yes," Ji-ji agreed. (*Way too many.*) "We can't stay the night in the rest station. Too risky."

"So we gotta sleep outside tonight?" Tulip asked. "You think there's ants round here?"

"Don't know," Ji-ji told her. "But we gotta get off the race path. S'not safe. What do you think, Sloppy? Delilah, I mean. Sorry."

"What do I know? You're our noble leader. An' from now on, you can call me Sloppy. You get it wrong every damn time. It's getting on my nerves hearing you trip all over yourself."

Ji-ji ignored Sloppy-Delilah's grumbling and focused on what she'd gleaned from Uncle Dreg, from other Friends, and even from Lotter himself about the area. This was the Piedmont, east of the Blue Ridge. In the old days, it was full of towns and cities, but natural and unnatural disasters had turned this inland mid-Atlantic region into a wilderness, pitted with ghost towns and abandoned cities. The race route steered them clear of old urban areas where Clansmen had taken over and established autonomous districts, but inter-Clan warfare was common. Find yourself in the middle of that and it could be worse than ending up in NoVA.

Tulip looked so terrified that Ji-ji whispered to Afarra, asking if it was okay for her to reveal Afarra's secret. Afarra gave her a thumbs-up and Ji-ji broke the good news. Tulip was ecstatic.

"So she can speak to mutants for real? . . . Calm 'em down when they try to eat us?"

"Yeah," Ji-ji said. "Seen her do it with my own eyes."

"Wow! Think it works with Clansmen too?"

"Don't see why not," Ji-ji said.

"Guess you both got special powers," Tulip concluded. "Guess that means we're safe."

Ji-ji, grateful Tulip hadn't revealed to Sloppy what her special power was, agreed.

"Give me a break," Sloppy muttered. "If the Cloth speaks Mutant, I'm Mary Poppins."

"Who's she?" Tulip asked, peeling her eyes from the trucks.

Sloppy, who seemed caught off-guard by the question, winged it: "Mary robbed the banks cos they're a swindle, an' gave spoonfuls of sugar to the poor. Fed the pigeons too, cos they were undernourished. You had more birds all over the place in those days, 'fore things got contaminated.

Mary P's iconic. If you picked up a goddam book once in a while, you'd know all about her."

The pickers rolled past in their tarpaulin-covered picking trucks. At the rear of one of the trucks, the tarpaulin flap was drawn back. A small, yapping dog peeked out.

"You see that?" Ji-ji said. "It's *him*!"

"Who?" Afarra asked.

"Chaff Man!" Ji-ji said. "Planting 437's executioner! In the back of that truck with Circus! How'd he get off the planting alive? An' what's he doing with pickers?"

"Who gives a damn?" Sloppy said. "Come on. Let's get out of here 'fore they catch us."

They agreed to abandon the race path and avoid the rest stations, which meant they would have to spend the night in the open. Afraid to stray too far, they kept to within a few hundred yards of the route and made their way through the dense undergrowth as best they could. Ji-ji wanted to warn the runners ahead and behind, but that would mean abandoning the others. Tulip and Afarra begged her not to go. As a compromise, the group quickened their pace and Ji-ji crept back to the path every mile or so to see if she could spot the other runners.

Dusk brought gunshots behind them, followed by the screams of girls and cries of pickers, followed by a choice none of them wanted to make.

IIIIIIIIIIIIII

"It's too risky, Ji-ji," Tulip whispered. "We should keep going. Pickers'll be satisfied. Won't pick no more. We don't make it to the gates in time we don't get in."

"He left the key near the door—on that string, see? By the lamp?" Ji-ji said. "We unlock the door an' Free them."

"An' how you plan on doing that," Sloppy said, "with a damn picker on the porch guarding the place? He's a big one too. Six-four, I'd say. An' there are seven others. That's eight altogether, one of which happens to be a fucking executioner if you were right about seeing the Chaff. You an assassin in your spare time? You up for killing eight pickers? You even got a weapon?"

"No," Ji-ji admitted.

"You got that potato peeler?" Afarra asked.

It took a second or two for Ji-ji to figure out what Afarra was referring to. "You mean the knife I used to slit his throat?"

Sloppy perked up: "You slit someone's throat already?"

"Didn't work," Ji-ji confessed.

"Shame," Sloppy said.

"No. Not a shame," Afarra insisted. "He was our friend. Do not worry, Tulip," she added. "Elly is not for killing friends now."

Tulip, who didn't look very reassured, posed the question she'd posed repeatedly: "How come there are no guards at this rest station? The monitors said the route would be guarded."

"I told you," Ji-ji replied. "The pickers must've bought 'em off."

"I'm scared," Tulip confessed. Her breathing was shallow and fast. "I was up for seedmating this fall. I was a Cropmaster Pick cos of my hair. Fairskins like it cos it's long an' not too nappy. He sampled some of us Picks early. He made us . . . do things. . . . I ain't going back. I gotta save Rose—"

Sloppy interrupted her. "Listen, Saint Jellybean. If you really are planning a suicide mission, this is where I say goodbye. For all we know they brought the Chaff along so he could lynch every last one of us. Wish I could say I'll miss you suckers but it'd be a lie."

They watched Sloppy creep backward on all fours for several yards so as not to be spotted. She scrambled to her feet and limped off.

Stunned, Tulip said, "Sookie's in there. Sloppy said she was her friend."

"We do better without the Delilah," Afarra said.

Ji-ji couldn't say she was sorry to see the back of Sloppy either. Huddled there in the dark with Afarra and Tulip, she listened to the frantic weeping inside the rest station and struggled to decide what she could live with and what she couldn't. If she didn't try to set the others Free, would she hear them weeping for the rest of her life? Was Sloppy right about this being a suicide mission? If so, she couldn't ask Tulip and Afarra to embark on it too. She forced herself to think things through logically. The pickers roasted their kill on a spit about fifty yards away in a small clearing. Rowdy and drunker by the minute, they couldn't see the cabin from the clearing or hear much if their buddy on the porch made a ruckus—two pluses. On the other hand, the pickers were armed to the teeth—a huge minus. The one man they'd left on duty was drunk. He had a bottle of liquor in his hand. He'd gulped it down at first; now he took a swig every now and then. An expert when it came to inebriation, Ji-ji figured if he was anything like her mam, he'd be out cold soon, mouth open, dribbling on his shirt—another big plus. They could do this.

As luck would have it, they didn't have to wait for him to pass out. The picker drained the last of the whiskey, tossed the bottle aside, staggered to his feet, cussed, and tottered off in the direction of the campfire. Must have got tired of smelling meat and not tasting it.

"This is my chance!" Ji-ji whispered. "Afarra, you can head on out now. Follow Sloppy. Skirt the race path for a mile or two. Don't get back on the route till you're sure it's safe, okay? Then keep running an' don't look back. Even if you hear all kinds of stuff, don't look back, understand?"

"What about me?" Tulip asked.

"You go with Afarra. I'll catch up with you when I got the others." Ji-ji moved to stand.

Tulip caught her arm, said, "No. We stick together. You got magic powers, right?"

"Yes," Afarra agreed. "We are sticking. With magic."

Ji-ji's throat swelled with gratitude, but she'd have to thank them later. "Tulip, I'm a Wild Seed an' none of 'em know me. They trust you more than us, so you speak first." Tulip nodded.

"Afarra, we gotta get 'em out quick 'fore the pickers realize what's happening. You lead 'em out. Don't let 'em get back on the race route, understand? Not till it's safe. Run in that same direction we were running in 'fore we circled back. If we get split up, we keep on running. We gotta make it to Dream Corridor by early afternoon tomorrow to make it to the gates by six. Tiro an' the flyers'll be joining us then. We can race the corridor together. Okay—it's now or never. Run quick an' run quiet."

The three girls dashed out from the bushes and ran toward the rest station.

They mounted the porch. Ji-ji removed the key dangling from a rusty nail and inserted it in the lock. The string got in the way of her trembling hands. She tried again. It worked this time.

She pushed the door open and pocketed the key. Not much light entered the cabin through its small windows. As Ji-ji's eyes adjusted to the dark, Tulip reassured the runners.

"It's Tulip, the one punched an' kicked at the Jefferson Arch. I'm with the Wild Seeds who got magic powers. We come for a rescue. Don't be scared. You can trust us."

"Stay real quiet!" Ji-ji added. "The pickers are nearby."

"*Hurry! Please!*" the runners begged.

Their hands had been bound behind their backs—some with tape, others with rope. Ji-ji counted nine captives altogether. She asked if there were others. "None that's alive," they told her. She looked around for something to cut the bindings. As Tulip and Afarra helped the runners stand, Ji-ji remembered something. She rushed out to the porch, found the discarded whiskey bottle, and hurried back inside. She took off her cape and wrapped it around the bottle to muffle the sound; then she grabbed the only chair in the cabin and brought the chair leg down on the bottle. It broke in half. Nice, jagged edges. There were smaller pieces too. She handed the top of the broken bottle to Tulip and kept the bottom for herself. She also handed out a few of the sharpest pieces to Afarra, who began using them to Free runners' hands. Ji-ji warned them not to cut anyone's wrist by accident, knowing how easily someone could bleed to death if that happened. When one of the runners asked her if she was an alien sent by God to save them, Ji-ji noticed her writhing feelers. She shook out the shards of glass from her short-cape and slipped it back on.

Soon, almost all had been Freed. Ji-ji creaked the door open and looked out. "All clear. Afarra, lead the way." Quiet as mice, the runners filed out into the night behind Cloth-33h/437.

Ji-ji helped Tulip cut tape from the wrists of Sara-May, the last of the runners. Her leg was injured. Running with her hands bound would be almost impossible. They had just managed to cut through the tape when they heard someone singing: "*She'll be comin' round the mountain when she comes!*" The drunk picker! It was too soon! If he raised the alarm, the runners would be picked again!

For a split second, Ji-ji hesitated. Then she closed the door with them inside.

A frantic whisper from Tulip: "He's coming back! He'll find us! What're you doing?"

"The others need more time," she whispered back. "Stay in the shadows."

"Why?" Tulip asked.

"Start sniveling like before, else he'll know they've gone," Ji-ji hissed. "*Do it!*"

Tulip and Sara-May whimpered with fear. Ji-ji took up a position behind the door. In her hand she clutched the broken whiskey bottle. He was tall. She'd need to remember that.

They heard the drunken picker fumble at the door for the key. "Where's the damn key?" he slurred. "Yeah, you dusky cunts! That's right, keep it up! You'll be weepin' buckets soon cos Rudy's about to teach you a lesson. . . . Where'd I put that fuckin' key?"

Ji-ji grasped the door handle. Slowly, as if it were the result of the breeze, she pulled the door open. Rudy stepped into her trap. With every ounce of strength she had, Ji-ji raised her arms and embedded the broken bottle into the tall picker's neck. He slammed up against the wall and tried to wrench her hands away from the bottle, away from his neck! He had a slab of cooked meat in his hand. He jammed it against her face and pushed! She bit down hard and tasted venison. She bit down harder—a finger this time. He let out a whimper of pain, couldn't shriek with the bottle lodged in his neck. She felt his warm blood on her hands, felt it run down her arm. How could he still be struggling!

One of her sproutings squeezed itself up through the neck of her cape and moved toward the man's horrified face. It wasn't long enough to strangle him; it brushed his lips instead. The bottle was slippery with blood. She lost her grip on it. His eyes told her he believed she was the devil come to claim him. Mad with a terror that gave him superhuman strength, he grabbed her by the throat. So much blood! Exhausted, she couldn't fight him anymore.

At that moment, Tulip plunged her broken bottle into his side. The picker slumped to the floor of the cabin. . . . Sara-May sprang to life, punching him over and over, sobbing as she did it.

Rudy lay on the floor, convulsing. He stopped mid-shiver. Tulip and Sara-May were crying. Ji-ji threw up; then she hauled herself to her feet. Rudy's body blocked the door.

"Help me move him!" Ji-ji said, grabbing one arm. "Stop sniveling! Can't do this alone!"

Tulip reacted first, grabbing Rudy's other arm. Sara-May grabbed his legs. They dragged him away from the door, sliding him over a glassy wet sheet of his own blood.

Ji-ji checked outside. "It's all clear," she said.

"What about you?" Tulip asked.

"I'll catch up. She can't run fast. We gotta help her. *Hurry!*"

The two girls took off, Tulip helping Sara-May limp-run for her life.

Ji-ji stared down at the picker. He looked like a photo of someone who'd been told to act shocked. Ji-ji searched him and found a knife strapped to his ankle. If he'd been sober enough to pull it out and use it, they would be the ones lying in a pool of blood right now.

She slipped his knife into her backpack and stepped outside. She smelled the roasting meat and popping grease. They would find Rudy eventually. Not for a while, she hoped.

She retrieved the key from her pocket, locked the door, and hung the key on the nail by its string. Her bloody hands had bloodied the key. Like a lynched seed it swayed back and forth.

Wait! Why was she making it easy for them? She snatched the key off the nail and flung it into the wilderness. Her sproutings shuddered. Were those the ones whispering or was it the trees?

"*Run!*" they whispered in unison. "*Beat the drum of the earth!*"

It was instinct. It was wisdom. She obeyed.

25 WALLS

Twelve was an unlucky number. Ji-ji counted again. Twelve, including her. The nine they'd rescued and the three rescuers. The logical part of her suspected she was suffering from shock, which would explain why she'd stopped running less than a mile away from the pickers and leapt into a swollen creek, rolling over and over to cleanse herself. Stupid to get her clothes wet like that on one of the chilliest nights of the spring. Stupid to delay when pickers could be on her tail. She didn't care that the stones in the creek bruised her body. She had to rinse off his sweat, his blood, and the stench of charred meat. Rudy's look of surprise lodged in her brain like shrapnel. Not easy to kill up close like that. You had to concentrate, not let yourself be distracted. Not easy to dislodge the face that saw you push the bottle harder into his stubble-neck. For an instant, Rudy had looked like a scared little boy. . . .

At the moment when her feelers had stroked Rudy's mouth and sent him into paroxysms of fear, something had awoken inside her. She'd felt what Lotter must feel, what the Lord-Secretary's face told her he felt when he'd stood in the doorway of Storeroom 2—absolute power over someone else's life, the most addictive high in the world.

Eleven runners had looked to the twelfth, begged the serial killer to save them. She'd told them to keep running. They hadn't listened. Tulip and Sara-May had waited a couple of miles from the rest station for her to catch up. Stupid. They could've been killed. She'd arrived soaking wet and shivering. Tulip hugged her. Seemed to understand why she'd had to wash. They ran some more, helping Sara-May, whose knee could be badly bruised or twisted or fractured or broken or shattered. They came upon Afarra and the others waiting only three miles farther on. All of them waiting for Ji-ji to tell them what the hell they needed to do next.

How dare they expect more from her. Hadn't she already given them everything she had?

Twelve. She counted them again, included herself as they looked at her expectantly. With three injureds and nine to help them the odds looked lousy. "They coming after us?" a runner asked, the cue for Sara-May to explain how Ji-ji and Tulip had killed the picker. "It was mostly Ji-ji," Tulip confessed. "She was the one did him in. Plunged that bottle into the bastard's neck an' hung on for dear life."

Eleven pairs of eyes waited for her to lead them to the Promised Land. Pastor Gillyman would put it like that, but then he was an Uncle Tom, a parrot. And what was she? Ji-ji Moses? Jellybean Un-Pyred? Killer Lottermule? She counted again. Including herself, still twelve. But the number was taken, so how could it be *their* number? Twelve father-men on each planting if you didn't count the cropmaster, twelve of everything—homesteads, Cropmaster Picks, chief overseers, full-time kitchen-seeds. (Yes, she'd had her disciples too.) Twelve dents in the floor of her room in her mam's cabin, each one marking a leg of her lost siblings' beds. Each night and each morning she'd counted them. A ritual she'd imposed upon herself. Lotter's followers called him the Twelfth. He'd sat next to Fightgood Worthy at the Last Supper of the Spring. She'd cooked them food that helped to grow the Territories one seed at a time.

"How we gonna run with the injureds?" someone asked.

"Who are you?" Ji-ji demanded.

"Sookie. From the 700s. We gonna take 'em with us?"

The three injureds pleaded with Ji-ji for mercy as if she had the power to grant it to them. She nearly laughed. She wanted to laugh so badly her stomach hurt. "Don't leave us here! Please don't leave us!" No she wouldn't leave them. Did she say this or think it? Must've said it, cos Sookie was sulking and they were all running, hopping, and limping through The Margins. Someone had set up a rotation so they could take turns helping the injureds. Was that her? No. Tulip did it, with Afarra. *I'm in shock,* Ji-ji said to herself. *Not thinking straight. "You can make yourself or let others make you." Who said that? The Tree Witch.*

And there was the Tree Witch's hand reaching out to her. Fall-leaf brown, sympathetic. No. Not the Gardener of Tears—Afarra. "I got you, Elly. You did good back there. I got your hand."

Twelve could be a lucky number. They'd made their own luck back at the rest station. She'd thrown away the key, wiped her hands on her shorts, cleansed herself. The pickers hadn't followed them, hadn't yet realized their prisoners had escaped. She was thinking more clearly now. If they discovered the raid before morning, the pickers might not be willing to hunt them on foot. Tulip kept checking to see if the gravel access road used by the trucks continued to parallel the race route. In the faint light provided by a watery moon, Tulip said it was impossible to know if the access road had ended. Next thing Ji-ji knew, Tulip said it had disappeared. The pickers couldn't follow them in the trucks. *See, what did I tell you?* Ji-ji thought. *The number twelve can be lucky.*

IIIIIIIIIIIIII

SNAP! No more than a one-second delay, then Simply Brownseed, the smallest and youngest among them, shrieking the way Rudy would've shrieked if the bottom of a whiskey bottle hadn't been lodged in his gullet.

The runners tore over to the screaming. In the thick undergrowth, they couldn't see at first what had happened. It hit them all at once. Simply had stepped on an ant trap! The savage metal jaws had all but severed her little foot! The victim's screams and sobs echoed through The Margins. "Don't scream, Simply!" the other runners pleaded. "Pickers'll hear! Or ants!"

When Ji-ji saw what the trap had done she knew those pleas were ridiculous. It took four of them—Ji-ji, Tulip, Sookie, and a runner called Hopeful—to pry open the trap. Meant to cripple a much larger creature, it left Simply with a crushed foot that no longer looked like a foot. Ji-ji used the bandages for her sproutings to bind Simply's wounds as best she could.

Ji-ji gave two painkillers to Simply, who weighed about eighty pounds. Less than a minute later, she passed out. The superstrong killers might have killed her. Another murder to confess.

The undergrowth became too dense to traverse. Forced to return to the path, the runners took turns carrying Simply between them. Though she weighed very little, they could only manage an arduous jog when they carried her. The three other injureds—Helen, Sara-May, and Honeybun—limped along with help from others.

Afarra spotted him first: a tall male speeding toward them. It was too late to hide.

The runner carried something. Ji-ji peered through the dark. It wasn't some*thing* on his shoulder, it was some*one*.

"*Tiro!*" Ji-ji cried. He must've sensed how much trouble they were in and come to the rescue. But why would he be carrying someone else? *It wasn't Tiro. . . . It wasn't a male either.*

"*Big Pike!*" Hopeful yelled. "*She's come back to help us!*"

The tall, powerful runner, who'd led after the first leg, raced to their rescue.

Some of the runners took off to greet her only to careen back a moment later when Pike screamed out a bone-chilling warning: "*Snarlcats! RUN!*"

"*Find a tree an' climb!*" Ji-ji shouted.

The runners abandoned the race path and tore into the wilderness. A frantic search led them to climbable trees. They clawed their way up them; even the injured runners managed it. All except Simply. Afarra, Tulip, and Hopeful hoisted her up into a bough and laid her in Ji-ji's lap.

"You sure we're safe up here?" Tulip asked.

"Yeah. I'm sure," Ji-ji lied.

Lotter used to tell her you could escape a snarlcat that way. Claimed they didn't climb trees unless there was a threat below. She'd been a seedling back then. He could easily have been lying to make her less afraid on the hunt. She'd soon find out.

Pike, perched up in a neighboring tree, discovered that the mauled runner she'd been carrying was dead. She climbed back down with the corpse and sat at the foot of the tree where Ji-ji and the others hid. She rocked the girl's limp body for a while. They urged her to climb up and join them. She wouldn't—said there was something she needed to do.

Pike called up softly, "Hey, Wild Seed!" *She means me, Killer Lottermule,* Ji-ji thought, struggling to hang on to Simply, who lay unconscious in her arms. "I'm taking Penny's body and leaving it for the cats," Pike said. "It'll keep 'em busy for a while. Forgive me, Pen."

Big Pike took off. The runners groaned when they saw her go. She was older, taller, and stronger than any of them, and she'd earned their respect repeatedly during the first leg. Pike had come in first, Tulip said, but she'd never crowed about it. During the first leg, she'd sprinted off several times to get water for the other runners and returned with full canteens.

Pike's exit jogged Ji-ji back into the present—sort of. She told the others Pike had promised to come back—not exactly true but an encouraging thing to say at that moment. The girls tried not to imagine what their fellow runners had just endured. Too horrifying to contemplate.

Once again, Tulip reassured the others. "We got ourselves a ant talker in Afarra here," Tulip said, tremulously. "If they come, she can sing 'em lullabies an' such. Ji-ji's seen her do it. Right, Ji-ji?"

Ji-ji lied again. She was getting good at it. "Seen it with my own eyes. Snarlcats turned into pussycats, an' stripers into puppy dogs."

Sookie didn't buy it. "You're lying," she said. "Delilah said you were a liar. A parrot too."

Tulip happened to be sitting next to Sookie on one of the tree's higher limbs. She leaned over and smacked her hard on the mouth. "Ji-ji saved your sorry ass. Think we would've gone back for you if she hadn't? Say she's a parrot again an' I swear I'll push you off this damn tree!"

Every sound terrified them. Most hadn't ventured off their plantings before, but they'd all heard stories about the big cats in The Margins. To fill the silence, Ji-ji told them she'd seen one. She said they usually didn't attack unless provoked, and failed to mention that the snarlcat she'd seen had been tearing a hunter to pieces.

Lotter had shot the cat six times with an assault rifle before he'd dropped his prey and slumped to the ground. By then the hunter's wounds were fatal. His great legs trussed up like a chicken, the ant had taken up most of the truck bed in Lotter's full-size Chevy. Lotter had given the beast to Herring, who had mounted the head on the wall of his study in Cropmaster Hall. Ji-ji still couldn't figure out why Lotter hadn't kept it. A taxidermist had stuffed the snarlcat, though Ji-ji had only seen the result after Lotter became cropmaster, when she'd delivered lunch to his study and seen the snarlcat's severed head affixed to the wall above the fireplace. The creature had been caught mid-roar. Its glass eyes looked real. Ji-ji had the strange sensation that the cat had been caught and held by the wall itself and that, if she walked round to the sitting room on the other side of the study, she'd see his back end sticking out from the wall.

Fifteen minutes later, Big Pike reappeared. The ecstatic runners implored her never to abandon them again. Pike didn't say one way or another whether she planned to hold herself to that. In silence, she climbed up into the tree where Ji-ji hid with Simply and settled back into the branches. Ji-ji could see how shaken she was, but the tall, dark-skinned woman didn't give in to panic. After several minutes, she described what had happened.

At least five runners had been killed during the attack by a pride of four or five snarlcats, big as ponies. The five had fallen back behind the lead group and been picked off by the ants. The ones running in the lead group with Pike had taken off like bats out of hell when they heard the commotion behind them. Pike said she couldn't help herself—had to run back: "Was like the screams lassoed me. You know what lassos are? We use 'em where I come from. . . . The ones attacked didn't stand a chance. I snatched Penny from under the cats' noses. She was flung a little ways off from the rest an' still moving some. The cats was busy with . . . busy. So I slung Pen over my shoulder an' ran like the devil. Came back this way cos I was scared runners behind us would be next in line for ambush. Had almost given up. You seeds were further back than I thought."

Hopeful explained they'd been picked—told her how Ji-ji, Afarra, and Tulip had rescued them. Big Pike said getting picked saved their lives. "You were real lucky. Those cats would've attacked you if you'd been further on down the road."

Tulip returned to her old refrain: "They promised there'd be guards along the route."

"Since when do steaders keep their promises?" Pike replied. "Seems to me the Districters, some of 'em anyway, are in cahoots with the Territories. Sure looks like they don't want us females to make it."

The runners clung to the trees. Occasionally, they heard roars in the distance; mostly there was an eerie silence. "Sounds like they're full," Big Pike said.

"*Oh god!*" Hopeful moaned. "Cats is worse than pickers. We're doomed."

Pike disagreed, echoing something Man Cryday had said: "Pickers is much worse. Cats are clean, kill you quick. . . . We can try an' make a run for it now. I'll take the little one. Can't weigh more'n a peanut. Stepped on a ant trap?"

"Yes," Ji-ji said.

"Foot's gonna detach then, guaranteed. Those picker-jaws don't mess around. Let's hope she don't bleed to death. I'll run on ahead with her. Cats may smell fresh blood an' attack again."

They coaxed the other terrified runners from the trees and returned to the race route.

Pike pulled Ji-ji aside. "Listen, Wild Seed. If they go for me an' Simply, get the others to cover their ears an' run like hell."

"I'm not their leader," Ji-ji said.

"Looks like you are from where I'm standing."

"I murdered a picker," Ji-ji blurted out. "Had to."

"Up close?" Ji-ji nodded. "Did the bastard deserve it?"

"Yeah."

"Then it won't be the worst thing you ever do. Trust me."

With Pike leading the way, the group stumbled along for a few more miles. Thirteen runners now, but if Simply died, twelve again. Pike loped ahead with Simply on her shoulder and returned to let them know the coast was clear. The group's pace was dangerously slow. By the time they passed the site where the attack had occurred, the victims had been dragged from the road and into the wilderness. Trails of blood and gore were the only things left.

The injureds kept pleading with the others not to leave them behind. Ji-ji promised they wouldn't. After hours of slow progress and a night without sleep, exhaustion took its toll, forcing the runners to take a nap. The pickers had stolen the runners' backpacks, so the others shared their supplies. They'd come upon another creek and drank from that, but with only a few canteens to fill, they'd need more water soon.

Not surprisingly, their brief naps afforded them little rest. Sara-May woke up and began to scream, convinced she was still being raped by pickers. At one point, they heard the roars of snarlcats way off in the distance and panicked. Tulip calmed them again by revealing details of how Afarra had tamed a pride of snarlcats.

"It's like hynotics," Tulip said. "Puts cats to sleep in less than *five seconds.* I seen it."

Pike, who wasn't fooled for a moment, said, "Is that so?"

Sookie put it more bluntly: "You're lying through your buck teeth, Tulip," which struck Ji-ji as odd cos Tulip didn't have buck teeth but Sookie did. In spite of Sookie's derision, Sara-May inched closer to Afarra, and later, one or two other runners moved in closer too.

Ji-ji didn't sleep even though she trusted Pike to keep watch. They'd hit a wall. As the red light of dawn bled onto the horizon, Ji-ji pulled up her knees, rested her head on them, and wished for the kind of strength she'd possessed just before she'd boarded the Liberty Train.

Afarra scooted up beside her. "It is right to do it," she whispered.

"You know what I'm planning?" Ji-ji asked, even though she knew the answer.

"You are planning a split, yes?"

"Yeah. The injureds will be devastated. I promised we'd stay together."

"We stay together an' no one is Free. To leave behind Sara-May and the injureds is very sorrowful, so I will stay with them and magic-talk the ants. You ask the monitors to be rescuing us soon. And if not, you petition me when you reach the city, yes?"

"Oh, Afarra, of course we'll come back an' find you! But I'm hoping there's another way."

Ji-ji conferred with Big Pike and Tulip, who confirmed her worst fears. The injureds couldn't make it without more help.

Ji-ji woke the runners and endeavored to sound more confident than she felt. "I figure we're only about fourteen or so miles from the start of the Dream Corridor segment. The deadline for runner arrival is late afternoon, depending on how the Freedom Race Council averages the start time an' calculates . . . never mind. That's not important. The main thing is, we gotta get to the city gates as quick as we can. Me, Tulip an' Pike are the fastest runners. The three of us will sprint to the corridor an' persuade the flyers to come back an' help carry the injured ones. Tulip an' Pike'll keep going to the city an' I'll guide the flyers back here. Most of the fly-boys are real strong. They get lots of time to make it to the gates, which means they got time to spare. They'll do this if I ask . . . I promise."

Helen, a Muleseed from a progressive planting in the 400s, wasn't the only one who felt betrayed: "You promised you wouldn't leave us behind! I can walk pretty good with help. Those fancy flyers won't come back for a few runners in a *million years*! You're leaving us to *die*!"

"I know at least two, maybe three flyers who'll for sure come back," Ji-ji said, counting on Tiro and Marcus, and hoping Laughing Tree would be the third, his grief over Ink's injury evidence of his compassionate nature. "I can help carry Simply. She's real small. So that's four, pretty much."

"Won't be enough," Helen said. She nursed what seemed to be a sprained knee and ankle. Ji-ji had used Rudy the Picker's knife to cut Helen's swollen foot out of her shoe. "You gotta leave one of us behind. Me an' Honeybun are the heaviest, an' I beat her by a mile." Helen broke down. "Don't leave us out here alone! Not with them mutants on the prowl!"

Big Pike stood up. At six-six, she towered above the rest of them. "I can carry Simply on my shoulder and run the rescue sprint easy. She weighs no more'n a mothball, an' she needs a medic to take a look at that dangle foot sooner rather than later. Then there's only three needs carrying."

"You sure?" Ji-ji asked.

"I'm sure," Pike replied.

Tulip had reservations. "No way you can make it back here an' then reach the city in time on the way back, Ji-ji. Let the flyers come back on their own. You done enough rescuing."

"Won't work," Ji-ji said. "The injureds need to remain hidden. The flyers'll run right past their hiding place if I'm not here to guide 'em. I'm real fast. I can still make it in time."

Sookie demanded to know what would happen to the able-bodied. "I'm not injured," Sookie said. "How come I'm not running with the rescue sprinters?"

"Those without injuries can run too," Ji-ji said. "You can run with us, if you can keep up."

Sara-May burst into tears: "You're l-leaving us here a-all a-alone," she sobbed.

"Afarra has offered to stay with you," Ji-ji told them.

"For real?" Sara-May asked. Afarra nodded. Sara-May flung her arms around her.

"What's the Cloth gonna do?" Sookie sneered. "Sing the ants a lullaby?"

Tulip was livid: "So I guess you're volunteering to stay here an' protect 'em instead? No, didn't think so. You been griping ever since the rest station. You owe 'em a debt of gratitude."

"I don't owe nothing to no Cloth," Sookie grumbled. "Could be all this is their fault. Could be the Cloth an' the Hunchback brought a hex down on us."

Tulip broke in: "Let's leave the whiny bitch here for the ants' dessert!"

"There's no time for this," Ji-ji said. "I'll never get there an' back in time if we don't leave now." She took out the knife she'd stolen from Rudy's corpse. "Afarra, I'm leaving this knife with you. Here's the rest of my food an' water. There'll be water along the way so I don't need the canteen." Tulip and Pike left Afarra their supplies too.

Ji-ji looked around. "It's pretty hidden down here off the road. You can't be seen, an' there's a cluster of climbing trees way back there. See 'em?"

A shy runner named Poppet raised her hand. Ji-ji told her she didn't need to do that but she kept it raised anyway. "Can the uninjureds head off now?" she asked.

"Don't need the witch's permission," Sookie said. "Who made her overseer? Not me. These injureds're slowing us down. See some of you in the city."

Sookie took off for the race path and didn't look back. Poppet, Hopeful, and a runner named Mabel followed.

Nymee, a shy, uninjured runner from the 600s, stood up. She surprised all of them by offering to remain behind with Afarra and the injureds. "Don't think I got the strength to make the rest of the run. Don't wanna fall back an' wind up alone. Pickers picked me first cos I was in the rear. Been throwing up ever since. If there's a flyer to spare, maybe he can carry me partway?"

"Thanks, Nymee," Ji-ji said, grateful that Afarra wouldn't have to look after the others alone.

Big Pike bent down, picked up Simply as if she were a seedling, and eased her onto her shoulders as gently as she could. Simply moaned in pain before plunging into unconsciousness again.

"Those pills should last all the way to the gates," Ji-ji said. "She's real small. You think two pills was too many?"

"No," Big Pike assured her. "A shoulder ride's rough at the best of times. Better if she's out cold. Not sure she could stand it otherwise."

Ji-ji grabbed hold of Afarra and hugged her. She whispered in her ear, "You're in charge now. Look after the others, little sister. I'll be back with help. I promise."

Ji-ji tore herself away and only looked back three times to wave.

Soon she was tearing along the path, Pike and Simply on one side, Tulip on the other. In no time, they overtook Sookie, Mabel, and Poppet.

"Hey!" Tulip called out. "You always run that slow, Sookie, or you doing it to make us feel good?" Sookie, who was already lagging behind Mabel and Poppet, gave her the finger.

Big Pike's stamina was astonishing. She ran as if she carried nothing at all—the great loping strides of a practiced runner. She told them she was from a planting close to the Territories' western border. "It's desert out there. Hot as the devil most of the time. You train in that an' you can run anywhere. My fathermate was decent. Didn't beat his seedmates, didn't plow us without our say-so. Made the mistake of trying to sneak us off the planting. Got accused of Unnatural Affiliation an' was shipped to some labor camp in the Delta. Name's Charlie Fortinum. Bald as a coot an' ugly as a weasel. Will be tracking him down after I get my papers."

Tulip understood. "Guess you got a lot o' pent-up vengeance to go after him like that."

"Not tracking down Charlie to kill him," Pike replied. "Tracking him down to save him."

Tulip was so shocked she stopped running and had to race to catch up. When she made it back she demanded to know why Pike would do something as crazy as that.

Pike thought for a minute, said, "You'd be shocked how many fairskins hate the planting life much as we do. Some get caught up in it young, some are born into it. Traps 'em like it does us."

"Long as I live I'll never forgive 'em," Tulip vowed.

"You got your road an' I got mine. But I got a good ten years or more on you, Tulip, so here's a word of advice. You keep nursing that crap steaders dole out an' one day you'll sniff under your armpits an' discover you stink too. Trust me. I seen it time an' again."

Later on, out of the blue, Big Pike said, "If you're a hunchback, I'm the Queen of Sheba."

Ji-ji began to stutter out an explanation. Tulip didn't help, launching into a bunch of ludicrous lies. Big Pike warned them it was impossible for them to pull the wool over her eyes.

"Guessed your secret soon as I saw you," she said. "You got a couple extra arms under that cape, am I right?"

"Yeah," Ji-ji said, exhaling for the first time in several seconds. "Extra arms."

"How'd you guess?" Tulip asked.

"We get a lot of superfluous limbers on Planting 777," Pike explained. "It's the groundwater. Contaminated. Seen a dozen pigs with spare eyeballs an' some with three tails. We had a four-legged Muleseed on our planting an' at least two dozen other abnormals seedbirthed in the past few years. If anyone messes with you let me know. Never had a problem with freaks. Figure you've waded through a purple river on account of your deformity. Besides, you two an' the Cloth went back for the others. Far as I'm concerned, that makes you worth protecting till I can set off after my Charlie. An' now I'll be picking up the pace. Try an' keep up."

IIIIIIIIIIIIII

There it was, Dream Corridor—the only multipurpose road leading into the city from that part of The Margins, the primary trade route between the Homestead Territories and the rest of the nation. The race path did a sweeping turn to the north to intersect with the Main Toll Road at the mouth of the corridor—a sixteen-mile passageway into D.C. and the source of the greatest joy and greatest anguish for thousands of refugees. As they stood there catching their breath, Ji-ji rifled through all the information she'd stored about this region.

Forty-foot, spike-topped, reinforced walls flanked the corridor. A ditch, like an empty moat, branched off from either side of the corridor's entrance and stretched for miles into The Margins. The ditch made it impossible for refugees and Novans living on either side of the wall to gain entry into D.C. without venturing deep into the wilderness. Circumventing Devil's Ditch was a treacherous enterprise; many seeds' bodies were said to have "fallen through the cracks."

Because there were no bridges and few access roads between Northern NoVA and Southern NoVA, and because warring gangs controlled the two areas, it was very difficult for Novans to cross from north to south. If the runners were turned away at the city gates, Ji-ji would have to make sure she and Afarra wound up on the same side of the corridor. At least then they could comfort each other and hope that Tiro would find and petition for them.

Beyond the tollbooths, the great steel-and-concrete corridor coursed like a river through the heart of NoVA. The Dream Corridor had many names—the Throat of the Gate, the One Road, even the Seed Canal—but its official name was the one Ji-ji loved as a seedling. When Uncle Dreg used to tell her stories about a corridor of dreams, she'd believed you only had to step onto it to be magically transported to a land where dreams came true, as if one of the most fiercely guarded roads in the trifurcated nation were a magic carpet. Even though she now knew the truth, her heart still swelled in her chest as she looked at it.

Inside the corridor of dreams ran a four-lane highway, two train lines (one heading into the city, one heading out), a two-lane dirt road for horse-drawn wagons and horses from the Territories (cars and trucks were in short supply), and two side-by-side walkways for pedestrians. Uncle Dreg used to say that entering the city from The Margins via D.C.'s southwestern gate was like time travel. At the end of Dream Corridor, the forty-foot gates to the City of Dreams opened, and you stepped into a brave new world. Until Zyla Clobershay explained to her why the phrase "brave new world" wasn't as complimentary as it seemed, Ji-ji had been convinced that the corridor led to an earthly paradise—a notion that Uncle Dreg, for whatever reason, hadn't disabused her of.

As they drew nearer, Ji-ji and the others saw that the Dream Corridor tollbooths at the entrance looked like small fortresses. No one traveling on foot, by car or truck, by train, or by wagon was granted access into the corridor without the right paperwork. Ji-ji was pretty certain most of the runners still had their papers. Some would have slipped them into their pockets while others would have stored them inside their belt pouches. An unlucky few would have put them in their backpacks, and all of the backpacks had been stolen by the pickers. It was unlikely runners who'd stored their paperwork in their packs would be allowed in. "One step at a time," Ji-ji told herself.

"We made it!" Tulip cried, as they jogged toward the booths.

"Not yet," Ji-ji warned. "Gotta be admitted first. The flyers'll be on the other side."

"Let's hope our timing's good," Big Pike stated. "If not, it's you an' me an' the injureds."

"You mean . . . you're offering to come back with me?" Ji-ji asked.

"Been mulling it over," Pike said. "Can't see how you'll swing it if I don't. Soon as I find a flyer willing to carry little Dangle Foot to the gate, I can pick up a coupla stretchers or something. The rules don't let us use wheeled transportation, so carts are out. But maybe with stretchers we could find a way to manage. I know you planned on hoarding all the glory for yourself, SuperSeed One. But after the previous daredevil rescue, that'd be plain greedy."

Pike had begun calling Ji-ji SuperSeed One and Tulip SuperSeed Two as they'd sprinted along the race route. Presumably, Afarra was Super-Seed Three. Ji-ji knew that if anyone deserved the title of SuperSeed it was Big Pike. She stuttered out her thanks.

Tulip said she wished she could head back with them but she just couldn't.

Ji-ji patted her arm. "It's okay," she said. "You did great back there. I won't forget it. Let's get through this toll and find Tiro."

A special tollbooth had been set up for the runners. Above it flew the runner flag with the lone runner on a winding path. The tollbooth officer was shockingly friendly for a fairskin official. He seemed genuinely concerned about Simply and called ahead to the city to have medics on standby. "No medics allowed in Dream Corridor to tend to seeds," he said. "Sorry. Mayor's orders. Here's some water. Looks like you need it. She step on a ant trap?"

"Yes," Ji-ji said.

"Thought so, poor little thing."

Ji-ji asked if the flyers were there yet.

"Flyer vans dropped 'em off for the sprint a few minutes ago. Probably two or three miles down the corridor by now."

They'd almost given up finding Simply's papers when Tulip spotted them tucked inside her underwear. The guard looked as relieved as they did. He stamped their papers, wished them luck, and raised the toll gate. The runners stepped onto Dream Corridor together, but Ji-ji had no time to savor the moment. "I gotta find Tiro," Ji-ji said.

"Go for it," Pike told her. "If you're alone when you run back, I'll follow soon as I can."

The wide, deserted pedestrian sidewalk headed into the city. Next to it, separated by a concrete median and a mesh fence, a more populated path took folks back to the tollbooths. A steady stream of people shuffled along on the tragic side of the mesh. A few pounded the mesh and called out to Ji-ji when they saw her running toward the city. "*Stop, seed! Petition for my little angel!*" a woman implored, holding her son up to the fence. "*See this poor seedling!*" begged another, holding her infant up for Ji-ji to see. "*He's gonna die in NoVA without medicine!*" Others called out their stories: they'd been living paperless in the city for years, not doing harm to no one; they'd been nabbed for jaywalking and expelled. "*You fancy racers'll be next!*" a man cried, spitting at her as she ran past. "*No dusky's safe in the City of Dreams!*"

Ji-ji pushed herself to run faster. Her back propelled her forward, almost as if fuel in her sproutings was being injected into her legs so she could fly. A few spectators lined the corridor's right shoulder, adjacent to the inbound walkway. Tiro had told her that Districters got passes to come out and cheer the racers on. She worried about her back and checked to make sure her backpack was securely tied over her cape. Her sproutings had retracted fully, thank god, so no one had noticed them so far. Nothing she could do about it if they did.

It wasn't long before Ji-ji passed a flyer bringing up the rear. Soon afterward, she passed a cluster of eight or nine more, then another and another. She heard one spectator chant, "*My oh my, that seed can fly!*" Others joined in. A fairskin spectator with a beard stepped into the walkway and waved a large Freedom Race flag over her head. "*Whoo-whee! Fly, girl!*" he shouted, as if "fly" and "girl" weren't one hyphenated word but two separate words. Lucky had called Afarra that—a girl. *Please don't let her die,* she prayed. *I can't lose another friend. Uncle Dreg, if you're listening, look after her.*

At last she spied them up ahead: Tiro, running with Marcus and Laughing Tree. *Yes!*

She called out Tiro's name. He heard, turned, saw her, and ran back. The spectators went nuts. "*The Wild Seed's running the wrong way!*" they cried.

A small group of reporters and cameramen who'd been following the famous Wild Seed fly-boy were soon at his heels. A few of the reporters rode on pedal bikes; most were on foot. As fast as she could, Ji-ji explained to Tiro what had happened. Tiro shouted to Marcus and Laughing Tree to join them. They came running.

"How many are there?" Tiro asked her.

"Three injureds," she said. "Nymee's bad off too. May need to carry her as well. An' Afarra'll need help too. Think you can help us? You can still get back in time. You sure your ankle's okay?"

"It's fine. Don't worry 'bout that. We'll help 'em, right Marcus?"

"Sure," Marcus replied. "You're our sister-seeds. We look after our own."

"Tree—you in?" Tiro asked.

"Yeah, I'm in," Laughing Tree said. "I can carry two. No problem."

"Not if you've gotta run for miles," Marcus pointed out. "Ideally, we need four flyers. Maybe more, so we can take turns. Where are they exactly? Hey, Ji-ji. Is that blood? You hurt?"

"It's not my blood. An' they're off-road. I need to show you where they are."

"No way," Tiro told her. "You can't do that run again. You won't make it back in time."

"You won't find 'em if I don't. If we stop talking and start running I can make it."

One reporter was live-broadcasting what was going on: "Looks like Wild Seed Dregulahmo and his fly-boy buddies are heading out into the ant-infested Margins to rescue a bunch of female runners attacked by vicious mutants!" The reporters wanted a quote from the "poor seed who begged for help." "Are you grateful, hon?" one of them asked. "Yes," Ji-ji replied. "Very grateful. But we gotta head back now."

Tiro and Marcus found half a dozen more flyers willing to make the journey back down the race path. Now they had nine altogether—even more than they needed. Four security guards jogged up to the flyers. One of them said they'd been sent courtesy of the Dreamfleet to accompany the flyers on their quest to save the seeds. Ji-ji turned around to see a spokesperson for the fleet telling *City News Live* that this selflessness proved what flyer recruits were made of.

"We got to *go,* Tiro," Ji-ji urged. "*We got to go now!*"

Laughing Tree saw how anxious she was and made a path for them through the reporters.

The flyers ran the wrong way down the pedestrian walkway. They passed the other flyers first, and then they saw Tulip running alongside Big Pike, who carried Simply in her arms. Laughing Tree called out to Pike by name, asked her if she needed help. "I got it under control, Tree," Pike replied. "Yep," Laughing Tree called back, "I can see you do." Tulip cheered when she saw the armed escort. "You did it, Ji-ji!" she cried. "I knew you'd find a way!"

Ji-ji prayed there was nothing in the Freedom Race rule book about being disqualified if you were carried to the gate. She prayed that the injureds still had their papers and that Afarra's ability to speak to mutants would not be put to the test. Talking to a stallion, to Drol, or even to a domesticated striper wasn't the same as talking to wild snarlcats. Did Afarra realize that?

Being on the way to rescue them made Ji-ji even more nervous than she'd been before. She remembered Fester's letter and suspected the Dreamfleet guards would turn their weapons on them; she wondered whether the reporter-cyclist with his recording device, who insisted on accompanying them on the "rescue mission," was a traitor; she was afraid that when they got back all the tollbooths would be closed. She was afraid, period. Because she'd left little Afarra to fight off a pride of snarlcats. What had she been thinking? *Hold on, Afarra! Hold on!*

They came upon the other uninjured runners heading toward the city. All of them were overjoyed when they saw Ji-ji's entourage—all except Sookie, who refused to look at them.

Ji-ji and Tiro ran side by side most of the time. "Let me know if you need a ride on my back, Ji," Tiro said. "I'm fresh as a daisy."

"Me too," she replied. He thought she was joking till she picked up the pace.

"You think they're still alive!" the reporter shouted. "Hey! You think they got eaten?"

None of the racers deigned to respond.

IIIIIIIIIIIIII

Ji-ji began calling Afarra's name when they were still on the race path. She told herself they were too far away from the road to hear her. She left the path and tore through the wilderness till she reached the place where she'd left them. She scanned the area. The runners were gone! Her heart was splitting in two. She couldn't breathe. Her sproutings hammered at her back.

"*Afarra!*" she cried, sinking to the ground. "*Afarra!*"

The fly-boys and the guards were calling too. "*Afarra! Afarra!*"

Ji-ji called again: "*Afarra! Nymee! Sara-May! Honeybun! Helen! Anyone!*"

Ji-ji couldn't breathe. She'd left Afarra to fend for herself. Unforgivable.

Tiro pointed to a cluster of trees in the distance: "Look, Ji!"

Off in the distance a thin, dark figure was running toward them with her arms wide open, listing like a drunk. There was only one person Ji-ji knew who ran like that.

"I am saying you will come! We are okay! We are safe in the trees! We are not being eaten!"

Tiro swept Afarra up in his arms like a sister and swung her around and around as the flyers and guards ran to help the others climb down from the trees.

Ji-ji herself was useless. All she could do was repeat two words over and over again to something invisible and merciful: "Thank you . . . thank you . . . thank you. . . ."

IIIIIIIIIIIIII

At the tollbooths they were waved through, even though two of the injured didn't have paperwork. "Thank the Dreamfleet," the toll guard said. "Got instructions from Wing Commander Corcoran. All the runners are to be admitted into the corridor—papers or no papers."

There was still a way to go, but they could make it in time if they kept up the pace. Marcus told her not to sweat it. "Districters fancy themselves Freedom lovers," he said. "They just wish their Freedom could be seedless. Makes things awkward when they gotta keep spitting us out. This won't cost them much. All they need to do is let in a handful of desperate seeds an' they can rerun their compassion for months."

The closer they got to the city, the more spectators lined the shoulder. News had spread of the fly-boy heroes who'd risked everything to head out into The Margins and rescue the hapless female runners. There were also cheers from beyond the wall. Marcus, who'd gotten chummy with a guard, said the District had turned on the giant screens that lined the top of the walls so Novans could watch the race. "We're a phenomenon on both sides of the wall," Marcus said, as he ran beside Ji-ji with Sara-May clinging to him. "Makes your heart go all warm an' fuzzy, don't it?"

"Yes," said Sara-May, blissfully unaware of the flyer's sarcasm.

Marcus stripped all the sarcasm from his voice and said, "You okay, Sara-May? I'm not jostling you too much, am I, sweetie?"

"No, Marcus," she said. "You're amazing." Sara-May wrapped her arms around the flyer's strong neck and held on tight.

Traffic stopped as the runners and flyers made their way down the last mile of Dream Corridor. A few steaders glared down at them from the halted wagons, but they dared not comment too much when they spotted their armed escort. When they arrived at the city gates, First Monitor Schultz stood with Inquisitor Pious, surrounded by reporters and cameras. The two welcomed the flyers and runners. There had never been a race like it before, they said. There were eighteen minutes to spare, Inquisitor Pious told them, but who's counting? All the runners who made it to the gate that day would be granted admittance. "Told you so," Marcus whispered.

A Dreamfleet spokesman advertised the final segment of the race. The flyer-battler match in the new Dream Coop had been rescheduled for tomorrow night so the flyer heroes could recover.

With great fanfare, the forty-foot reinforced steel gates to the city opened; the fly-boys carried the injured and exhausted runners through the gates. Ji-ji and Afarra followed. A reporter who wasn't able to get to the fly-boys because of the swarm of fans around them settled for runners instead. He shoved a mic into Ji-ji's and Afarra's faces.

"Johnny Sanderspool, *City News Live.* We're live. What are your names, seeds?"

"I'm not a seed, I'm a girl. And this is my friend and sister. Another girl."

Cheers came from somewhere. Ji-ji didn't know where, or if it was in response to what she'd said. She didn't care. All she wanted was to find out how Simply and the others were doing. Tiro pried himself away from the gaggle of reporters begging for interviews. He hurried over to Ji-ji and Afarra. "They're taking the injureds to City Hospital," he said. "Nineteen runners made it altogether. Make that twenty," he said, looking over their heads toward the gate.

Sloppy, in racer's shorts and T-shirt but without the runner's cape she'd craved, hobbled into Dream City. A reporter rushed up to her and seemed to be asking for her story. She shoved him aside. Just then, a man grabbed Sloppy roughly from behind. He had a little dog tucked under his arm.

At last Ji-ji understood how Sloppy had done it. She must've ridden with Chaff Man and the pickers. Had she been in league with them the whole time? Ji-ji, too exhausted to be outraged, watched as Sloppy and her executioner friend disappeared into the crowd.

Tiro was swept up by reporters again. There was a Dreamfleeter among them; his yellow wing insignia identified him as a scout. He patted Tiro on the shoulder like a proud uncle.

Afarra turned to Ji-ji and declared, "You are not staying in this City of Dreams."

Ji-ji smiled. "I won't ask how you know that. I'll rest up, get my kith-n-kin petitions filed, get you settled, and then head to the Madlands to find Charra, assuming my back cooperates."

"Okay," Afarra said. A flyer had carried her on his back most of the way, so she wasn't winded at all. "You are watching the battle tomorrow night?"

"No," Ji-ji said. "It's a foregone conclusion. An' if it's not, I don't want to see him get hurt."

A small military jet rose into the air, taking off from the airport in the city.

"I fly south too," Afarra stated. Again, it was not a question. "On your back."

Ji-ji laughed. "If only," she said, as they followed the plane's steep, awe-inspiring rise.

A woman embraced Ji-ji so fast she didn't have a chance to see who it was. "*Ji-ji!*" the woman cried. Ji-ji could tell she'd felt her sproutings. She was about to make some excuse about superfluous limbs when she pulled back and saw the woman's face.

"Welcome to the city! I've been waiting to say that for a long time! Come quickly."

"Wait! Afarra comes too!"

"Of course!" the woman said. "Hurry." She lowered her voice. "It's not safe for you here." The woman grasped Ji-ji's hand and Ji-ji grabbed Afarra's.

"Where are we going?" Ji-ji asked, as they threaded through the crowd.

"Home, of course."

Ji-ji didn't ask where that was. All she knew was that Zyla Clobershay had a tight hold of her hand. Her teacher and mentor had felt the weird sproutings under her cape and still had no intention of letting go. Maybe they'd arrived in the City of Dreams after all.

26 SO THIS IS HOW IT ENDS

A few hours after her arrival, at a party in the home of her teacher to celebrate the runners' success, Ji-ji fainted. The Friends' chief physician, Dr. Narayanan, who happened to be a guest at the celebration, ordered her straight to bed. His diagnosis: she was suffering from exhaustion due to overexertion. Later, however, when they assumed she was sleeping, Ji-ji overheard the doctor whispering to Zyla about the seriousness of her condition. He uttered phrases Man Cryday had used: *extracorporeal liberation* and *ingrown colonization*. Though the doctor acknowledged these weren't medical terms, he said ingrown colonization could, in a general way, characterize her condition. Ji-ji still wasn't sure what the terms meant, but she knew how painful an ingrown toenail could be and braced herself for a continuation of the throbbing pain in her back.

Ji-ji and Afarra had fallen in love with Zyla's modest two-bedroom apartment as soon as they'd stepped inside. In a rambling apartment building not far from the river, it had been repeatedly flooded before the new levee system had been built. Ben and Germaine had an apartment across the hall, and Miss Alice, the leader of the Friends, had the top floor all to herself. Surrounded by Friends of Freedom, Ji-ji felt safer than she had ever felt in her life.

Zyla Clobershay instructed Ji-ji and Afarra to call her by her first name. Initially it felt disrespectful to be on a first-name basis with her beloved teacher, but Ji-ji soon grew accustomed to it. For the first few days, Ji-ji and Afarra slept in the double bed in the guest room. Soon, however, Ji-ji's back was so inflamed and the pain so intense that the risk of Afarra accidentally brushing against her became too great. Zyla told Afarra to sleep in her, Zyla's, room. Afarra refused. "I am being with Elly all the time," Afarra insisted. "So is he." By "he," Afarra meant Uncle Dreg, whose necklace she wore everywhere, even to bed. (She would have worn it in the bath too, if Zyla hadn't convinced her soap stung the Eyes.) After a series of fairly heated arguments, Afarra wound up sleeping on a mat on the floor in Ji-ji's room, though Zyla caught her half a dozen times curled up at the foot of Ji-ji's bed.

During the race, the Friends had been hard at work in the city. Though the editors of the *D.C. Independent* decided not to publish Fester's letter (or to admit they had a copy in their possession), they quoted "sources" outlining Territorial plans for a "cleansing" of Toteppi. They'd done their own investigations to supplement information in the Lord-Secretary's disturbing letter and found documentary evidence of a plan to move against Toteppi throughout the Territories. The public outcry that ensued jeopardized the new trade talks, forcing the Supreme Council in Armistice to back off their plans. At the Dreamfleet, Commander Corcoran, whose son had been secretly detained in the Territories on trumped-up "espionage" charges, announced his son's detention and spoke out forcefully against Territorial deception. Soon afterward, public pressure forced the Lord-Father of Lord-Fathers to release Corcoran's son and claim it was all a misunderstanding. For now, Zyla said, the city and the Dreamfleet were safe.

The Friends had no doubt, however, that Ji-ji remained a target. Armed Friends of Freedom guarded the door to Zyla's apartment; more stood guard at the entrances to the building. Visitors were frisked before they entered, and the Friends purposely leaked the news that Ji-ji's condition was deteriorating fast.

Afarra never left her side, except to go to the bathroom and to bathe, usually after Zyla Clobershay told her she stank. Tiro visited Ji-ji every day, bringing stories of the city with him, promising she'd get better. Tulip visited too, ecstatic because her kith-n-kins had sailed through, and she'd successfully snatched her little sisters Rosemary and Thyme from the mouth of Clownfish.

As people tiptoed around her, Ji-ji realized she might be dying. Sometimes that scared her; at other times it didn't. She'd never been so tired in her life. She made Afarra promise to prevent them from amputating her wings, if that's what they decided to do—not that Afarra needed convincing. "*No one* is taking them!" Afarra pledged, resting her hand on the Seeing Eyes. "This is why I stay here day out day in. To bodyguard.

The sproutings are belonging to you. We are needing them to fly to the moon."

Ji-ji didn't tell Afarra she'd given up on the whole damn flying business—an old man's impossible dream. Nor did she ask Tiro to repeat his promise not to let them amputate. She suspected he would betray her, hang on too tight cos he needed her to be there for him. Hard though it was for Ji-ji to admit it, she couldn't trust him to respect her wishes. When she confided this to Afarra one evening, Afarra touched the necklace and said, "He is saying he will catch up one day. He is saying give him time."

"I wish I could," Ji-ji said. "But I don't have much left. If something happens, Zyla an' the others will look after you. You know that, right?"

"Oh yes. Something will happen," Afarra replied. "He is saying it is a certain almost."

Ji-ji smiled. A "certain almost" would have to suffice.

||||||||||||||

To Ji-ji's surprise, Doc Riff showed up one day. Ben accompanied him, reunited at last with Germaine, who'd been very anxious about the mission he'd undertaken to deliver a copy of Fester's letter to Man Cryday. Germaine flung herself in Ben's arms and gave him one of the longest kisses Ji-ji had ever seen, involving tongues and what looked like a decent amount of saliva. Ji-ji and Afarra found it fascinating.

Doc Riff took a long time examining her back and prescribed something even stronger than his usual horse pills for the pain. He told her Man Cryday had requested he make the house call and asked him to report back his findings. The Gardener of Tears had hoped to make the journey herself, but the threat to Dimmers Wood and Memoria prevented her from leaving right now.

Having observed Doc Riff interact with the others, Ji-ji realized he must have been a Friend of Freedom for years. He urged her not to tire herself and to drink as much fluid as possible. It worried her when he said that. She couldn't get to the bathroom these days without assistance. She wanted to mention this to Doc Riff but she was afraid he'd insist on a catheter, and it would have mortified her if he had. She wished Man Cryday could have examined her instead. Doc Riff's good looks made it difficult for her to confide in him about urination.

In the next few days, the pain in Ji-ji's back soared to a new level. It had been agonizing before but nothing had prepared her for pain as vengeful as this. It came at her in waves. Zyla called it her "high tides" and "low tides." During high tides, Ji-ji wished for death; during the low tides, she wished for death less frequently.

As the pain increased, Zyla and Germaine, close friends, took turns tending to her round the clock. Ji-ji felt time slipping away. Though she'd reached the City of Dreams, she didn't have the strength to see it. Couldn't even stand at the window to catch a glimpse of some of the city's war-ravaged buildings being restored. Hours ran into days. Racked with migraines, she begged her teacher to keep the curtains drawn. She asked to wear her minstrel-mouse watch. Afarra fetched it (Germaine had carried her possessions safely to the city) and strapped it onto Ji-ji's thin wrist. It didn't help. In the room where it was always dark, Ji-ji couldn't tell whether the mouse's white-gloved hands indicated ten in the morning or ten at night.

Whenever the pain was at low tide, she sat propped up with pillows and conversed as much as she could with visitors. Usually, she had an hour or two before the pain jackhammered a path up her spine and forced her to ask visitors to leave.

She asked about Dip. Had they heard from her? No one had. Not from Sloppy either. Tiro said if Sloppy really had betrayed them, she deserved to be flogged. Ji-ji could see his point, but she couldn't help thinking about Sloppy's big toe (the one Casper mashed because his biscuits and gravy were cold) and what she'd said about running alone through the dark in The Margins. Hard to forgive someone for their cowardice—not so hard to forgive them for their fear.

Sometimes, Tiro brought Marcus with him. Although he wasn't a Friend of Freedom, he knew the truth about Ji-ji's condition and was privy to most of the Friends' other secrets. The two fly-boys filled her in on all the latest news from the coop. Their performance in the final Freedom Race battle in the Dream Coop, when they'd once again taken the top spot with Laughing Tree, had earned offers for the three from the Dreamfleet Flyers. Marcus decided to take his time and mull it over. Tiro, on the other hand, had signed on the spot so he could use his signing bonus to sweeten his kith-n-kin petitions for Zaini and the boys. It would work, he told her. It had to.

Soon, the relentless pain responded only to a morphine drip. Medicine was extremely expensive, but Tiro, who claimed Ji-ji as a member of his medical kith-n-kins, obtained whatever she needed.

"You gotta be able . . . to manage without me," she told Tiro at the conclusion of a visit during low tide. She felt the tide rising and had to struggle to get the words out.

"Don't talk like that, Ji. How many times I got to tell you? You ain't going nowhere. Not while I'm around."

"That's what I'm afraid of," Ji-ji said.

IIIIIIIIIIIIII

Her condition steadily worsened. The Friends tried to honor her request to see Charra, or speak to her if that was all they could arrange. They sent multiple messages into the Madlands, all to no avail. Ji-ji knew her sister would never ignore a message like that. Either she was in such deep hiding that even the Friends' network couldn't locate her, or she'd been killed. Ji-ji said she would have to settle for meeting up with her sister in the afterlife. If the two of them decided to Dimmer a few people—Lotter, Williams, Casper, Worthy, and Tryton, for example—they could team up and do it together.

These days, her dreams were invariably about flight. Once, she flew to the moon, where twelve white men waited for her, all of them delighted to see she'd joined them. In her dreams, she wasn't *like* a bird, she was a bird: her whole body spoke the language of flight. She would awaken in the wake of her flight dream and feel it pulling her into its vortex again. Each time this happened, she found it harder and harder to resist.

IIIIIIIIIIIIII

One after another they came to visit. They trod softly, as if Death were a light sleeper they were terrified of waking.

The Friends had been praying for a miracle. Ji-ji wanted to tell them not to be sad, but the avalanche of pain raking her back wouldn't let her. More morphine . . . rest. . . .

The next time she looked over—a minute later? an hour? a day?—Ji-ji saw Zyla with something in her hand. A folded-up piece of fabric. A story-cloth!

"Is it the one about the birds?" Ji-ji asked. "That's my favorite."

"Yes, it is," Zyla replied. She unfolded it.

Not the story-cloth after all, but it was still the one about the birds. It came with a note. Zyla warned her it might be upsetting. "If it is, tell me to stop reading," she said.

Dear Ji-ji

Thought youd appreciate a gift from the 437th. I salvaged it before he burned her cabin to the ground. I hear your sick. Thought this quilt could cheer you up. (I asked a trusted friend whose alot better at spelling to look over this note and help me make a few corrections. Writing isn't my strong suit. You may not know this but A-Is don't have to pass things through the censors on account of our status as Indigenous. So don't worry about this winding up in the wrong hands.)

I want to ask a favor. I know I don't deserve it seeing as how I was always short with you but if we all got what we deserve the world would be a pitiful place and you did get on my nerves and thats the truth.

If things go south and you pass to the Other Side, please tell Lua-Dim not to Dimmer me anymore. Tell her I did my best under the circumstances. Tell her Bettie's sorry her wombling died. Real sorry.

We got a plague of Dimmers on the 437th. Uncle Dreg come back as a Dimmer too. You hear about that? Wafts round PenPen shaking the bars and vowing to help the prisoners fly away. Hasn't worked so far.

Lua was a good girl but Lua-Dims a devil. Braids detaching and wafting down, her shrieking all the time cos he refuses to nurse. Deadborns dont nurse, I tell her. She says to me all smartass, Dead don't shriek neither, but here I am a-shrieking. Lua-Dims nothing like the live version. Can't take the nighttime din no more.

Tell her Betties sorry as sorry can be for what happened. And give little Sidney a hug from his mama. (Sid was my onlyborn. Sweetest seedling there ever was.) Tell him, before Lua-Dim, no night went by when I didnt rock him in my arms in my dreams. Kiss him for me, Jellybean. Tell him his mother sent that kiss. If Sidney wants to Dimmer me tell him go ahead. Tell him I wouldnt mind one bit. Don't forget.

Best regards,

Bettie (no ann at the end. The anns are their doing not mine.)

"Sounds like Bettie Plowman's dealing with a lot of guilt," Zyla said.

"She deserves it," Ji-ji told her. "She killed Silas. Wexcisioned him. I'm glad Lua-Dim's making her life hell."

"That doesn't sound like you, Ji-ji."

"You weren't there," Ji-ji said. "You didn't see what I saw."

"No. None of us really sees what another person sees," Zyla said. "But guilt's a hard thing to deal with without forgiveness."

Ji-ji closed her eyes to get Zyla to stop talking. Moral lessons were irrelevant if she didn't have time to practice what Zyla preached. She said the pain was approaching high tide again and asked that Bettie's gift be laid on her bed. Zyla and Afarra arranged the quilt Zaini made for Silapu on top of the sheets. Three blackbirds nesting in an Immaculate tree, a flock taking off from the tree like fireworks. Everything quilted together. Wounds patched and sewn.

IIIIIIIIIIIIII

Tiro sat in the vigil chair by the bed, shaken. Afarra, fists raised, straddled Ji-ji's bed.

"What the hell just happened?" Tiro asked. "How'd she do that? Freaked me out the way she spoke. His same exact voice—like Uncle was in the room with us! *Jesus!*"

Afarra brandished the living will Ji-ji had signed. "*No touching!*" she cried.

Ji-ji indicated she wanted to speak. She took a deep breath. The pain in her lungs made her wish she hadn't.

"You . . . snuck in . . . when Zyla and Germaine . . . were out."

"*Sneak!*" Afarra yelled.

"I'm sorry, Ji. But you got any idea how much work it took to get that surgeon to come here? Thought he could take a look—see if there was anything could be done. Riff an' Narayanan ain't surgeons. Man Cryday ain't either—not anymore. Hasn't practiced in years. Probably why she botched Charra's amputation."

"My . . . choice," Ji-ji said, her voice barely above a whisper. "Not yours."

"Okay. I get it. I do. . . . Brought you something. Tickets to the big battle in the fall. First time me an' Laughing Tree'll fly with the pros. One for you an' one for the harpy over there." Afarra gave him the finger. "Think it's the necklace makes her spout that weird shit?"

"Ask . . . her," Ji-ji suggested.

"Hey, Afarra. You can get down off the bed now. Surgeon's gone. You scared the crap outta him. How'd you do Uncle Dreg's voice like that?"

Afarra jumped down off the bed and glared at Tiro. "*He* is doing his voice, *dumbass*!"

"But it came out of your mouth. How'd you do that?"

"Moron," Afarra said.

"Now you sound like Aunt Cryday. Give a fly-boy a break, okay?"

He turned to Ji-ji, said, "Listen, in a few weeks, after . . . you know . . . I gotta head on back to the 437th. Got official word yesterday. Williams is keeping 'em. Bastard says he looks forward to guiding Bromadu an' Eeyatho 'away from the path of Deviancy.' Says he'll auction 'em off soon as they 'ripen.' Hate to deliver bad news."

"I'm real sorry . . . to hear . . . this," Ji-ji managed to say.

"Guess I should've expected it from that bastard. . . . Georgie-Porge an' Orlie send their love. Arrived yesterday. Their petitions sailed through. Zyla told you all six of yours were granted, right? Six kitchen-seeds just got tickets to Freedom. You did it, Ji. . . . An' thanks for trying to petition for Mother an' the boys. I know it was risky filling out the forms. I appreciate it."

Tiro looked at Afarra, who still scowled at him. He tried to make it up to her, said, "Wish Cloths got kith-n-kins, Afarra. Bet you'd choose some great ones to petition for. Hey, I almost forgot." He reached down and picked up a bag. "Marcus loaded me down with chocolates. Fly-boy's enlisted in the fleet at last. Told him you got no appetite, but Marcus says everyone loves chocolate, an'—"

Afarra snatched the bag from Tiro's hand and offered the chocolates to Ji-ji. When Ji-ji waved them away, Afarra dug in, humming contentedly to herself as she did so.

"How's Tree?" Ji-ji asked.

"Tree's Tree. Know what he went an' did? Petitioned for Ink. Paying his medical. Tree's having this basket contraption made for Ink to sit in. Plans to carry him around like some damn parrot. Marcus calls Tree *Trink* to rile him up. Tree likes it. Says it's a compliment."

"Trink is a good name," Afarra said in a deep voice, through bites of chocolate. "I like it."

"You hear that?" Tiro exclaimed. "She did it again! Sounded just like him!"

Ji-ji moaned. The pain was rising fast. *High tide! High tide!*

"You need more painkillers, Ji? More morphine?" She shook her head. "Who knows? Could be I won't be missing you for long. Chances of me getting 'em out is next to nothing, an' the chances of me swinging from Sylvie are pretty damn good. If the worst happens, give Amadee a message for me. Tell him I miss him like it's me who got tractor-pulled. Hey, Ji. Think you get put back together? Don't think I could bear it if he was all pulled apart like he was at the end."

She reached out to comfort him but the vigil chair was empty. How long had it been since he'd sat there? She had no idea. What a shame he was gone when she still had so much to tell him. . . .

||||||||||||||

Germaine burst in at two in the morning, waking Zyla, who sat in the vigil chair, Afarra, who was curled up at the foot of the bed, and Ji-ji, who'd finally fallen asleep about an hour before.

Zyla leapt up, alarmed. "Have they found her? Are the steaders here?"

"No," Germaine said. "Sorry. Thoughtless of me to burst in like that. Got a message to deliver. Thought Ji-ji would want to hear it."

"It better be good news," Zyla said, "or I'll strangle you. Took us ages to get the pain down to where she could sleep. Riff only just left."

"It *is* good news, Zy. Real good news."

Ji-ji indicated she wanted to sit up. The three of them propped her up with pillows.

"You ready?" Germaine said, so excited she hopped from one foot to the other. Ji-ji nodded.

"It's addressed to G. Judd, and it was sent to this address. It says:

"Dear G. J. (that's me, of course)

I hear from a little dickybird there's been some developments. Can't wait to see what they are.

Ask the Ex if she's still got that timely gift I gave her. Tell her it's almost impossible to rid yourself of a Brit once they've decided to be your friend.

Tell her I hope she's steering clear of cutlery.

Tell her I am, as always, lucky.

P.S. And give her these."

Germaine placed a pair of dice in Ji-ji's hand.

"Lucky's *alive*!" Ji-ji murmured. "How?"

"Beats me, kid," Germaine told her. "Guess we'll have to wait to hear the details. But it's definitely him. His handwriting—everything. Man Cryday'll know more I bet. But for now, I thought you'd want to know. Was I right to wake you?"

"Oh yes," Ji-ji said, happily.

The Existential closed her eyes and slept like a baby.

IIIIIIIIIIIIII

Afarra sat beside her on the bed and stroked her hair. Uncle Dreg had told her to look after Elly, to stay close because hard times lay ahead. Afarra had promised to do exactly that.

In her heart she knew Elly would never die. But no one believed her. And sometimes, when she looked at the girl she loved more than life, a tiny seed of doubt sprouted in her brain.

Today had been hard. Agony! The sproutings swollen and raw, covered in pus and scabs. Man Cryday had said they needed to be vivacious. Afarra didn't know what that meant exactly, but she did know the worms were poison now. Even his necklace hurt her when she put it on—*heavy, heavy!* His voice ricocheting inside her head.

Yesterday she'd heard him weeping. Found him sitting on the vigil chair all hunched over like an ordinary old man. She'd tried to find words to comfort him but he'd used them all up to comfort her.

"I am being scared," she whispered to the Eyes. She held them up to her ear. For once, they told her nothing.

She stroked Elly's back. *Hot! Hot!*

Elly moaned, opened her eyes.

Afarra spoke to her: "You are wanting to hear the song again? The 'Purple Rain' song you like?"

"Yeah," Ji-ji said. "I'd like that."

Afarra leapt up and pressed the play button on the old player Zyla had borrowed so they could listen to music. "I am liking Prince," Afarra said.

"Me too," Ji-ji agreed. "You think that's where . . . the seeds' nursery rhyme comes from? 'Purple pain . . . is . . .'" Ji-ji was too weak to continue.

Afarra took up the slack. "'Purple pain is prince again / Rain tears, and wince again,'" she said.

"Thank you, Afarra," Ji-ji said. "Thank you for . . . everything."

Afarra was desperate to cuddle her. Would it hurt if she did? Yes. Zyla said no more cuddling. Too sore. Afarra settled for words, even though she knew she wasn't very good at them.

"All these weeks in this room . . . two together. . . . Heaven! At night I hear. Them sing to me. The angel-birds. Up high. In the nest in the sky. High, high, blackbird. They are singing us to sleep."

"Who are?" Elly managed to ask.

"Your wings," Afarra said.

IIIIIIIIIIIIII

Ji-ji woke from the deepest sleep she'd ever had. The three of them were together: Afarra lying beside her, Tiro asleep in the vigil chair next to her bed. She figured she was dead or dreaming, because there was no pain.

She pushed the blackbird quilt aside, raised herself from the white sheets, and stood, unsteadily at first. She was dizzy. She waited for it to pass.

Something was weighing her down. She leaned forward a little, found her balance.

She shuffled to the window, drew back the curtain, and looked out. Dawn. A murmuration of starlings drawing patterns in the sky like a great body of black-winged water—in and out and up and down and around and around!

She looked to her right and her left. On either side sat two enormous furled scrolls. They reached to the floor and rose above her head. As she turned back to face the room, they unfurled themselves. When they brushed the walls and touched the ceiling, they curled to accommodate the room, which wasn't wide enough to let her unfurl them fully. They didn't look like flesh or feathers or keratin. The thousands of tiny translucent scales didn't hook together to form a seal the way feathers did. But she knew she wasn't dreaming this time. She knew this was real.

Ji-ji brushed the filaments with her fingers—threads of light, delicate and responsive. She felt the interlocking flaps that opened, closed, and rearranged themselves in different patterns, moving synchronously. The tiny flaps on her wings caught and held the light like tears. Some flaps had ridges on them—so tiny she could feel but not see them. Her wings were an intricate, gossamer latticework of light, a dance on something unlike skin. Their translucence captured the dawn's maroon, scarlet, pink, fuchsia, and violet in tiny drops of color, each one trembling like a jewel-leaf.

Afarra sat up in bed, the prophet's Seeing Eyes looped around her neck. "You have come! We have been waiting!"

Tiro woke from his vigil sleep. He leapt up so fast he stumbled over his own feet. "I must be dreaming!" he cried. He walked toward her with his arms outstretched and his eyes wide open. He touched the wings he'd feared. "They don't look like anything real!" he murmured.

"They *are* real," Afarra insisted, coming up behind him. "Purple tears, all bound together."

IIIIIIIIIIIIII

Far more people than expected attended Ji-ji's memorial service. The runners showed up; so did most of the fly-boys. The Friends of Freedom too.

Germaine cried. Zyla cried more.

Tiro didn't attend, said he couldn't bear it. Marcus stood in for him.

Afarra attended but didn't say a word to anyone. Underneath her blouse, the wizard's Seeing Eyes saw everything.

"She was an angel," Sara-May said, speaking for the runners. "She came back to save us."

A reporter came from the *D.C. Independent.* He asked the late runner's teacher for a quote: "She was my student," Zyla told him. "And she was my friend. We'll miss her very much."

IIIIIIIIIIIIII

Afarra saw someone watching from the window as she, Zyla, Germaine, and Ben pulled up in an alley beside a derelict building in D.C.'s flood zone. The city had stopped trying to save this area, which was flooded four or five times a year. Warning signs ordered everyone to KEEP OUT!

Afarra grabbed her bag and leapt out before the car came to a complete stop. Zyla scolded her but she ignored it.

She ran forward, arms outstretched, reeling like a drunk, and flung herself into Tiro's arms.

"Did you keep your mouth shut like I told you?" he asked.

"I am not saying one single word about nothing!" Afarra replied.

"Good," Tiro said. "Let's keep it that way."

The building was damp and moldy. They walked up three flights of stairs, then three more. At the top, they knocked on a door marked THE AERIE.

Ben explained to Zyla: "They may've closed down this practice coop years ago, but it's still got its uses."

Someone on the other side walked toward the door.

IIIIIIIIIIIIII

Ji-ji stood at the window watching them pull up. Afarra leapt out before the car came to a standstill. For four whole weeks, they'd managed to keep Afarra away. The Friends needed to make sure no one suspected a thing.

Tiro had rushed downstairs to greet them. Just as he'd done when she'd been so sick, he'd shown up each day to spend time with her. He still found it hard to believe she was well—kept rebuking himself for doubting Uncle Dreg.

Soon they would knock on the door. She would show them round the apartment—more of a hideout really—where she'd been staying with her bodyguards. Afarra would ask her if she was flying yet. She would say no, but that was okay cos she wasn't knocking on death's door anymore, or in agony either. She would tell Afarra things were looking up, which would be true. She would tell her how much she'd missed her, which would be truer still. She would show her to the room they'd set up for her, show her the mural Ji-ji had drawn of a birdgirl with a girl on her shoulders, flying to the moon.

Ji-ji glanced over at her writing desk—something Tiro had made for her. In the hours she had to kill she wrote down her story—Zyla's idea. "The Friends need Root Voices," Zyla said, sounding like Man Cryday. "Doesn't matter how rough it is. I can help you smooth it out."

Today, perhaps because of all the excitement, Ji-ji had writer's block. She didn't know what the next words would be, but she knew how much rested on getting them right. So hard to write your own story without knowing its end.

Under a Dreamfleet snow globe featuring the Capitol in a blizzard and a flyer-battler swinging back and forth on a trapeze lay a note Germaine had given her. It arrived a few days ago. "*Dying is easy,*" it read. "*We've done it before. Looking forward to seeing you again in the afterdeath.*" It came with two more dice. Ji-ji kept all four dice on the writing table for luck.

She hadn't told anyone her plans, or mentioned the fact that, whether or not her wings functioned by then, she planned to leave for the Madlands after Tiro, Marcus, and Laughing Tree made their professional debut in the Dream Coop in the fall. She would persuade Charra to raid the 437th and save Tiro's family. She'd managed to keep him in Dream City until now, but it would eat him up soon if he couldn't get his family out of there. After they'd liberated seeds on the 437th, she, Charra, Afarra, and Tiro (along with some Friends, she hoped, and Charra's raiders) would rescue Bonbon from Armistice. On the way back, they could raid the 368th in memory of the boy in ass's ears.

It was a silly, impossible dream. A child's dream; she knew that. But she also knew what Lua told her: "Oh, the *rising*! From the cradle to the grave! See it? *See?*" Yes, Lua. She could see it now.

On their Death Day, Lua's words had been echoed by the words of Uncle Dreg: "Black, brown, and white flocking together! Heads of midnight, heads of earthlight, heads of moonlight! Faith and Hope will nourish you, but only Love can dream you Free! My beautiful birds of paradise, you are destined to fly the coop and bring together the tribes of the world!" Ji-ji didn't know if they could dreaminate them true, or even find words of their own. She did know she could choose to try.

A knock on the door. She had learned to unfurl herself at will, to balance without stooping way over or falling backward. She unfurled herself to welcome them, made the moment stretch out and arch its back like a cat so she could savor it, and felt the yearning of the Tribe. Jubilation.

IIIIIIIIIIIIII

Beyond the Window-of-What's-to-Come, high above the City of Dreams, birds curled and dipped and rose as One, preaching their wordless, wondrous gospel of flight.

AUTHOR NOTES AND ACKNOWLEDGMENTS

Typically, acknowledgments are expressions of gratitude to the people who have made a book possible. In this instance, however, I would like to begin by acknowledging the genre of speculative fiction itself, and, more specifically, Afrofuturism, the hybrid form that is redefining the narrative landscape.

Speculative fiction is inherently inclusive. It embraces a range of phenomena—realism and worlds invented; the past, the present, and the future; personal vision and collective imagination. It can be satirical, urgent, celebratory, and/or subversive. It allows us to unchain ourselves from time and formulate narratives inside an imagined future. If the spell works, the story's future reverberates back to a roiling present, whose roots extend deep into the past. This braiding of tenses is what endows speculative fiction with its unique potency and makes it so well suited to survival narratives. Inside Afrofuturism, in particular, race and gender can be realigned, reconstructed, and reimagined. The genre enables us to explore sociopolitical, psychological, collective, and deeply personal landscapes as we draw upon the tropes and figures that have sustained or devastated us. Even for those writers among us, myself included, for whom realism is a primary touchstone, speculative fiction releases narrative from the compulsions of majority-built realism as it takes characters to the impossible-made-possible, which is, after all, the very definition of the future. So for this journey, I am grateful to have relocated myself inside the borderless, dangerous, lawless, infinitely inclusive genre of speculative fiction.

In order for a novel to take root, many different scraps of fabric are quilted together. If writers are lucky, we make our literary journeys alongside writing professionals we trust. The best of them create a safe space in which we can uncover the voices we need to tell our stories. Over the years, the guidance fine editors give us accumulates. In the solitary dark that is the writing process, their feedback serves as a lighthouse. As a writer of mainstream literary fiction, poetry, and nonfiction, I have learned from extraordinary editors and publishers like Joelle Delbourgo, Tim Duggan, Carolyn Marino, Ruth Gundle, Heather Buchanan, and John Glusman, the last of whom helped me sift through horror and find a way into narrative in the wake of the mass shooting tragedy at Virginia Tech.

In Jennifer Weltz, I have an agent who is also a trusted friend and valued reader. As I tried to escape the repercussions of tragedy by avoiding the narrative my characters needed me to write, Jennifer was there, as Jean Naggar had been before her, offering sage advice. I can't wait for this pandemic to be over so that I can celebrate with them and their staff at the Jean V. Naggar Literary Agency.

For this Dreambird Chronicle series, Jennifer sent a draft of the manuscript to Dr. Jen Gunnels at Tor, who embraced its quirks and differences and understood where it was trying to go. She has shepherded it through the house with a fierce dedication. Part of the reason I am able to tackle this novel series and the world it depicts (one that has become increasingly and horrifyingly similar to the world we face today) is Jen Gunnels' inspired feedback and advocacy, and Tor's determination to include a diversity of voices in its lineup. Writers don't always realize that it takes a team of dedicated people to usher a novel from manuscript to finished product. My thanks to the copyediting, design, marketing, and publicity teams at Tor, especially my publicist Saraciea Fennell, designer Jamie Stafford-Hill, editorial assistant Matt Rusin, cover artist Eli Minaya, and copy editor Terry McGarry.

My friends and colleagues at Virginia Tech have put up with my reclusiveness over evenings, weekends, and summer and winter breaks as I tackled a daunting story. They have inspired me in ways they probably don't recognize. My thanks to the Magnificent Four—Glenda Scales, Barbara Pendergrass, Bev Watford, and Menah Pratt-Clarke. The four Black women understand why Blackness in the rural American South requires a recharging of batteries in rooms where backstory and explication are unnecessary.

My thanks to faculty and staff in English and the Creative Writing Program at Virginia Tech. Like writers whose work I love—writers like Hurston, Morrison, Bessie Head, Octavia Butler, Terry Tempest Williams, George R. R. Martin, Tolkien, James Baldwin, Zadie Smith, and Marilynne Robinson—my colleagues' work has inspired my own. My thanks to Ed Falco, Matthew Vollmer, Jeff Mann, Fred D'Aguiar, and Erika Meitner, for decades of dedication to the craft and to students; and to Carmen Giménez Smith and Evan Lavender-Smith for adding their voices to the wonderful mix that constitutes our MFA Program. My thanks to the incomparable Nikki Giovanni, who has never stopped dreaming large and flying along her own inimitable path to the stars. My thanks also to Virginia Fowler, who, when I first arrived at Virginia Tech as a so-called affirmative action hire, understood the struggle and helped guide me through it with wisdom and patience. Thanks to Peter Graham, Gena Chandler-Smith, Sheila Carter-Tod, and Tom Gardner, whose intellectual curiosity always stimulates my own; and the army of dedicated instructors like Aileen Murphy, Jane Wemhoener, Lissa Bloomer, Gyorgyi Voros, and Robin Allnutt, who remind me every day why teaching is a vocation we must never undervalue. My thanks to Provost Cyril Clarke and fellow ADPs Rosemary Blieszner and Jacqueline Bixler, and to Carolyn Rude for doing a fine job in administration so that former administrators like myself can return to writing and teaching. I'm grateful to students I've taught in the U.K., Africa, Arkansas, Massachusetts, and Virginia who remind me why the present is miraculous, in spite of its steady refrain of suffering, and why the future is the place most in need of investment.

With thanks to gifted poets I read and reread, including David Wojahn, Judith Barrington, Randall Horton, and Terry L. Martin. Thanks to scholar Bob Siegle and artist Jane Vance, who were there in the early days and told me how much words mattered. With gratitude to novelist Katherine Neville and poet Annie Finch, whose generosity to other writers is legendary. With thanks also to cherished friends Richenda Kullar, Tina Theis, and Denise Dowd, whom I've loved ever since we went to school together, and who always welcome me back to the U.K. with open arms. And the late, great Siobhan Dowd, with whom I used to walk to La Retraite Catholic convent school, and whose magnificent words live on.

I am grateful to Helene Gayle, Michelle Nunn, and the people at the humanitarian organization CARE, for inviting me to serve as part of a delegation to Sierra Leone, where I used to teach. Thank you for fighting the global struggle against poverty, especially as it relates to women and children. You never forget how much pain there is and how great is our capacity to relieve it, if we choose to do so.

Now for the scraps of fabric that form the quilt's familial center. My sisters-in-spirit (so much more than sisters-in-law) Linda, Dolores, and

Doris, who have made me a part of the Jackson family. My little sister Paula and her husband, Mike, whose passion for literature and desire to celebrate the extraordinary journeys made by a kidnapped people brought me to a reading at the Smithsonian's National Museum of African American History and Culture, where pivotal scenes later in this series take place. My sincere thanks to my brother Tamba and his wife, Gail, our travel kin, who have journeyed with us and helped us laugh like fools with our whole bodies, without giving a damn if people think we're insane.

My thanks to my long-dead-but-always-with-me parents, Yvonne and Namba Roy. The love between my White English mother and Black Jamaican father flourished at a time when marriages like theirs were despised and ridiculed. They taught me that when two "unlikes" combine through love, the metaphor they make is always a source of joy. My thanks to my beloved Joseph and Austin, who prove to me every day why the world is filled with delight if you only remember, once in a while, to look up from the page. And my thanks, most of all, to my darling Larry for accompanying me on this long and difficult journey, and for his faith that this story of race and resurrection was worth the telling.

—Lucinda Roy, December 2020